WHAT REAL

What a beautiful novel. Cynthia's heart shone in every line. I smiled and cried as though I were part of the Gallagher family. Will and Lydia's story gripped my heart, taking permanent root. Their struggles challenged me to take a deeper look inside of myself. Thoroughly moving, authentic, and deeply engaging. A triumph of joy over sorrow.

— CANDACE WEST, AWARD-WINNING
AUTHOR OF THE VALLEY CREEK
REDEMPTION SERIES

When life deals us unexpected blows, and we don't see God's blessings or hear His voice, our faith can falter. Beyond Shattered Dreams reminds us that He's always working, turning tragedy into beauty if we will trust Him. Out of loss and pain can come abundance we've never imagined. In this well-written, introspective third installment of her Wounded Hearts series, Cynthia Roemer reminds us of the promise of restoration, the deep joys of family, and the gift of unexpected love. Superbly done!

— DENISE WEIMER, AUTHOR OF *WHEN HOPE SANK* OF BARBOUR'S DAY TO REMEMBER SERIES AND THE SCOUTS OF THE GEORGIA FRONTIER SERIES

Roemer possesses such a rich, authentic historical voice, and Beyond Shattered Dreams is another beautifully written exploration of love and loss against the backdrop of the Civil War. Readers will be captivated by the emotional depth of the characters and the gripping plot that unfolds. This compelling story of love's redeeming power is sure to resonate with readers long after they turn the last page.

— MISTY M. BELLER, USA TODAY
BESTSELLING AUTHOR OF THE BROTHERS
OF SAPPHIRE RANCH SERIES

BEYOND *Shattered* DREAMS

Wounded Hearts • Book Three

Award-winning Author

CYNTHIA ROEMER

Scrivenings PRESS

Quench your thirst for story.

www.ScriveningsPress.com

To my family,
Marvin, Glenn, Megan, and Evan.
You are what I treasure most in this life.
True gifts from the Lord.

Paperback ISBN 978-1-64917-418-5
eBook ISBN 978-1-64917-419-2

Editors: Amy R. Anguish and Kaci Banks

Cover by Linda Fulkerson, www.bookmarketinggraphics.com

Beyond Shattered Dreams is a work of fiction. Where real people, events, establishments, organizations, or locales appear, they are used fictitiously. All other elements of the novel are drawn from the author's imagination.

All other scriptures are taken from the KING JAMES VERSION (KJV): KING JAMES VERSION, public domain.

"And ye shall seek Me and find Me,
when ye shall search for me with all your heart."
(Jeremiah 29:13)

1

Mississippi River near Memphis, Tennessee
April 27, 1865, 1:50 a.m.

W ill Everett smacked a hand to his neck, ending the annoying buzz of a mosquito. He huffed. Between the biting insects and the mob of fidgety soldiers vying for a spot, how was a man to get any sleep?

Not to mention having no bed to lie on.

He snugged his uniform collar higher and scratched his neck. Already, an itchy welt was forming below his ear. One of many bites since last evening's sendoff from Vicksburg. He'd been eager to leave Camp Fisk and board the *Sultana* but hadn't expected such a hoard of passengers. The notion of remaining aboard the frenzied, overcrowded steamboat all the way to Indiana turned his stomach.

Yet, he'd not complain. So long as the vessel carried him home to his family.

Heavy clouds overhead shielded the moon and stars from view, leaving the night eerily black. A nearby soldier stirred awake, his sleep no doubt hindered by the awkward conditions.

Sitting taller, he glanced at Will. "Still black as pitch, I see. You got the time, fella?"

With a yawn, Will reached into his trousers and pulled out his brass pocket watch, a gift from his folks when he'd turned eighteen. He ran his thumb over the watch's smooth casing. He'd gone to great lengths to keep it hidden from the Rebs during his imprisonment. So much had happened in the nearly two years since he'd left home. His family would likely not recognize him with his scruffy beard and gaunt frame. Even now, weeks after eating something besides scanty prison rations, his uniform sagged on his malnourished body like a boy who'd donned his father's breeches.

The war and prison life had scarred him in more ways than physically. He'd witnessed appalling images no person should.

Popping the watch open, Will strained to see the thin hands in the dim light. He kept his voice low to not disturb those fortunate enough to sleep. "Just shy of two a.m."

His companion scrubbed a hand down his face. "Arr. This night seems endless. I've known better conditions in a Confederate prison camp."

"That may be, but this steamboat is ferrying us home."

"You've a point there, soldier." With that, the private settled back in his spot.

As Will slipped the treasured watch back into his pocket, a spray of fine mist dampened his cheek. He pulled his kepi down over his face and leaned his head against the stair rail. For lack of a better place, he'd settled on the *Sultana*'s stair landing between the steamboat's boiler and hurricane decks in an attempt to catch a few winks of sleep. Yet, the boat's noisy boiler engines and rough sway over the swollen Mississippi made rest near impossible.

A year of battle, followed by nine months of wasting away in a congested, disease-ridden prison, had taken its toll on the lot of them. A good number of his regiment hadn't survived. This mosquito-infested steamboat teeming with rank, unwashed soldiers was little improvement, but at least something better was on the way.

A weak smile tugged at one corner of his mouth. Nothing could faze him now that home was within reach. He could almost taste his mom's fried chicken and fresh apple pie. He subconsciously licked his lips, the very thought of the delicacies causing his deprived stomach to rumble.

A deafening blast erupted from the rear of the boat, followed by a flash of brilliant light. A surge of pain tore through the side of Will's head as his body catapulted into the air like a stone from a slingshot. For a brief moment, his world fell to silent darkness. He startled awake as his body smacked against frigid water and plunged beneath. Dark murkiness engulfed him. Unable to tell up from down, he held his breath and struggled to regain his bearings. Panicked, he batted his arms and kicked his legs, praying he would reach the surface before his lungs filled.

A moment later, he emerged, gasping for air. He fought to keep his head above water, the engorged river lobbing him along like driftwood. What had happened? How had he ended up stranded in midstream in the dead of night? His mind whirled, too foggy to recall anything outside of landing in the murky water.

Bright light pulled his attention upstream, and he struggled to see past blurred, water-streaked vision. A wave of nausea coursed through him at the sight of a wrecked steamboat, its back half engulfed in flames. With shrill cries, soldiers plunged from its decks. Countless others thrashed along in the water, clamoring for debris, while those less fortunate floated lifelessly on the current.

Fatigue tore at Will's limbs as he latched onto a large slab of wood drifting past. Breathless, he heaved himself onto it, pain throbbing in the side of his head. He shivered, colder out of the water than in. Drowsiness tugged at him as he drifted farther from the wrecked boat. Merciless cries beckoned around him in the darkness. He closed his eyes, his mind cluttered and confused. A lost feeling engulfed him. None of this made sense.

He shivered. So cold.

His heartbeat slowed as if his very life were being snuffed out. Had he survived the blast only to freeze to death or drown in the river?

His heart sank. *Lord, have mercy.*

2

Memphis, Tennessee
April 29, 1865

"No!" Will's eyes jerked open, and the swirl of water engulfing him vanished. Instead, rafters stretched out above him. His breaths came fast and shallow.

Hurried footsteps padded closer. A gentle hand restrained his shoulder. "Easy, soldier. You're safe now."

The woman's gritty southern drawl sounded strange in his ears. He veered his head toward her and immediately regretted the action. A surge of pain shot through his already pounding head. He reached a hand up, fingering bandages rather than hair. "What happened?"

The short, squat woman leaned closer, her fleshy face framed by a loose chignon of auburn hair. Given her bloodied white smock, he presumed she was a nurse. "You don't remember?"

Will scoured his mind for some recollection but came up lacking. He pinched the bridge of his nose to ward off the blur in his vision, as well as mounting confusion. "Not really. My mind's awful foggy."

"You've taken a nasty blow to the head. Your memory will

clear in time." She straightened and patted his arm. "What's your name, soldier?"

Though a simple request, he struggled to comply. "I ... I don't remember."

The nurse blinked, the creases above her nose deepening. "Where are you from?"

Will opened his mouth to answer but drew a blank. "I'm not sure."

With a shake of her head, the woman rested her hands on her hips. "We'd best have the doctor take a look at you. I fear you may have a concussion. Have you no recollections at all?"

The more Will sought answers, the more his head ached. "Only darkness, being in water, and seeing a fiery boat and lots of debris." His eyes glossed over from the memory. "Men were moaning in pain, and there were ... dead bodies floating all around." Shaking off the morbid scene, he peered over at her. "I don't know what, but something terrible happened."

The nurse smoothed her soiled smock over her ample middle, her lips flattening in a thin line. "Two days ago, the steamboat you were on, the *Sultana*, exploded."

"Two days ago?" He mumbled, then glanced at the caregiver. "Have I been asleep all that time?"

"More or less. You thrashed about from time to time but never fully awakened until now."

Will tried to wrap his mind around the incident. "What caused the explosion?"

She checked the bandages on his chest and left arm. "Apparently, the boat was grossly overloaded, which strained the boiler engines. A majority of those on board didn't survive. You were one of the fortunate ones. Rescuers discovered you unconscious, adrift on some debris, and brought you here."

"Where's *here*?"

"Gayoso Hospital. Memphis, Tennessee."

"*Memphis*? What am I doing in Memphis?"

"From what I gather, the *Sultana* was traveling north from

6

Vicksburg. You must have boarded there with the other parolees."

He swallowed, his mouth suddenly dry as cotton. Just what sort of man was he, to have been imprisoned? "Parolee?"

One of the nurse's brows shot up. "You must have suffered quite a blow indeed not to recall a stint in one of our Confederate prisons." She gestured to the room lined with patients and the dingy blue uniform jackets scattered about. "From what I hear, you Yankee prisoners were paroled and sent to Camp Fisk outside Vicksburg when the war ended. You were headed home when the explosion happened." She bent lower, crossing her arms over her chest. "You do recall the war, don't ya?"

Will closed his eyes, attempting to squeeze even one telling image into his thoughts. Though he had a sense the nurse's words rang true, his wounded head and body hurt too much to concentrate. With a sigh, his eyelids bobbed open. "I'm sorry."

The nurse rested a hand on his arm, her countenance softening. "Rest easy then while I fetch some broth. After two days without food, you must be famished."

Indeed, he should be, but instead, his stomach bordered on nausea. He dampened parched lips, unwilling to refuse her kindness. "Thank you."

A faint smile edged onto her mouth, then vanished just as quickly. She patted her skirt pockets as though in search of some forgotten object. Her creased brow relaxed as her hand apparently latched onto what she sought. With a satisfied nod, she drew the item out and shoved it toward him. "Perhaps this will help you remember. It was in your trousers when you arrived."

Something weighty and smooth dropped into Will's palm. He brought the object closer, squinting to clear his jumbled vision. *A pocket watch?* He turned it over in his hand, brushing his thumb over the emblem etched at its center. Though the brass timepiece felt strangely at home in his hand, he had no recollection of owning one. "I don't recognize it."

The nurse's lips lifted in a weak grin. "Well, perhaps in time. I'll let the doctor know you're awake and see to your dinner."

As she strode away, Will popped the watch lid open. Moisture had gathered under the crystal, making the long, thin hands difficult to read. The lack of ticking, coupled with the motionless hands, likely meant the plunge in the water had rendered the watch useless. To be certain, he wound the crown a few half-turns and placed it near his ear.

Nothing.

As he started to close the ruined watch, he noticed a small word etched into the lid of the casing. Concentrating, he held it closer and squinted. His eyes widened as he made out the word Will, followed by a capital *E*. *Will*. Was that his name? And did his last name start with E? The name Will sounded as foreign to him as the nurse's southern drawl.

The E could stand for any name. Edwards, Ellis, or Enos. None of which sounded familiar.

With a heavy sigh, he snapped the lid closed and stared up at the wooden rafters, his mind swirling. Who was he? Why couldn't he remember?

Apparently, he'd been through a lot. He lifted his head high enough to see a blanket covering his lower half while much of his upper body was swathed in bandages. By the looks of him and the level of pain he was in, it was a wonder he'd survived.

The throbbing intensified and he closed his eyes, shutting out his ponderings as well. Maybe the nurse was right. He simply needed time to collect his senses. Yet, judging by what she'd said, he couldn't help but wonder if some of what he'd been through would better remain forgotten.

3

August 28, 1865
(Four Months Later)

"Ticket, please."

Sweaty palmed, Will handed the steward the note the hospital had provided, assuring free passage north as far as Evansville, Indiana.

The spindly crewman studied the handwritten note, then peered over at Will. "This is dated June. Why the delay?"

"I was injured aboard the *Sultana*. It's taken me time to recuperate and find my bearings."

"The *Sultana*, eh?" Something akin to compassion flickered in the steward's close-set eyes. "You're fortunate to be alive."

"I'm aware of that, sir."

The steward returned the paper to Will. "Let's hope this voyage ends differently."

With a nod, Will slipped the letter back into his pocket, shouldered his duffel bag, and stepped aboard the steamboat. Upon release from the hospital in June, he'd received a red union suit, a set of clothes, and $13. Not much. But a start. A few odd jobs over recent weeks had earned him enough to travel north in an attempt to find some answers.

A sense of lostness kneaded through him as he took in the array of passengers. All strangers. Despite the doctor and nurse's assurance his memory should return, months had passed with only vague snippets of what his life had once been. Restless nights filled with random, unsettling dreams hounded him relentlessly. Many bore nightmarish images that often woke him in a sweat. Other more pleasant visions ended too soon, taunting his inability to piece them together.

None had provoked a memory of who he was or where he was from. Did he have family awaiting his return? Parents? Siblings? Likely in his early twenties, might he have a sweetheart or even, perhaps, a wife? If so, by now, they'd probably given up hope of ever seeing him again. The thought of causing loved ones undue concern or heartbreak bothered him.

He fisted his hands. If only he knew where to begin.

Information he'd gleaned from other survivors revealed the vast majority of soldiers aboard the *Sultana* had originated from Indiana or Ohio. Such a sizeable area could take years to comb. Seeing as he'd been guaranteed passage to Evansville, he'd begin there, following every lead until he uncovered his roots. For lack of a better name, he'd taken on the surname Evans, after his destination. Will Evans was as good a name as any until his true identity came to light.

Music and laughter poured from within the heart of the steamboat, grating on Will's nerves. He wove along the deck, avoiding eye contact with those he met. Shamed by his inability to initiate even a simple conversation, he wandered the unfamiliar steamboat like a stray dog searching for a home. The rest of the *Sultana* survivors had departed months ago. Although they, too, had been strangers, at least Will and they had a shared experience to draw upon. But any attempt at small talk with these steamboat travelers was sure to end poorly.

Finding a vacant spot near the massive side paddlewheel, he

gazed over the vast Mississippi River. Despite the humid air, a cold chill worked through him at memory of the murky water that had encompassed him months earlier.

A memory he longed to forget but couldn't.

As the steamboat disembarked, he clutched the side rail, still unsteady on his feet from long weeks of recovery. The floorboard creaked beneath his boots, stirring a vague recollection, as did the uneven sway of the steamboat. The hum of the boiler engines and the sooty smell of coal pulled his attention to the stern and the enormous smokestacks billowing black smoke.

His breaths shallowed as his mind revisited the disturbing images of the fiery steamboat and piercing cries all around. His shoulders shook from the dread of repeating them.

Yea, though I walk through the valley of the shadow of death, I will fear no evil, for Thou art with me.

The verse of Scripture coursed through his thoughts as clearly as if he'd had a Bible before him. Though the words should have brought reassurance, instead, they frustrated him. How could he recall the verse so plainly and not even remember his name? Why had he even survived the tragic incident? What sort of life could he have without purpose or identity? Utterly alone? Right now, God seemed as aloof as his past.

Will fingered the two-inch scar above his left ear. The slight bulge, devoid of hair, no longer pained him, but remained a vivid reminder of his lost self. He tugged his cap lower on his head and slid the pocket watch from his trousers. The ruined trinket remained his only link to his identity. Running his thumb over the smooth casing, he released a determined breath. No matter how long he had to search or how far he had to travel, he would not stop until he found home.

Gallagher Home near Elmira, New York
August 28, 1865

SOMETHING WAS UP.

Lydia Gallagher eyed her older brother Luke. He'd instigated this family gathering, and by the curious grin he and his sweetheart, Adelaide, were sharing, Lydia had an inkling why.

Intent on finishing their meal, her brother Drew, his wife, Caroline, and Mama seemed oblivious to the inconspicuous goings-on. Lydia's gaze slipped to the empty chair at the head of the table, and a twinge of regret rippled through her. She forced a grin. If Papa were here, he'd have noted the couple's silent exchange, winked at her, then made some off-handed remark to force their hand.

But the war between the states had stolen Papa away. By God's grace, Drew and Luke had both been spared. But her stomach had been in knots until their return, fearful the same fate might befall them. How blessed she and Mama were to have them home again ... and for them to have brought such fine ladies into their family. Who would have thought both brothers would fall for Southerners? And yet, over the past few months, Caroline and Adelaide had become like sisters to her.

Lydia never wished to be apart from any of them again.

With a loud clearing of his throat, Luke leaned forward in his chair. "Uh, folks? Adelaide and I have something we'd like to share."

Clasping her hands together under her chin, Lydia held back a squeal. She'd known Adelaide was the girl for Luke since she'd come to live with them earlier that spring. After her devastating burns during the fall of Richmond.

When everyone stilled, Luke slipped an arm around Adelaide's shoulders, looking as though he might burst. She returned his warm smile, eyes filled with admiration. Blotches of red tainted Luke's cheeks as he turned his gaze on the rest of them. "There's no simpler way to say it. I've asked Adelaide to be my wife, and she's agreed!"

Joyful chatter erupted throughout the dining room, everyone talking at once like a barnyard of cackling chickens.

When the group quieted, Mama was the first to speak. "Your father would have been very pleased, as am I." Her eyes grew misty as her gaze drifted to the far end of the table where Papa had sat. Though she rarely spoke of it, his passing had left a fearsome void in her heart.

As it had Lydia's. She'd been twelve when the telegram arrived, relaying news of Papa's death. It had taken her months to accept the fact he wasn't coming home. How she missed his wit and amity.

Luke leaned to kiss Mama's cheek. "Thank you."

Sated with questions, Lydia refocused. "How soon will you marry? Have you decided upon a date?"

With a shake of his head, Luke eased back in his chair. "Not yet. We'll need time to find a place to live."

"Uh ... that may not be a problem." Drew scratched his cheek and cut a glance at Caroline. At her discreet nod, he clasped her hand. "Caroline and I have an announcement as well."

Lydia grinned. *A baby. It had to be.* But at their somber expressions, her smile faded.

"What announcement is that?" Mama's unsettled tone hinted she'd noted their hesitancy as well.

Releasing a long breath, Drew swiped a crumb from the table. "That ... Luke and Adelaide can have the cottage house because we won't be needing it much longer."

Luke's brow furrowed. "Then where will you and Caroline live?"

The conflicted expression on Drew's face was telling. A hush fell over the gathering in eagerness for an explanation. At last, he met Mama's gaze square on, a tinge of sadness in his eyes. "Washington."

"Washington?" The word burst from Lydia like a cannon blast.

"What do you mean, son?" The slight quiver in her mother's

voice was disturbing enough to incite Lydia to go and stand behind her, hand on her shoulder.

With a quiet cough, Drew leaned forward in his chair. "As you know, General Grant was recently promoted to General of the Army. I worked a special assignment for him during the war. Now he's asked me to serve under him again ... on a more permanent basis."

Mama's tone deepened. "And you've accepted?"

Drew and Caroline exchanged glances ahead of Drew's response. "The work suits me, and the move would give Caroline more opportunity to pursue her nursing. We've prayed about and discussed it, and ... feel it's the right decision."

All the air fled from Lydia's lungs, her hopes of the family remaining together shattering like broken glass. "But you've been home such a short time. Washington is so far away. We'll never see you."

Drew offered a weak smile. "'Course you will. We'll only be a few hours away by train." He turned to Luke. "Though I hate the thought of burdening Luke here with the brunt of the farm work. I promise I'll do my best to take time off when I can to help with planting and harvest."

The pledge did little to bolster the group's dampened spirits. At last, Luke stretched out his arm. "A fella can't ask for more than that. Congratulations, big brother. We hate to see you go, but the cottage house will sure ease our situation in finding a place to live."

Drew stood and clasped his hand, the tension in his face ebbing. "Thanks, Luke. We were hoping you'd see it that way."

Numb, Lydia wrapped an arm about her middle. She'd thought after returning from war, her brothers would never wish to leave again. And now, mere months later, Drew was going away. For good. Weren't families supposed to stay together?

"How soon will you leave?" Though still somewhat strained, Mama's voice was again calm.

Settling back in his seat, Drew appeared more at ease. "Not until the first of the year. We'll leave shortly after Christmas."

"Just the right amount of time to plan a wedding." With a grin, Luke turned to Adelaide. "What do you say to a Christmas Eve wedding?"

Adelaide's lips lifted. "I can't think of a better time."

Luke gave a brisk nod. "Christmas Eve it is, then. Come the new year, we'll all make a fresh start. I, for one, can't wait to see what the Lord has in store."

Lydia gnawed at her lower lip. What did He have in store for her? Loneliness? Boredom?

She suppressed her growing angst. So much change at once. Just when she'd come to enjoy having everyone around, they were leaving, resurrecting all the scars of losing Papa.

In a few short months, she and Mama would be by themselves again in this big old farmhouse once so full of life. Her brothers were grown men now with lives of their own.

And it appeared there'd be no holding them back.

4

Corydon, Indiana
Christmas Eve Day, 1865

"There you are, Will. One month's wages ... along with a Christmas bonus."

"Thanks, Mr. Hastings. I appreciate it." Will took a quick count of the bills in his palm. Twenty-five dollars would be enough to shoulder the expense of relocating until he found another place of employment. He seemed to have a knack for any job he set his mind to do, which wasn't much help in determining his chosen trade. But outdoor work suited him best.

The storeowner leaned on the countertop, his thinning hair combed to one side to conceal his balding head. "Sure you won't stay a while longer? You're a good worker. I hate to lose you."

"Thanks, but I'd best be on my way. I'm obliged to you for the work." Will tucked the money in his trousers pocket along with what he'd saved from previous jobs. Over the past four months, he'd worked as a farmhand, for a sawmill, a cooper, and now a mercantile. Of his employers, Mr. Hastings had been his favorite. But Will couldn't afford to stay in an area once he'd exhausted his efforts to locate his family.

He'd covered many of the southernmost counties, but Indiana was a big state. If he was ever going to locate his kin, it was time to press farther north. And if nothing turned up there, he had all of Ohio to tackle.

With a brisk nod, Mr. Hastings straightened. "Have you somewhere to go for Christmas? You're welcome to spend it with my family. I'm certain the missus won't mind. Our son and daughter will be there with their families. One more wouldn't be a bother."

A lump lodged in Will's throat. The thought of spending Christmas with a real family was definitely enticing, but he wouldn't feel right intruding upon a household not his own. "Thanks, but I have other plans."

It wasn't a lie. He had his hotel room paid up through tomorrow and likely would head out midday in search of his next locale. Besides, it was best not to get too attached.

Mr. Hastings thrust out his palm. "Well, Godspeed to you, son."

"Thank you, sir." Will gave the proprietor's hand a hearty shake, then donned his cap and took up his box of supplies. He'd purchased only what was necessary, hoping one day to buy a horse. Not only would the animal provide an easier mode of travel but company as well.

But horses required care and money. As long as he was transient, owning one would prove difficult. He glanced at his worn boots, already dreading the day he'd have to break in a new pair. Sore feet and travel didn't mix.

The bell jingled above his head as he opened the door to leave. His gut clenched at the thought of spending another night alone. He'd had too much solitude, and that likely wouldn't change anytime soon. Though more than one employer had offered him room and board, he'd opted to bed down in an outbuilding or hotel room, fearful his frequent nightmares would infringe on his host's sleep.

A chilling wind pushed him along as he ambled down the

street toward the hotel. He tugged his coat collar higher on his neck, loneliness gnawing at him. How many more months would he drift aimlessly about with no place to call home?

He'd like to think he and the Lord had grown closer over the months of solitude, but the truth was, the longer his quest went unfulfilled, the more callous his heart became. Like his half-hearted, unanswered prayers, he was losing hope of ever finding his family.

Or himself.

Gallagher Home

"I NOW PRONOUNCE you man and wife. You may kiss your bride."

Lydia's lips spread in a wide grin, her heart melting as Adelaide leaned into Luke's tender embrace, sealing their marriage vows with a kiss. How beautiful her friend looked in her cream, off-shoulder taffeta fringed with lace. Thick ebony ringlets danced along the nape of her neck beneath a simple veil. It seemed only a short while since Adelaide had come to live with them as a stranger needing a place to heal.

Now, she was family.

Luke's vivid blue eyes sparked as he stole another quick kiss from his bride before turning to greet the small gathering of family and friends. The parlor furniture had been moved aside to make room for rows of chairs to accommodate the dozen guests.

With a radiant smile, Adelaide turned to hug Lydia. "We're truly sisters now."

"Yes." Moisture pooled in Lydia's eyes as she held her friend close and whispered in her ear. "I'm going to miss you."

Releasing her hold, Adelaide voiced a soft chuckle. "We'll only be gone a few days and living not far away when we return."

"I know. It's just going to be different with Drew and

Caroline gone and you and Luke living at the cottage house instead of here."

Adelaide placed a gloved hand on Lydia's cheek, a slight pout on her lips. "We'll see each other often, I promise."

With a half-hearted nod, Lydia smiled, hopeful her friend's words would ring true. She gave Luke a warm hug then stepped aside to allow others a turn. Looking on, the moment seemed bittersweet. Tomorrow's Christmas would likely be the last time the family would be together for a long while.

Drew and Caroline had moved into Drew's old room for the night to allow Luke and Adelaide the privacy of the cottage on their wedding night. They would leave the day after Christmas for Pennsylvania for a short honeymoon. By the time they returned, Drew and Caroline would have left for Washington.

Lydia sighed. Everything was happening so fast. She'd waited years for the family to be together again. Yet, it seemed her dear brothers had returned from war merely to go their own way. Chastening herself for her dismal mood, she drew a determined breath. She was happy for them. Truly.

Her shoulders sagged. Then why this overwhelming sense of loss?

A hand touched her arm, startling her from her reverie. She turned to look into Mama's moist, joy-filled eyes. "Come help in the kitchen, will you?"

Though preparing meals wasn't Lydia's favorite task, helping ready the food would prove a welcome distraction from her clash of emotions. With a final glance at the happy couple, she fell into step behind her mother. As they reached the entryway to the kitchen, Mama moaned softly and leaned into the doorframe, clutching a hand to her chest.

Rushing to her, Lydia slipped an arm around her waist. "What is it, Mama? Is something wrong?"

Though Mama seemed to struggle for breath, she shook her head. "No. Just a bit winded from all the excitement."

"Are you sure? You look pale." It wasn't like Mama to tire or turn pallid when hosting a small gathering. Something wasn't right. "I'll have Drew fetch Doctor Royce."

Straightening, Mama flashed a tepid grin. "Nonsense. I'm fine." With a steadying breath, she took a determined step forward. "Come. We have guests to tend to."

Unconvinced, Lydia pinched her brows, intent on keeping a watchful eye on her mother.

Festive fiddle music drifted from the parlor, lifting Lydia's spirits. This was a day of joy and celebration. And yet, she couldn't help but feel it was also the onset of a new chapter in the Gallagher household.

One she wasn't certain she would relish.

5

Outside Baldwin, New York
Monday, May 4, 1868
(Two Years Later)

W ill shifted his duffel higher on his shoulder, eyeing the stalled carriage up ahead. By the looks of things, the young couple was in a bind. One of the rear wheels lay flat on the road, the carriage cocked to one side. Uncertain what the trouble was, Will hesitated, then increased his pace.

As he neared, the man veered toward him, his dismayed expression brightening. "Mornin'."

Will nodded and edged closer. "Looks like you could use a hand."

"Sure could." The good-natured fellow looked to be about Will's age, if not younger. He flashed a lopsided grin. "The wheel nut worked its way off, and I neglected to pack my axle jack. I could use someone to lift while I fasten it."

"I can manage that."

Wrapped in a shawl, the raven-haired beauty resting against the front wheel stood upright, her dark eyes hopeful. "Oh, thank you. We've been stranded here more than an hour."

Will tipped his cap. If he wasn't mistaken, the woman's thick middle bore signs she was with child. "Glad to help, ma'am."

The young man stuck out his palm. "I'm Luke Gallagher, and this is my wife, Adelaide."

Giving his hand a shake, Will dipped his chin. "Will Evans." He still felt a bit phony using a borrowed name, but what choice did he have? He knew no other.

"Good to meet you." With an amiable nod, Luke slipped on a leather glove and slathered the axle spindle with grease. "We appreciate you lending a hand. We're on our way home from a trip, and you know how kinfolk fret if you're late."

The casual remark pricked Will. Actually, he didn't. The only sense of being missed he knew was his recurring dream of a golden-haired female dressed in black running to meet him. For better than two years, he'd puzzled over the image. The face remained too obscure to distinguish the woman's age or features. Whether wife, mother, or sister, she'd likely long since given up hope of his return.

Luke set the wheel upright and gestured for Will to lift the axle. "Where ya from, Will?"

The question jarred him back to the task at hand. Bending over, he gripped the back axle and held it level, grateful the carriage wasn't too weighty. "Indiana." *Or Ohio.* He still couldn't be certain.

Luke slid the wheel into place, then eased back on his haunches, peering up at Will. "You're a ways from home. What brings you out east?"

To be honest, Will had tired of his endless search for his identity, hopped a train, and rode until the appealing landscape compelled him to stop. But he wasn't about to admit that to a stranger. "I'm looking for employment."

Standing, Luke brushed his hands together. "Is that so?" He shared a look with his wife, unspoken words seeming to pass between them before he returned his gaze to Will. "Ever do any farm work?"

"A bit. I've tried my hand at most everything."

Luke's eyes brightened. "You, uh, headed anywhere in particular?"

Will got the sense he was about to be hit with a proposition. He stepped away from the carriage and slid his duffel strap over his shoulder. "One place is as good as another as far as I'm concerned."

"So, you don't have any obligations or anywhere you need to be?"

Sadly, Will hadn't even one. "Not to speak of."

A wide grin spilled onto Luke's lips. "Then what would you say to working for me?"

Will chuckled. "Just like that? Without knowing anything about me?"

"You were kind enough to help a stranger in need. That says a lot about a person."

Something within Will thrilled at the offer. He could see himself working for this agreeable couple. He moistened his lips. "Farming?"

"Yep. Our place isn't far. Just a few miles outside of Elmira. A couple hours ride from here." Luke leaned against the carriage, crossing his arms over his chest. "The farm's a bit much for one fella to manage. My brother Drew moved to Washington a couple years back. He comes to help when he's able but, with his job and growing family, those times are fewer nowadays." He squinted against the waning sun. "So, how about it? You want the job? We don't have a lot of ready cash, but we'll provide room and board as well as a share of the crop for wages."

Scratching his cheek, Will weighed the offer. Being paid a crop share meant he'd need to stay at least through harvest. Longer than he'd remained in one place since leaving Memphis. But the way the job fell into his lap, it seemed foolhardy to turn it down. And gauging by the couple's hopeful expressions, to decline would bring certain disappointment.

Maybe this was where the Lord intended him to be for now. His lips lifted. "I believe I'll take you up on that arrangement."

Thumbing his hat higher on his head, Luke slipped an arm around his wife's waist, a pleasant grin lining both faces. "Well, all right then. Hop on. We'll give you a lift."

Will obliged by hefting himself on back. Leaning against the side of the carriage, he crossed his legs at the ankles. He flexed his tired feet inside his worn, dusty boots, feeling bits of grit inside where slits in the back of the heels had allowed caked dirt to settle. Staying in one place would have its benefits. Maybe now his calloused feet could have a much-needed rest and he could afford to break in another new pair of work boots.

Mrs. Gallagher chuckled. "Won't Ma and Lydia be surprised."

Will knit his brow. *Ma and Lydia?* Just how many folks were in their household? After being on his own so long, living around a passel of people would take some getting used to.

As the carriage jerked forward, Will cast a glance at the couple in the front seat. Strangers moments ago. Now, his employers. They knew hardly anything about him, and yet they'd offered him a place to stay and a job to sustain him.

Barging in on the Gallagher family felt intrusive.

But then, so far as he knew, he had no family to call his own.

And likely never would.

LYDIA SNAPPED her book shut and glanced out the sitting room window, sighing. Not even Charles Dickens could hold her interest for any length of time, it seemed.

Lonesomeness crept in whenever Luke and Adelaide were in Pennsylvania visiting Adelaide's cousin, Clarissa. The ventures came far too frequently for Lydia's liking. With them away, she was hard-pressed to occupy herself.

At seventeen, she should have scads of social engagements.

Luke and Adelaide had wed shortly after their eighteenth birthdays. But other than an occasional church gathering, most of Lydia's time was spent at home. Not that she hadn't had suitors come to call. None simply struck her fancy.

Then there was Mama. Though Mama often made light of her occasional "spells," as she referred to them, Lydia had finally persuaded her to visit Doctor Royce. When told she had a weak heart, Mama requested Lydia not share the diagnosis with anyone, not even Drew or Luke. Despite Doctor Royce's warning to limit activity, Mama insisted on doing more than she ought. Someone needed to stay nearby to keep an eye on her.

A job that necessarily fell to Lydia.

She stood and paced the length of the room, her boot heels clicking a steady rhythm along the floorboards. "When do you suppose they'll be back?"

Intent on her knitting, Mama sat contentedly in her wingback chair. "They'll be home when they get here."

A firm knock at the door stilled Lydia mid-stride. She paused, listening. Had she missed hearing their approach? It couldn't be Luke. He always gave three brisk raps and then trod in. And the strikes were much too heavy-handed to be Adelaide's.

Unless something was wrong.

Her eyes locked with Mama's, a flicker of unease washing over her. "I'll answer it."

Setting her knitting aside, Mama pushed up from the chair. "I'll go with you."

Eager to shield Mama from ill news, Lydia quickened her pace, her ample skirt swishing side to side as she walked. With a steadying breath, she eased the door open. Her eyes flared at the unexpected visitor. "Mr. Malloy. Good afternoon."

Guthrie Malloy bobbed his head, tipping the brim of his dust-covered hat. Close-set gray eyes peered down at her, a wiry beard and mustache concealing the lower half of his face.

"Afternoon, Miss Gallagher." His thick neck lengthened as he looked past her to the hallway beyond. "I'd like a word with your ma."

Reluctantly, Lydia stepped aside to let her mother approach. The last time the neighbor paid them a visit, it was to ask permission to run his cattle across their land to shorten his trip to market. He'd neglected to mention he would allow them to trample their fields. What would he plead for this time?

Mama shouldered her way through, mouth taut. "What is it you need to speak with me about, Mr. Malloy?"

He took a step back, motioning to the pair of wicker chairs on his left. "Could we sit?"

Lydia's shoulders clenched at the unusual request. Guthrie Malloy had never been one to socialize. He was the type to state his business and be on his way without so much as a "good day." Warily, she followed Mama onto the veranda, trying to make sense of the unannounced visit.

"You sure have a nice place here, Mrs. Gallagher." The compliment came off a bit thick from Malloy's lips.

"Thank you." Smoothing her dress out under her, Mama took a seat, meeting the neighbor's gaze straight on. "What can we do for you, Mr. Malloy?"

When Lydia remained standing, Malloy eased into the chair across from Mama and peeled off his hat. "I'll get right to the point." Lips spread in a tight grin, he raked a hand over his thinning chestnut hair flecked with gray. "I wanna make you an offer."

Lydia gripped the back of Mama's chair and arched a brow. That sounded more like the Mr. Malloy she was acquainted with. She didn't trust the man. He liked to twist situations to his advantage.

He cleared phlegm from his throat as though fighting nerves.

Another guest, Mama might have offered a cup of tea, but she posed no such amenity with Mr. Malloy. Though Mama never spoke ill of their neighbor, Lydia sensed her mother's feelings for the man mimicked her own. "An offer? What sort of offer?"

"Like I say, ma'am, this is a right fine piece of property. Your husband and boys kept it up real well for a good many years." He leaned forward in his chair, calloused hands on his knees. "I mean no disrespect, but since your husband's passing and your older son left, it seems more than your younger boy can handle."

Lydia bristled, biting her cheek to keep still. What business was it of his to keep account of their property's state of affairs?

Mama sat taller, her shoulders stiffening. "Luke manages quite well considering, Mr. Malloy."

He raised a hand to quiet her. "Now hear me out, Mrs. Gallagher. I won't dispute that, but if I was to take a portion of your land off your hands, he might fare better. Just a portion, mind ya."

"And what portion would that be?" A hint of coolness seeped into Mama's tone.

Mr. Malloy's eyes took on the look of a ravenous dog. "The stretch of land adjacent to mine. I'd pay you a fair sum, and the extra acreage would sure come in handy for my herd."

At last, he spoke his true intentions. Lydia gritted her teeth, unable to hold her tongue any longer. "Mr. Malloy, if you think ..."

Mama's slender fingers gripped Lydia's arm firmly, stilling her sure-to-be hasty words. "We appreciate your concern, Mr. Malloy, but we have no wish to sell our land."

Their surly neighbor edged forward in his chair. "At least give it some thought. I only hope to ease your boy's load."

Lydia pursed her lips. Like pigeons swim, he did. The man had his sights set on owning more land, was all. The last thing Papa told her before he left for war was to take care of Mama and the farm. And that's what she intended to do. Leaning to the side, she studied her mother's expression, grateful it displayed no weakening of her resolve.

With a composed smile, Mama tipped her chin higher. "If

need be, Luke will take on a hired hand to aid in the demands of the farm. I'm confident the Lord will provide the help we need."

As if sensing her mind was made up, Mr. Malloy slowly rose from his chair. "With so many young men lost to the war, good workers might be hard to come by. In time, I think you'll find my offer a sound one." He donned his hat, all the pleasantness fleeing from his expression. "The offer stands. When you're ready to sell, you or your boy come see me."

Without another word, he pivoted and downed the veranda steps.

Heat burned Lydia's cheeks as she stifled the urge to spout a harsh reply. The fellow was much too sure of himself. Mama would never sell even an acre of the family's property to the likes of him.

Would she?

Lydia waited until the neighbor was out of earshot, then dropped into his vacated chair. "That man is far too bold and ambitious."

Mama sounded a soft chuckle. "I'm sure his offer was well meant."

"More like greedy." Lydia said under her breath.

"Now, now, child. You mustn't judge too harshly. He did offer to buy the land, not steal it."

Lydia scoffed. "Like he did Mrs. Lansing's after her husband passed, paying half what the property was worth when he knew she had little choice but to sell?" Edging forward in her chair, Lydia clasped her mother's arm. "Promise you won't sell. Please, Mama? This should remain Gallagher land. Grandma and Grandpa bought the property. Papa was born in this house, as were Drew, Luke, and me."

A hope Lydia had for her own children, as well, one day.

Mama's gentle hand cradled Lydia's chin. "I can promise you this, dear. I won't do anything I feel would go against your father's wishes and that I haven't thoroughly talked over with the Lord."

Mustering a slight grin, Lydia breathed a bit easier. She knew in her heart Mama would never go against Papa's or the Lord's will. But while the words brought her some semblance of reassurance, she also recognized something disturbing in them.

Mama hadn't said she *wouldn't* sell the land.

6

"Well, here she is. The Gallagher farm."

Will gazed at the quaint house flanked by fallow land, rolling hills decked with trees in the distance. Small, but homey-looking. He could get used to this picturesque landscape.

Hopping from the carriage, he perused the cottage. It seemed a bit slight for a farmstead. Four people living in such close quarters would leave little room for privacy. And where were the outbuildings? Other than a small garden shed, there were none. Where would he sleep? Hopefully not in that tiny home. His cursed nightmares would drive everyone out.

He gripped his duffel, wondering if he'd made a mistake. Shifting his weight from one foot to the other, he mustered the courage to speak. "I don't wish to put you out. I'd be happy to bunk with the horses if you show me where that might be."

Luke's mouth cracked a wide grin as he helped his wife from the carriage. "You aren't putting anyone out. This here is where Adelaide and I live. I only stopped to unload our things and drop her off." He gestured behind Will. "The main farmhouse is over yonder. There's plenty of room for you there."

Pivoting, Will breathed a sigh of relief to see the two-story house and barn in the distance. That was more like it.

"You can head up that way and introduce yourself to Ma and my sister, Lydia, if you like. I'll be along once I finish here."

With a reluctant nod, Will started down the path. The breeze held a chill as afternoon gave way to evening. The sun dipped lower in the west, casting long shadows over the landscape. Snugging his coat collar higher on his neck, Will studied the two-story farmhouse. Ample space for only two people. Would they think him odd for requesting to bed down in the barn? Regardless, he refused to subject them to his disruptive dreams.

Movement on the porch caught his eye. In the diminished light, a woman appeared to be either pacing or sweeping. He swallowed. Despite being constantly on the move, meeting new people had never been his strong suit. He only hoped Luke's kin would prove as welcoming as he and his wife.

As he neared, the woman paused at the top step. Will's breaths shallowed, and he slowed his pace. Her blonde hair and petite frame closely resembled the girl's in his dream. Yet, instead of running to greet him, this young lady remained in place, gaze fixed intently upon him.

Who's that fellow?

Lydia leaned her broom on the porch rail and stared harder at the man walking toward her. He didn't look to be anyone from around here. More like a drifter or vagrant. Worse yet, had Mr. Malloy sent one of his farmhands to coerce them into selling? She set her jaw, crossing her arms over her chest. If so, she'd fetch her rifle and send him packing. She'd put a bullet in one man in defense of this family. If she had to, she would do it again. Anything to protect this place and her loved ones. Though, she admitted, the thought made her queasy.

As the fellow drew closer, she caught a better glimpse of his features—his chiseled jaw and straight nose. Not a bad-looking sort, from what she could tell. And young. Around Luke or Drew's age, she would venture. His eyes were too shadowed beneath his cap to view, but he seemed to be peering back at her, his thin lips growing taut as his steps slowed. Someone so easily intimidated should prove simple enough to bluff.

Stretching her five-foot-three-inch frame to full height, Lydia waited until the fellow was within speaking distance and then called out in as stern of voice as she could muster. "This is private land, mister. State your business."

The stranger jolted to a stop about twenty paces from the house. Still too far away to readily read his expression. "I'm your new farmhand. Your brother hired me."

Taken aback, Lydia gawked at him. "Which brother?"

"Luke."

Her gruff pretense forgotten, it was all Lydia could do to squeak out a reply. "Luke ... hired you?"

"He did."

She gnawed at her lip. Only that morning, following Mr. Malloy's visit, she'd begun praying the Lord would send someone to ease her brother's burden with the farm. Could her prayers have been answered so quickly? *Thank You, Lord.*

The man ventured a step closer, his voice less strained. "You must be Miss Lydia."

She blinked. "Yes. Yes, I am." He knew her name? What else had Luke told him?

More than he'd told them about this fellow, obviously.

Heat singed her cheeks as she recalled her rude greeting. What an impression she must have made. Hopefully, he would overlook the matter. Eager to deflect attention elsewhere, she let her gaze slip past him. "They're home?"

"Just arrived."

The door creaked open, and Lydia turned to see Mama striding onto the veranda, a shawl wrapped around her shoulders. Her gaze shifted from Lydia to the stranger. "I wasn't aware we had company. Good evening, young man."

The nameless visitor lifted off his hat and sauntered closer. "Evenin', Mrs. Gallagher. Name's Will Evans. Luke sent me on ahead to introduce myself. Said you could use some help with the farm."

"Praise be." Mama clamped her hands together at her chest and smiled down at him. "You, sir, are an answer to prayer."

His eyes flared as if the comment surprised him. "That's good to hear, ma'am."

Lydia's gaze locked with his for an instant before he lowered his head, a hint of a smile touching his lips. Now that she'd had a better look at him, he was more handsome than she'd first thought. She held back a sigh. *Will Evans.* What a fine sounding name. Suddenly she wanted to know more. Where he was from. How he and Luke met. What his interests were. Was he a believer?

A thousand questions begged to be asked. But one dogged her more than any other.

How long would he stay?

The clop of hooves and whir of carriage wheels gripped Will's attention from behind. He turned just as Luke reined in his horse. He grinned up at his kinfolk then at Will. "Hello. I see you're getting acquainted."

With a brisk nod, Will shifted his duffel higher on his shoulder.

Mrs. Gallagher inched closer to the porch rail, the creases at the outer edges of her eyes deepening with her amiable smile. "Good to have you home, son. Yes. What a pleasant surprise. How did you two meet?"

"We crossed paths over near Baldwin. Adelaide and I had wheel trouble, and Will happened along to aid us. Found out he was in need of a job, and here he is."

Mrs. Gallagher's expression brightened as her gaze drifted to Will. "A godsend for certain."

"And he couldn't have come at a better time." As soon as the words left her lips, Luke's sister clamped her mouth shut as though she'd spoken out of turn.

Luke hopped from the carriage, shooting her a quizzical look. "Why's that?"

Seeming hesitant to respond, Lydia traded glances with her mother, then posed a question of her own. "You're needing help, aren't you?"

"'Course I am, and blessed to have it."

Will sensed there was more to Lydia's comment than she was telling. Judging from Luke's bewildered expression, so did he.

Yet, the remark didn't puzzle Will nearly as much as being told he was an answer to prayer. Whether the Lord had had a hand in him coming or not, he had a feeling he'd landed in a good place. He glanced over at Lydia, amazed at how much she resembled the girl in his dream. Could he have inadvertently stumbled upon a place he'd once been?

Not likely. There wasn't an ounce of recognition in any of their eyes.

Mrs. Gallagher motioned to them. "Come on in. We were just about to set down to stew and biscuits. It won't take long to add a few plates." Her brow creased. "Where's Adelaide?"

"At home. The trip tired her. I'm sort of bushed myself." Luke thumbed over his shoulder at the barn. "I'll just unhitch Angel and, if you don't mind, do our visiting in the morning."

"All right, son." Her smile returned as she pivoted toward Will. "Well then, that gives us the opportunity to get better acquainted with our new boarder. Bring your things, Mr. Evans, and I'll get you settled in your room while Lydia puts supper on."

Not wishing to seem ungrateful, Will weighed how to respond. A warm bed sounded so much more inviting than a barn floor. If he only had the courage to explain his predicament instead of making lame excuses. He gripped the rim of his hat. "I appreciate the hospitality, Mrs. Gallagher, but if it's all right, I think I'd rather bunk in the barn."

All three Gallaghers stared at him as if he'd grown a second nose. Luke chuckled. "May as well take advantage of the spare room. Your pay's the same whether you sleep on a hard barn floor or a cozy bed."

Will dampened his lips, doing his best not to appear unsociable. "I thank you for the offer, but the barn will suit me fine."

With a shrug, Luke motioned for him to follow. "Suit yourself. I'll fix you up a place in one of the empty stalls."

"Sounds good."

"Oh, Mr. Evans."

Will took a step toward the barn, then halted at Mrs. Gallagher's plea from the porch. He spun toward her. "Please. Call me Will."

She gave a slow nod. "Will." Though her tone was difficult to read, her penetrating stare made clear his need to note what she was about to say. "You might reside in the barn, but you'll take your nourishment in the house with us."

"Yes, ma'am." Will wouldn't argue that. He might have to forego the comfort of a warm bed, but he had every intention of enjoying hot meals from the table.

He only hoped they wouldn't ask too many questions he couldn't answer.

Lydia peered out the kitchen window at the lantern light flickering inside the barn. "Why do you suppose Mr. Evans chose to stay in the barn?"

"Men have their own way about them, I suppose." With a grin, Mama patted Lydia's arm. "You'll discover that when you marry."

A surge of heat pricked Lydia's cheeks. She'd not much

considered the ways of a man. Nor marriage, for that matter. Having two older brothers had given her some insight into a male's way of thinking. Most of which she found a challenge to grasp. But Will seemed altogether different than Drew or Luke. Quiet, reserved, shrouded in mystery.

He'd said little during supper, offering only vague comments in response to their attempts at conversation. Yet, there was so much she wished to know about him. Like how he'd gotten that sizeable scar over his left ear. Had he been wounded in the war? Or in an accident? She hadn't dared ask. Not when he was unwilling to answer even simple questions about his upbringing.

Their new guest seemed to have a knack for diverting conversation away from himself. Twice, he'd complimented Mama on the meal in lieu of responding to inquiries about his family.

Lydia pried herself from the window with a sigh. "Will must be a very private man. He doesn't seem to like talking about himself. Maybe that's why he chooses to stay in the barn."

"Perhaps it's for the best." Mama touched a hand to Lydia's cheek. "After all, we don't know the man. The idea of a stranger staying down the hall from my young daughter is not very comforting."

"Oh, but Will would never harm me. He's a good man. Of that much I'm certain."

"Is that so?" Mama's voice held an element of humor. "He did clear his supper dishes away and compliment my cooking. That's the mark of at least a considerate man." Tiredness brimmed in her eyes as she removed her apron. "Time will tell his true nature. But despite his guardedness, I can't help but feel the Lord had a hand in bringing him here."

With another glance out the window, anticipation brewed inside Lydia. "So do I."

Her lips lifted in a grin. *For hopefully more reason than one.*

W ill stared at the log rafters, the first hint of daylight finally beginning to stream through the crevices of the barn. Between the scratchy bed of straw, the animal noises, and his maddening dreams, he'd lain awake off and on much of the night. Without a working pocket watch, he never knew for certain how much time elapsed.

Starting a new job was always a bit nerve-racking. Hopefully, he would live up to Luke's and his family's expectations. They all seemed so sure he was an answer to their prayers. Just why, he couldn't say. Luke seemed a capable, easy-going fella. Was the work simply too much for him or was there more to it than that?

Light footsteps sounded outside the barn door, jolting him to a sitting position. Luke wasn't kidding about getting an early start. Working a long day on half a night's rest wasn't a good way to begin. By tonight, maybe he'd be so whipped he'd sleep straight through. Wouldn't that be a miracle?

"Mr. Evans? Are you up?"

The female voice brought him to his feet. *Lydia? What was she doing out here?* He brushed straw from his backside. "I'm up."

The barn door eased open and large eyes peered in at him. "I've come to milk Penny." In response to her voice, the cow gave a mournful bawl, and the cat that had climbed atop Will more than once in the night appeared from nowhere.

He smothered a yawn. "You always up this early?"

Snatching the metal pail from inside the door, Lydia gazed at him with doleful eyes. "I'm sorry. I didn't mean to wake you. It's just, Penny gets out of sorts if not relieved of her milk."

"It's no problem." He just wasn't expecting company at the crack of dawn.

A smile touched her lips as she edged closer. "How did you sleep? I hope the animals didn't keep you awake."

If he was honest, he'd admit to the fact. But not wishing to dampen her cheerful mood, he chose to bend the truth a bit. "Not bad for the first night in a new place."

"That's good." She glanced at his meager bedroll. "It gets a mite chilly of a night. Would you like another blanket?"

The girl was indeed thoughtful, though a bit overly alert for such an early hour. "If you have one to spare, I'd appreciate that."

With a nod, she took up the three-legged stool propped in the corner and set it beside the cow. "I think you'll like working for Luke. As brothers go, he used to be quite a tease, but he's always looked out for me."

Will knelt to roll up his blanket, half amused and half dazed by the talkative young lady. After living in solitude the past couple of years, the constant chatter was a bit overwhelming. Yet, there was something intriguing about the girl. He glanced over at her as she set to work milking. She was certainly fetching with her golden locks, trim figure, and big blue eyes. Nonetheless, a smidge young and talkative for his liking. Not more than sixteen or seventeen, he would wager.

His chest clenched. He couldn't get past his first glimpse of her on the porch and how she reminded him of the girl in his recurring dream. Vague though it was, the woman in his dream rushed toward him with outstretched arms then vanished like mist just as he sought to embrace her.

Who was she? Sweetheart? Sister? Wife?

If he could only get a good glimpse of her face. He had a feeling finding her would prove the key to unlocking his forgotten past.

And perhaps his future.

A soft nicker sliced through his thoughts. The horse in the stall next to him stuck her head over the side wall, her dark eyes full of spark and vigor. Standing, Will reached a hand up to stroke her face. He'd admired the bay mare since he'd first laid eyes on her hitched to the carriage.

The steady ping of the milk hitting the pail stopped, and he sensed Lydia's eyes upon him. "That's Angel."

Will ran his fingers across the mare's soft muzzle. "She's a fine animal."

Nimble footsteps trekked through the straw-covered floor to the front of the stall. "She belongs to my brother Drew, but he had no place for her in Washington so left her here. She's good with the carriage, but Drew's the only one who can ride her."

"Why's that?"

The faint scent of lilac wafted at Will as Lydia leaned against the stall post. "The two of them went through a lot together during the war. She won't let anyone else ride her. Rears and sidesteps any time Luke or I try to mount her."

Will stroked a hand along the bay's neck and withers. "The name Angel doesn't quite seem to fit, then."

"Oh, but it does." The candor in her voice surprised him. "She saved Drew's life more than once. Like the Lord sent her to watch over him. So, he called her Angel."

The horse sounded a soft nicker as Will looked her in the eyes.

"She likes you. I can tell. Do you have a knowledge of horses?"

Something stirred deep inside Will. The feel of the soft coat beneath his fingers. The firm, muscled neck seemed so natural to his touch. "I think so."

"You *think* so?" Lydia studied him like a schoolmarm weighing the motives of a tardy student.

"Mornin'."

Luke's spry greeting spared Will from answering. Relieved, he swiveled toward his new boss. As he opened his mouth to reply, Angel nuzzled his shoulder, nearly throwing him off balance.

A sideways grin stretched across Luke's lips. "Looks like Angel approves of you." He moved beside Will, giving the horse a pat on the neck. "Lydia probably told you she gets special treatment 'round here. Drew credits her and the Lord for bringing him home from the war in one piece."

Something within Will balked. Too bad the Lord hadn't sent an angel to see that he made his way home. Instead, he'd been left to flounder in endless searching that had led him nowhere.

He felt a light cuff on his arm, jarring his attention back to Luke. "I promised Ma we'd all be in for breakfast. Afterward, we'll start plowing the east field."

With an affirming nod, Will followed his boss from the stall, feeling every inch an intruder. He'd committed to staying through harvest, but as soon as his obligations here were through, he'd be on his way. He still needed answers, and until he found some, he'd never belong anywhere.

LYDIA KEPT one eye trained on Will as she poured sorghum over her pancake. There was something not right about the man. He seemed to know as little about himself as the rest of them. Or at least that's the impression he gave. No matter how attractive or agreeable he appeared, she was beginning not to trust him.

Though Will had been there but a day, she found it odd he'd divulged nothing personal, saying very little unless spoken to directly. His diversions seemed more out of confusion than outright concealment. And yet, why would he not admit to something so harmless as having experience with horses? It made no sense.

"So, tell us about your trip. How did you find Clarissa and Mr. and Mrs. Banks?" Mama's inquiry to Adelaide sliced through Lydia's ponderings.

Adelaide wiped syrup from her lips and returned a courteous grin. "They're well. Clarissa seems to grow more ladylike every time we see her. It's hard to believe she's already fifteen."

Though Lydia had never met Adelaide's cousin, she almost felt she knew her. With only a couple of years separating their ages, Lydia had often wondered how they would get on, should they meet. "Was she excited to learn of your baby?"

A hint of pink spilled onto Adelaide's cheeks at Lydia's query. "She was overjoyed at the news."

Luke bent to give Adelaide a peck on the cheek. "As am I."

They shared a grin, deep love in both their expressions.

Lydia stifled a sigh. Would she ever experience such heartfelt devotion from a man?

Clasping Adelaide's scarred hand in his, Luke turned to face the rest of the group. "Something else noteworthy happened over our visit as well."

Mama laced her fingers together over her half-full plate. "Oh? What's that?"

He leaned over the table, a curious glint in his eyes. "I've been asked to give a sermon at the church where Clarissa and her parents attend. Isn't that incredible?"

Lydia nearly choked on her glass of milk. Her brother speaking before a church? Though his faith and deep devotion to the Lord were admirable, he'd never given any indication he could ever preach to a congregation. "How did that come about?"

"At the end of Sunday's service, the pastor announced he needed to travel out of town the last Sunday in May. Conversation afterward turned to who might be able to fill in. The elders asked if I would be willing."

Lydia swallowed the dryness in her throat. "Are you going to do it?"

Luke's smile deepened as he shifted his gaze to Adelaide. "I'm considering it."

"I think you'd do a fine job. You certainly have the Bible knowledge and a heart to share your faith."

At her sister-in-law's words, Lydia's chest tightened. They'd just returned home. Were they so eager to talk of leaving again?

Taking up her fork, Mama flashed a grin. "I wouldn't mind hearing you myself, son, should you decide to speak."

A spark of interest sliced through Lydia's angst. Making the trip *with* them put a different slant on the venture. "Oh, could we go? I'd love to meet Clarissa."

Luke snickered. "I don't see why not. I'll need all the support I can muster." The sheen in his eyes and the confirming words clearly hinted his decision was all but made. He turned to their guest. "That is if Will here has no qualms about looking after the place while we're away. You should have your bearings around here by then."

Emptying his mouth of food, Will cleared his throat. "All right by me."

Lydia tensed, her momentary lapse in scrutinizing their new employee resuming. The thought of leaving the entire place under the care of someone they knew so little about was a bit unsettling. After Mr. Malloy's unexpected visit, entrusting everything they owned to a stranger seemed risky.

She peered across the table at their handsome guest. By all appearances, he seemed trustworthy. Yet, his elusive nature had her bemused.

Someone needed to find out more about him.

She stifled a grin, the thought not an unpleasant one.

May as well be her.

8

W ill took a swig from his canteen, the cool water edging
out the dryness in his throat. For early May, the air
seemed more humid than he was accustomed to. He glanced at
the portion of the field that he'd run the plow and harrow over.
The soil had turned nicely, with just enough moisture to break
into workable clumps.

He slid a hand along the nearest horse's sleek, dark neck.
Luke took good care of not only his equipment but also his
horses. The team was well-trained and groomed.

His new employer sauntered up beside him, having spent the
past couple of hours sawing overhanging branches from the
outer edges of the field. "Whew. I'm about ready to call it a day,
how about you?"

"Sounds good to me." With a brisk nod, Will shouldered his
canteen.

"What do you think of the team?"

"Fine horses. They pull well together." He gave the darker
horse a pat on the neck. "Part Shire, aren't they?"

"You have a good eye. They're sisters, we're told. Bought at
auction shortly after the war." Luke ran a gloved hand over the

white blaze on the far horse's face. "Molly is seven. Her sister, Chloe, there is six."

Will moved to unhitch the horses. "A good age. Old enough to know what they're doing and young enough to have some useful years left."

"My thoughts exactly." Luke loosened the leather breastplate. "Lucky for you, they're pastured this time of year. Come winter, the barn gets a mite crowded. By then, you may change your mind about staying out there."

Metal clanked as Will unhooked the harness from the plow. He straightened, unable to look his employer in the eye. "Maybe so." He hated to mislead or disappoint, but come winter, he likely wouldn't be here. As tempting as staying in one place sounded, he couldn't rest until he'd uncovered his past.

Glancing over the plowed ground, Luke jutted out his lower lip. "You handle them well. Cut a pretty straight furrow."

"The horses deserve most of the credit. They made it easy."

"I don't know. Drew used to say I plowed as crooked as a chased rabbit." Chuckling, Luke made a zigzagging motion with his hand.

Will stifled a grin. He'd liked Luke from the start. Anyone who could see their failings in such a light-hearted manner had his admiration.

"But then you know how older brothers exaggerate. Or maybe you don't have an older brother."

Mouth growing taut, Will took up the reins. How should he respond? If he made up an answer, it would only lead to more deception. Best to remain vague but truthful. "I haven't seen my family since I left for war."

Squinting against the evening sun, Luke stepped from in front of the team. "Sorry to hear that. I figured you for a soldier. You serve under Grant or Sherman?"

Images that often plagued Will's dreams flashed to the forefront of his mind. Drawing a jagged breath, he trained his gaze on the horses. "I don't much like talking about the war. Too many bad memories."

"I know what you mean. Nothing good about war."

With a click of his tongue, Will tapped the reins across the horses' rumps and steered them toward the pasture. Maybe in time he'd feel comfortable divulging his confidences, but it was simpler to keep them to himself for now.

Luke strode alongside, hands in his pockets. "'Course, that doesn't mean the Lord can't bring something good out of it."

Guessing the comment was meant to spur a response, Will decided to oblige. "Such as?"

"Such as allowing Adelaide and me to meet. She was nearly dead when my men and I found her in the burnt rubble of Richmond. We'd never have crossed paths if not for the war."

Will had noticed the scarring on Adelaide's disfigured hands, but hadn't wanted to ask how it happened. "A lot of pain and bloodshed just so you two could meet up." He didn't wish to sound cynical, but he was on the other end of the spectrum—having lost all sense of who he was and where he'd come from.

The crunch of grass beneath the horses' hooves intensified in the terse stillness. At last, Luke gave a noticeable sigh. "True. But I believe that even amid pain and suffering, the Lord has a plan. If you look hard enough, you'll find a blessing in every heartache."

"Even war?"

"Even war." After a long pause, Luke glanced over at Will. "Adelaide suffered tremendously before we met. She was bitter toward God and full of hatred, having lost her family and nearly her life to the war. But in time, God renewed her faith. All the hardships she went through, while still a part of her, faded into restoration and peace."

Will turned away, the muscles in his shoulders tensing. He wasn't bitter or hateful toward God. Just disappointed. His prayers had gone unanswered, and in response, his faith had disintegrated to almost nothing.

Luke was obviously a man of great faith. If that worked for him, fine. But if the Lord wanted Will to believe, He'd have to prove Himself.

"WHAT ARE YOU DOING?"

Sucking in a breath, Lydia straightened and whirled toward the voice. Luke gaped at her from the barn entrance, a yoke and harness draped over his shoulder. She drew a hand to her chest, heart pounding. "You startled me. I—I thought you were Will."

Her brother's brow furrowed as he hung the harness on its peg. "And if I had been? What do you suppose I would think of someone rummaging through my belongings?"

Heat singed her cheeks as she ventured a step toward him. "I'm sorry. It's just—we know so little about Will. He's so ... secretive."

Luke turned to face her. "A man's got a right to his privacy. Will's a hard worker and a good man, that's plain enough. And that's all we need to know. So, no more snooping through his personal possessions."

Lydia wrung her hands. "But that's just it. He has no personal effects. Won't share where he's from or what he's done. It's like he didn't exist before coming here."

"He's from Indiana. He told me so himself."

"But *where* in Indiana? He won't give a straight answer. When I asked if he knew horses this morning, he said he *thought* so. Don't you find that odd?"

Luke gripped her shoulder, peering down at her like a scolding father. "Like I say. It's his business. Not ours."

Confident she was getting nowhere, she reneged with a sigh. "All right. No more meddling. I promise."

"Good." Placing a finger under her chin, he cautioned her with his gaze. "I have a feeling Will has some deep hurts. Only he can decide if and when he's willing to share them. Our job is to pray and accept him as is."

She offered a slight nod and then grinned. "Spoken like a true pastor."

A reluctant smile played on Luke's lips, and he gave her shoulder a soft nudge. "Go on. Get out of here."

Chuckling, she made her way to the barn door, nearly bumping into Will as he entered, arms laden with the other harness. She jolted to a stop, her expression sobering. Their eyes locked momentarily before Will stepped aside to let her pass. Mustering a weak grin, she dipped her head and strode by, pangs of guilt hounding her every step. Luke had been right to chasten her. If Will had happened in first, she'd have had a lot of explaining to do.

Memory of his gentle expression sent a flutter through her. His eyes were much too kind to warrant suspicion. Maybe he had no personal items because he was an angel sent to help them. Luke didn't know about Mr. Malloy's offer to buy their land. Will coming at just the right time seemed more than coincidence. After all, didn't Scripture say some had entertained angels unawares?

Her lips lifted in an impish grin. Maybe that's why Angel had taken to him so.

With a quick backward glance, Lydia trudged toward the farmhouse. The more she learned of Will, the less she understood.

And the more she ached to know.

Yet, she'd promised Luke she wouldn't meddle.

She hiked a brow. But that didn't mean she couldn't attempt to penetrate Will's silent shell. Given the opportunity, she could be pretty persuasive.

Her insides churned at how close she'd come to destroying her chances of ever gaining his confidence. What would he think of her if he knew she'd rifled through his things? Would he have been so put out he'd have up and left?

Troubled by the thought, she whispered a prayer of both gratitude and forgiveness.

All the while wondering if she could forgive herself.

9

Friday evening, May 8, 1868

Will stood and pushed in his chair. "Thanks again for the victuals."

The comment garnered a smile from his hostess. "You're welcome, Will. But don't feel you have to thank us for *every* meal."

He'd like to say that was the way he was raised, but then he couldn't rightly make that claim. "It's hard not to voice appreciation when it tastes so good."

Mrs. Gallagher gave a good-natured chuckle. "What a nice compliment."

Will was glad to see even Lydia crack a slight grin. He let his gaze linger on her a moment. She'd seemed subdued the past few days. Almost as if he'd offended her, though he couldn't imagine how. They'd hardly spoken. Even of a morning while milking the cow, she'd kept to her duties, giving him little attention. He'd caught her looking at him a few times, quickly turning when he glanced her way. Though he didn't know her well, plainly something wasn't right.

Stepping from the dining room, he donned his hat. Soft

footsteps followed him into the hallway, and he turned to see both ladies looking on. "Evenin', Mrs. Gallagher. Miss Lydia."

Mrs. Gallagher nodded. "Good night, Will."

Lydia's lips parted slightly as if she had something to add, but then her head dipped. Whatever had a chokehold on her tongue wasn't loosening easily.

A gentle breeze met him as he ventured outside. The steady drone of frogs pulsed in the distance, marking out his steps to the barn. He glanced over the landscape, the last rays of sunlight turning the Western sky a vibrant pink. There was a peacefulness here. The closest thing to a home he could recall. The Gallaghers were fortunate to have this place ... and each other.

"Mr. Evans ... Will?"

He jolted to a stop, the soft-spoken voice jarring him from his thoughts. Pivoting, he was stunned to see Lydia perched at the top porch step, her eyes tainted with uncertainty. He stepped toward her. "Did you need something?"

"Yes. I mean, I need to tell you something." Without waiting for a response, she downed the steps, her face so pale she looked as if she might lose her supper. She glanced behind her as if assuring they wouldn't be overheard. Clutching her hands together at her front, she walked toward him, eyes trained on the ground ahead. "Could we walk a bit?"

"Sure." Sinking his hands in his pockets, he fell into step beside her. The girl was making him antsy. What was troubling her?

About ten paces from the barn, she came to an abrupt stop and turned toward him. Keeping a respectful distance between them, he swiveled to face her. She moistened trembling lips, wringing her hands as if attempting to find the right words. Her gaze trailed up him but stopped just below his Adam's apple.

When she said nothing, he attempted to spur her along. "Did I do something wrong?"

"No. I did." She gave a loud huff, still not looking him in the eyes. "I ... searched through your things one day when you were in the field. It was wrong of me. I'm sorry." The anguished words gushed out like water over a burst dam.

Unsure how to respond to the confession, Will stared at her, jaw slackened. "What did you expect to find?"

Long, dark lashes fanned her cheeks as she dropped her gaze. "You've told us so little about yourself. I ... just wanted to know more."

The tremor in her voice sparked of sincerity. Half flattered and half disturbed by the notion, Will tried to decipher the reason behind her curious deed. Out of awkwardness, he scratched at his cheek. "Not much to tell."

"Oh, but there is." Her head lifted and large, sky-blue eyes stared up at him, their vibrancy returning. "Everyone has an upbringing, family, and experiences to share."

Will shifted his feet, years of unrest roiling inside him. Enough secrecy. Whatever the girl's motives, he'd grown weary of excuses. He firmed his jaw. "I don't."

"'Course you do."

He met her gaze, a bit shaken by the intensity. Maybe it was the genuineness in her expression or that he'd tired of concealing his unknown past, but for the first time in nearly three years, he *wanted* to own up to the truth. As he released a long breath, the tension seeped from his shoulders. "I have no memory of my background *or* my family. Really not much of anything."

A flicker of compassion flashed in her eyes. "Wh ... what happened? Were you injured in the war?"

"After the war." With a sigh, Will stared at the three-quarter moon shimmering in the eastern sky. He ambled forward down the worn path. Lydia strode with him, the top of her head barely level with his shoulder. He liked the feel of her walking alongside. "Ever hear of the steamboat *Sultana?*"

"I think so. Didn't it sink a couple years back and a lot of soldiers lost their lives?"

Will's stomach lurched at the very mention of it. "That's right."

Like sunlight bursting over the horizon, Lydia seemed to sense the connection. "You were on it?"

Unable to find his voice, he merely nodded.

Her tone softened to almost a whisper. "The scar on your head. Is that how you got it?"

He swallowed, wavering between brushing aside the question or spilling every detail. The need to clear his head finally won out. "I don't recall much, but best I can tell, when the boilers exploded, I was thrown from the *Sultana* and hit my head. Rescuers found me floating unconscious on debris."

Moisture glistened in her eyes as she stared over at him. "So, you have no memory of your life before the incident?"

"Not even my name."

Her brows pinched. "But your name is Will Evans. Isn't it?"

He shrugged. "*Will* anyway. I'm not sure of my surname." Uncertain why, he stopped walking and reached into his pocket. Maybe it was that Lydia had owned up to her mistake and been truthful with him, or maybe he was just done with pretense, but something about this girl had him baring his soul. He held his watch out to her. "This is the only tie I have to my past. It was in my pocket when they found me."

Taking it from him, she ran her fingers over the smooth surface, then popped it open. After a moment, she peered up at him. "It doesn't work?"

"The plunge in the water must have damaged it. Don't know if it's repairable or not, but see that name etched in the casing?" He pointed to the lower rim of the lid.

She moved it closer to her face and shifted it toward the moon's brightness, the darkening sky making it difficult to see. "Will E." Her head lifted. "So, Evans isn't your actual last name?"

"Most likely not."

She handed the pocket watch back, her small hand near his a

bit unnerving. "Then you've been unable to find out anything about yourself?"

With a shake of his head, he slipped the ruined watch in his pocket. "I've spent the past two and a half years searching for answers and gotten nowhere."

"I'm sorry." Her eyes locked on his, glistening in the moonlight. "Your family must be devastated not knowing what happened to you."

There was something freeing in finally revealing the burden he carried. "That's the hardest part. Not knowing what or who is out there hoping for answers, same as me."

She rubbed her arms against the chill. "How sad for both you and your family. I hope someday you'll be reunited."

The sincerity in her tone sapped some of the lonesomeness that had plagued him these many months. There was comfort in being understood. He touched a hand to her elbow. "We'd better get you back inside."

She nodded a sweet smile and pivoted toward the house. "Thank you for sharing about yourself with me, Will. And for accepting my apology."

He snickered. "Guess it did us both good to clear some air."

"So it seems." Her mouth twisted as if stifling a grin. She tipped her head to one side, her expression sobering. "I'll pray for you. That the Lord will one day restore your memory."

Though Will nodded his thanks, his stomach gripped. He resisted the urge to tell her prayer would do no good. His own unanswered pleas convinced him the Lord had better things to do than look out for *him*.

If his memory hadn't returned by now, it likely never would.

UNABLE TO GET Will out of her head, Lydia stared up from her bed at the darkened ceiling. The poor man. She ached to think how dreadful it would be to lose memory of everything, even who she was. At least now he made sense—his vague responses, his diversions, his quietness. They were meant to conceal his lack of knowledge about himself.

She chuckled at having thought him an angel. Though, she agreed with Mama that he was an answer to their prayers. Her first impression of him had been accurate after all—that the Lord must have sent him to ease Luke's load and spare them further pressure from Mr. Malloy.

The question was, how could she use the newfound insights to help Will? Should she share what she knew with Luke and Mama?

No. Will had entrusted his secret to her. If he wished the others to know, she would leave it for him to tell. She nibbled her lip. At least, she would do her best. Holding in her thoughts had never been a strong point for her. But, if she earned Will's confidence, perhaps he would open up to her again.

She'd sensed their friendship begin to bud as they strolled together in the moonlight. Would that same amity remain or vanish with the light of day?

A nervous tingle rippled through her. Though she might, for her part, wish their bond to deepen into more, she couldn't consider that now. She'd promised to pray for Will, and pray she would. Though his dubious expression when she'd made the offer had been telling. Did he blame God for his troubles? If so, he had a spiritual wound in need of healing as well.

Lacing her fingers together over her chest, she closed her eyes and whispered a heartfelt prayer on his behalf.

10

Saturday, May 9, 1868

Will straightened and wiped the sweat from his brow as a rider reined his horse to a stop at the edge of the field where he and Luke were working. Luke leaned in close, keeping his voice at a murmur. "Guthrie Malloy. Our neighbor to the east."

Luke's tone was enough to convince Will the neighbor was not on his employer's list of favorite people.

The man's scrutinizing stare swept over Will before settling on Luke. "I see you didn't waste any time hiring a hand."

Striding over, Luke peered up at him. "Pardon?"

"Like I told your ma. You could spare yourself the bother of hiring out if you'd take me up on my offer."

Clearly confused, Luke's brow puckered. "What offer is that?"

Malloy sat forward in his saddle, the leather creaking under his weight. "Didn't your ma tell you? I offered to take a portion of your property off your hands. Seems a bit more than a young feller like yourself can handle."

Though not directed at him, Will gritted his teeth against

the veiled slur. He'd not known Luke for long, but it was plain he was a hard worker who took great care in what he did. True, the farm was a lot for one man to handle, but something told him Malloy's proposition had little to do with easing Luke's load.

With uncanny composure, Luke tossed his neighbor an affable grin. "Well now, that's right kind of you, Mr. Malloy, but it seems the Lord supplied us Will here at just the right time. The two of us ought to be able to handle the farm just fine."

Stifling a grin, Will tipped his chin higher. If he'd not already committed to staying through harvest, Luke's comment would have convinced him. For no other reason than to keep Malloy from making good on his intentions.

Sitting taller in his saddle, the neighbor raked a hand over his scruffy beard. "Suit yourself. Just being neighborly." His gray eyes crimped slightly as he nodded toward Will. "But if this feller doesn't work out, come see me. I'll give a fair price for whatever land you and your ma are willin' to sell."

Will met the man's steady gaze. He had a feeling he'd been sized up and found lacking. Or, more likely, taken the blame for standing in the way of Malloy's plans. Either way, Will wouldn't be intimidated.

Luke nodded. "I appreciate the offer, but I've no doubt Will here will work out."

At last, Malloy broke off his stare and nodded to Luke. "Well then, I'll be seein' you."

Will waited until Malloy was out of earshot then turned to Luke. "I don't think that man likes me."

With a soft snicker, Luke clapped him on the arm. "It's you foiling his plans he doesn't like. If Malloy had his way, he'd own half of Chemung County." Luke crossed his arms over his chest. "What troubles me is why Ma and Lydia didn't tell me of his offer."

"Maybe they didn't see any need, since you have my help now."

Nodding, Luke jutted out his lower lip. "Maybe so."

Will stared after Malloy. Something about the man didn't set right. Will had to admire Mrs. Gallagher and Lydia for handling the incident themselves. Come to think of it, maybe that's why they'd deemed him such an answer to prayer. Whether he was or wasn't, he couldn't say. But for the moment, he was thankful to be here.

The question was, what would happen when he left?

A FAMILIAR HUM sent Lydia dashing onto the veranda to greet the regular Saturday morning visitor. She smiled at their dark-skinned neighbor toting what Lydia knew to be a basket of eggs and honey. "Mornin', Mrs. Perkins."

The aging woman hiked a brow. "Well, ain't you the perky one this mornin', all smiles. Must be somethin' extra special to bring on such a cheery look."

Lydia snuck a glance at the field where Luke and Will were hard at work. "Not really. Just ... happy for the company."

Mrs. Perkins cut a sideways glance from her to Will and back again. "I, uh, noticed Luke has a young man helping him. Have you hired on?"

Despite every attempt not to let it, a smile seeped across Lydia's lips. "Yes. That's Will. Will Evans. He's working for us now. He's already proven a huge blessing." She slipped another glance toward Will. "We've enjoyed having him here."

"I can see that."

The woman's knowing tone and expression hinted Lydia was much too transparent. She couldn't help herself. Since last night's stroll with Will, she'd thought of little else. Smitten was what she was. For the first time in her life, a man intrigued her. Though she'd be hard-pressed to admit it to anyone.

Reeling in her smile, Lydia did her best to compose herself. "With Drew away, Luke truly needs the help."

"Mm-hmm. And where did you find this young fellow?"

"Luke and Adelaide met him on their way home from Pennsylvania. Their carriage broke down, and he stopped to help. Luke offered him a job, and he accepted."

"Sounds like a right, fine fella." Mrs. Perkins dipped her chin, grinning slyly. "One you might wish to keep around."

Warmth flooded Lydia's cheeks. Mrs. Perkins was indeed wise to her. But somehow, she didn't care. So long as the dear neighbor kept the knowledge to herself. "Yes ... for Luke's sake."

"Oh, of course. For *Luke's* sake."

The woman's amused gaze penetrated Lydia's defenses, and the two shared a light-hearted chuckle.

The house door creaked open, and Lydia turned to see her mother, bearing a basket containing a jar of milk and tin of butter. Mama's glance wavered between the two of them, eyes full of question. "What have I missed?"

Sobering, Lydia took the basket from her. "Nothing, Mama. We were just chatting."

She handed Mrs. Perkins the dairy items and took the eggs and honey basket in exchange. For years, the two families had traded goods to supply what the other lacked.

Mrs. Perkins tilted her head to the side, her smile fading. "How are you, Martha? You look a mite peaked. Are you ailin'?"

Mama pressed a hand to her middle. "No. Just seems I tire easier these days. My age must be catching up with me."

Lydia's stomach gripped. She knew better. Mama's weak heart was the cause. Mrs. Perkins had several years on Mama and walked the mile distance from her house to theirs without strain. Often, Mama grew short of breath merely climbing to the upstairs bedrooms.

"Well, you take care now. And if there's anything I can do to help, you jus' say the word."

Mama spawned a weak grin. "Thank you, Celia. I'll be fine."

Would she? Lydia wasn't so certain. The pallor in Mama's cheeks had become more evident over recent weeks. Even Adelaide had mentioned it a time or two. Though Lydia did her best to shoulder some of her mother's load, Mama was not one to accept help willingly. She insisted on doing much of the cooking, stocking of supplies, and garden tending herself.

Would the trip to Pennsylvania be too much for her? A night away from home and two long days of travel? As much as Lydia wished to go, the thought of putting her mother's health at risk stymied her enthusiasm. She could only pray Mama would do what was best.

"I MET YOUR NEIGHBOR TODAY."

At Will's comment, Lydia's fork stilled. "Mrs. Perkins?"

Clearing his throat, Will stabbed at the layer of greens on his plate. "No, Guthrie Malloy."

Will didn't have to look up to sense the tension that accompanied the name.

After a long pause, Mrs. Gallagher spoke. "Oh? What did he have to say?"

Confident his hostess already knew the answer, Will didn't hesitate to disclose the matter. "That if I don't work out, he'd be happy to purchase some of your land to ease Luke's load."

The huff from Lydia was not a contented one. "The old coot."

"Lydia!"

Will suppressed a grin at Lydia's candid response but sobered at her mother's firm rebuff. He'd not meant to spark trouble.

Lydia slumped back in her chair. "I'm sorry, Mama. But that man is sticking his nose where it doesn't belong. Of course Will is going to work out, so Mr. Malloy needn't bother himself with any more offers to buy our land. And if he comes around again, I'll tell him so myself."

Tossing her a glance, Will made every effort not to smile. The girl's spirit was invigorating, and her faith in him was astounding, given their short acquaintance. She obviously held a very strong attachment to this place and her family. Will couldn't blame her. If he owned such a fine spread, he'd likely respond in much the same manner.

"You leave Mr. Malloy to me." Mrs. Gallagher's pale blue eyes were firm but gentle as she leaned closer to her daughter. "He knows where I stand on the matter. The land belongs to me, and no daughter of mine need do my talking for me."

"Yes, Mama."

Until now, Will had pegged his hostess for a sweet, genteel woman. But he was beginning to understand where Lydia had inherited her gumption. Beneath Mrs. Gallagher's matronly exterior lay a heart of quiet strength and character.

Traits the entire family appeared to possess.

In fact, if Will had handpicked a place to stay, he couldn't have done any better than here.

A disquieting thought rippled through him. Maybe meeting up with Luke and his wife on the road that day hadn't been by chance after all. Could the Lord truly have had a hand in him coming? If so, for what purpose?

The Gallaghers all credited God for bringing him here. Maybe He had. But Will's mind kept drifting to his recurring dream, convinced somehow it tied in with this family.

This place.

He just wasn't sure how.

11

Friday Morning, May 29, 1868

The barn seemed all too quiet as Lydia slipped the cloth over her milk pail. The weather had warmed enough that Angel now spent nights in the corral behind the barn and pastured with the other horses by day. Bridle in hand, Will had left shortly after Lydia arrived to milk Penny. Even their cat, Basil, had abandoned her to the outdoors in search of field mice.

With a disgruntled huff, Lydia stood and hefted the full bucket. Nearly three weeks had passed since Will confided in her. She'd anticipated the private stroll and conversation to be the first of many, but Luke kept him so busy, she and Will barely spoke outside of mealtime. Not lending opportunity for their friendship to deepen as she'd hoped.

An odd, rhythmic scuffing sounded behind the barn. A man's murmured voice was answered by a horse's soft nicker. Curious, Lydia set down her pail and cracked open the rear barn door leading to the corral. She caught a glimpse of Will's back just before he veered out of view. Several more darts back and forth demanded a better look. Widening the door, Lydia poked her head out, stunned to see Angel several paces from Will, mimicking his every move. She scrunched her nose. What were they doing?

At first, she determined the horse was deliberately making it difficult for Will to catch her. But the longer Lydia watched, the more she realized the sidestepping on both parts was deliberate. Almost as if they were ... dancing.

A smile edged across Lydia's lips. Were they playing?

Angel's head jerked up, breaking off the movements. She whinnied softly as Lydia stepped into full view. Will turned, cheeks blotching red and hazel eyes flashing wide.

Not wishing to add to his discomfort, she stifled the giggle bubbling in her throat. "Drew would be happy to know Angel is receiving so much attention." She ventured a step closer. "Although he might be a tad jealous she's so taken with you."

Regaining his composure, Will shrugged. "I don't know about that. She has a lot of personality. Sort of fun drawing it out."

"Ah, I see." Lydia gnawed her lip, watching Angel nuzzle Will as he ran his hand along her smooth, reddish-brown coat. Was it possible to be envious of a horse?

She clamped her hands together behind her back. "You're good with horses. Were you in the cavalry?"

No sooner had the words left her mouth than she regretted them. She grimaced. "I'm sorry. I forgot."

"That's all right. I've wondered the same." He stroked Angel's face, looking deep into her eyes. "Something in me says I had a horse of my own either before or during the war. It's frustrating not being able to recall something so trivial."

"It must be." Hoping to draw him out further, Lydia grappled for something to add. "So, you don't recall anything at all about your past?"

His eyes momentarily clouded, as if searching the far recesses of his mind. At last, he shook his head. "Only jumbled bits and pieces, mostly in dreams. Nothing solid."

Lydia moistened her lips, praying he wouldn't find her next question too intrusive. "Are the dreams pleasant or unpleasant?"

Will cut her a sideways glance as though she'd hit upon something significant or unsettling. He reached to give Angel another pat on the neck. "Mainly ones I'd just as soon forget."

"But there are a few agreeable dreams?"

A hint of red seeped into his cheeks. "A few."

Though Lydia ached to know just what those dreams entailed, she bit back her curiosity. Too many questions were bound to ruin any trust she'd gained.

"Well, I'd best get the team hitched." Snatching up the bridles he'd laid aside, Will started toward Molly and Chloe.

Lydia fell into step beside him, struggling to match his long strides. "Where are you headed?"

"Elmira, to pick up the seed corn. Luke wants it here ready for when he gets back from Pennsylvania."

The three-day trip to Copperville had seemed a pleasant idea, but part of her hated leaving Will behind. Holding her skirt up to quicken her pace, Lydia tossed him a sideways glance. "Will you get lonesome while we're away?" She was baiting him, she knew, but how else could she learn if he had any sort of attachment to her?

"I don't know. Sorta used to being by myself." The words rolled off his tongue much too easily for her liking.

Lydia's shoulders sagged, the response not what she'd anticipated. She forced a smile, hoping her face didn't convey her disappointment. May as well give up the notion of being courted by this fella. He was far too self-sufficient and obviously not interested. With a weighted breath, she mustered one last attempt. "Surely you'll miss something."

Or someone.

With a shrug, he slid one of the bridles from his shoulder. "Reckon I'll miss your and your ma's cooking." He nodded toward Angel. "Oh, and my stablemate over there."

The corners of Lydia's mouth made a hasty downward

retreat. The admission delivered the final blow. What hope was there when a horse held a higher place in Will's heart than her?

———————

WILL DROPPED the bag of seed corn into the wagon bed atop the others, then stepped aside for Luke to do the same.

Swiping corn dust from his hands, Luke surveyed the stack. "That's the last of it. We'll be all set for planting when I get back."

The thought of a whole weekend alone with nothing to do left Will hollow. He'd told Lydia he'd not mind being by himself. But the truth was, he'd grown accustomed to having the family around. Too much time on his hands wasn't good. Not the way his mind tended toward the negative. He dusted off his pants. "Don't suppose you'd want me to get started while you're gone?"

The offer brought a questioning gaze from Luke. "I can't ask that of you. Weekends are your own time."

"I wouldn't mind. Truth is, I'd welcome something to do."

Luke's eyes crimped. "You sure?"

Shrugging one shoulder, Will leaned against the sideboard. "May as well. We'd be that much further ahead."

A lopsided grin slipped in to replace Luke's indecisive stare as he fastened the end gate in place. "Wheat harvest will be here before we know it, so I suppose it wouldn't hurt to get started on the corn." He paused and turned to Will. "All right. I'd be a fool to pass up that offer. Much obliged."

Will gave a satisfied nod as he rounded the side of the wagon. Out of the corner of his eye, he spotted a man on horseback riding toward them. He turned for a better look, recognition settling over him like a thousand-pound boulder. Guthrie Malloy's pointed glare landed firmly on Will, and his gut clenched. The man obviously had no use for him.

Refusing to be intimidated, Will broke off his gaze and

heaved himself onto the wagon seat. He'd let Luke handle this. The less contact Will had with Malloy, the better.

Stilled hoofbeats and the creak of a saddle announced the neighbor's unwelcome presence. "Gettin' set to do some plantin', I see."

"Sure are." Luke fired back the chipper response without hesitation and hopped up on the wagon seat next to Will.

"I finished plantin' well over a week ago." Arrogance oozed from the man's gruff tone, touching off a raw spot within Will. He had a feeling every encounter with this fella was bound to turn sour.

As though sensing where the conversation was headed, Luke gave no answer but took up the reins, seeming as eager as Will to be on their way.

Malloy reined his horse closer, his solid frame casting a shadow over them. "I thought with your *worker* here, you'd be all but done yourself."

Will shot a glance in Luke's direction, expecting a sharp reply in his defense. Instead, a weak grin crept onto his employer's lips. "All in good time, neighbor. All in good time."

Malloy's shadow shifted as he leaned in closer, voice low. "Maybe he's not the worker you thought he'd be."

Will clamped his jaw against the insult and forced himself to keep still. No doubt the barbed comment had been meant to rile him.

Unfortunately, it was working.

With a soft chuckle, Luke tipped his hat higher on his head. "Oh, I don't know. I wager Will here can hold up to any of your boys."

Amazed at Luke's cordial, yet pointed response, Will was grateful he'd left the confrontation to his even-keeled employer. Had he handled things, he'd likely have popped the insolent neighbor in the jaw and escalated the incident.

Malloy's mouth worked side to side as though formulating a snide retort. His chin jutted. "Well, dry as it is, you'll need a good rain to get your seed corn up. Your pa would've knowed better than to wait till the ground was sapped of moisture to plant."

Luke's mouth twitched, the only notable sign the man's cutting remark bothered him. Releasing the brake, Luke dismissed the jab with a firm, "You needn't worry about us. The Good Lord will see fit to send rain when it's needed."

With a tap of the reins, the wagon jostled forward, Luke's words hopefully leaving Malloy something to gnaw on. As they maneuvered along the crowded street, Will blew out a breath. "I wish I had your knack for handling people. That fella's about as irritating as they come."

"Ah, deep down, he's harmless. Just has a few rough spots."

Will scoffed. "A few? Seems rough spots are all that man's made of."

A good-natured laugh sounded from his companion. "There's a bit of good in everyone. You just have t' look for it harder in some than others. Guthrie's biggest shortcoming, other than greed, is having his way. I figure he sees you as a threat to getting what he wants." Luke gave another tap of the reins. "Even if you weren't here, he still wouldn't get our land."

Though the words were reassuring, Will wasn't convinced Malloy was as harmless as Luke supposed. There was something deceitful about the man. Conniving.

Will only hoped the Gallaghers wouldn't find that out the hard way when he left.

12

Gallagher Farm
Saturday, May 30, 1868

Lydia fastened her satchel and glanced around her sparse bedroom, a twinge of nervous excitement threading through her. She'd not been away from home since she and Mama went to meet Adelaide in Washington more than three years ago. What a grand venture that had been—riding the train and staying at the lavish Willard Hotel.

This journey would be different, traveling long hours in a dusty carriage and staying with people she wasn't acquainted with. Her shoulders drooped. Maybe it was the fact she was older now or that her sense of adventure had curtailed a bit, but her heart wasn't in going.

True, she wished to meet Adelaide's cousin and hear Luke give his sermon, but if she was honest, her greatest motivation was a selfish one—to keep what remained of their family intact. Luke and Adelaide seemed far too eager to return to Copperville.

She needed to know why.

Leaving her travel bag where it lay, she strolled to the

window, eyes surveying the newly worked fields and pastureland. She breathed a soft sigh. Perhaps Will had something to do with her hesitancy to leave as well. Though she couldn't imagine why. He obviously held little regard for her. Why should she fret over leaving him when he cared so little for her? The time apart might do her good—take her mind off a relationship that seemed doomed to go anywhere.

"Lydia!"

The strain in her mother's hoarse cry jolted Lydia from her musings. "Coming, Mama." Hiking her skirt, she fled the room. Mama stood hunched at the bottom of the stairway, one hand clutching the railing, the other at her chest.

With a sudden intake of breath, Lydia rushed to her, the milky pallor in her mother's cheeks shooting a tremor through her. "Mama, are you all right?"

"Help me to the ... parlor. I need to ... lie down."

With slow strides they edged toward the parlor entry, Mama's labored breaths marking out each step. Lydia eased her onto the settee and leaned over her. "Is it your heart?"

Taking a hard swallow, Mama stared up at the ceiling, sweat droplets dampening her brow. "I just need to rest a moment."

Lydia pulled a handkerchief from her skirt pocket and dabbed Mama's forehead. A glance at the mantel clock assured Luke and Adelaide would arrive any moment. "Perhaps we should stay home. I fear the trip will be too much for you."

With a shake of her head, Mama moistened her lips. "I'll be fine. I want to see my boy give his sermon. The Lord will lend me strength."

A tap on the door stilled any further argument Lydia might have voiced. She started to rise. "There's Luke. We'll see what he has to say."

Belying her weakness, Mama's firm tug held Lydia in place. "Don't deny me this. Please."

Mama's lipid blue eyes beckoned, sapping Lydia's resolve. She hesitated, fearful her silence could prove detrimental to Ma's wellbeing.

Boots treaded in the hall. "Ma? Lydia? You ready?"

"Help me up." Mama's whispered plea came a moment too late.

Luke rounded the doorway and frowned at them. Three swift strides landed him beside Lydia. "What's wrong?"

She floundered for words. "She ..."

"I'm fine. Merely a bit winded from the excitement of readying for the trip."

Mama's half-truth settled heavily within Lydia. It didn't feel right keeping Mama's weak heart from her brother.

Something in her expression must have alerted him there was more to Mama's dilemma than fatigue. "You sure you're all right? You're pale as chalk."

With effort, Mama sat upright and pressed a shaky hand to her forehead. "I just need to sit a moment. I'll be fine once I'm out in the fresh air."

Seeming unconvinced, Luke shot Lydia a questioning glance.

Torn between revealing what she knew and honoring her mother's wishes, Lydia averted her gaze to the braided rug at her feet.

Mama's voice rallied. "My satchel's in my bedroom. Would you fetch it, son?"

After a moment's hesitance, Luke nodded and backed toward the parlor entrance.

When his footfall faded, Lydia sat on the settee beside her mother, thankful some of the color had returned to her cheeks. "You can't go on hiding the truth from Luke forever, Mama."

She patted Lydia's hand, the creases at the corners of her eyes deepening. "I know, dear. But he has Adelaide and their coming baby to consider. I don't wish to add to his worry."

Lydia gently squeezed her mother's hand, certain the dear woman would take any measures necessary not to be a burden, least of all to her children. "He's not blind, Mama. Whether you tell him or not. He can sense you aren't yourself."

Her thin lips angled upward in a faint grin. "When the time is right, I'll tell him." Drawing a breath, she sat straighter. "I'm better now. Shall we go?"

Like a fledgling bird hesitant to leave its nest, Lydia perched on the edge of the settee, vacillating between good sense and the yearning to comply. Lord willing, they would make the trip without incident.

If not, she would regret it the rest of her days.

WHILE LUKE HELPED Adelaide onto the front seat of the carriage, Will stepped to aid Mrs. Gallagher, her movements stiff and slow. More than once since his arrival, he'd noticed her shortness of breath and wondered if she suffered from a health condition. With nothing being said by any of the family, he'd thought no more of it. But if the creases in Lydia's brow while observing her mother were any indication, his assumption had been right.

Mrs. Gallagher huffed as she settled onto the bench. "Thank you, Will." She dabbed at her forehead with a handkerchief. "Make yourself at home while we're away. There's a loaf of fresh bread, boiled eggs, and smoked ham in the kitchen. And you'll find greens in the garden out back."

He tipped his head, a bit amused by her motherly concern. "Yes, ma'am."

With Mrs. Gallagher properly situated, he turned to offer Lydia a hand up. She looked rather fetching in her navy and white travel dress and a mite more mature with her hair up.

Seeming hesitant to take the hand he offered, she merely stared up at him, her sky-blue eyes full of expectancy.

Taken aback by the potency of her gaze, he struggled for something to say. "Safe travels, Miss Lydia."

"Thank you." Her gaze trailed to his outstretched hand, and a flash of crimson shaded her cheeks.

Had he embarrassed her?

At last, she slipped her gloved palm into his and allowed him to help her onto the carriage. The intimate feel of her hand in his brought an uneasiness he hadn't reckoned on, and he quickly released his hold as she took a seat beside her mother.

The awkward moment melted away when Lydia turned to him with a shy grin, the blue in her bonnet bringing out the vibrancy in her eyes. "Watch over Penny and Basil for me."

He returned a firm nod. "Will do."

Taking up the reins, Luke hollered over his shoulder. "Thanks for looking after the place, Will. We'll be back sometime Monday evening."

"I'll be here."

As the carriage rolled forward, Lydia pivoted to face him. "Take care of yourself."

Will barely heard the soft-spoken words over the click of the wheels. Before he could respond, she turned away. Something deep within him thrilled at the directive, not only due to the genuine show of concern, but also the tender look in Lydia's eyes as she'd spoken.

A twinge of uneasiness rippled through him. Until now, he'd thought of her as nothing more than Luke's younger sister. Yet, in that moment, she seemed more woman than he'd given her credit.

And he wasn't sure what to do with it.

13

Copperville, Pennsylvania

Lydia arched her neck for a better look at the sizable estate in the distance. "Is that it?"

"Sure is."

Luke's response could not have been more welcome. The lengthy journey and firm seat had left Lydia's backside and legs numb and eager for movement. A mere two stops along the way hadn't proven sufficient to undo the seemingly endless hours of jostling. She couldn't imagine making the trip in Adelaide's condition. Though her sister-in-law had uttered no complaints, her constant shifting hinted at discomfort.

"Praise be." Mama's weary response and haggard appearance told how strenuous the trip had been on her as well.

Placing a hand on her mother's arm, Lydia gave a soft squeeze. "You can rest now, Mama."

Mama leaned her bonneted head against Lydia's and mustered a weak grin. "I admit that sounds most inviting."

With a glance back at them, Adelaide draped an arm over her rounded middle, her complexion a mite peaked. "I heartily agree."

Lydia's mouth twisted. No matter how difficult the journey for her, Mama and Adelaide had endured worse.

The sun hung low in the west as Luke eased the carriage to a stop outside the lavish Banks' residence. Four white columns lined the front of the two-story brick house flanked by outbuildings and an expanse of fenced-in acreage. One thing was certain—Clarissa's adoptive parents wanted for nothing.

Before they even stepped from the carriage, the door swung open, and a fair-haired girl Lydia assumed was Clarissa darted onto the veranda, all smiles. Her fitted buttercream dress revealed the lanky frame of a girl still maturing, with pleasant features faintly resembling those of Adelaide's.

A well-dressed couple strolled out after her, refined in both poise and presence. Lydia subconsciously straightened her back and held her chin a notch higher, fearing her modest appearance wouldn't meet their standards. Yet, their welcoming expressions did not tend toward arrogance.

The girl quickly downed the steps and greeted Adelaide with open arms. "It's so good to see you. You look wonderful. Motherhood agrees with you."

With a weighty chuckle, Adelaide pressed a hand to her expanded waistline. "That's sweet of you. Though I'm not sure *traveling* agrees with me at present."

Striding over, Luke met Mr. Banks halfway up the steps and shook his hand. The man clapped him on the shoulder. "How are you, my boy? We're glad you've come."

Lydia's chest tightened. Perhaps coming hadn't been such a good idea. At home, she could envision a mediocre reception from the Banks. Here, she glimpsed firsthand their glowing reception, like the prodigal's father welcoming his wayward son.

"Good to see you again, sir." Turning, Luke gestured toward Mama and Lydia. "I'd like you to meet my mother, Martha Gallagher, and my sister, Lydia."

With a dip of his chin, Mr. Banks glanced their way. "Pleased to meet you."

Mama smiled up at him. "Kind of you to put us up. Are you sure we'll not be an imposition?"

He shook his head. "Not at all. We're pleased to have you."

Mrs. Banks motioned to them. "You must be exhausted and famished. Come inside. I'll have Cook get you something to eat."

Slipping an arm around his wife's waist, Mr. Banks nodded. "Yes. Do come in. I'll send Michael for your luggage. Reggie will tend to your horse and rig."

Lydia hadn't noticed the slender young man standing at Angel's head. It seemed Mr. and Mrs. Banks had a servant for every need. For the stable boy's sake, she hoped the horse took to him. Else he may be in for a long night. She grinned. Will had easily won Angel over.

As well as her.

Awaiting her turn up the steps, Lydia peered at her gloved hand, warmth trickling through her. Hours after parting, she could still feel the gentle strength of Will's fingers enveloping hers. How silly of her to blush over the innocent gesture. But she'd never held a man's hand other than Papa's. Will's touch nearly stole her breath.

She shook off the memory as she started up the steps alongside her mother. The sooner she rid herself of aspirations involving Will, the better.

A carpeted hallway awaited them inside. Mr. and Mrs. Banks led them to a spacious parlor, the likes of which Lydia had never seen. So different from their simple farmhouse, and yet, the memories within the four walls of their modest home meant more to her than a dozen houses equivalent to the Bankses'.

She edged toward the lengthy table lined with portraitures of the family, most of Clarissa at various stages of childhood. But what truly caught her eye was the sleek, mahogany piano situated in front of the curtained bay window. Though she'd ever longed to play such an instrument, the opportunity had never presented itself.

Clarissa likely had every advantage a girl could wish for and more. While Lydia had spent her days milking cows, digging potatoes, and walking to school, this girl had had servants to do her bidding, traveled, and learned the fine arts. Regardless, Lydia would not trade her family and upbringing for all the finery the world could offer.

"Do you play?"

Pivoting, Lydia saw Clarissa's wide eyes fixed on her in expectation. With an adamant shake of the head, Lydia answered, "No, I don't."

"Then I'll have to teach you a simple tune while you're here. Come. Sit." Before Lydia could respond, Clarissa took her by the hand and guided her to the plush settee before the huge stone fireplace. "I've been so eager to meet you. Adelaide told us all about you."

Taken aback by the girl's earnestness, Lydia's mouth slackened. "Has she?"

"Yes. And I have a feeling we're going to get on just grand."

With a weak grin, Lydia cast a glance over her shoulder to where Luke, Adelaide, and Mama were thoroughly engaged in conversation with Mr. and Mrs. Banks. Obviously, the family had a gift for hospitality.

Lydia's stomach tightened. She just hoped Luke and Adelaide didn't find the family's allure too enticing.

WILL YAWNED as he set the lantern on the wash stand and eased onto the quilted bed. With the sun barely set, it seemed too early to go to bed, but his muscles ached from the long day of planting. Besides, he had nothing better to do. Thank goodness for Mrs. Gallagher's thoughtfulness in leaving enough victuals to fill his belly. Fresh bread and smoked ham beat anything he'd have conjured up. Tomorrow, he'd try his hand at frying eggs.

He glanced around the unfamiliar room, hands propped on

his thighs. It felt strange to take up residence in the house with the Gallaghers away. But Mrs. Gallagher had told him to make himself at home. And after the tiring day, a bed sounded much more appealing than a hardened dirt floor. He rubbed a hand over his forehead. Maybe the more comfortable setting would keep his menacing dreams at bay.

He jostled the bed, the mattress a bit firm for his liking. Yet, it beat the thin layer of straw he'd become accustomed to. The room's musty smell and lack of personal items assured him this was either Drew or Luke's vacated room and not Lydia's. He'd leave it just as he'd found it. Even sleep atop the covers so as not to muss the bed.

A sweat droplet slithered along his temple, and he wiped it away. One thing was certain. He'd not get much sleep in this muggy upstairs bedroom, all closed up. Hoping to alleviate some of the stuffiness, he strode to the window and slid it open. A chorus of crickets carried on the gentle breeze as he breathed in the fresh air.

Much better.

Thick clouds blanketed the night sky, concealing most of the moon's glow. A bit of rain would be just what the newly planted seeds needed to sprout. Tomorrow being Sunday, he'd not work anyway. He supposed he should attend church service, though his heart wouldn't be in it. Out of respect for the Gallaghers, he'd gone previous weeks. But with them away, he was tempted to keep to himself. Not being on the best of terms with the Lord, it seemed hypocritical to sit in the pew.

A sigh escaped him as he straightened and backed from the window. No one would miss him anyhow. He was as obscure as the images that plagued his muddled mind.

Dropping back down on the bed, he tugged off his boots. He might have enjoyed hearing Luke's sermon. The fella was as genuine a Christian as they come, evidenced in how he handled himself around Guthrie Malloy. That alone had Will's utmost respect. Luke lived out the faith he professed. A quality Will admired but couldn't much relate to.

Dousing the lantern, he laid back on the bed. He locked his fingers together behind his head, listening to the rhythmic rasp of insects outside the window. By now, the Gallaghers were probably enjoying a leisurely dinner at a fine restaurant or settling in for an evening of stirring conversation with their hosts.

A grin wedged through his cloud of fatigue. He had to admit it was pretty quiet around here without Lydia's lively chatter. There was something about the girl that roused his senses. The look in her eyes when they'd parted lingered in his mind like a summer sunset. She seemed to truly care about him. Why, he couldn't fathom. Maybe she thought of him as a lost puppy in need of coddling.

He blew out a breath. More than likely, she pitied him, now that she knew his plight. He'd probably shared more about himself than he should have. But, he had to admit, after years of keeping his predicament locked inside, it felt good to tell someone the truth. Surprisingly, Lydia had listened without voicing judgment or bludgeoning him with questions.

His eyes bobbed closed, the lure of sleep tugging hard at his senses. A good night's rest would rejuvenate his body, but his memory had a mind of its own.

PANIC SEIZED Will as a blast of cannon fire and smoke spiraled toward him. He startled awake just as he was struck and thrown back. He stared at the darkened ceiling, breaths shallow and body damp with sweat. His hands flew to his chest to ensure he was still intact. With a relieved huff, he raked a hand through his hair. There was no escaping the bleak images that had become as familiar as the sunrise. Would his sleep forever be plagued with dark, random remembrances of war and imprisonment that he otherwise couldn't recall?

The distant rumble of thunder brought him fully to his senses. Maybe the sound was why this dream seemed so vivid. Even now, he thought he smelt the faint scent of smoke. He glanced to the window, surprised by the brightness of the moon. Hours earlier, clouds had hindered its shine. Now, the amber glow seemed to dance along the windowsill.

A cow's frantic "moo" sounded from outside. Odd Penny would bellow in the middle of the night. In the month he'd slept in the barn, the worst she'd done was chew her cud or stomp her hoof.

He scoffed. Maybe she missed him.

The swelling breeze rustled the linen curtains, ushering in a pungent odor along with a crackling noise. Will tensed. That was no imagined cannon's gunpowder he smelled. It was the singed scent of smoke. And that was no moonglow.

It was fire.

Scrambling to his feet, he lunged toward the window. Orange flames danced along the north side of the barn. Will gripped the windowsill, jaw clenched. The seed corn and all the farm provisions were in there. "No!"

If the fire continued to spread, it would devour the entire barn and everything in it. Much of the Gallaghers' livelihood would be lost.

He couldn't let that happen.

Will groped in the dark for his boots and franticly slipped them on.

Rushing from the room, he sought the only source of assistance he could. "Lord, I've no right to ask, but if ever I needed Your help, it's now."

14

Sunday morning, May 31, 1868

Will plopped down on the seed sacks, elbows on his knees, exhausted and soaked to his skin. Still in disbelief. Some might call it coincidence, the way the storm blew through just as he stepped outside. After all, he'd heard rumbles of thunder and felt the upsurge in the breeze from the bedroom window. But, he had to admit, the timing seemed more than happenstance.

Though he wasn't ready to assert the Lord had answered his prayer, either. Too many disappointments stood in the way.

Whether the rain had arrived by chance or Divine intervention, Will was grateful. From the way the fire was spreading, there'd been no possible way he could have stopped it. And yet here he sat, barn intact, with Penny and Basil safe inside. Though several boards along the north wall were either charred or eaten away entirely, the damage was minimal compared to what might have been. Amazingly, the stack of seed corn didn't have a singed mark on it.

Other than stomping out a few stray flames along the straw-covered barn floor, Will hadn't so much as scooped a solitary bucketful of water to stop the fire. The rain had poured just long enough to douse the flames and then shut off like a busted pump.

Nothing short of a miracle.

Will hated to think how Luke would have reacted had he come home to a burnt barn and ruined seed corn. The whole Gallagher family likely would have thought Will inept. Possibly even sent him on his way.

The notion of which bothered him more than he cared to admit.

The strong scent of smoke lingered, settling heavily in Will's chest. Now that he'd had time to mull things over, the whole incident didn't set right. No fire just happened.

His shoulder muscles knotted. Someone had set it. And he had a pretty good suspicion who.

"Mr. Evans? You about?"

The female voice brought Will to his feet. "In here."

Scuffing sounded at the barn door, and Mrs. Perkins peered in at him, face puckered. "You all right? Hal and me was on our way t' church service an' noticed the smoky smell. With the Gallaghers away, we thought we'd best check an' see if all is well."

"It is now. Just thankful the rain came when it did."

Her gaze drifted to the charred timbers, and her eyes flared. "Lan'sakes. Lightnin' must've been somethin' fierce over this way."

Will considered setting her straight—that lightning wasn't the culprit—but determined it best not to make premature accusations. "The storm did come on rather sudden."

Mr. Perkins shouldered his way through, perusing the damaged barn before his gaze settled on Will. Though the two hadn't been formally introduced, Will had seen the neighbor stop by from time to time. The stocky, dark-skinned man gave a brisk nod. "Seems you had yerself an interestin' night."

Will held the man's gaze. Something in his dark eyes conveyed a deeper assessment of the damage than his wife's. "Not one I care to repeat."

Mrs. Perkins crossed her arms over her chest, hugging her worn, leather Bible. "The Lord surely was lookin' out for you, t' douse the fire afore it got outta hand."

Unwilling to argue the point, Will nodded. "Yes, ma'am."

Mr. Perkins stepped closer, a notable limp in his gait. "If you need help patchin', I'll come by t'morrow and lend a hand."

Though Will regretted inconveniencing the man, he disliked more the thought of Luke returning home to a charred, gaping hole in his barn. Even a temporary fix would be better than nothing. "That's right kind of you, Mr. Perkins. I'll see what materials I can muster."

With a good-natured smile, Mrs. Perkins wagged her finger at him. "And I'll bring ya both a basket of victuals for your lunch."

Touched by the couple's generosity, Will dipped his chin. "Much obliged for your kindness."

Seeming satisfied, Mrs. Perkins brandished a wide smile. "We'll be on our way then and let you get cleaned up, lest you be tardy to church service."

In attempt to pacify the kindly neighbor, Will nodded and forced a grin. Looking like a vagabond in his soiled, drenched clothes and tousled hair, he'd given up the idea of going in for church service. And, truthfully, leaving the place unattended seemed foolish. No telling what might happen with him away. Come to think of it, he hadn't even had breakfast. And those eggs were calling.

Mr. Perkins hung back as his wife vacated. Looking Will in the eyes, he lowered his voice. "Keep alert. Not everyone 'round here can be trusted." Without waiting for a response, he ducked outside.

The directive was enough to convince Will the neighbor was

mindful of the fire's origin. Did he also suspect who might have set it?

Will gave the damage another glance over. Odd how situations play out. The one night he hadn't slept in the barn, it'd been set ablaze. And just after they'd brought home the bags of seed corn.

Coincidence? Not likely. Had he been in here, would he have seen or heard something?

If someone kept a close watch on the place, they might even be aware the Gallaghers were away. Will clenched his jaw at memory of Guthrie Malloy taking note of the seed corn purchase. He would certainly have something to gain by damaging it. If he was out to do the Gallaghers harm, destroying their future income would prove an effective means.

Was he truly so desperate to get his hands on their land?

Will's belly rumbled, spurring him to take up the pail of milk outside Penny's stall. The first order of business was breakfast and a change of clothes. Afterward, he'd take a look in the loft to try to drum up a few planks to fill in the hole.

Exiting the barn, he squinted against the brightness of the sun. Mud from last night's rain oozed over the edges of his boots, making a squishing sound as he sauntered toward the vacant house. Though he'd planned to take advantage of sleeping another night in a bed, that idea now seemed a luxury he couldn't afford. He'd take no more chances. Tonight, he'd be back in his usual spot in the barn.

A rifle at his side.

———

LYDIA PEERED over her shoulder at the array of people continuing to file into the church building. Having arrived early for Luke's sake, Lydia and her mother had planted themselves in the second pew, awed by the intricately carved wood and arched ceiling. A dozen pews lined both sides of the aisle, more than twice the number of those back home. And one by one, they had filled almost to capacity.

Stationed at the back, Luke and Adelaide greeted each person entering, looking very much at home in the role. Quiet chatter had gradually blossomed into a steady buzz as the building filled. Lydia felt a tug on her dress sleeve and turned to see a smiling Clarissa pointing to the wall clock. "Almost time. Do you suppose Luke is nervous?"

Cutting another glance over her shoulder, Lydia raised a brow. "He doesn't seem to be." With all these people, *she* certainly would. The very thought of speaking before so many left her sweaty-palmed. Turning back around, she brushed a stray hair from her travel dress, feeling as out of place as the lost strand. Though the Copperville church was striking to visit, she missed the familiarity of her church back home, surrounded by friends and neighbors, her family ... and Will.

A nervous tingle rippled through her. Was he attending service on his own? She'd longed to ask if he intended to, but feared he'd find the query intrusive. Had she crossed his mind even once since they'd parted? She'd thought of him dozens of times.

For what good it would do her.

Heaving a sigh, she laced her fingers together in her lap, her attention drawn to a slender, long-legged fellow in a dark suit coat making his way to the front. The congregation quieted as the last of the stragglers found their seats. Luke and Adelaide slipped into the empty front pew just as the song leader gestured for the congregation to stand. At the man's directive, the congregation sang several stanzas of *Amazing Grace,* the blend of men and women's voices echoing through the building in a heavenly peal.

Several hymns later, the man pushed a swath of chestnut hair from his forehead and motioned for the congregation to sit. When the assembly quieted, the song leader strode from behind the pulpit, his beady eyes skimming the crowd. "With Pastor

Lindquist away, we've asked Luke Gallagher to speak in his absence. While Luke isn't a preacher, those of you who've become acquainted with him know him as a man with a heart for the Lord. And we're pleased he's willing to step up in our time of need."

Whispers spattered through the congregation. Out of the corner of her eye, Lydia saw Luke blow out a long breath, a red streak climbing his neck into his cheek. Perhaps his nerves were a smidgen frayed after all. She longed to give him a reassuring touch on the shoulder, and was pleased to see Adelaide offer him a smile of encouragement.

The song leader's gaze settled on Luke, his thin lips spread in a wide grin. "Come up and share what the Lord has placed on your heart, Brother Gallagher."

Without a moment's hesitation, Luke jolted to his feet, Bible clutched firmly to his chest. He shook hands with the man in passing, then strode to the pulpit, his short blond waves combed neatly in place. Drawing a deep breath, he perused the congregation, vivid blue eyes gleaming. "I'm honored to have been asked to speak. Like Brother Conway says, I'm no preacher, but I pray something I say today will encourage you or give you somethin' to ponder."

The rustle of dresses and shifting of feet echoed loud against the quiet. Lydia longed for a glimpse of the people's faces, but was too self-conscious to turn for a look. Were they scowling and critical or boasting smiles of encouragement? She lifted a silent prayer for her brother, that what he had to say would be well-received.

Luke cleared his throat as if to rid the shakiness from his voice and continued. "During the war, my sergeant told me I'd missed my calling as a preacher. Now, I wish I could say for certain the remark came out of a genuine regard for my convictions. But I suspect it was more because he wished I'd throw my efforts to share my faith in a different direction than him."

Soft laughter vibrated through the congregation, and Lydia's spirits lifted. She should have known Luke's charm would outweigh any qualms the listeners might have.

As if the confining chains of insecurity had crumbled to his feet, Luke's stance relaxed. He strolled to one side of the pulpit, leaving his Bible open atop it. "At the time, I chuckled at the idea. And yet, here I stand before you, doing something I never thought possible. The Lord indeed works in ways we cannot see or know."

A volley of "amens" peppered the building, and a touch of pride washed through Lydia. Though she'd never imagined her teasing, full-of-life older brother preaching before a congregation, she'd always respected the sincerity of his faith and his way with people.

He paused, his expression turning more solemn. "There's a reason I share my faith so freely. His name was Jacob."

Lydia's chest squeezed. She knew well the story of Jacob, Luke's friend who'd perished without knowing the Lord. And how deeply that tragic loss had affected Luke. She glanced at her mother, not surprised at the moisture pooling in her eyes. Tranquility streamed from every angle of her face. In that instant, Lydia knew the sacrifice in coming had been worth every ounce of struggle.

She reached to clasp her mother's hand, and warm, frail fingers encircled hers. A tear tumbled down Mama's cheek as she turned toward Lydia with a gentle smile. There was something sacred and enduring in the moment, like a precious memory was being chiseled on both their hearts. That they were among strangers in a far-off place no longer seemed important. They were together, reveling in the specialness of the occasion.

Luke's enthusiasm trickled through her like a breath of spring as he conveyed his story. All apprehension seemed to have fled, as if he'd spoken before a crowd a hundred times. A contented smile wedged across Lydia's lips. If only Drew and

Caroline could be here. Then her heart would be full to perfection.

Her smile deepened. *Well, almost.*

For a brief moment, her mind traveled back to the two-story farmhouse nestled amid fields and meadows and to the man they'd left to tend it.

True perfection would be to have Will listening at her side.

15

Monday Evening, June 1, 1868

Will rubbed a hand over the back of his neck to knead the tightness from his muscles. Hal Perkins might be more than twice his age and have a bum leg, but Will had struggled to keep pace with the man. The two of them had worked long into the afternoon to replace the burnt-out section of the barn. Hopefully, the planks Will found in the loft hadn't been set aside for another use.

Slipping on his soiled gloves, he gave the barn wall another once-over. A few more boards to cover the remainder of the hole and there'd be little evidence the fire ever happened. He peeked through the opening. Other than the blackened bits of straw and charred smell lingering inside the barn.

With a step back, he blew out a breath. The incident still galled him. What sort of fella set fire to his neighbor's farm? Though he felt certain Malloy was the culprit, he needed to be careful not to make accusations he couldn't prove. His duty was to relay what happened and let the Gallaghers form their own conclusions.

Evening shadows spilled across the landscape as the sun sank below the tree line to the west. Will glanced around the corner of the barn to the lane, wondering if the Gallaghers would make it home as planned or if they'd been detained. He cringed. Hopefully the wheel he'd helped repair hadn't worked loose again.

He stooped to gather the last bits of charred timbers. Taking on full responsibility of the place hadn't panned out so well. He'd hoped to prove himself capable to Luke. And, for some odd reason, to Lydia. His lips tugged in a weak grin. At least he'd kept his promise to look after Penny and Basil.

He tossed the armload of rubble on the pile of debris he and Hal had erected. Though they'd stacked the ruined planks a safe distance from the barn, the stiff breeze had deterred them from setting the heap aflame.

Lifting his hat, Will swiped his sleeve across his sweaty brow. With the passing of the sun, the wind had begun to settle. Maybe it wasn't too late yet to start a fire. An evening blaze would definitely be cooler. In truth, he wasn't sure he wished the Gallaghers to witness the full extent of the damage. No one liked to return home to a mess.

He'd nearly convinced himself to fetch the matches when the jingle of a harness and clomp of hooves curtailed the notion. A glance to the roadway assured him the Gallaghers had returned. His jaw tensed. Too late. Time to own up to the mishap and hope his best was good enough.

AS THEY NEARED THE HOMESTEAD, Lydia scoured the farmyard for Will, finally spotting him coming around the corner of the barn. She suppressed a grin, a nervous tingle rippling through her as he came into fuller view. Though mere days had passed since she'd last seen him, it seemed like weeks.

With eager anticipation, she smoothed her dress and touched a hand to her ringlets, hoping she looked presentable after the long, dusty trip. Would he be happy to see her ... er, them?

Will sauntered out to meet them, his expression difficult to read in the shadowy light.

As if in greeting, Angel sounded a soft nicker. With a chuckle, Luke pulled her to a stop beside Will. "Sounds like somebody missed you."

A hint of a grin edged across Will's face, and he rubbed a hand along Angel's forehead. "So it appears."

Will's smooth, masculine voice sent a shiver through Lydia. She tried to catch his eye, but instead, his gaze landed on Luke. "How was your trip?"

"It was good. Long, but good. Things go all right here?"

"For the most part." A shadow fell across Will's face, and he shuffled his feet like he had something to say but couldn't quite manage it.

Lydia eyed him. He was holding back. Why? Had there been a problem of some sort? From the rear seat, she couldn't read Luke's expression, but his silence implied he shared similar thoughts.

At last, he nodded. "I'll get Ma and Lydia settled in, and we can catch up on things in the morning."

"Yes. That sounds most agreeable." Mama's breathy response hinted she was eager to again enjoy the comforts of home.

As they pulled away, Will's eyes finally lifted to meet Lydia's. Her attempt at a smile fell short as, with a quick tip of his hat, he pivoted toward the barn. Her heart sank, the reunion not what she'd envisioned. Plainly, Will hadn't missed her nearly as much as she'd missed him. Not only had he barely glanced her way, but he was remaining tight-lipped regarding some unknown mishap that had befallen the place.

With a quiet sigh, she eased back on the seat. Perhaps it was time to give up her infatuation with a man who seemed to care so little for her.

Her stomach clenched. The one man who'd caught her eye had her wishing he hadn't.

WILL LOCKED his fingers together behind his head and blew out a long breath, staring at the barn rafters. Of no fault of his own, he'd let the Gallaghers down. Lydia, especially. He'd sensed it in her expression.

After their long trip, he hadn't the heart to mention the fire in the barn. Thankfully, the damage to the back corner of the barn had faded into the shadow of darkness and gone unnoticed. Though he was surprised, no one mentioned the charred smell.

Tomorrow, he would explain the incident to Luke. At least what he *presumed* happened. Not wishing to alarm Lydia or her mother with the assumption the fire might have been maliciously set, he'd keep his speculations to himself.

They'd find out the truth soon enough.

But he had a feeling Lydia held something more against him than half-truths. Either that or she was tired and out of sorts from the trip. He wasn't sure what to make of her. He only knew the usual luster in her eyes had faded like a worn-out coat.

So different from the attentive stare she'd given him as they'd driven away.

He closed his eyes. Just as well. Given time, he could get accustomed to her company. Something he couldn't afford to do. Come the end of corn harvest he'd be leaving, and how would that set if they became attached? As things were, he had no business pursuing any sort of relationship. For all he knew, he could be married or otherwise committed. Though by now, any wife or sweetheart he might have had had probably moved on in life, thinking him dead.

Still, he couldn't get that vision of the fair-haired girl running to greet him out of his head. Hardly a week passed that he didn't have the dream. It must carry some sort of significance. And until he discovered its importance, he wasn't at liberty to lend his attentions to any female.

A tromping noise outside the barn brought him to a sitting position. Scrambling for his rifle, he stared into the darkness, trying to make out what had invaded his solitude. At Angel's soft whinny, all the air expelled from his lungs. Evidently, she'd found the hole left by the torn-away boards and stuck her head through.

Standing, Will raked a hand through his hair. "You stole half a night's sleep from me, girl. What're you doing there?" More gentle nickers sounded as he propped his rifle against the stall and ambled over to her. He rubbed a hand down her face, and she leaned into him, head bobbing up and down. Will reached to scratch behind her ear. "At least you're one female I can coddle without regret."

His stomach twisted as his thoughts returned to Lydia. He'd confided in her more than anyone he could recall. She'd proven a worthy confidant, lending a listening ear when he needed one. But until he knew the truth of his past, friends were all they could be.

16

Tuesday, June 2, 1868

Luke scratched at his cheek, surveying the barn repairs and the pile of rubble in the early morning light. "So, you think the fire was set?"

"I don't see any other explanation. It started ahead of the storm, and there weren't any close lightning strikes. Thankfully, the rainstorm doused the flames before they got out of hand." The words rolled off Will's tongue rather reluctantly. It wasn't easy suggesting someone had maliciously set fire to his friend's property. The question was, should he share his suspicions as to who the culprit was?

"Sounds like the Lord was looking out for us." With a shake of his head, Luke crossed his arms over his chest. "It's hard to fathom why someone would do this, though. Must have been some troublemakers out on a late-night binge."

"Could be." Though Will had to admire Luke's loyalty to his neighbors, deep down, he thought his boss a bit too trusting. He offered a weak nod but couldn't resist conveying his doubts. "But that sort usually makes a ruckus. It's more likely someone caught wind you folks were gone and decided to take advantage of the situation."

Luke's eyes crimped. "It does seem suspicious. You didn't see or hear anything?"

"'Fraid not." Will hesitated. "I ... uh, took the liberty of sleeping in the house that night."

A hint of a grin spilled onto Luke's lips. "Well, now, glad to hear it. You might want to consider bunking there more often. The barn's no fit place for a man to sleep."

He shrugged. "I don't wish to burden your mother and sister."

"You'd be no burden. Why, quiet as you are, they'd hardly know you were around."

Heat rose in Will's cheeks. There was no easy way to explain his predicament. He gave a low sigh. "It's on your ma and Lydia's account I stay in the barn."

"How's that?"

Will hesitated, shoving his clammy hands in his pockets. "I have dreams. Nightmares, really. Noisy enough to wake me in a cold sweat. As well as anyone else within earshot."

Understanding seemed to dawn in Luke's eyes, and he nodded. "War does terrible things to a man. You've not offered much about your past, nor have I asked. I figure there's good reason you don't wish to talk about it. But I appreciate you sacrificing your comfort on behalf of my family."

The tension eased from Will's shoulders, his respect for Luke raising a notch at his response. Will *couldn't* share about his past because he had no known past to share. And judging by the few shreds of it he'd witnessed in his dreams, there wasn't much he cared to recount anyway.

With a wry grin, Luke nudged Will's arm. "You might find them heavy sleepers who wouldn't mind the noise."

Will mustered a weak smile. "Could be." Though he doubted it.

Shifting his attention to the freshly worked field to the west, Luke jutted his chin. "Looks like you got a fair amount of planting done while we were away."

Grateful for the change in topic, Will followed his friend's gaze. "Not as much as I'd hoped, but it's a start."

"You're a good worker, Will. A trustworthy one at that. I'm thankful the Lord sent you our way."

The unexpected praise took Will off guard. Rarely had previous bosses taken notice of him, let alone viewed him as a godsend. "That works both ways. I'm grateful for the job."

"Well, it brought me peace of mind knowing the place was well looked after while we were away."

A glance at the pile of ruined timbers made Will hesitant to accept the compliment. He purposely steered the conversation in another direction. "You never said how your sermon went."

The comment sparked an immediate glow from Luke's face. "Ah, it was great. I was nervous going into it, but once I was up there, I felt as at home as honey in a beehive."

Will smirked. "You're a lot different than me. I could no more speak before a crowd than squeeze lemon juice from an apple."

Confidence and vitality seemed to ooze from Luke. "Ah, for me, there's something special about standing before a group of people sharing faith and the truths of Scripture. I've not felt anything quite like it."

"You'd do it again then, I take it?"

"Oh, you bet, if I'm asked. Though I'm sure Adelaide would prefer the baby come first."

A twinge of longing gnawed at Will. Luke had such zeal for his faith. Such joy and zest for life. Will envied him that. Traveling from place to place, never setting down roots or feeling a part of anyone or anything had become his way of life. How he ached to experience a depth and vibrancy for God, for *anything,* the way Luke did. "I think I'll stick to farming."

A spurt of laughter erupted from Luke. "Then what say we go

have our breakfast? Afterward, I'll head to town for more boards while you plant."

"Sounds good."

"What happened to the barn?"

Will cringed and spun toward the frantic feminine voice. Milk bucket in hand, Lydia perused the damaged section of the barn before turning her wide-eyed stare on him and Luke. Thankfully, Luke took the initiative. "Just a little mishap. Nothing to concern yourself with."

She strode over for a closer look. "But that pile of charred boards. Looks like the barn caught fire."

Will floundered under her pointed gaze. Taking his cue from Luke, he kept his answer vague. "Pure carelessness on my part."

Her blue eyes bored into him as if extracting the truth. Keeping secrets from her was like trying to stem the flow of a flooded creek. He cut an uneasy glance at Luke, who was edging toward the path to his house, clearly wanting no part in further explanation. "I'd best see if Adelaide has breakfast ready."

Unwilling to face Lydia alone, Will backed toward the water trough, thumbing over his shoulder. "And I'd better wash up." He skittered away, leaving a slack-mouthed Lydia alone with her milk pail.

And likely a head full of questions.

———

"WHO WERE THEY TRYING TO FOOL?" Lydia tugged at Penny's udder with more force than intended, and the cow issued a bellow of complaint and swung her head around. Easing her grip, Lydia cast the Jersey a repentant scowl. "Sorry, girl. It's not your fault those two dullards can't give a straight answer."

She blew out a breath. "Carelessness. Ha!" From what she could tell, Will wasn't careless about anything. He was as cautious and steady as they came.

Were they trying to protect her from the truth? Or did they think her too immature to handle it?

A faint singed smell, mingled with the scent of straw and hay, pulled her attention to the far wall where daylight streamed through the gap left by the missing boards. The way Will was acting, something malicious must have taken place. Lydia's mouth twisted. If she'd get no answers from Luke or Will, maybe the barn itself would give clue as to what happened. She poured a meowing Basil a small bowl of milk and then set aside her half-filled bucket.

As Lydia rose to her feet, Penny turned big brown eyes on her as if wondering why she'd not been fully milked out. Lydia gave the inquisitive cow a pat on the rump. "Don't worry. I'll be back." Seeming unconcerned, the cow returned to her breakfast.

With quick strides, Lydia crossed the barn. Dusty beams of early morning sunlight filtered in, turning patches of the straw-covered floor golden. Lydia slowed as she neared the section of the wall that had been replaced. Bits of charred straw lined the edges. Lydia shook her head. "It's a wonder the entire structure didn't go up in flames." *Thank You, Lord, for Your mercies.*

Stooping over, she rummaged through the singed straw with her fingers, not sure what she was searching for. Just some sort of explanation for the cause of the fire ... other than Will's "carelessness." After searching from one end of the burnt section to another unsuccessfully, she wiped the soot from her fingers and gave a disgruntled huff. Straightening, she planted her hands on her hips. "There must be something."

A gentle breeze drifted through the foot-wide gap in the boards. Lydia poked her head out, squinting against the mounting sunlight. Sight of the charred boards and scorched grass turned her stomach. They might have been ruined.

Her gaze dropped to the ground outside the hole. A small sliver of wood several feet to the left caught her eye. Unable to reach it from inside and not wishing to soil her dress, she rushed outside to retrieve it. Bending down, she clasped the sliver of wood between her fingers and pursed her lips. Just as she'd suspected.

Something was amiss, and she intended to find out what it was.

17

"Why didn't you just say the fire was set?"

Will paused mid-bite, his cheeks warming as he met Lydia's pointed glare. The girl was too perceptive for her own good. Lowering his forkful of scrambled eggs back to his plate, he gave a slight cough. "What makes you think it was set?"

"Fire?" Metal clanked as Mrs. Gallagher's fork dropped to her plate. Her saucer-like eyes shifted between him and Lydia. "What fire?"

Expelling a long breath, Will bowed his head. There was no sense denying the fact any longer. "The north side of the barn was set ablaze while you were away. Thankfully, a rainstorm doused the flames before they got out of hand."

"So you admit the fire was no accident."

Lydia's forthright tone drew Will's eyes back to hers. "I suspect so, though I can't say for certain since I didn't see it happen. Just woke to the smell of smoke."

Leveling her gaze, Lydia slid the stub of a wooden match from beneath her plate and held it out. "I found this on the ground just outside the barn. So, unless you're in the habit of tossing lit matches where they'll easily ignite, I'd say the fire was intentional."

"Intentional?" Martha's brow creased. "Who would do such a thing?"

Setting the match bit on the rim of her plate, Lydia leaned back in her chair. "Guthrie Malloy, that's who. He's after our land and apparently willing to acquire it any way he can."

Amazed at the girl's astuteness, Will squelched the urge to nod in agreement. Though he'd come to a similar conclusion, he was in no position to voice his suspicions.

Mrs. Gallagher raised a hand to her chest. "Don't be absurd, Lydia. Mr. Malloy wouldn't stoop to such dishonest tactics."

Lydia's mouth flew open as if to speak, then clamped shut. Her penetrating gaze landed on Will an instant before she silently returned to her meal.

Something within him wished to assure her of the fact that he agreed with her assumption. Maybe they were simply less trusting than kindly Mrs. Gallagher, but someone had set that fire.

And his bet was on Malloy.

LYDIA RUBBED her fingers along the new oak boards which replaced those damaged by the fire. She breathed a gentle sigh. If the Lord hadn't sent rain to quench the flames, the damage would have been so much worse. Having completed the patch job earlier in the day, Will and Luke had gone to finish planting the field Will had started.

Feeling weighted by her accusing tone earlier in the day, Lydia had helped Mama ready the evening meal and then slipped outside to try to gain a few moments alone with Will to right her wrong. Nearly a quarter-hour passed before she heard the team approaching the barn. Keeping out of sight, she listened to Will and Luke's murmured voices mingling with the clank of metal as they unhitched the team at the far side of the barn. As the horses trotted out into the pasture, they kicked up their heels and snorted, glad to be free of their trappings.

Lydia lingered in the shadows of the barn's north side until Luke's footfalls fell away. Expecting Will to head toward the house, she edged closer to the front of the barn and watched for him to pass by. Instead, he rounded the corner and jolted to a stop, clasping her arm as if instinctively trying to steady her. He peered at her with rounded eyes. "Sorry. I didn't know anyone was over here."

A nervous tingling vibrated through her at the warmth of his touch. Facing him square on, she melted under his steady gaze, the tip of her head barely reaching his chin. Never had she stood so near him, or noticed the flecks of gold in his eyes, or the slight dimple in his left cheek. The day's growth of stubble gave his complexion a rugged appeal.

As he slid his hand from her arm, she shook off the entrancement and scrambled for a viable reason to be there. "I ... uh ..." She glibly gestured behind her, heat burning her cheeks. "I was looking over the repairs to the barn. You did a fine job."

"I had good help. Hal Perkins worked all day on it with me."

"We'll be sure to thank him." Lydia pivoted as Will slipped past and stooped to pick up stray shards of wood from the ground. She swallowed the dryness in her throat. "I also wanted to ... apologize for my short tone this morning." The admission came out more rushed and breathier than intended. Was there such a thing as being too straightforward? If so, she had the knack for it.

To her relief, Will merely shrugged and continued to gather broken bits of wood. "No need. I'd be upset, too, if this were my place."

She hiked her skirt and bent to help. "I suppose you think me presumptuous to assume Mr. Malloy is to blame."

The moment's pause made her question if he'd even heard. But slowly, he looked her way, propping his forearm on his thigh. "Not really. I tend to agree."

Lydia straightened to full height, dropping some of the board fragments she'd gathered in the process. "You do? Why didn't you say so?"

"It's not my place. Besides, there's no proof, so it does little good to make accusations." He stood and carried his armload of splintered boards to the pile, leaving her to digest his all-too-truthful confession.

It did her heart good to know he shared her conviction. She hurried after him. "Then, what are we to do about it?"

Shifting toward her, Will brushed his hands together. "Not much can be done except to keep watch for anything suspicious."

"Does Luke know?"

"I mentioned the possibility, but I'm not certain he's sold on the notion."

She mustered a faint smile. "Well, at least you and I are in agreement. That's something."

He stared at her, and for a brief moment, Lydia sensed he wished to confide in her more deeply. But the impression soon passed, and he glanced toward the farmhouse. "We'd best not keep your ma's supper waiting."

With a nod, she fell into step beside him. Amber rays of sunlight streamed through the pair of elm trees to the west, casting dappled patches of light along the ground. Lydia clasped her hands together behind her, intentionally slowing her gait. It wasn't often she was able to engage Will in private conversation. No matter the topic, she longed to squeeze out every morsel and moment she could.

WILL LOCKED his hands together behind his head and blew out a breath. Avoiding Lydia was going to be tough. About as unlikely as reclaiming his forgotten past. The girl was hard to figure. One minute, she was all fired up at him. The next, she was gazing at him with those sky-blue eyes like he was someone grand. He wasn't sure which was harder to take.

A grin tugged at his lips. The latter was definitely more pleasant.

Lydia was bright, attractive, vibrant. Someone who, in other circumstances, he wouldn't mind pursuing. But he couldn't afford to become attached to someone when he was set on leaving. Not to mention her being his boss's sister.

Both very good reasons to keep his distance.

But it was the third reason that haunted him most. A deterrent he couldn't let go of—the notion he may have a wife or sweetheart awaiting his return. No matter how much time elapsed, if he'd pledged himself to someone, he was bound to honor that vow.

Whether he had any memory of it or not.

Angel's muffled nicker sounded outside the barn, slicing through Will's thoughts. He arched a brow. As far as females were concerned, he'd best stick to horses.

18

Wednesday, June 3, 1868 (1 a.m.)

L ydia turned on her side, sleep eluding her. Between the knowledge that Guthrie Malloy had likely set the barn ablaze and her invigorating encounter with Will, her mind was too frazzled to rest. She yawned and tried to still her churning thoughts.

To no avail.

Flipping onto her back, she stared at the ceiling, listening to the drone of insects outside her window. Would Mr. Malloy make another attempt to waylay their efforts at a crop? The Lord had come to their aid once. Would He again? Convincing Mama and Luke the man was trying to force them to sell their land would likely not be easy. At least she and Will were of the same mind.

Warmth flooded her chest. She could still feel his strong fingers gripping her arm when they'd nearly collided. And the way he'd looked at her. Almost as if he cared something for her. Such a lingering gaze offered her some semblance of hope.

An odd sound outside her window penetrated her thoughts. She sat up, tension pulling at her brows. *What was that?* Tossing her sheet aside, she swung her legs over the side of the bed and listened more intently.

She sucked in a breath. There it was again, barely audible over the prattle of nightlife. Yet it sounded almost ... human.

Her heartbeat pulsed in her ears as she eased over to the window and glanced around. Though nothing looked amiss, the moonless night provided little help in spotting movement. The sound came a third time, this time leaving no doubt.

It was a man ... moaning.

With jittery fingers, Lydia fumbled for her night-jacket. If the moans were Mr. Malloy, she hoped he'd stumbled in the dark and injured himself, spoiling his evil intents. Tightness tore at her muscles as she slid her arms into the garment. Would Will hear and take action before she could investigate? Though she prayed so, she couldn't depend on it.

Show me what to do, Lord.

Pushing aside her fears, she drew a steadying breath. She'd fetch Luke's old hunting rifle, the one he'd left for their protection during the war. She hesitated. Not since the night she'd shot that awful Simon Banner when he'd tried to take off with Adelaide had Lydia touched the weapon. The memory of him writhing on the ground still made her queasy. Though she had no love for Mr. Malloy, she had no wish to shoot him. Perhaps a warning shot would be enough.

Not wishing to wake Mama or alert Mr. Malloy to her presence, she opted not to light a lantern. Instead, with trembling hands, she groped her way along the hall to Luke's bedroom door. She eased open the door and scrunched her nose against the staleness fanning out at her. Slipping inside, she reached behind the door. Her hand gripped the metal rifle barrel, and she hesitated. She didn't enjoy the thought of putting a bullet in anyone. Not even an ornery ol' coot like Malloy.

But, Lord forgive her, if she had to, she would.

Gun in hand, she felt her way to the dresser. Unless Mama had removed them, there should be several cartridges and musket caps in the top drawer. Giving the handles a firm tug, she cringed at the squeal the movement produced. She stilled, hoping the noise hadn't awakened Mama. When there remained only silence, Lydia reached a hand in the drawer and felt for the ammunition. She suppressed a whisper of triumph when her fingers snagged on the cartridges and cap pouch.

Thinking it too risky to load the rifle indoors, she snatched up the supplies and tiptoed from the room. With slow, careful steps, she eased down the stairway. Mama's heavy breathing drifted from the downstairs bedroom, masking Lydia's descent.

The tension in her muscles eased as she slipped down the hall, out the front door, and onto the veranda. The vastness of the stars shed only a faint glimmer without aid of the moon. Squinting against the blackness, she perused the yard. Nothing stirred. Whoever was out there was well hidden by the dark night.

As she started to load the rifle, another moan sounded. Lydia's hands stilled. The noise originated from somewhere near the barn.

Heart hammering, she gripped the rifle barrel tighter. Had something happened to Will?

Quickly, she finished loading the rifle and slid the ramrod into its holder, jaw clenched. If Mr. Malloy had harmed Will, she'd not feel one bit of remorse for putting a Minié ball in his chest. Downing the steps, she cut another glance around. Likely if Malloy had been here, he'd either been scared off or done the damage he intended and left.

As she stumbled her way to the barn, a thrashing sound accompanied another moan. Perhaps Malloy was still inside along with Will. Hands atremble, Lydia eased the barn door open a crack and positioned herself behind the rifle. How could she possibly shoot straight with her hands quivering so? And in such darkness?

Much too risky.

The writhing and moans continued, drawing her attention to

the stall where Will typically slept. Though she could barely make out his form, the movement in the straw didn't sound like a scuffle. More like someone stirring in his sleep. Lowering the gun slightly, Lydia spoke in a whisper. "Will? Are you all right?"

Another groan sounded, along with more thrashing. Lydia stepped closer, wishing the night wasn't so dark. She moistened her lips, debating whether it was safe to lower the rifle. At last, convinced she and Will were alone, she edged to within feet of where he lay and knelt beside him. "Will?"

"No!"

Lydia startled at the frantically spoken word. It seemed less directed at her than one voiced in the throes of a troubled dream. Laying the rifle aside, she placed a hand on Will's arm, his muscles firm beneath her grasp. Dankness seeped from his shirtsleeve onto her fingertips, the scent of sweat drifting up at her. Was he feverish from a wound or merely in the midst of a nightmarish dream?

She placed the back of her hand against his forehead. Though damp with sweat, his face did not feel overly hot. She gave his arm a nudge. Still, he did not awaken.

For lack of anything better, she removed her night-jacket and dabbed sweat from his brow. She tucked her lip under her teeth. How would she explain herself should he awaken? Yet, he seemed much too enthralled in his dream to rouse. Gingerly, she felt along his midsection for any sort of wound. But the longer she observed, the more convinced she became his mind—not his body—was in torment.

His head wagged side to side, the barn too shaded to distinguish his features. But judging from the puckered skin beneath her fingertips as she wiped his forehead, his facial muscles were drawn tight. Was he remembering unpleasant memories of the war? Experiencing dreadful images of his injuries and the fateful night of the doomed *Sultana*?

What sort of torturous trials had he walked through?

He released another loud moan, his breaths fast and heavy.

At a loss what else to do, she prayed, longing to somehow ease his anguished soul. *Bring him comfort, Lord. Still his troubled mind.*

With quivering hands, she continued to dry his sweat-drenched face and neck. It was bold of her, she knew, to be so near a man alone. In her night clothes, no less. But there was nothing unseemly in her motives. The Lord could judge that. So far as she knew, Will was unaware of her presence. If he did wake, she would slip into the darkness without a word.

Setting her now sopping night-jacket aside, she brushed dampened hair from Will's forehead with her fingertips and whispered, "Shh. You're safe here." Gently, she stroked his brow and temples until his movements gradually eased and his breathing quieted. She could barely make out the contours of his face in the dim light. A few more moments of unhindered slumber assured her his restlessness, at least for the moment, had passed. Would he sleep peacefully for the remainder of the night?

Her eyelids grew heavy, the late hour and sleepless night taking their toll. She tucked the rolled-up blanket he used for a pillow more firmly under his head. His eyes flickered open. She cringed, frozen in place, praying he would be too drowsy to stir. When he settled back into restful sleep, every muscle in her body fell limp. How awkward for both of them if he'd awakened.

As soundlessly as she could, she eased from the stall and groped for the rifle. Clasping it by the barrel, she took a backward glance and whispered a silent prayer. Now, more than ever, her heart ached for Will. Though likely he'd not recall she'd been there, it did her heart good to know she'd helped ease his discomfort.

If only a little.

Stepping lightly, she wedged herself through the doorway and out into the night air. The yapping of coyotes sounded in the distance, overshadowing the rhythmic chatter of insects as Lydia strode toward the unlit house. Despite the warm, late-spring night, the mournful cries made the hair on her arms stand on end. Such a lonesome sound.

As she strolled, she set the rifle to the half-cocked position. Though relieved Mr. Malloy hadn't been about the place, her heart troubled over Will. Did he have these nightmarish dreams often?

She paused and spun toward the darkened barn. Was that why he insisted on staying out here? To spare her and Mama his outbursts?

With a low sigh, she continued on. Such a selfless gesture only increased her regard. Though Will had given her no reason to assume he might one day care for her, try as she may, she couldn't rid herself of the hope.

He'd come to them a stranger but had proven himself trustworthy and a friend to their family. And yet, like the lonesome coyote, he remained aloof, guarded. Would he be content to remain with them indefinitely?

Or would his longing to uncover his past lure him away?

The uncertainty should stay her fondness toward him.

But her heart whispered otherwise.

19

Will scrubbed a hand over his face, as tired as when he'd fallen asleep. Early morning light seeped through cracks in the barn walls. What a night. His dreams seemed to have gone on endlessly. Though he only remembered bits and pieces, he recalled more than he cared to. Everything from being corralled in a pen with other soldiers like cattle to being submerged in water, feeling as though he couldn't breathe, only to emerge to the mournful cries of people in agony.

The only redeeming part was the vague recollection of soft fingers stroking his brow and a momentary glimpse of someone leaning over him in the darkness. A woman. Or had it been an angel of mercy? Either way, it was the only part of his nightmarish dreams he wished to cling to.

He sat up and arched his back, stretching weary muscles. He would never take to the hardened dirt floor, the thin layer of straw offering little padding. Yet, it didn't seem to matter how comfortable or uncomfortable he was. The same appalling dreams tormented him.

Shaking off his fatigue, he raked a hand through his hair. Lydia would be in soon to milk Penny. If he was going to avoid her, he'd best get moving. His fingers brushed against something smooth and damp in the straw. He glanced down, his brow furrowing at sight of a piece of feminine clothing. Drawing his hand back as if bitten, he veered to one side. How in blazes did that get there?

He scratched his stubbled jaw, staring down at the misplaced garment. Maybe the "angel of mercy" hadn't been a dream after all. Come to think of it, she'd looked a lot like Lydia. Reaching down, he gripped the thin ivory fabric between his thumb and forefinger and held it up. The smell of sweat mingled with the scent of lilac. Though he wasn't sure of the source of perspiration, the lilac scent was one he'd come to associate with Lydia. What would possess her to come here in the middle of the night? It made no sense.

Unless ...

He swallowed, dryness cleaving to his throat. Unless his restless dreams had awakened her.

The sound of approaching footsteps stymied his thoughts. Quickly, he stuffed the garment under his bedroll and sprang to his feet. Whether it be Luke out for an early start to the day or Lydia coming to milk Penny, he didn't wish to be caught holding the rather delicate piece of woman's clothing.

Either way, his day was likely off to a shaky start.

LYDIA'S HEART thudded against her chest, hasty steps propelling her toward the barn. After her sleep-deprived night, she'd lingered in bed, indulging in a few extra moments of leisure. Until she'd recalled leaving her soiled bed jacket on the floor next to Will. At that recollection, she'd leaped up as though the mattress was overlaid with daggers.

She pressed a palm to her forehead. How could she have been so careless?

The bucket handle grew slippery beneath her moist fingers. She tightened her grip, slowing her pace as she neared the barn door. How would she explain the mislaid clothing to Will? Better yet, how would she even face him?

She gnawed at her lip. She'd been diligent to remember the rifle. How could she have been so addleheaded to forget the night-jacket?

Perhaps with her being a tad late, he'd be gone, and she could snatch the garment without a word. Though he'd surely noticed it, removing it might deter any mention of the incident.

At least she prayed so.

Giving her usual knock on the door prior to entering, Lydia stilled, hoping the plea would be met by silence. Instead, she wilted at the sound of Will's hesitant, "Come in." With a deep breath, she bolstered her courage and edged her way inside. Though keenly aware of Will's presence, she trained her focus on Penny in the opposite stall and did her best to will away the heat mounting in her cheeks.

The barn seemed much less confining in light of day and a great deal easier to maneuver. Basil scampered into her path, and Lydia reached to give him a scratch on the back, the action momentarily easing some of her pent-up angst. Out of the corner of her eye, she could see Will setting up for a shave. Neither spoke, foregoing their usual morning exchange of greetings.

Silently, she set to milking. Tension as thick as misty morning fog hung in the air as though unspoken strain had wedged its way between them. When certain Will wasn't looking, she ventured a glance in his direction, hoping for a glimpse of her forgotten night-jacket. To her relief ... and disappointment, the quick perusal came up short. Either he'd disposed of it or, from her vantage point, it wasn't visible.

She slowed her milking, hoping to outlast Will's stay in the barn. Once he left, she could make a thorough search. And pray by some miracle he'd overlooked the jacket.

But judging by his silence, he hadn't.

WILL PUT away his razor blade, his empty belly eager for another of Mrs. Gallagher's fine breakfasts. He glanced at his bedroll, uncertain what to do about the wayward bed jacket. If it *was* Lydia's, asking about it would likely embarrass her. And if it wasn't, he'd have a hard time explaining how such an item had come into his possession.

The awkward silence was enough to convince him it was best not to broach the topic. He couldn't remember a time when she hadn't offered a morning greeting. Had he said or done something upsetting in his sleep? Or was it embarrassment that had her tongue-tied?

Part of him was eager to learn more of what had taken place. But Lydia obviously wasn't in the mood to explain. Maybe later, he could smuggle the garment onto the porch and none would be the wiser.

He tried to catch her eye to offer a nod of reassurance as he made his way to the door, but she kept her gaze rigidly fixed on the task at hand. He paused, troubled to see her acting so unlike herself. Not knowing how to rectify the situation, he moved on. Half a dozen steps out of the door, he slowed his pace, curiosity nipping at his heels. With him gone, would she search for the jacket?

He wavered, the lure to find out too strong to resist.

Faint noises inside the barn hinted Lydia likely had either finished milking or was making an effort to find the missing garment. Fearful she might be watching, Will continued to stride toward the house. When he felt certain she'd no longer track his steps, he doubled back.

Easing toward the barn, he peeked through a knothole in the door and spied Lydia rummaging through the straw near his sleeping quarters. With brows pinched and rosy lips taut, she swiped franticly at the bedding, searching from one end of the stall to the other, never disrupting Will's belongings.

He stifled a grin, her desperate attempt to find the lost piece of clothing tugging at his sympathy. Should he put her worries to rest?

At last, she sat back on her haunches with a huff, eyes perusing the stall area.

A roguish grin crept across Will's lips. He really shouldn't embarrass her. Though watching her in a dither seemed nearly as agonizing. Easing the door open, he cleared his throat. "Lose something?"

Her face snapped toward him, eyes flared and face blanched. Thrown off balance, she dropped onto the straw with a soft squeal.

He moved to help her up. "Sorry. I didn't mean to startle you."

"I thought you'd gone." She accepted his outstretched hand, a reddish glow replacing the pallor in her cheeks. "I wasn't snooping. I-I was looking for something."

"You'll find it under my rolled-up blanket there."

Turning loose of his hand, she brushed straw from her backside, her azure eyes lifting to meet his. "I will?"

He gave a slight nod.

Slowly, she bent for a look, easing the bedroll up as if a snake might be coiled beneath. Quickly snatching up the bed jacket, she concealed it behind her back, the crimson in her face deepening. "I ... suppose you're wondering how it got here."

He leaned against the stall post, tamping down the overwhelming sense of awkwardness. "I'll admit I'm curious."

Finding it hard to look him in the eyes, she stammered. "I-I heard moaning and thought perhaps Mr. Malloy had returned. Instead, I found you very troubled in your sleep and perspiring heavily." She cleared the hoarseness from her throat. "I had nothing else, so used my bed jacket to wipe your brow. I never intended you to know I'd been here."

He sank his hands in his pockets, softening his tone. "That was kind of you."

The reply seemed to catch her off guard, for she hesitated before inhaling a jagged breath. "I hope you don't think my actions ... inappropriate." Her fawnlike gaze flickered downward.

Drawn by her sincerity, he stepped toward her, resisting the urge to touch a hand to her cheek. "It's a kindness I won't soon forget."

A gentle smile touched her lips as her eyes lifted, and something melted within Will.

In that moment, the thought of leaving became that much harder.

20

Sunday, June 7, 1868

Lydia rose from her wicker chair on the veranda, too fidgety to enjoy the leisure of Sunday afternoon. Since her encounter with Will earlier in the week, her stomach had been tied in knots while her spirit had been feather-light. Though they'd spoken little since, she had the distinct feeling something substantial had passed between them that day. A tenderness which had wound its way to her core.

She leaned against the railing, the absence of a breeze making the warmth of mid-afternoon a tad stifling. Out of the corner of her eye, she caught a glimpse of Will in the pasture behind the barn, and her heart sped. Repositioning herself for a better look, she watched him pause to give Angel a pet, then amble toward the pond, hands in his pockets, hat tilted low over his brow. The poor fellow looked so forlorn, like he hadn't a friend in the world. Even during church service, he'd stared out the window through much of the sermon as if he truly didn't wish to be there.

What was troubling him?

Lydia snuck a glance back at the house. Mama had lain down

to rest. She seemed to tire far too easily these days—a concern Lydia continually lifted to the Lord. Though Mama had had no more episodes with her heart that Lydia was aware of, her fragile health remained a constant worry.

Returning her gaze to Will, Lydia donned her bonnet and edged toward the veranda steps. She'd never be missed in venturing on an afternoon stroll. She thrummed her fingertips on the railing. Would Will resent her joining him?

Lydia hesitated but an instant more before hiking her skirt and downing the steps. With hurried strides, she crossed the yard and slipped through the gate to the pasture beyond. Perspiration lined her brow as she trekked through the tall grass, careful to watch her step lest her foot land in an undesirable spot.

The three horses grazed beneath the canopy of a sprawling bur oak to her right, paying her little heed. Up ahead, Will had found a shade tree of his own beside the pond to lounge against. His head veered toward her as she neared, his hat concealing much of his face. Lydia offered a tentative grin, her breaths shallowing. There'd be no turning back now. Would he welcome her company or think her a pest?

Her mouth grew cottony, and she longed for a sip of water to ease the dryness. With a hard swallow, she risked a greeting. "I hope I'm not intruding."

He nudged his hat higher, allowing her a better glimpse of his handsome features. The stormy look in his eyes seemed to calm at her approach. "I don't mind."

Tension eased from her shoulders as she leaned against the tree trunk. She stared out over the tranquil water, a layer of moss and cattails fringing the far end. A few moments of silence passed between them, the rasp of frogs and chortle of robins and cardinals in the trees serenading them. Despite the peaceful setting, Lydia's thoughts churned. She snuck a glance at Will. There were so many questions she wished to ask him. Many of which he would not have an answer for.

Yet, she longed to know this complex man who stood beside her.

Her heart thudded against her chest as she mustered courage to speak. "Are you happy here, Will? I mean, helping Luke with the farm?" She kept her eyes trained on the pond's smooth surface, watching a small ripple fan out over the water where a fish or turtle had poked its head up.

Heat flamed in her cheeks at his lack of response, and she chided herself for asking.

As she opened her mouth to retract the question, Will spoke instead. "I suppose workin' here's about as much as someone like me can ask for."

The odd statement gave her pause. "Someone like *you?*"

Nodding, he reached for a pebble and tossed it into the pond. "Someone who has no place of belonging, no real sense of purpose."

Lydia's heart squeezed. "Of course you have belonging and purpose. I know for certain Mama and Luke are overjoyed to have you here." As was she. Though she was hesitant to say so.

Some of the luster in his eyes returned. "Well, I'm glad of that, at least."

She shifted toward him, gaining confidence. "What is it you wish for in life, Will? Truly wish for?"

He looked her square on, his gaze so intense the specks of gold in his hazel eyes seemed to shimmer. "To know who I am."

The candid response caught her off guard. Though she'd known he was troubled by his forgotten past, she'd not realized how deep-rooted the need to rediscover his identity ran. She moistened her lips, wishing for a way to ease his longing. "Have you considered your loss of memory might be the Lord's way of sparing you some heartache from your past?"

Will scoffed. "If the Lord wished to spare me, He'd not plague me with relentless dreams that provide only enough of my past to keep me guessing."

It was a point she couldn't argue. "Your unsettling dreams happen often, then?"

"Most every night. That's why I took up residence in the barn. I'd rather disturb livestock than you and your ma."

Her heart plunged at the confession. "How considerate of you. That's quite a sacrifice."

He shrugged. "I've slept worse places."

Leaning into the rough tree bark, Lydia drank in his crooked grin. Though she could never say so, she wouldn't mind smoothing the tension from his brow and calming him in the night should he choose to move to Drew or Luke's room. Instead, she ventured a suggestion. "I understand why your dreams are disturbing. But perhaps ... if you'd simply let go of your past, the troublesome nightmares would let go of you."

Will's head drooped downward, and Lydia feared she'd said too much. He reached for another pebble and skipped it across the water's surface. When he looked at her again, his eyes were filled with quandary. "If you lost your family and were hounded by dreams with bits and pieces of your past, wouldn't you want answers?"

Pricked, Lydia shifted her gaze to a button on his shirt. Until now, she'd neglected to put herself in Will's place. Losing Papa to the war had been difficult enough. She couldn't fathom what it would be like to be stripped of childhood memories and her entire family. Her heart softened, fresh awareness mellowing her voice. "I suppose I would."

"Then you'll understand why my mind won't rest until I learn who I am and where I came from." His tone was gentle, almost pleading.

The statement weighed heavy on Lydia, for it could only mean one thing. She lifted her eyes to meet his, the expectancy in his gaze wrenching the unpleasant words from her. "Does that mean you intend to leave here and continue your search?"

He kicked at the ground with his boot, mouth pulling taut. "Someday."

The vague response left her with more questions than answers. She willed the shakiness from her voice and forced herself to hold his gaze. "Soon?"

The dimple in his left cheek became more prominent as the muscles in his mouth constricted. "After fall harvest."

Lydia managed a slight nod, disappointment marring any attempt at a response. She'd hoped he'd stay on longer, for Luke's sake. Even more so for her own. Perhaps she'd been wrong in thinking Will was beginning to care for her. "Does Luke know?"

"Not yet. I've not had the heart to tell him." He met her gaze. "I'd appreciate if you wouldn't say anything. I'd rather he heard it from me."

"All right." The words squeaked from her like an ungreased hinge.

Crossing his arms over his chest, Will peered out over the pond. "I've worked a number of places over the past three years. This will be the first one that'll be hard to leave."

The words were bittersweet. She'd been so certain the Lord had sent Will. Now, a month later, he already had plans to leave. Likely, he had from the start. A hard notion to accept. She couldn't deny Will the chance to rediscover his identity, but she could pray, Lord willing, he'd decide the life he had now was worth holding onto.

WILL SWIPED the brush along Angel's neck and withers, his conversation with Lydia still foremost in his thoughts. That girl could loosen his tongue faster than he could raise his defenses. Without even trying, she'd wrenched as much information about his circumstances from him as he knew himself.

Shifting to Angel's side, Will gave a half-hearted swish of the brush, then paused. He'd had no intention of sharing his plans to leave or to confess doing so would be hard. He may as well have come right out and admitted it was largely on Lydia's account he'd regret leaving.

With an agitated huff, he gave Angel's coat another swipe. At least now, when the time came, she would understand why he had to go. Leastwise, he hoped so. The tremor in her voice when she'd asked how soon he planned to leave made him wonder if she'd miss him. Maybe it was selfish of him, but he hoped she would.

If only a little.

Angel ventured a step forward in search of fresh grass. Will slid a hand along her smooth side. Her reddish-brown coat had shed its winter hair and shone against the amber glow of evening. He would miss her as well. There was something about the scent and feel of a horse that soothed him.

Lydia seemed stunned Angel had taken to anyone other than her brother, Drew. Maybe the horse understood something about Will he didn't know himself. His lips twisted in a lopsided grin. Would she let him ride her if he made an attempt?

Someday, he aimed to find out.

Dropping the grooming brush to his side, Will gazed into the distance at the stand of wheat and freshly planted fields. If not for the relentless unknowns in his life, this was just the sort of place he could settle down to.

His stomach clenched. Was there any truth in what Lydia proposed? Was it possible the curse of not knowing his past would lose its grip if he'd simply stop searching?

He dipped his hand in his pocket, letting his fingers glide over the smooth surface of his pocket watch. If things didn't work out as he hoped, would the Gallaghers welcome him back?

Or would his restless spirit plague him the rest of his days?

21

Monday, June 8, 1868

A rigid scowl wedged across Dr. Royce's lips as he removed the stethoscope from his ears.

Unsure what to make of his gentle sigh, Lydia wrung her hands and waited, her gaze wavering between him and her mother.

Mama sat forward in her chair, one eyebrow tipped higher than the other. "Don't look so glum, doctor. It can't be all bad."

He slipped the instrument into his black bag, his somber expression easing slightly. "I was merely wishing your heartbeat was as strong and steady as that of your future grandchild's."

With a soft chuckle, Mama tapped a hand to her chest. "Mine has a bit more wear on it, don't you think?"

"That it does. Though you're too young for such a sluggish heart."

Lydia moved to stand beside Mama, placing a hand on her shoulder. "Is her condition worsening?"

Dr. Royce smiled, easing some of the tension brewing inside Lydia. "There's little change since my last visit. Just see that she behaves herself and doesn't overdo."

Lydia leaned to look her mother in the eyes. "I'll make certain of it."

Mama looked past her, a rare frown lining her brow. "I'll not be coddled like an infant. The Lord knows the day and the hour my life will end. I'll not add a single minute by letting myself be pampered or having others do the work."

"No one's asking you to stop being active, Mama. Just to limit how much you do."

"That's right, Martha. Moderation is all I ask." Tossing Lydia a quick wink, Dr. Royce closed his bag and stood. "I'll leave her in your capable hands, then." He wagged a finger at Mama, feigned sternness in his tone and demeanor. "But no more lengthy carriage rides, mind you. Excessive travel at this point can only weaken you."

Mama reached to clasp Lydia's hand, her chin angling upward. "The trip to Pennsylvania was well worth it. I have no regrets."

Lydia gave Mama's fingers a gentle squeeze. She knew well the sweet balm attending Luke's sermon had been for Mama. For both of them. But no doubt, the trip had taken a toll on her. Lydia smiled at the elderly doctor. "In this one instance, I think the good outweighed the bad. But from now on, I assure you we'll stay closer to home."

"That's good to hear." His expression sobered, and he patted his suit pocket. "Oh, I nearly forgot. Mrs. Flynn at the post office sent me with a couple of letters for you."

"Letters?" Mama's voice held a trace of curiosity. One letter was a rarity. Two at once was nearly unheard of.

Slipping the missives from his inside pocket, Dr. Royce glanced at the writing. "Let's see. There's one for you ..."

The doctor handed Mama the letter, and her face lit like candles on a Christmas tree. "It's from Drew."

Lydia bent for a closer look. "How wonderful. It's been months since we've heard from him and Caroline." She peered at Dr. Royce. "And the second? Who is it for?"

The doctor jutted out his lower lip and ventured a glance. "It's addressed to Luke and Adelaide. From a Mr. and Mrs. Banks of Pennsylvania."

Lydia's brow pinched. Perhaps a note of gratitude for filling in.

Flicking the letter with the back of his fingers, Dr. Royce shook his head. "Had I realized that, I'd have left it with Adelaide while I was examining her." He started to return the missive to his suit pocket. "Well, no matter. I'll drop it off on my way."

"I'll take it." Lydia announced rather boisterously, her offer fueled by more than helpfulness. Since yesterday's conversation with Will, she'd been eager to speak privately with Adelaide. With Luke and Will on the far acreage planting corn, the letter would provide the perfect excuse to pay her a visit.

Dr. Royce pushed the letter in her direction. "Fine. Fine. I'm overdue at Mrs. Baxter's. That will save me a stop."

Taking the missive, Lydia returned a quick smile. "I'll see they get it."

With a brisk nod, Dr. Royce inched toward the parlor doorway, hat in hand. "Good day then, ladies. I'll see myself out and leave you to your reading."

"Thank you, doctor." Mama replied haphazardly, her fingers vigorously working to break the seal on Drew's letter.

Slipping the other into her inseam pocket, Lydia moved to the settee. She perched on its edge, eagerly awaiting to hear what Drew had to say.

Holding the letter out in front of her, Mama cleared her throat.

"Dear Family, I've been in Chicago a few days for the Republican Convention with General Grant. As you may have heard, he has been nominated for the presidency. I plan to stop by the farm for a short visit before I head home to Washington later in the week. I'll be arriving in Elmira on the Tuesday afternoon train. I look forward to seeing all of you soon. Fondly, Drew"

Bubbling with anticipation, Lydia clasped her hands together. "Oh, that is good news, though it doesn't sound as if Caroline or little Mary are with him. Still, it will be so wonderful to see Drew. It's been much too long."

Mama lowered the note, eyes round as walnuts. "Yes, but that's tomorrow afternoon. Hardly enough time to prepare. His bedroom will need aired and cleaned and fresh linens put on the bed. Not to mention ..."

Lydia placed a restraining hand on Mama's arm. "Did you not hear what Dr. Royce said, Mama? You're to take things easy. Drew won't care if the place is spotless."

Worry lines creased the outer edges of Mama's eyes. "But he comes so infrequently. I want everything to be perfect."

"He would rather find you well rested and up to his visit than to have a clean or fresh-smelling room, I assure you." Lydia gave Mama's arm a gentle pat. "We'll work at preparations as soon as I return from delivering Luke and Adelaide's letter."

A gentle smile edged out the tension on Mama's face. "All right, dear. Be sure to let Adelaide know of Drew's coming."

With a satisfied nod, Lydia rose to her feet. "I will."

She fingered the paper in her pocket. As eager as she was to share the news of Drew's visit, she was even more anxious to speak with Adelaide about Will.

LYDIA'S gentle tap produced the creak of a chair and stirring within the cottage. She smoothed her dress, pressing down the swath of nerves threatening to overtake her. Adelaide was the one person she could confide in about matters of the heart. When Adelaide had come from far-off Richmond to stay with them three years ago, she'd been but a stranger. It hadn't taken long for her to gain the regard of the entire family. She'd soon become the sister Lydia had always wished for. And yet, the thought of baring her innermost feelings to even Adelaide was discomforting.

The door clicked open, and Lydia dropped her arms to her sides, fighting awkwardness. Adelaide smiled, her dark eyes and raven black hair striking against her ivory skin. But for the noticeable rise in her middle, she remained as slender and delicate as ever. "Lydia. Come in."

Lydia stepped over the threshold, nearly bursting with the news she had to share. Swiveling, she flashed a wide grin. "Guess who's coming for a visit?"

Adelaide nudged the door shut. "Who?"

"Drew."

"How wonderful. Caroline and little Mary, too?"

Lydia shook her head, some of the enthusiasm seeping out of her. Though her niece was over a year old, she'd seen her only twice—about a month after her birth and at Christmas. "Drew is stopping on his way home from the Republican Convention in Chicago. It seems General Grant has been nominated for president."

"Grant nominated for president? Now that's something." One of Adelaide's brows lifted, a slight upturn to the corners of her mouth. "Though, in my opinion, Lee would have made a better one."

Lydia shook her head. "That's no surprise." Though having married a "Yankee" and transitioning north, her friend's southern roots had never fully lost their hold.

With a soft chuckle, Adelaide motioned to a chair. "Sit down. Would you like some tea?"

"No, thank you." As jittery as she was, Lydia doubted she could hold a cup steady.

Adelaide reached for a cup and saucer, then paused, placing a hand on her rounded belly.

"Are you unwell?"

"I'm fine. Just feeling movement." Adelaide poured herself

some tea and then took a seat across from Lydia. "Ever since Dr. Royce's exam, the baby has been quite active."

Lydia gave a contented sigh. "It will be so nice to have a niece or nephew within walking distance. Mary will be a grown woman before she even knows I'm her aunt."

A smile edged across Adelaide's lips. "Well, I'll be thrilled to have your help. Especially when the baby is fussy, and I'm in need of rest."

"Happy to oblige." Lydia quipped. "Although calming a crying baby isn't what I intended." She drew the missive from her pocket. "Dr. Royce brought our mail from town and neglected to give you this." She passed it to Adelaide.

With a nod, Adelaide studied the address. "Oh, from Mr. and Mrs. Banks. They must be thanking Luke for providing the sermon while their pastor was away." She smoothed a hand over the letter but made no attempt to remove its seal. "I'll wait for Luke to open it."

A lull fell between them as Lydia considered how to broach her main purpose in coming—Will. She traced a finger along the oak table's wood grain. Perhaps she should forget the whole thing and go help ready the house for Drew.

"Is there something more on your mind?" Adelaide took a sip of tea, a hint of inquisitiveness in her dark eyes. "You suddenly seem miles away."

Her friend's intuitive remark jolted Lydia from her stupor. Gathering courage, she laced her fingers together on the table. "I-I was wondering if I could ask you something."

Setting her cup on the saucer, Adelaide eased back in her chair. "Go right ahead."

Lydia swallowed the dryness in her throat, at a loss how to proceed. She drew a steadying breath. The straightforward approach seemed best. "What do you know of Will?"

Adelaide blinked. "Will? Uh ... not much really. He's a hard worker. Luke says he's very trustworthy and dependable. Truly, I've not spent much time with him other than the ride here. He was so gracious in helping to fix our carriage wheel. That alone earned my regard. Why do you ask?"

Not wishing to betray Will's trust or her own feelings, Lydia sought her words carefully. "I *have* spent a bit of time with him and ... have a similarly favorable opinion. I do hope Luke will encourage him to remain here."

A teasing grin edged out the uncertainty on Adelaide's face. "Why, Lydia Gallagher. I believe you're smitten."

Heat flared in Lydia's cheeks. "No, I ..." She tensed, then slumped back in her chair. There was no use denying it. Adelaide had seen right through her. Relieved to have it out in the open, Lydia allowed a faint smile to seep onto her lips. "Perhaps I am a bit smitten."

A snicker erupted from her companion. "Forgive me. It's just I've never seen you take interest in a man, let alone become besotted. It's rather refreshing to see." She leaned over the table and wiggled her eyebrows. "Tell me. Does Will share your infatuation?"

"I don't know." Lydia twisted her mouth to one side. "At times, I've wondered if he does. Other times, not. He ... confuses me."

Adelaide touched a hand to Lydia's arm. "Trust me. You're not the first woman to find a man perplexing. But then, I imagine they feel much the same about us."

"Did you ever wonder about Luke's feelings for you?"

"Oh, a number of times. As well as mine for him. But our situation was different. If you'll recall, I wasn't too fond of Yankees when I met Luke. We had that barrier to overcome as well as our varying level of faith."

Lydia released a soft sigh. "I'm not sure where Will stands with the Lord. I know he seems indifferent to faith at times. Not bitter as you once were. Just calloused, as though he's closed himself off from God."

"Nothing prayer can't penetrate, I'm sure. If the Lord can

change my embittered heart, I'm certain He can change anyone's."

It was true. God had worked wonders in Adelaide's life, transforming her from a withdrawn, broken person to one who was whole and loving. Given time, would He do the same for Will? Tempted to aid the situation along, Lydia moistened her lips, struggling for the right words. "There are ... circumstances that might pull Will away from here. That's why I ask you to encourage Luke to persuade Will to stay."

Even as she spoke the words, Lydia's stomach knotted. Was it wrong to attempt to manipulate Will? Was she usurping her will above God's?

Adelaide gave Lydia's arm a gentle pat. "I'll see what I can do."

"Thank you." Lydia forced a weak grin. Right or wrong, she was determined to do all she could to ensure Will stayed put.

22

"Here they come!"

The enthusiasm in Lydia's voice compelled Will to stop what he was doing and follow her gaze to the approaching carriage. Luke had gone to retrieve his older brother, Drew, from the Elmira train depot earlier in the day, leaving Will to ready the McCormick reaper. The grains of wheat were nearly hardened, indicating harvest was days away. Likely, they'd put the task off until after Drew's visit.

The click of boots descending the veranda steps pulled Will's attention back to Lydia. Even from across the yard, he could see the glow of excitement streaming from her face as she rushed to meet her brothers. The image caught in Will's throat, reviving the vision of the blonde girl from his persistent dream dashing to meet him. Except the girl in his dream wore black. Was there someone out there as eager for his return as Lydia was her brother?

Unable to stomach the thought, Will turned away, a stab of unrest coursing through him. Plainly, the fragmented unknowns of his past weren't going to let go. He could no more stem the flow of shattered remembrances than he could undo the events that stole his past.

Lydia's giddy laughter became swallowed by the rhythmic clomp of hooves and the whir of carriage wheels. Mrs. Gallagher had ventured onto the veranda, smiling radiantly as she leaned into the railing to welcome her eldest son. Adelaide joined her, the growing babe in her womb more evident than when Will had arrived.

He resisted the urge to watch the joyous reunion, choosing instead to busy himself sharpening the cutting blades on the reaper. Not that he wished to deny the family happiness. It was simply not his to be a part of.

And somewhat painful to endure.

Elated voices filled the evening air as the carriage came to a halt outside the house. Will attempted to drown out the cheerful voices and laughter with his grinding, but moments later Luke called to him, "Will! Time to quit. Come meet Drew."

The muscles in Will's shoulders tensed as he lifted his head. "Be right there." Reluctantly, he returned the metal file to the barn and brushed himself off. His dirt-stained trousers and unkempt appearance weren't likely to impress an important fellow from Washington. He smoothed his tousled hair. Would Drew be as hospitable toward him as the rest of the family? Or find his presence here intrusive?

Weighted steps carried Will from the barn to the farmhouse, where the family stood gathered on the veranda. Angel's soft nicker as Will passed garnered a quick pat on the neck. He lingered at the bottom step, a bit intimidated by the broad-shouldered figure at the top. Drew pivoted toward him, his chestnut hair and chiseled jaw far different from his siblings.

Luke clapped him on the shoulder. "Big brother, this is the fellow I was telling you about. Will Evans."

With a brisk nod, Drew stretched out his arm. "Good to meet you, Will. I've heard a lot about you."

Edging up the steps, Will clasped the newcomer's hand, matching his firm grip. "Same here." He mustered a weak grin, uncertain how to read Drew's stoic expression. He seemed a contrast to Luke and Lydia. Serious in nature, though not ill-tempered. As though his stint in Washington had sapped his humor.

In truth, Will wasn't much different. Unwanted circumstances had drained the wit right out of him. *If* he ever possessed any.

"Luke tells me you've been a big help to him this spring."

Will met Drew's focused stare. "I do my best. I'm grateful for the employment."

"Knowing he has good help takes a burden off my shoulders." A hint of remorse marred Drew's expression as he shifted his gaze to his family. "I've not made it home as much as I'd hoped."

"Well, you're here now. That's what counts." Mrs. Gallagher looped her arm through his, admiration in her pale blue eyes. "Why don't we all go inside and visit whilst we have our supper. The girls and I have it all ready. Just need to put it on the table."

Drew leaned to kiss her forehead. "After all the hubbub in Chicago, a good homecooked meal with family is just what I need."

Will eased back down a step, intent on slipping away unnoticed. Not wishing to intrude upon the family gathering, he'd see to Angel and make do with smoked jerky and the handful of wild berries he'd seen growing in the pasture.

"You're coming, aren't you, Will?"

Lydia's pleading voice stopped him in his tracks. Heat flared in his cheeks as all eyes trained in his direction. He thumbed over his shoulder. "I ... thought I'd see to Angel."

"I'll do that." Drew loosened his mother's arm from around his and gave her hand a soft pat. "I'll be in before the food's on the table." He downed the steps until he was at eye level with Will. With a tip of his head, Drew motioned toward the house. "You go on and make yourself at home. Angel and I have some catching up to do."

Before Will could protest, Drew strolled past, leaving him without an excuse not to join the family. With a reluctant sigh,

Will turned and upped the steps as the others filtered inside. He had a feeling not much got past the eldest Gallagher sibling.

The question was, how many of Drew's questions would Will not have the answer to?

LYDIA PLACED the steaming bowl of string beans on the table, then took a seat beside Will. He looked on edge, mouth pulled taut, shoulders stiff. The reassuring smile she flashed him garnered little response. What could be wrong? Luke and Adelaide had joined them for supper on occasion and Will hadn't seemed ill at ease. Was he nervous meeting Drew?

If so, Will would soon find he had nothing to fear. Drew might be a bigwig in Washington, but here at home, he was simply her big brother. Someone she saw far too little of these days. He reminded her so much of Papa—his build, his dark features, his intuitive nature. While Luke had always been the fun-loving brother who teased her unmercifully in his younger days, Drew had been the protective one, always looking out for her. She loved them both dearly. To have them here filled her with such joy and contentment. Hopefully, Will would feel more at ease once he and Drew became better acquainted.

No sooner had they all taken their seats than Drew tromped through to wash his hands in the kitchen basin. "Angel looks as fine and fit as I've ever seen her. Someone's taking good care of her."

"That's Will's doing." Lydia couldn't contain the pride in her voice as she glanced first at her brother, then Will. "Angel has taken quite a fancy to him. Almost as if she favors him in your absence."

"Is that so?" Surprise showed on her brother's face as he dried his hands. He peered at Will. "You'd best take that as a compliment. Angel's choosy about who she likes." He gave Luke a gentle nudge as he passed. "Just ask Luke here."

Fully expecting Luke to respond with a clever quip, Lydia knitted her brows when his only response was a weak grin and a nod of his head. It wasn't like Luke to accept a jest without some sort of counter. Adelaide, too, seemed a bit subdued. Had they quarreled? Doubtful. Lydia could count on one hand the number of times they'd had a disagreement. And their countenances had looked more miffed than melancholy.

Though she couldn't place it, something wasn't right.

With all other spots filled, Drew settled into Papa's place at the head of the table. Since her father's untimely death early in the war, the chair had remained empty. Though Mama rarely voiced her grief, there were times sorrow shone in her eyes as she gazed at the vacant seat. Tonight, her moist eyes boasted contentment as she glanced around the full table. "Drew, would you speak the blessing?"

As they bowed their heads, Lydia snuck a glance at Will, their chairs so close her skirt spilled over to touch the edge of his seat. Though his head dipped downward, his eyes remained open, as if speaking with the Lord was not foremost in his heart. Closing her eyes, she resolved to pray that whatever barrier stood between Will and the Lord would be removed.

The blessing said, Lydia lifted her head, letting her gaze travel over the family she held so dear. All too soon, this table of six would dwindle to two, and it saddened her. Within days, Drew would leave, and if Will held true to his intentions, he would abandon them as well in a few short months. Lydia pushed aside the unwelcome thought. At least Luke and Adelaide would remain nearby, and there was the baby's coming to look forward to.

With a decided breath, she determined to make the most of every moment and not allow disagreeable thoughts to ruin the day's blessings. "It's wonderful we can all be together. Too bad Caroline and little Mary couldn't have taken the train from Washington to join us."

Drew arched a brow, taking the platter of meat passed to

him. "Another time, perhaps. Right now, I doubt Caroline's ... queasy stomach could withstand the trip."

Mama paused from spooning potatoes onto her plate. "I didn't realize train rides bothered Caroline. She never mentioned it."

"Nothing a few more months won't cure."

An audible gasp seeped from Lydia. "Another baby?"

A hint of a grin edged across Drew's lips. "Around Christmastime."

She clasped her hands together. "Oh, how wonderful!"

Pressing a palm to her chest, Mama's eyes filled with tears of joy. "Another grandchild. What a blessing."

"Congratulations, big brother." Luke's smile, though genuine, lacked its usual luster.

"Thanks."

Lydia rocked forward in her chair and laced her fingers together on the table, her plate of food forgotten. "So much excitement with another baby coming and you traveling to important events with General Grant. Possibly our next president."

Setting her fork on her plate, Mama peered across the table at Drew. "Do you think he stands a chance of winning?"

"More than likely, I'd say. He was the only nominee even considered at the convention, and the vote was unanimous among the 650 delegates. He hasn't formally accepted the nomination yet, but I expect he will soon."

"My—brother. Aide to the president." With a smirk, Lydia leaned toward Drew. "Just don't forget about us little people."

Drew thrust the meat platter toward her. "Let's not get ahead of ourselves."

With a soft giggle, Lydia glanced around the group, noting only Mama's smile appeared unhindered. Will seemed more intent on eating than the family's conversation. And while Luke and Adelaide's expressions held an element of interest, there was a definite shadow over their countenances.

"Will your position with General Grant change, should he be elected?"

Mama's query produced a nod from Drew. "Most likely. Though I'm uncertain just what it will entail."

"Whatever it involves, you can be sure it will keep him away from the farm," Luke interjected.

Adelaide placed a steadying hand on his arm, and his head dipped.

Cutting Luke a sideways glance, Drew took a sip of tea, choosing not to respond.

In the moment of terse silence, Lydia's stomach clamped tight. Even Will paused in mid-chew, his gaze shifting between the two brothers. It wasn't like Luke to complain. Especially since the Lord had provided Will to work in Drew's stead. Until now, Luke had seemed happy with the arrangement.

Something more than Drew's absence was bothering Luke.

Had Will shared his intentions to leave so soon? Doubtful. Not when he'd made it clear he didn't want the information told. Though such unwelcome news might account for her brother's uncharacteristic sour mood.

Luke raked a hand through his hair and blew out a breath, his chair creaking under him as he slumped back. "Sorry, Drew. I didn't mean that."

"No offense taken." Drew took up his fork. "If you need the help, I'll—"

With a shake of his head, Luke gestured toward Will. "It's not that. Will here's good help. I … just have a lot on my mind right now."

No one ventured to ask what that might be, but a twinge of melancholy dampened Lydia's spirit as the clank of silverware replaced conversation. Being surrounded by those she loved was what her heart longed for most. She'd never expected strife to seep in and spoil it.

She only prayed whatever was troubling Luke would resolve itself as quickly as it had come.

23

Wednesday, June 10, 1868

"That reaper sure beats a sickle or cradle for harvesting wheat."

Will stopped filing and glanced toward the voice. His shoulders tensed when he recognized Drew approaching. As accepting as the newcomer had been, something about Drew intimidated Will, whether the man's prominent position or intuitive nature. He wasn't sure what had taken place between the two brothers last night at supper, but he'd never seen Luke so on edge.

With a brisk nod, Will again began grinding, the sound of metal against metal relieving the hesitancy of his response. "Saves a lot of hours and manpower, I imagine."

His companion gestured toward the wheat field dampened from last night's gentle rain. "As boys, Luke and I were out there binding sheaves and stacking them in stooks from mid-morning till sunset while our father wielded the cradle. By day's end, it seemed we'd hardly made a dent in the field. We were never so glad as when Pa purchased this McCormick reaper. Ever run one?"

With a shake of his head, Will kept filing. "This'll be my first time."

Drew touched one of the cutting blades. "Well, it's plain you know how to sharpen a blade. What was your trade before coming here?"

The query stalled Will's hands. He'd rushed through breakfast and headed outside to avoid such inquiries. Now, there seemed no escape. "I've tried my hand at a number of things."

"A sort of jack of all trades, huh?"

"You might say." Will peered in the direction of Luke's house, his restlessness mounting. Of all times for Luke to run late. He was usually so prompt in starting the day. Lydia, too, would be a welcome sight about now to help defray her brother's probing. It wasn't that he was afraid of Drew unearthing his confidences. He just didn't want to be found lacking or incompetent. There was a shame in having a blank mind with no clear answers.

Edging closer, Drew propped his boot on the edge of the reaper. "I noticed the scar above your ear. That a war injury?"

The question resurrected images Will would sooner forget. He clenched his jaw, reliving the one true memory ingrained in his mind. "Of sorts. I was thrown from the *Sultana* when she exploded."

Drew's head dipped. "Sorry to hear it. Terrible tragedy. You're fortunate to have lived through it."

With a nod, Will returned to work, the steady movement of his arms and shoulders easing some of the pent-up tension sifting through him.

Though he sensed the conversation wasn't through.

"Who'd you serve under?"

Will stifled a sigh. Another question he could only guess at. Fabricating responses was sure to land him in deeper water than he could swim out of. And vague replies wouldn't satisfy a man of Drew's perceptive nature for long. Best to end this interrogation before he completely botched things.

Pausing, Will wetted his lips and squinted up at Drew. "I'd

rather not talk about my stint in the war. Not much I care to recall."

Drew studied him, his dark eyes seeming to coil their way inside of Will. At last, Drew's expression softened. "I can appreciate that. There are battles I'd like to purge from my memory as well."

The scuff of boots broke off their conversation, and to Will's relief, Luke sauntered over, eyes a tad bloodshot.

Turning to face him, Drew crossed his arms over his chest. "There you are. I figured you'd be up and raring to go long before me."

Luke met his brother's gaze, his vivid blue eyes turbulent. "Been up. Just needed some extra prayer time this morning."

Drew hiked a brow. "Sounds serious."

"Yep, well, if you've got a minute, I could use some brotherly advice."

With a brisk nod, Drew clapped his brother on the back. "Let's take a walk."

The pair sauntered along the worn path, leaving Will to his work. Plainly, whatever had Luke uneasy last night had trailed him into today. It didn't appear his marriage was the issue. More than once during last night's meal, Luke had reached for his wife's hand or cast her a loving glance. And despite the minor mealtime clash, he didn't seem angry with his older brother either.

Whatever the problem, it appeared to have him in a dither.

But somehow, Luke always seemed to place God at the center of a situation. Good or bad. Though Will couldn't fully fathom that degree of loyalty to God, he had to respect it. His own devotion to prayer had deteriorated when his pleas to find his family went unanswered.

Though relieved the probing questions had ended, Will's heart ached for his friend. In the short time they'd worked together, Luke had become almost like a brother to him. Though apparently Drew was who he needed right now.

Will's stomach gripped. When it came to family, it seemed there was no substitute for the real thing.

As the brothers veered toward the pasture, Luke sank his hands in his pockets and shuffled his feet like a scolded schoolboy. Obviously, something important was bothering him.

Though Will had little faith it would do any good, he lifted his eyes heavenward and whispered a prayer. Maybe Luke's strong faith would make up for Will's lack. "Whatever the problem be, Lord, lend him Your help."

Taking up the file, Will forced out a breath. In time, maybe Luke would entrust his problem with him as well. But for now, sight of the two brothers strolling side by side only heightened Will's need to find his family.

If there was a family to be found.

LYDIA RAISED a hand to Drew's bedroom door, hesitant to knock. She'd waited all day for the opportunity to speak with him alone. But somehow, now, the thought of presenting her request stymied her. Would he be willing to help?

In the stillness, Mama's steady breathing drifted from her downstairs bedroom, assuring Lydia the impending conversation would go unheard.

The "thunk" of a boot on the floorboards echoed from inside Drew's room, prompting her to act. With a steadying breath, she rapped her knuckles against the pine door.

"Come in."

The swift response spawned an uptick in Lydia's heartrate. She gripped the door handle, then paused. Would Drew think her request odd? Worse yet, would he see through her as readily as Adelaide had?

Heat singed her cheeks. Too late to reconsider now.

Pasting on a smile, she pushed open the door and stepped inside.

Drew sat perched on the corner of his bed, rubbing one of his socked feet. He stared up at her as she entered. "Thought you'd gone to bed."

"Not yet." She gestured to his feet, hoping a bit of small talk might ease the awkwardness of her unforeseen visit. "Feet sore?"

A faint grin seeped onto her brother's face. "It appears living in Washington has made me soft. A few hours walking the fields and my feet are paying the price."

Lydia returned a slow nod, her smile more genuine. "Ah. Then you'd best come home more often."

"Maybe so."

Venturing a step closer, she latched her hands together behind her back. "I saw you and Luke walking. Is everything all right between you?"

Drew's eyes crimped. "Shouldn't it be?"

"Of course." She lowered her gaze to the floorboards. "He just seemed a bit annoyed you aren't here to help more."

The clipped silence made her wonder if she'd said too much. When Drew spoke, his voice had deepened. "It's not me Luke's frustrated at."

Lydia's eyes flicked back to Drew. "What then? He was fine until yesterday."

Instantly, Lydia regretted asking. She knew full well Drew could hold a person's confidence—it was partly why she'd come to him.

His mouth grew taut. "I'd rather he tells you himself when he's ready."

The room grew quiet again but for the steady rasp of insects outside the window. Though there was a foreboding nature to his words, it was plain Lydia would get nothing further from him. She moistened her lips, considering how to shift the conversation to the topic she'd *truly* come to discuss.

Lowering his foot to the floor, Drew leaned his elbows on his knees. "Now, was that what was troubling you, or is there something more on your mind?"

Her brother's pointed question left little room for delay. Tamping down her unease, she gathered her wits and plunged ahead. "I-I have a favor to ask regarding Will."

"What sort of favor?"

Lydia swallowed the unsteadiness in her voice. "He ... he needs help."

Drew's furrowed brow demanded more. "Is he in some sort of trouble?"

"No. Nothing like that." She released a soft sigh. "First, you have to promise not to say anything to him or anyone else. I vowed not to tell."

"Then maybe you'd best keep that vow."

She shook her head. "I can't. It's tearing him up inside and, with all your resources in Washington, you may be able to help."

Drew ran a hand over his stubbled chin. "Just what *resources* are you referring to?"

"Records."

"Records? What sort of records?"

Striding over, she eased onto the bed beside him. "Do you remember when the *Sultana* steamboat sank just after the war?"

His brows pinched. "Yes. What of it?"

"Will was aboard when it exploded. He was thrown overboard and suffered a head injury."

Drew nodded. "He told me as much. But was pretty vague when I asked about his scar. In fact, he seems vague about a lot of things."

With a tentative glance at her brother, Lydia softened her voice. "Because he doesn't know. He has no memory of his past."

Crossing his arms over his chest, Drew raised a brow. "Huh. I sensed something wasn't right. I guess that explains it. He doesn't remember anything?"

"Nothing. Not even his full name."

"I thought his name was Will Evans."

"His name is *Will*. He's just not sure about Evans." Seeing the confusion warring on her brother's face, Lydia gnawed at her lip. "He has a pocket watch with the name Will E. etched in it."

"So, Evans isn't his real last name?"

"Not likely." With an apologetic scrunch of her nose, Lydia shifted to face him more squarely. "That's where you come in."

Drew gave a soft snort. "You expect a lot of me. How am I supposed to retrieve the man's memory?"

"By learning who he is." She draped her hair behind her ear, her confidence mounting. "There must be records of which soldiers were aboard the *Sultana*."

"There should be. Yes. Though I'm not sure how thorough or accurate they'd be." Drew scratched at his cheek. "And the name Will E. is not much to go on."

"I realize that, but could you maybe jot down the names of all the Williams with a last name starting with E?"

Drew scoffed. "There must have been dozens of soldiers aboard the *Sultana* fitting that description. It would be nearly impossible to track down someone with so little information."

Sensing he might refuse her, Lydia placed a hand on his arm, her voice pleading. "Please, Drew. Won't you at least try?"

He scrutinized her with an inquisitive, older-brotherly glare. "Why is this so important to you? Is there something between you two I should know about?"

Warmth flooded her cheeks, and her pulse quickened. She slid her hand from atop his arm, averting her gaze to the quilt between them. "No. He just seems so distraught over not knowing his family or background. I only wish to help him learn who he is."

She sensed Drew's eyes upon her as though weighing her true motives. An answer she wasn't certain of herself.

At last, he blew out a long breath. "If I recall, the majority of those on the *Sultana* were from Indiana and Ohio."

Her head lifted. "That's right. Will told Luke he's from Indiana. Likely he presumed as much."

A wrinkle creased Drew's forehead. "There's nothing else you can tell me about him? Surely there's something more."

Lydia's mouth twisted, her mind riffling through the conversations and encounters she'd had with Will over the past month. Like a pinhole of light on a dark canvas, a ray of hope shot through her. She sat taller. "I think he might be cavalry. He seems to have a knack for horses. And the way Angel took to him. It was like she knew he was someone she could trust."

Drew released a long breath. "Well, it's not much, but perhaps that would narrow the search a bit."

"Then you'll do it?"

"I can't promise anything, but I'll try."

"Thank you. That's all I ask." Lydia leaned to give him a peck on the cheek, her joy mingling with a twinge of unease. As deeply as she wished Will could learn the unknowns of his past, she feared the knowledge would hasten his desire to leave.

Standing, she pushed aside the unsettling thought. It was a risk she had to take. Until he knew the truth, his spirit would never find rest.

And there could be no hope of a future for them.

Without warning, Drew slapped his hands on his thighs, jarring Lydia from her thoughts. "Now, I've a question for you."

With a calming breath, she peered down at him. "What's that?"

"What's ailing Ma?"

24

Friday, June 12, 1868

Lydia waved from the veranda stoop, shielding her eyes against the morning sun as Luke and Drew drove off in the carriage. A swirl of dust rose in their wake, hanging in the humid air like a fog. Drew's short visit had come and gone in a flash, leaving her a bit dizzy from what had transpired.

Her mother stared after the carriage, eyes moist, chin held high, paleness marring her complexion. Lydia shouldn't have been surprised by Drew's inquiry into Mama's health. It seemed nothing escaped her oldest brother's notice. Perhaps his infrequent visits made it easier for him to note the change in her appearance. With him living far away, Lydia had found it impossible to deny what she knew of their mother's weakened heart. He deserved to know something of what was transpiring.

To her knowledge, he'd kept their conversation to himself in the two days that had passed. His ability to keep a confidence ensured little danger of him slipping up and letting Mama know Lydia had betrayed her secret.

Or Will's, for that matter.

Luke, on the other hand, seemed much too preoccupied

these days to take notice of anything besides Adelaide, the coming baby, and whatever situation had him troubled. Even harvest didn't seem a priority. Will had done most of the reaper preparations. The bowed heads of the bearded wheat hinted harvest was imminent. And yet, Luke seemed distracted, indifferent to the fact.

"It's hard to see him go." Mama's voice sounded hushed and raspy, as though something deep within her ached for Drew to stay.

Edging closer, Lydia draped an arm around her mother's waist. "He'll be back, Mama, and hopefully bring Caroline and Mary with him."

"I know, dear." Mama leaned her head against Lydia's, watching the carriage disappear from view. "I just pray they don't tarry too long."

Lydia tensed and unwittingly tightened her hold on her mother. Something in Mama's tone sounded foreboding, as though time was a commodity she had little of.

With a sigh, Mama straightened. "Well ... I don't suppose those breakfast dishes will wash themselves."

Pushing aside her misgivings, Lydia groaned. "Unfortunately."

They turned and walked arm-in-arm to the house. Twenty minutes later, Lydia reemerged, the dishes washed, dried, and put away. The air had warmed considerably in the short span of time, the sun deepening its hold as it rose higher. It seemed the Lord always reserved the hottest of days for wheat harvest.

She caught a glimpse of Will as he strode around the far corner of the barn, and a stab of guilt buffeted her. Would he be angry if he knew she'd petitioned Drew to delve into his private information? Or would he be as eager as her to learn the outcome? Not wishing to give him false hope or risk his ire, she dared not say anything. Likely, Drew would come up short anyway.

Or forget the matter altogether.

A man on horseback appeared along the road to the east. Squinting against the glare of the morning sun, Lydia struggled to make out who it might be. But as he veered toward the house, she caught a clearer image, and her stomach twisted. Guthrie Malloy. What did *he* want?

She stifled the urge to retreat inside, bolt the door, and pretend no one was home. But by now he'd seen her, or at least Will. She couldn't shove the responsibility off onto him. Besides, Mama would never agree to such a farce. Yet, the last thing she needed was to have the fractious neighbor upsetting her. If the man had to show himself, why couldn't he have come when Drew and Luke were still here?

Or had Mr. Malloy planned it this way, keeping watch on their place to know when and who was around? The thought made the hair on her neck stand on end.

With heavy tread, Lydia exited the veranda and strolled into the yard to meet the unwanted visitor. Thankfully, Will had seen him, too, and was making his way over. A sliver of relief coursed through her at the thought of having Will at her side to face the intrusive visitor.

Mr. Malloy brought his hefty roan mare to a halt several yards from Lydia, casting a dubious glance at Will as he wedged his way past to stand beside her. With a tip of his hat, Malloy's gaze settled on Lydia. "Mornin'. Luke or your ma around that I could speak to 'em?"

Willing the shakiness from her voice, Lydia lifted a silent prayer and mustered her courage. Rather than answer him directly, she met his gaze square on. "What is it you've come for, Mr. Malloy?"

He eased forward in his saddle, his gloved hand holding his horse's reins taut. His gaze slipped to Will and back again. "No offense, miss, but I'd rather do my business with someone other than a girl or hired hand."

She slid her tongue over her teeth, seething inwardly. Will, too, seemed to bristle at the insolent remark. Lydia tipped her chin higher. "Luke isn't here, and Ma isn't currently receiving visitors." She swallowed, hopeful Ma hadn't noticed the visitor's approach and that they were far enough away from the house the conversation couldn't be heard through the open windows.

"Oh? Somethin' ailing her?"

Lydia gnawed her cheek, debating how to respond. The last thing she wanted was for Malloy to think he could take advantage of Mama's failing health. "She's fine. Just ... indisposed at the moment."

Eyes firmly fastened on Malloy, Will took a step forward as though shielding Lydia from further questioning. "State your business or be on your way."

Lydia inadvertently edged closer to Will, warmed by his show of support, while something akin to contempt flared in Malloy's eyes. For a long moment he made no answer, then his mouth twitched. "I'll come back another time. You let Luke and your ma know I was here."

He reined his horse in the direction he'd come and stared out over the field of ripened wheat. "You've a good-looking crop there," he called over his shoulder. "Be a shame if it didn't get harvested." With that, he goaded his bulky mare into a sluggish trot.

Lydia balled her hands into fists and tromped after him, voice raised. "Oh, it'll get harvested, all right. You can count on it."

Will's strong but gentle hand clasped her arm. "Don't let him rile you."

Lydia's harried breaths gradually calmed, the invigorating feel of Will's touch warring with the fury coursing through her. She stared after Malloy. If she'd had any doubts about him setting the fire, they were relinquished. Yet, only she and Will seemed savvy to the truth.

Somehow that had to change.

***

"I TELL YOU, Mama, the man's up to no good."

Mama raised her glass to her lips and took a quick sip. "Perhaps you mistook what Mr. Malloy said. I'm certain he means no harm."

Lydia clanked her fork down on her plate, jaw slackened. "He intends to ruin us, is all. So he can get his hands on our property."

A humored chuckle rippled through Mama. "What an imagination you have, child."

Heat flared in Lydia's cheeks. Both irritated and embarrassed by her mother's reference to her as a child, Lydia gestured to Will. "If you don't believe me, just ask Will. He heard Mr. Malloy's threat."

Will's eyes widened like those of a deer caught in the sites of a shotgun. His chair creaked under him as he eased forward and scratched at his cheek. Obviously, he'd intended to stay out of the dispute.

Lydia intensified her gaze as if doing so might extract the words to corroborate her story.

At last, he cleared his throat and crossed his hands over his chest. "He does seem to have his eye on the place, ma'am."

Though the backing wasn't as strong as Lydia might have liked, a wave of satisfaction coursed through her as she shifted her gaze back to her mother. "And we've little doubt but that he set the fire as well."

All traces of humor fled from Mama's lips. Her eyes oscillated between the two of them. "Though I have my doubts Mr. Malloy would stoop to any such vile measures, I admit he has a tendency to acquire property not his own. Have you voiced your concerns to Luke?"

"I merely pointed out the fire seemed suspicious."

Lydia arched a brow at Will. So he *had* brought the incident to Luke's attention. She'd had a feeling the two men were discussing the topic when she'd happened upon them that day.

Evidently, Luke hadn't taken the occurrence any more seriously than Mama.

Lacing her fingers together on the table, Mama focused her attention on Will. "And what was his response?"

"He seemed to agree there was cause for speculation."

Mama dipped her chin. "Then perhaps one or both of you should state your concerns regarding today's visit."

Lydia slumped back in her chair. "Luke's too preoccupied to care."

A sigh escaped Mama. "He and Adelaide do seem to have a lot on their minds, but regardless, Luke needs to be kept abreast to the goings on here."

Lydia glanced at Will, his hazel eyes meeting hers an instant before he returned to his meal. His comradery meant more to her than he likely knew. Though their efforts may not have entirely convinced Mama of the neighbor's evil intentions, just maybe they'd succeeded in slipping a chink in his armor.

25

W ill cut a glance at Lydia, her straw hat shading much of her face from view. She'd worked tirelessly all afternoon in the hot sun, binding sheaves of wheat while he and Luke took turns running the reaper and stacking the sheaves into stooks.

Lydia had barely spoken a word since her unsuccessful attempt earlier that morning to convince Luke of Mr. Malloy's ill intentions. The rebuff seemed only to fuel her efforts to speed harvest. A smile tugged at Will's lips. She was one determined lady, that was certain. He had to admire her that. Though having witnessed her irritation toward her brother, Will was grateful to be on her good side.

The sluggish stride of the team hinted another round or two would be all they could manage for the day. Will returned to stacking sheaves. Already dozens of stooks dotted the field, left to dry in the summer breeze. The thought of the harvested wheat sitting idle in the field for better than a week left him a bit nervous. The valuable crop would make an easy target for someone to set ablaze.

Too bad Luke couldn't recognize the danger. But, with no

real evidence against Malloy, Will hesitated to voice a grievance. Still, that didn't mean he couldn't take precautions. Even if it meant sleeping under the stars a few nights with a rifle at close range.

Luke's mind was obviously on other things besides the wheat crop. Instead of his usual easy-going, amiable nature, he'd retreated inside himself, his expression and eyes stormy. But until he was willing to share what was bothering him, Will could only speculate what the trouble might be.

Metal clanked as Luke brought the team to a halt at the edge of the field. "Let's call it quits for the day," he hollered back at Will and Lydia.

Will returned a nod, while Lydia's only response was to straighten and press a hand to the small of her back as though the constant stooping had left her muscles stiff.

Luke quietly unhitched the team from the reaper and led them to the barn for feeding and a much-deserved night's rest. The waning sun lost its fury as it sank lower in the west. Stillness settled over the landscape, the only sound the rustling of leaves and trill of insects.

Tossing a sheaf of wheat onto the pile, Will glanced at Lydia, who seemed to be struggling to tie a piece of straw around a wheat bundle. The strand broke, sending some of the hewn stalks tumbling to the ground. With a sigh, Lydia rolled her shoulders then bent to retrieve the wayward wheat. Clearly, she was exhausted. Yet, he knew her well enough to realize she wouldn't quit until every last bundle was tied.

Brushing bits of straw from his wrists and gloves, he strode toward her. Lydia straightened and pivoted his way as he neared, her face flushed from heat and exertion.

Will reached for the loose sheaf of wheat in her hands. "It must be near suppertime. You go on to the house. I'll finish."

Though fringed with fatigue, her vivid blue eyes flashed what appeared to be a mixture of relief and gratitude. "Are you sure?"

Nodding, he took the bundle from her, his gloved hands grazing hers.

The rosiness in her cheeks deepened as she lifted the hat from her head and fanned herself, glancing over the acres of harvested wheat. "We must've harvested ten acres. What do you suppose it's yielding?"

Quickly tallying the stacks of wheat, Will drew an estimate. "Near eighteen or twenty bushels an acre, I'd say."

"Truly?" She gazed up at him, a glimmer in her eyes. "The Lord blessed us with a fine crop."

Will tried not to notice the way the sunlight glistened on her hair or the smoothness of her skin. Raw beauty poured from within and without of this young woman at his side. He resisted the urge to brush his fingers along her cheek. If not for the fear he might be obligated to someone else, Lydia was just the sort to take his heart captive.

Yet, the unknowns of his past rose up between them like a stone wall he couldn't scale.

And until he knew the truth, he'd never be free to love.

———

LYDIA SHIFTED IN HER CHAIR, trying to decide which was worse —the overwhelming fatigue or the stiffness in her muscles. She hadn't noticed it much until she'd sat down for supper, but after relaxing for a time, she could hardly move without discomfort. Forcing down a last bite of biscuit, she pushed aside her empty plate. All she could think of was drawing a bath of Epsom salt water and soaking in it for a solid hour before easing into bed.

"Thanks for another fine meal, Mrs. Gallagher."

Will's soothing voice sliced through Lydia's misery as he stood and retrieved his hat from the back of his chair. How was it he looked so fresh and unhindered by the day's work while she was completely spent?

"You're welcome, Will. I'm glad it suited you."

Lydia grasped her plate and cup, emitting a quiet moan as she rose from her chair. Both Mama's and Will's gazes landed squarely on her, and she worked to conceal her soreness.

Mama's brows pinched. "Have you injured yourself?"

Embarrassed by her lack of stamina, Lydia glossed over the incident. "Just a bit stiff from all the stooping. I'll be fine." With slow, rigid steps, she carried her dishes from the table.

"T-They say walking helps ease stiff muscles." Will stumbled over his words.

The silverware on Lydia's plate jiggled as she jolted to a stop beside Mama's chair. Was he suggesting she take a walk or implying he might join her?

Mama caught her by the arm. "Why, that's a splendid idea. Why don't the two of you go for a stroll while I wash the dishes?"

Lydia's cheeks heated at Mama's assumption. Keeping her eyes trained away from Will, Lydia sounded a nervous chuckle. "Will likely has better things to do than escort me on a walk."

"I don't know. A leisurely walk might do us both good."

The unexpected response ripped through her like lightning. She shot him a questioning glance, her thickened throat nearly choking off her words. "It would?"

Meeting her gaze, he twisted his hat in his hands. "If you're up to it."

If anyone else had suggested the idea, Lydia would have told them she'd sooner wrestle a muddy pig than take ten paces she didn't have to. But coming from Will, the notion was hard to resist. She swallowed and mustered a tired smile, thoughts of a hot bath swept aside in lieu of time spent with Will. "Perhaps a short one. Let me just finish clearing away these dishes."

With a brisk nod, Will edged toward the hall. "I'll wait outside."

Ignoring the soreness in her arms and thighs, Lydia deposited her dishes near the wash basin and returned to the dining hall, where Mama now sat alone. "Are you sure you don't want help with dishes?"

Mama shooed her toward the doorway. "Go."

Unable to stifle her eagerness, Lydia headed toward the door. It was the first time Will had asked her on a walk. Whether out of pity, compassion, or companionship, she couldn't say, but the very notion he sought her company elated her.

A brilliant sky greeted her as she stepped onto the veranda, vibrant rays of sunlight blanketing the evening sky with color. "Oh, how lovely."

"Sure is." Will turned toward her, the brightness accenting the streaks of gold in his eyes. "All set?"

With a shy nod, Lydia ambled closer, cringing at the pull on her weary calves as she started down the steps.

Will placed a steadying hand on her elbow. "Pretty sore, huh?"

"Miserably." Conscious of his touch, she fought for breath. "You must think it shameful to be so stoved up after only a single day's work."

A rare chuckle fell from his lips. "Oh, I don't know. Anybody gets sore using muscles they haven't used in a while."

Lydia relaxed under his amiable companionship. As they strolled into the yard, he slid his hand from her arm, leaving a noticeable void. Though quite capable of maneuvering unaided, Lydia longed to loop her arm through his and savor the warmth of his nearness. Instead, she let her arms dangle at her sides, feeling both awkward and content. "I suppose you've not one sore muscle?"

"Not now, but when I first came, I did. Luke's a hard worker."

"Yes, he is." Recollection of her brother's untold stupor wedged its way into her thoughts. In the distance, light began to stream from the cottage windows as the vibrancy of the sky gradually faded to blue. She cast Will a furtive glance. "Have you noticed something troubling him?

Will shrugged. "He seems distracted. But I figure with the baby coming, his nerves are likely a mite raw."

Lydia shook her head. "It's more than that. Luke isn't easily rattled. He's been so excited about the baby and always optimistic. Lately, he seems more ... melancholy. I've rarely seen him so troubled in spirit."

"Well, I'm sure whatever it is will work itself out."

Lydia nodded and resisted the urge to ask if Will had shared his intentions to leave. Something told her he hadn't. And even if he had, Luke would have taken the news in stride rather than let it eat at him.

She tried not to think of Will leaving. Hoping. Praying. Something would alter his plans.

Perhaps even his feelings for *her*.

Lydia's stomach gripped. At times, she thought she detected a glimmer of affection in Will's eyes when he looked at her. Tonight gave her hope he at least thought something of her. But would it be enough? His desire to locate his family and learn of his past were strong lures.

Ones that seemed to reach Will's very core.

They strode in silence for a time, their boots marking out a slow, steady cadence along the dirt lane. At last, Will broke the stillness. "Is the walk helping?"

Resting her hands on her hips, she arched her back. "You know, I think it is. The soreness in my legs and back seem to have eased. Thank you for suggesting it."

"My pleasure."

Her steps lightened. Will was a good man. One she was eager to spend more time with. Yet one she knew she couldn't hold on to, should he choose to leave.

As they neared the edge of the wheat field, the scent of cut straw wafted on the gentle breeze, reminding Lydia of the hard labor that awaited them tomorrow and her need for rest. Reluctantly, she slowed her pace. "We should probably head back."

"Whenever you say." Will turned toward her, letting his eyes travel over her face as though he didn't wish their time to end any more than she did.

The first stars of eventide flickered overhead as they started back. Lydia laced her hands together at the small of her back, a shy grin tugging at her lips. She giggled. "When you first arrived, I thought you were an angel, the way you showed up just when we needed you."

"An angel?" Will snickered. "Far from it, I assure you."

"Well, regardless, I'm convinced the Lord sent you here."

Offering no reply, Will shifted his gaze to the amber glow lining the western horizon.

Troubled by his lack of response, Lydia studied him. "You don't agree?"

He sank his hands in his pockets and stared at his boots. "I don't believe God takes that much interest in people. Leastways, not me."

A lump rose in her throat. "Of course, He cares."

"Not enough to answer prayers."

The candid statement brought Lydia to a standstill. She placed a hand on Will's arm, and he turned to face her, his expression shadowed by the waning light. "You think God doesn't care because you haven't found your family?"

"More or less."

Sliding her hand from his arm, Lydia struggled how best to respond. "Maybe He's answering your prayers, but in a different way than you'd expect. Or maybe you haven't given Him enough time."

Will's eyes crimped. "Three years is a long time to pray and not get an answer."

"Yes, it is, but if you'll recall, Abraham waited more than two decades for God's promise of a son."

"Abraham?"

"Yes. In the Bible. The story of Abraham ... and ... Isaac?" Her words slowed as it dawned on her that while Will seemed to have some element of faith, she'd not seen a Bible among his meager possessions, nor had he carried one to Sunday service. She tempered her voice. "You don't own a Bible?"

With a shake of his head, Will shifted his feet. "No, but I figure at some point I did since I recall some of the stories and verses the pastor speaks of. But it's all pretty jumbled."

Heartened to know he'd at least been listening to the Sunday sermons, Lydia smiled up at him. "Then I'll refresh your memory."

Will fell into pace beside her as she ventured a step forward and pointed at the darkening sky. "The Lord promised Abraham his descendants would be as numerous as the stars, but he didn't even have a son. And though he was quite old, he believed God's promise and waited more than twenty years for the Lord to give him Isaac. The trouble was, he grew impatient and tried to hurry God by taking things into his own hands, which caused more problems than it resolved."

Lydia's mind fled to her appeal to Drew in seeking information about Will. Was she doing the same? Trying to hurry God? Or would her request prove the catalyst for reuniting Will with his family?

"So, you're saying I need to wait and do nothing, and God will set everything right?"

The terseness in Will's voice compelled Lydia to soften her tone. "I'm saying the Lord has a plan for you and may be working in ways you can't see." She braced herself for a dispute, but when Will offered no argument, she lifted a silent prayer of thanks and pleaded for wisdom.

They strolled in silence for a time, the glow of light in the downstairs windows of the farmhouse guiding their way. Lydia stole a glance at Will. Though his features were cloaked by the mounting darkness, he seemed more in deep thought than irritated.

As they reached the veranda stoop, Lydia paused and pivoted toward him. "Thank you for the walk, Will. It truly helped."

"That's good."

His voice held a somber tone, and Lydia almost regretted the conversation had taken the turn it had. And yet, she knew Will's relationship with the Lord wasn't what it should be, and her heart ached for his faith to be genuine.

A sudden thought struck her, and she clasped her hands together. "If I'm not mistaken, Drew's old Bible is still in his room. You're welcome to use it. Scripture is full of examples of people who waited for their prayers to be answered."

The slight shrug of Will's shoulder was enough incentive for Lydia. "I'll bring it to you first thing in the morning."

"No rush." With a nod, he tipped his hat. "Good night."

"Good night, Will." Her heart yearned as she watched him go, realizing the soreness in her legs and back was nothing compared to the raw ache within Will's spirit.

26

Tuesday, June 16, 1868

Luke lifted his hat and scratched at his head. "I don't understand it. The reaper was in perfect shape when we finished yesterday." Letting out a huff, he jiggled the busted reel. "This will set us back a couple of days. Maybe longer." He peered at the mixture of blue and clouds blanketing the sky. "Hopefully, rain will hold off a few more days."

Fingering the broken reel, Will couldn't get past the memory of Malloy's ominous words a few days earlier. He'd have had easy access to the reaper out in the open. Had he snuck over during the night and tampered with it? Lydia had little success in convincing Luke of the neighbor's wrongful intentions. Will wasn't likely to convince him either. It wasn't his place to even try, yet he felt obliged to say something. He'd come to value this family and this place too much to keep silent. "Uh, Luke?"

"Yep?"

Straightening, Will let the piece of broken reel flop. "This didn't happen on its own."

Luke pushed his hat back on his head. "You think someone did this intentionally?"

Swallowing the awkwardness, Will nodded. "I'm almost certain of it."

"I admit it seems suspicious, but I can't feature anyone doing something so malicious."

Luke's ability to see the best in people had him blinded to the truth. Will plunged ahead, hoping to convince him of the neighbor's wrongdoing. "Lydia and I had a run-in with Guthrie Malloy the other day that didn't set well with either of us."

Nodding, Luke squinted over at him. "Lydia told me as much, but I figured she was making more of it than she ought. Seems to think he's out to ruin us and snatch up our land."

"I'm convinced he is."

Luke's expression turned stony. "The man's not the friendliest sort, I'll give you that, but I can't see where his ill-manners make him a land digger. Just what was said?"

"Not much. Only that his dealings were with you and your ma. But what he *did* say sounded pretty incriminating. Something to the effect that it would be a shame if the wheat didn't get harvested."

Luke scrubbed a hand over his face. "So, you think he's trying to force us into selling some of our land?"

Will nodded. "I believe those are his intentions. When he didn't get anywhere persuading you to sell, he set the fire. And now he's busted the reaper to hurt your chances of harvesting a crop."

With a disgruntled sigh, Luke fixed his gaze on the damaged reaper. "If what you say is true, it's time we find out what his intentions truly are. Offering to buy land is one thing. Destroying someone's property for your own gain is another." He gave the broken reel a partial turn. "We'll need some supplies from town to repair the reaper. Let's swing by our ill-tempered neighbor's place on the way home and have a talk."

Satisfied, Will gave a consenting nod. "I'll hitch up the wagon."

"Pick me up at my house," Luke called over his shoulder. "I

want to check on Adelaide before we head out and let her know we're going."

Will strode toward the barn, catching a glimpse of Lydia on her way to the house. She walked a bit stiffly, as though her muscles were still giving her trouble. Intent on toting her bucket of milk, she apparently hadn't noticed him. He slowed his pace, fearful if their paths crossed, he'd say more than he should. Though she'd be thrilled to know Luke had agreed to confront Malloy, it seemed wise to hold off telling her and see how things went.

Her slender frame and attractive features held his attention longer than public scrutiny would allow. He stifled a grin, grateful for the opportunity to observe her unaware. She was indeed fetching, and his heart felt knitted with hers in ways he couldn't explain. Part of him wished to give up his pursuit of his past and settle into this life. No longer hold Lydia at arm's length. But he knew his soul couldn't rest until he'd exhausted every possibility.

Last night's conversation had his mind spinning in all directions. He'd lain awake for hours after seeing Lydia home, contemplating what they'd discussed. While he'd felt at ease in her company, that comfort ended when their focus turned to God. As much as Will longed to share her conviction that the Lord had a plan for him and was somehow answering his prayers, he couldn't. If the Lord had given him one shred of hope, he might feel differently. But silence and a bunch of muddled dreams were all he'd been doled.

He blew out a breath as he entered the barn. As he lifted the harnesses from their pegs, his eyes instinctively drifted to his sleeping quarters. As promised, Drew's Bible rested atop his bedroll. He glanced at the worn leather binding but made no move to disturb it. Obviously, it had seen a great deal of use. He hadn't time now to read or even thumb through it. Wasn't certain he ever would. But it seemed important to Lydia for him to have it. At the least, he could carry it with him to use at Sunday service.

Looping the harnesses over his shoulders, Will headed to the pasture, his gut twisting. He wasn't sure which had him on edge more—talk of God or confronting Malloy. If Malloy didn't fess up, he might accuse Will of wrongdoing instead.

And Luke would have to choose who to believe.

———

LYDIA PEERED out the kitchen window, her jaw slackening at sight of the wagon disappearing down the path, barely able to make out the image of Will and Luke riding on the bench. "Where are they going?"

Mama edged beside her for a look. "I don't know, dear. Will said nothing about going anywhere at breakfast."

A sigh escaped Lydia. The warm, clear day should have afforded an early start for wheat harvest. Not that she was too disappointed in that regard. Despite applying liniment to her stiff, sore muscles before retiring, she wasn't eager to repeat the abuse.

Yet, it made no sense why they should leave with so much work to be done. Every day the wheat remained in the field was an opportunity for Guthrie Malloy to do it damage.

Turning from the window, she snatched her bonnet from its peg and tied it on. "I'm going to find out what's happened."

A knowing smile played on Mama's lips, and she waved Lydia on. "I thought as much."

Lydia stifled a grin as she swept past. Mama knew her all too well—that she would seek an explanation for any unknown. Perhaps that was one reason Will intrigued her so. There was so much she longed to know.

As quickly as her sore muscles would allow, Lydia made her way along the path to where the reaper rested at the edge of the field. At first glance, nothing appeared out of the ordinary. The stooks of harvested wheat stood unharmed, and the remainder of the field swayed in the gentle breeze, practically begging to be cut.

But as she turned her attention to the reaper, she sucked in a breath and then released a frustrated groan. "What happened?"

She fingered the damaged reel, her mind struggling to make sense of it. Then, like the sun bursting from behind a cloud, she knew. "Malloy! It had to be." Her insides roiled. He'd made good on his threat to stall harvest.

What else would the man try?

Drawing an agitated breath. she lifted her face heavenward. "Protect this crop, Lord. Don't let any harm come to it. And please allow Luke to see the truth of what's happening."

Luke.

Plopping down on the reaper platform, Lydia rested her elbows on her thighs and cradled her chin in her hands. She hoped Will held more persuasion over her brother than she did. He'd more or less passed off her concerns as girlish notions. It wasn't like him.

Something just wasn't right.

She stared down the lane where the wagon had disappeared. Had they gone to confront Mr. Malloy or merely headed to town for repairs? Regardless, she had a lot of time on her hands she hadn't anticipated. Her gaze trailed to the cottage in the distance. Perhaps now would be a good time to pay Adelaide a visit and see if she could shed insight into Luke's odd behavior.

A mystery Lydia was a bit reluctant to unravel.

27

"Afternoon, gentlemen. What can I do for you?" Malloy's amiable tone didn't fool Will. The man was conniving and rotten to the core.

Luke sat forward on the wagon seat, holding the reins taut. "You came to see me a couple days back. I'm here to find out why."

Casting Will a furtive glance, Malloy scratched at his beard. "I was hoping to talk privately with you on the matter."

"You can speak your mind. I've no secrets from Will."

The man jutted out his lower lip and crossed his arms over his chest. "All right. Then I'll say it outright. I was wondering if you'd given any thought to my offer to buy the east section of your property?"

"Not a lot. No."

Malloy widened his stance, the muscles in his neck bulging. "I'm sorry to hear it. I'd hoped by now you'd see how it might benefit you an' yer ma. Selling that strip of land would give your ma a sizeable purse, not to mention ease your work load."

Will expected Luke to say the two of them were handling things just fine and confront Malloy about the reaper. Instead, his companion seemed frozen in thought, his head dipped low.

Surely, after all Will had told him, he wouldn't consider selling to this ruffian?

Seeming heartened by Luke's lack of response, Malloy took a step closer. "I'd be willin' to offer a fair price, mind ya."

Luke gave a slow nod. "I appreciate the offer and will remind Ma of your interest." He cleared his throat, cutting a quick glance in Will's direction before settling his gaze on Malloy. "I do need to ask about a couple of suspicious incidents on our property recently."

"Oh? What might those be?"

Will's chest tightened at the man's guise of innocence. It was all Will could do to keep still. If he were a betting man, he'd wager Malloy knew well what mishaps Luke referred to.

With a scratch of his chin, Luke tempered his voice. "Our barn was set ablaze a couple weeks back. Then, this morning our reaper went busted, though it was in perfect working order when we finished last night's harvest."

Lowering his gaze, Malloy wagged his head. "You don't say? Well now, I hope you've not suffered too much loss."

The man's inflated tone turned Will's stomach. He glanced at Luke but couldn't decipher if his friend was fooled by Malloy's response or thought it phony.

Luke rallied a weak grin. "We'll make do."

Malloy's head lifted. "Glad t' hear it. Glad t' hear it."

Unable to hold his tongue any longer, Will cast the neighbor a pointed stare. "Don't suppose you know anything about either incident?"

A flicker of contempt flashed in the man's eyes before he again turned to Luke, his innocent air returning. "Why, Luke. You've known me your whole life. Surely you wouldn't suspicion me of anything so unneighborly? Er ya gonna let this new hired hand of yours accuse me of wrongful doin' when it was likely him who did the damage? Seems the misdeeds started after he arrived."

Bristling, Will sat forward on the wagon seat, intent on

giving Malloy a punch in the jaw or, at the least, a good tongue-lashing. But before Will could do either, Luke put up a hand to stop him. "What's done is done. The Lord knows who's to blame, and any revenge is His to divvy out." He leveled his gaze on Malloy. "But, be it known, malicious, ill-gotten gain is no gain at all and will come to naught."

The words went unchallenged as Luke released the brake and tightened his hold on the reins. With a brisk nod, he eased back on the wagon seat. "We've work to do, so we'll bid you good day."

As the wagon lurched forward, Will resisted the urge to cast Malloy a warning glance. The man might know how to put on a good act, but Will was wise to him ... and determined not to let him strike again.

"Don't forget to give my proposal some thought!" Malloy called after them.

Ignoring the comment, Luke kept his gaze straight ahead and gave another tap of the reins.

They rode in silence for a long while, each steeped in his own thoughts. Try as he may, Will couldn't rid himself of the unwelcome ball of fire in his chest. As infuriating as it was, Will had to admire Luke's ability to forgive a wrong and move on without a fight. Time and again, he'd proven himself a Christian in the truest sense. Had he believed Malloy? The very thought irked Will. He could see how the neighbor's words might plant a seed of doubt in his friend's mind. They hadn't known each other long, and it was true the misdeeds started after Will's arrival.

Fisting his hands, he squeezed until his knuckles turned white. He wished Luke would say something. *Anything.* Until he did, Will could only hope and pray his friend saw Malloy as the deceitful man he was.

"WHAT'S WRONG WITH LUKE?" The words poured from Lydia blunter and swifter than she might have liked.

Adelaide pressed a hand to her blossoming abdomen and motioned Lydia to a chair at the table. "Have a seat."

At the conflicted look on her sister-in-law's face, Lydia's stomach dipped. She perched on the edge of the chair, too disquieted to seek the comfort of a backrest. Luke's uncharacteristic moping had prompted the visit, but now that Lydia witnessed the worry notched in Adelaide's expression, her concern heightened. "Is it the baby?"

With a definitive shake of her head, Adelaide gnawed at her lip but offered no reply.

Lydia jiggled her foot up and down, reluctantly posing the only other possibility she could conceive. "Have you and Luke ... quarreled?"

Again, Adelaide adamantly shook her head. "No." She drew a long breath and released it slowly, pinning Lydia with a firm stare. "If I tell you, you must promise not to say anything until a decision has been made."

Lydia managed a slow nod, tightness coiling its way from her chest to her throat, nearly choking off her voice. "Decision?"

Lacing her fingers together, Adelaide moistened her lips. "It's the letter Luke received from Mr. and Mrs. Banks."

Lydia stilled her bouncing knee. "What's happened? Are they ill?"

"No."

"Did something happen to Clarissa?"

"No. Nothing like that." The tremor in Adelaide's voice was disturbing.

Resisting the urge to pummel her with further speculations, Lydia settled back expectantly in her chair. "What then?"

Adelaide brushed a strand of hair from her cheek, struggling to meet Lydia's gaze. "You'll recall Luke spoke to the Copperville Church a few weeks back."

The tentative remark prompted an uptick in Lydia's heartbeat. "Y-es."

Chin quivering, Adelaide seemed to pry every word from her lips. "It seems ... several in the congregation were ... quite taken with Luke's sermon."

Sitting forward, Lydia pinched her brow. "He did a fine job. What of it?"

Adelaide folded her hands, her gaze drifting to the oak table. "The church's current pastor has decided to relocate."

Lydia blinked, letting the words soak in. Something in her sister-in-law's tone and demeanor wedged a worrisome knot deep within Lydia's chest. "Surely they couldn't expect Luke to fill in until a replacement pastor is found? It's much too long of a trip."

"Yes, it is." Adelaide lifted moist eyes, her words spilling out in a whisper.

All the air fled from Lydia's lungs as she pondered the full implications of the admission. She swallowed, knowing the answer to her question before she even asked. "Then, what decision is Luke struggling with?"

Adelaide's lips pulled taut, her gaze more intense. "Remember, you mustn't breathe a word to anyone. Luke especially. He must make up his own mind and not be persuaded."

Lydia nodded. "Of course."

With a hesitant sigh, Adelaide eased back in her chair, cradling the babe in her womb. "The church has asked him to consider taking on the pastor position."

Almost without realizing it, Lydia sounded a nervous laugh. "Luke's not a preacher. Why, he would never give up farming to preach at a church so far away."

But Adelaide's arched brow and somber expression suggested otherwise.

"He's ... not seriously considering it? Is he?"

Brushing a crumb from the table, Adelaide pursed her lips.

"He's ... praying about the possibility. As you can tell, the decision is causing him a great deal of turmoil."

Lydia slumped back in her chair, her mind careening back to the day Luke had preached. With each word, his eyes had burst with vibrancy, every fiber of his being engaged. In her heart, she knew he was born for something other than farming. His love for the Lord superseded all else. It always had. She wrapped her arms around her waist, a sickened feeling washing through her. Already, they'd lost dear Papa and Drew and Caroline. To give up Luke and Adelaide would be more than she or Mama could bear.

"Please don't say anything to your mother." Adelaide's plea cut through Lydia's fog. "There's nothing settled as yet. No sense upsetting her needlessly."

"I won't." The hoarse words spilled out, hollowness clawing at Lydia's insides. Despite her promise, her mind instinctively began to concoct ways to dissuade Luke from making the decision he hadn't yet declared. Maybe if she convinced him that leaving would be the death of Mama, he'd stay. But that would require breaking not only her promise to Adelaide but Mama's trust as well.

Adelaide put a hand on Lydia's arm. "I know it's your desire for us to stay, but please pray for the Lord's will in this. No matter our own wishes, it's His plan we must seek."

A twinge of guilt burned inside Lydia. Though she managed a slight nod, inwardly, she balked. Family meant everything to her and wasn't something she could give up easily.

She clenched her jaw. This was one instance in which she would have a hard time seeking the Lord's will above her own.

AFTER MILES OF LONG SILENCE, a rut in the road seemed to jolt not only the wagon but Luke's tongue loose as well. "Ever wrestle with God, Will?"

The unexpected question caught Will off guard. *All the time,* he wanted to say but instead settled on, "We've had our differences."

Luke stared out ahead of them, seeming to speak as much to himself as Will. "Life's going along just fine and then the Lord throws something totally unexpected at you and asks you to make a choice."

A bit flustered, Will slid a glance at his companion. "If this is about what happened with Malloy, I ..."

With a shake of his head, Luke interrupted. "This has nothing to do with Guthrie Malloy. Though, depending on how things go, it may have a bearing on his offer."

Will knit his brows. "I'm not sure I follow."

Luke blew out a long breath and settled the team into a slow walk. "I'm sure you've noticed I've not been myself lately."

Uncertain how to respond, Will shrugged. "I figure you have your reasons."

"That I do, but I've not been fair keeping those reasons to myself. You see, about the time Drew arrived, I received a letter from the church in Copperville. It conveyed news the preacher I filled in for is leaving. They've asked me to take his place."

It took a moment for the words to sink in, but at last, Will understood. "So, are you going to?"

Luke's mouth twisted. "I haven't fully decided. If I take the church, it means Adelaide and I would have to move away, leaving Ma and Lydia without someone to look after them and no one to farm the ground." He looked Will square on. "That's where I haven't been fair."

"How's that?"

"I've given this a lot of thought and prayer but never considered your input. Or Ma and Lydia's, for that matter."

Will could understand Luke wanting his family's say, but why his? "My input?"

With a firm nod, Luke returned his attention to the road. "I wouldn't feel right leaving Ma and Lydia in the lurch. So, if I did take the position, I'd need a trustworthy man, like yourself, to manage the farm."

Will wiped clammy palms on his trousers. Him take over the farm? He'd planned to inform Luke shortly he'd be leaving after the fall harvest. He'd not anticipated this turn of events.

Luke cut him a quick glance. "There aren't too many fellas I'd feel confident entrusting my farm and family to. But I fully believe the Lord brought you here, maybe for this very reason."

Uncomfortable heat crept up Will's neck, and he tugged at his collar. There was that mention of God sending him here again. These Gallaghers seemed determined to convince him of the notion. "I don't know, Luke. I'm not sure I'm ready to settle in one place."

"I know it's a lot to ask. But at least pray about it and consider if you'd be willing."

"What about Malloy? He doesn't have much respect for me. You leaving would give him more cause than ever to try to get his hands on the place."

"Believe me. Malloy is the least of my worries."

"So, you still don't believe him to be a threat?"

"Oh, I've no doubt he's capable of some underhanded ways. I've seen how he takes advantage of people. But I also think you have what it takes to handle him."

At Luke's words, the tension eased from Will's shoulders. "But you'd still consider his offer to purchase some of the property?"

"Only as a last resort." Luke sat forward and tapped the reins down. "If I do leave, the upkeep of the property would mainly fall to you. Though I'd seek permission to take time off in spring and fall to help.

"Now granted, you're a hard worker, but I know how burdensome this much land can be for one man. Malloy's offer would ease your load as well as give Ma and Lydia extra money to live on. Of course, Ma would have the final say. I just need to know where you stand. If you'd be willing to carry the brunt of the load and commit to staying long-term."

A swirl of emotions coursed through Will. Being asked to commit to a place not his own and abandoning his search for his past would indeed be a sacrifice. He'd had every intention of leaving come fall. Luke's request shattered that idea completely. "I don't know, Luke. I'll need time to consider it."

"No hurry. Believe me, I understand." Luke tossed Will a lopsided grin. "I realize I haven't been easy to live with this past week. But this isn't a decision I take lightly. It affects not only Adelaide, me, and our baby but Ma, Lydia, and you as well. Either choice has its drawbacks and blessings." He gave a soft snort. "Here I resented Drew leaving me all the work, and now I'm asking the same of you."

Still struggling with the thought of forfeiting his plans, Will gently posed the question, "If I chose not to stay long-term, would it influence your decision one way or another?"

Luke's cheek flinched. "It might complicate things. But if I know for certain the Lord is calling me to go, no setback will keep me from it."

The avowal both amazed and baffled Will. To possess such strong faith as to put God's will above everything he'd ever known and everyone he held dear seemed unthinkable. Here, Will was desperate to find the home and family he'd lost, and Luke was willing to give his up at the Lord's bidding.

It seemed too great a cost.

Yet, in a way, he envied Luke. His depth of devotion to God went beyond head knowledge or half-hearted commitment. It was at the very center of his being.

What Luke didn't know was that his request forced Will to make an equally difficult decision—to continue his quest for his past or take on a new challenge he wasn't sure he was equipped for.

He was certain of one thing, though. Lydia would never be

content to see a portion of Gallagher land sold to the likes of Malloy.

And neither would Will.

28

Wednesday, June 17, 1868 (1 a.m.)

L ydia fumbled her way to the wicker veranda chair in the dark, still numb from her conversation with Adelaide. She smothered a yawn, fatigued from hours of tossing on her bed. And yet her unsettled mind had driven sleep from her. Try as she may, she'd been unable to pray. Though she'd promised not to attempt to influence Luke's decision, her focus seemed to continually shift to devising a way to convince him to stay.

A bitter root coiled its way deep within her spirit. Never in her remotest dreams had she imagined Luke would consider leaving. He knew the effort and upkeep the farm required and that, without a crop, she and Mama would have no means of income. Surely, he would have enough sense to turn down the church's offer.

Wouldn't he?

Her stomach tightened. Will would be leaving in a few short months as well. One more disappointment she couldn't bear to contemplate.

A tear slid down her cheek, and she swiped it away. She'd managed to brave her way through supper, ducking her head lest Mama or Will detect her red, puffy eyes. Having remained silent through much of the meal, she'd been grateful neither had pressed her for conversation. She'd not even inquired about the busted reaper or where else Will and Luke might have gone.

Nor had Will offered to explain.

The gentlest breeze stirred, carrying the scent of straw in the humid air. Lydia stood and clutched the railing, a serenade of katydids and crickets enlivening the night. Stars shimmered overhead, alleviating some of the darkness. In her sullen mood, the vast night seemed to beckon her, and her gaze fell to the path leading into the open fields. A quiet stroll sounded more enticing than returning to her stuffy bedroom.

With slippered feet, she ventured into the yard, snugging her bed jacket tighter around her. The still, unlit barn assured Will was resting peacefully. Or was he, like her, awake and deep in thought? Resisting the urge to find out, she padded past. Right now, she had no wish to speak with anyone.

An owl hooted in a nearby tree. She sucked in a breath and hugged her arms to her waist. Traipsing around in her night clothes in the middle of the night wasn't seemly. She should turn back. Instead, she trudged on, her mind too muddled to care.

As she neared the wheat field, a man's moan jolted her to a stop. Heart pounding, Lydia spotted movement several yards to her left.

She squinted in the direction of the sound, eyes searching.

Another moan split the night.

She swallowed. *Will?* She'd know that voice anywhere. What was he doing out here?

Following the disturbing noises, she inched closer until she came upon him sleeping at the base of one of the stooks of wheat. Even in the dim light, his restless thrashing gave clue to a violent dream. As Lydia knelt beside him, her foot knocked against something hard. She reached down, and her hand brushed the smooth shaft of a rifle barrel. A weak smile wedged its way past the bleakness in her soul as the reason for his presence became clear.

He was protecting the wheat.

She wiped dampened hair from his brow, longing to quiet his mind and ease his tortured spirit. His head shifted side to side, and she drew her hand away, a sense of helplessness spilling over her.

Placing a hand lightly on his arm, she closed her eyes and bowed her head. *Comfort him, Lord. Rid him of these nightmares that plague his sleep. He's a good man and has brought us so much blessing. Grant him Your presence and peace.*

Opening her eyes, she ran a fingertip over his puckered brow. How her heart ached to free him of this stranglehold that held him captive. She couldn't just leave him here. Not in such an anguished state.

With a determined slant of her chin, she moved down and laid crossways at his feet. She would stay just long enough for him to quiet and then slip away into the night. Nestling onto the stubbled straw, she peered over at Will. Lying so close to a man might not be considered proper, but in Bible times, hadn't Ruth visited Boaz at the threshing floor in the wee hours of the night to claim him as her kinsman redeemer?

This was different, of course, but Will was doing what he could to protect her and her family. How could she abandon him?

And truly, tonight, she needed the comfort of his nearness as much as he needed hers.

WILL STARTLED AWAKE, staring at the blackened sky. Sleeping under the stars, though not as stifling as the barn, hadn't proven any less fearsome where his dreams were concerned. His mind never ceased to fabricate some fiery snare to battle through.

He ventured a glance around, grateful all appeared peaceful.

As he shifted onto his side, his boot knocked against something. Pressing his chin to his chest for a look, he glimpsed a whitish object lying at his feet. Had some critter or stray dog taken him for a safe place to rest?

Propping himself up on his elbow, he pried his eyes wider.

His jaw slackened. That was no animal. It almost looked like ... Lydia?

Will raked a hand through his hair. What was she doing out here? In her night clothes, no less? How had she even known he was here? Surely his restless dreams hadn't awakened her this far from the house.

He considered waking her, then thought better of it. She'd been embarrassed the last time he'd found her out. No need to draw attention to what obviously was another attempt to comfort him. The least he could do was lie still and pretend to sleep, even if sleep alluded him.

Easing back onto the straw bed, he locked his hands together behind his head. She'd seemed upset about something at supper. Hadn't even asked what he and Luke had been up to. Such a lack of curiosity wasn't like her.

No. Something had her troubled. He knew that much.

Will was grateful not to have added to her sorrows by sharing what he and Luke had discussed on the way home. If she didn't have an inkling already, she'd find that out soon enough.

But he didn't intend for it to come from him.

LYDIA YAWNED AND STRETCHED, conscious of a painful kink in her neck. Her eyes shot open as she recalled where she was. She sat up, relieved to find Will resting peacefully.

She rubbed a hand over her neck. When had she fallen asleep? Will's restless dreams had seemed to last for hours. Pure exhaustion must have lulled her to sleep. How grateful she was he'd at last found peaceful slumber and that her presence had gone undetected.

The slightest glimmer of light dawned on the eastern horizon, hinting at the promise of a new day. Resisting the temptation to remain any longer, she soundlessly rose to her feet and brushed bits of straw from her nightgown. With a final glance at Will, she slowly padded toward the house.

A few sweet hours of slumber had dulled the turmoil inside her. But as she cautiously trekked back to the farmhouse, each step seemed to reawaken her restless heart. Her gaze drifted to the open fields, the faintest bit of daylight brightening her way and ushering the first robin's song.

Lifting her face to the heavens, she gazed at the retreating stars and whispered the burdens entwined around her heart. "I don't understand, Lord. Nothing makes sense. Why would You take everyone away? The church can find another pastor. Mama and I need Luke here. He's all we have to keep this place going."

Lips trembling, she brushed a stray strand of hair from her cheek and stole a glance over her shoulder. "Luke ... and Will. Please let them stay."

With a heavy sigh, she pressed on, her soul aching for answers. They were selfish prayers, she knew. But ones that came from the very depths of her soul.

Ones she refused to alter or regret.

29

"The reaper is damaged, you say?"

With a nod to his hostess, Will swallowed his mouthful of biscuit. "Yes, ma'am. We should have it fixed by the end of the day. Tomorrow at the latest."

Mrs. Gallagher wiped the corners of her mouth with her napkin. "Well, at least it's only a minor delay."

Will stole a glance in Lydia's direction, attempting to read the elusive expression in her eyes. For a moment, she looked as though she might say something but reached to sip her apple juice instead. It wasn't like her to hold in her thoughts. Whatever was troubling her had a firm grip. Shadows darkened the skin beneath her eyes. And, if he wasn't mistaken, her eyelids were a tad puffy as though she'd shed more than a few tears.

He didn't mean to stare, but she had him worried. Since he'd come, she'd either been rife with questions or eager to share her opinion. But now, there was a sorrow about her he couldn't place.

What had brought her to the field? Sleeplessness? A troubled mind? Or had his loud dreams truly awakened her? Whatever the case, he was touched by her compassion and ached to ease the burden she seemed to be carrying.

He tipped his coffee cup toward him, noting it was all but empty.

"You need a refill. I'll fetch the coffee pot." Mrs. Gallagher's chair toppled backward as she stood. Clutching a hand to her chest, she uttered a soft moan. She leaned over the table, face ashen.

Lydia flew to her mother's side, placing a hand on her arm. "Are you all right, Mama?"

Through jagged breaths, Mrs. Gallagher managed a slight nod. "I must have risen too quickly. I feel ... a bit faint."

Will stood and clutched his hat. "Would you like me to fetch the doctor?"

With a shake of her head, Mrs. Gallagher straightened. "No. I'll be fine. But perhaps I'd better lie down a spell."

Seeing Lydia's look of desperation, Will moved to offer Mrs. Gallagher his arm. A weak smile touched the older woman's lips as she clasped hold, her grip surprisingly strong. "Thank you, Will. If you'd kindly help me to my bed."

With slow, steady movements, they maneuvered through the dining room and out into the hall. Lydia trundled along beside, brows knit with worry. Though she'd never made mention of concerns over her mother's health, Will had witnessed enough to know something wasn't right. Clutching her skirt in one hand, Lydia rushed ahead to open the bedroom door.

Mrs. Gallagher's color rejuvenated as Will eased her onto the quilted mattress. She patted his hand before releasing it. "Thank you, dear boy. My apologies for not retrieving your coffee."

A sideways grin edged across Will's lips. "That's the least of my worries. You just get feeling better." His gaze flicked to Lydia. "Will you be all right?"

Lydia nodded, a flash of gratitude flickering in her eyes as she settled on the far side of the bed. "We'll be fine. I'll stay with her a while."

Donning his hat, Will dipped his chin. "Let me know if you need anything."

"Will?"

Mrs. Gallagher's breathy voice pinned him in his tracks. "Yes, ma'am?"

"Don't mention this incident to Luke. He has so much on his mind there's no need to worry him with anything more."

Will shifted his gaze from her to Lydia and back again, Mrs. Gallagher's pale blue eyes pleading. "If that's what you want."

With a satisfied nod, the older woman turned away and closed her eyes, arms draped across her middle. Why she'd choose to keep Luke in the dark about the incident, Will couldn't say. But who was he to question her reasoning?

He had his own problems to unravel.

LYDIA TAPPED her hands together behind her back, pacing back and forth outside the barn, evening shadows beginning to spill across the yard. She didn't wish to leave Mama by herself for long, but she needed to speak with Will.

Alone.

It had taken her all day to work up the courage to approach him. She'd not needed the added worry of Mama's health, but if she didn't clear her head, she was going to burst. Promise or no promise, she needed answers. And Lydia had a feeling Will knew more than he let on.

She stilled, her heart leaping to her throat when she saw Will part ways with Luke and head toward the farmhouse. Apparently, the reaper repairs had been more extensive than they'd thought. She'd resisted going out to check how things were progressing. Her emotions were still too raw to face Luke. There was no telling what might pop out of her mouth. And she didn't wish to shed tears before Will *or* her brother.

As Will neared, his gaze fastened on her, a mixture of unease and pleasure in his eyes. He lifted his hat and swiped his sleeve across his sweaty brow as he paused beside her. "How's your mother?"

Lydia warmed at his thoughtfulness. "Better. She slept much of the morning but insisted on helping in the kitchen this afternoon."

A soft smile edged across Will's lips. "She's a strong lady. Much like her daughter."

For a brief moment, their eyes locked, and a shy grin seeped onto Lydia's face. Even with hair in disarray and dirt smudges on his face, Will had never appeared more handsome than in that moment. His gentle spirit and heart of compassion, coupled with his rugged features, left her wobbly.

Shaking herself free of the entrancement, she reminded herself why she'd come. "I ... wanted to thank you for your kindness toward Mama."

He shrugged. "It's easy to be kind to someone who's shown such hospitality. Glad I was handy."

With a scrunch of her nose, Lydia cast him an apologetic glance. "I'm afraid she wasn't up to waiting supper on you. There's a plate of food keeping warm for you on the stove."

He started to back away. "I'll clean up and be right in."

"Will?" Lydia caught him by the arm, his muscles firm beneath her fingers.

"Yes?" His hazel eyes shone with expectancy as he stared down at her.

Lydia swallowed the dryness threatening to choke off her words. Yet, she was determined to speak her mind. "Mama thinks a great deal of you. As do ... I." She withdrew her hand, her breaths shallowing. Heat singed her cheeks as she lowered her gaze to the ground. "We both want you to stay."

A dozen anxious thoughts permeated her as she awaited his response. Did he think her impetuous? Childish? Too forthright?

At last, a warm hand cupped her chin, and her eyes lifted. Tenderness streamed from Will's eyes, and Lydia sensed him edging closer. Responding to his nearness, her pulse quickened.

A hint of a smile edged across his lips as his hand moved to her cheek. "I'm honored."

She leaned into his touch, longing to close the gap between them.

And hopeful he would.

Instead, he merely gazed intently at her as if contemplating whether his current life outweighed the lures of the past.

If he sensed he was truly needed, would he stay? Would he at last be willing to let go of his past and embrace a future here?

With her?

Moistening her lips, she forced out the words that pained her to speak. "Did you know Luke's considering leaving?"

Will's mouth grew taut, and he gave a slight nod. "He told me on our way home from town yesterday."

Relieved she hadn't needlessly broken her promise to Adelaide, Lydia couldn't resist prodding for more. "What did he say? Did he share his intentions?"

Will's hand fell away, the tender moment seeming to melt like springtime snow. Breathing a soft sigh, he eased back, leaving a noticeable void. "It's not my place to say. He'll let you know when he's ready."

Angst bubbled in Lydia's chest. "He's leaving, isn't he?" When Will remained silent, her shoulders sagged. "First Drew and now Luke. It's not right. Family should stay together."

Will's eyes grew distant, and her heart sank. She softened her tone. "I'm sorry. I know how you've longed and searched for your own family."

His pained expression eased slightly, bolstering her courage to speak her thoughts. "But ... could it be you're searching for the wrong thing?"

"How's that?" Will's hardened tone gave her pause.

With a hesitant step closer, she added, "Maybe ... instead of searching for who you once were, you need to seek the man the Lord wants you to be *now*."

Will's cheek flinched, and his whole body seemed to tense as he pinned her with his stare. "And maybe you should stop trying to sway your family to your way of thinking and let God do with them what He wills."

Lydia's mouth hinged open. Obviously, she'd hit a nerve. Though Will hadn't raised his voice, it wasn't like him to be so blunt. Pricked by the sharp retort, she stumbled back. As the full gist of his words soaked in, her emotions shifted from shock to hurt. Just what was he insinuating? That she was controlling, even manipulative, where her family was concerned?

Her chin quivered, and she averted her gaze, moisture brimming in her eyes. Unwilling to shed tears before Will, she hiked her skirt and sprinted toward the house, her spirit and hopes for the future crushed.

30

Will kicked the toe of his boot against the stall door, more ashamed than angry. He'd let his frustration get the better of him. Leaning against the oak sideboards, he raked a hand through his hair. He should have known better than to lash out at Lydia like that. Plainly, his words had hurt her deeply. But there'd be no taking them back. His hasty response would forever be etched in her mind.

It wasn't so much *what* he'd said as how he'd said it. True, Lydia needed to let her family make their own decisions. But declaring that fact in such a straightforward manner and out of resentment for her comment toward him had only made matters worse.

For both of them.

He'd only meant to imply change was inevitable, and the harder she fought against it, the more devastated she was destined to become.

But was he any different? If he was honest, he'd admit Lydia's words held merit as well—that he was so bent on uncovering his past that he was missing what the Lord intended for him in the present.

He glanced at the Bible resting untouched on his bedroll.

Did it hold the answers he longed for? Squatting down, he snatched the worn Book of Scriptures from atop the blanket. He thumbed through its thin pages, uncertain where to even begin. At church a couple of Sundays back, the pastor had quoted a verse that had stuck with him from the book of Jeremiah. How did it go?

Something about God giving His people an expected end.

As he lit a lantern, Will's stomach rumbled. That plate of food awaiting him on the stove sounded pretty good about now. But the notion of facing Lydia again stifled any urge to retrieve it. His appetite could wait. Hopefully later, before heading to the field for the night, he could slip in unaware and not disturb Lydia or her mother.

With a determined huff, he slid open the Bible's leather cover. Shifting toward the light, he ran a finger along the contents page until he located the page number for the book of Jeremiah. He thumbed through the pages to its beginning, then paused to scratch his cheek. Now if only he could recall the chapter and verse.

Uncertain how to locate the particular passage, he randomly leafed through a few pages at a time, finally recalling the chapter was twenty ... something. He flipped a bit farther, noting an occasional verse or two had been underlined. When he came to chapter twenty-nine, he paused. Verses eleven through thirteen were underlined and circled as if of great importance.

Will tapped his finger over verse eleven, immediately recognizing it as the one he'd heard in the sermon.

> *"For I know the thoughts that I think toward you, saith the LORD,*
> *thoughts of peace, and not of evil, to give you an expected end."*

His mouth twisted. It seemed odd to consider God giving thought to him personally.

To give you an expected end.

The phrase almost sounded like the Lord had a plan and a purpose for each individual.

Him included.

Maybe that's why he'd clung to the verse—because it gave him some semblance of hope.

Curiosity pulled his attention to the remaining circled verses, ones he didn't recall the pastor reciting. As he read on, the words seemed to call to his spirit in a way nothing else had.

"Then shall ye call upon me, and ye shall go and pray unto me,
and I will hearken unto you. And ye shall seek me, and find me,
when ye shall search for me with all your heart."

Will read and reread the verses, soaking in the words as if they were the very air he breathed. He'd spent years in search of an identity and his forgotten past, never once considering the importance of seeking the Lord.

Every thought and prayer had revolved around *his* wants and wishes. When they'd gone unfulfilled, he'd lost all interest in a relationship with God. In his disappointment, he'd more or less shut God—and everyone else—out of his life.

Until he'd come here, and the Gallaghers had taken him in as one of their own. Whether he'd fully admitted it to himself or not, he'd come to care for them like family.

Lydia, especially.

His chest tightened. And now he'd hurt her. Would she find it in her heart to forgive him?

She'd given him a lot to think on. As did these verses.

He read them again, trying to etch them on his fractured mind. What did it mean to seek God with all your heart? He wasn't sure what that looked like or how to begin. One thing was certain: if he'd put half the effort into seeking God that he'd put into finding his family, his soul would be in a lot better place by now.

Will bowed his head, his voice soft and low. "Forgive me for pushing You away, Lord. Lydia was right. I've had my priorities all turned around. It's *You* I need to seek. For whatever reason, my old self, my past, is gone. Show me how to become the man You desire me to be. Help me embrace the life You've given me here and now instead of longing for something that may never be."

Something rubbed against his leg. He opened his eyes to see Basil at his feet. Clutching the Bible close to his chest, he leaned to stroke the cat on the back, and a soft purr sounded. The amber streams of sunlight filtering through cracks in the oak boards began to fade as the dark shadows of twilight took hold in their stead. Will settled onto the strawed barn floor, not having the heart to cast Basil aside when he curled in his lap. The cat might be just the company he needed.

He reached to brighten the lantern flame, the glow of light growing more vivid. Having missed supper, he had a little time to burn before heading to the wheat field. Might as well start reading. Opening the Bible again, he turned to Genesis. If he was going to seek God, what better place to start than the beginning?

With a deep breath, he held the Bible closer to the flame and read. *In the beginning, God created the heaven and the earth ...*

LYDIA LAY face down on her bed, muffling her cries in her feather pillow. As if her worry over Mama's health and fears that Luke and Adelaide would soon leave weren't enough, now she was at odds with Will. Her insides ached from the crushing weight on her spirit. Thankfully, Mama had retired early, allowing Lydia to slip up to her bedroom unnoticed. Giving full vent to her sorrows, she could only pray her anguished cries wouldn't carry beyond her bedroom door.

Maybe you should stop trying to sway your family to your way of thinking and let God do with them what He deems best.

Will's candid words came rushing back, playing over and over in her head like an annoying crow cawing outside her window. To think, she'd been ready, eager even, for him to draw her into his strong embrace. Instead, he'd turned on her, more or less implying she was manipulative and conniving.

The thought triggered a fresh barrage of tears. She buried her face in her pillow once more, chest heaving from the intensity of her sobs. When she opened her eyes again, dark shadows had settled over the room. She blinked burning eyes and slid a handkerchief from her pocket. Giving her nose a firm blow, she curled up on her side and stared aimlessly at her surroundings.

Her gaze drifted to the daguerreotype photo of her family on the bedstand, and her chest squeezed. The photograph had been taken mere months before Papa and Drew left for the war.

A lone tear slid down her cheek as she reached for the treasured keepsake. With a sniffle, she traced a finger along each image, memories of better days flooding back. Though each face bore only a hint of a smile, there was no mistaking the love and admiration the family shared for one another in their pose and touch.

She heaved a jagged sigh. So much had changed since then. Barely eleven at the time, Lydia had had no inkling of what the turbulent years of war would bring—death, separation, hardship. Nor would she have guessed how fragmented her family would become so soon after the war.

Thoughts of Will wove their way in. Though she pitied his having lost contact with his family, his insensitivity to her family's plight hadn't set well. He had no right to judge her for wanting Luke and Adelaide to stay. After all, she was merely thinking of the best interests of the farm and Mama's well-being.

Wasn't she?

A catch in her spirit implied there was more. A reality she couldn't yet own up to. Unable to rid herself of the swirl of resentment clouding her mind, she snugged the photo to her chest and closed her eyes. Will could think what he wished of her, but she refused to let go of this family without a fight.

———

A DISTANT GUNSHOT echoed from outside the bedroom window, frightening Lydia awake. Enveloped in darkness, she sat up in bed, still fully clothed and clutching the photo of her family. She must have fallen asleep. Rising to her feet, she replaced the photo to the bedstand, curious why someone would be shooting in dark of night.

With soft bootsteps, she tiptoed over to the window for a look. An orange glow danced in the distance. She sucked in a breath, recognizing at once the fire was located near the stooks of wheat. Though the flames appeared rather minor, they would no doubt spread quickly amid the dry stalks. She could only pray Will was sleeping nearby and taken notice.

Had he fired the shot to alert them?

Or at an intruder?

She fumbled her way to the door and down the stairs, pausing momentarily outside Mama's bedroom. To her relief, steady breaths rose and fell. Lydia continued down the hall to the front door, heart pounding. She'd need something to help smother the fire.

The glow of starlight guided her way to the dark barn. Stepping inside, she groped for the shovel in the corner. "Will?"

Silence.

When no answer came, Lydia hurried outside and trotted along the path toward the field. To her relief, the fire seemed to diminish in size the nearer she came to it. In the flickering glow, she caught sight of Will slapping at the small flames with a shirt or blanket. She joined him, stamping out the flames spreading along the ground with the back of the shovel.

Setting grievances aside, they battled together to save the wheat crop. A charred smell hung in the air as the last of the flames was snuffed out. In the dim starlight, Lydia ventured a glance at Will, grateful he couldn't see her tear-stained face.

He swept an arm over his brow and stared back at her. "Thanks for the help."

Through shallow breaths, she forced herself to speak. "What happened?"

"Someone rode in on horseback and set the wheat ablaze. I hollered just as he was about to light another heap and scared him off. I fired a warning shot in his direction, and he groaned. So I'm pretty sure I winged him."

"If so, then we'll know who's to blame." Lydia stared in the direction of the cottage, too far away to see in the dark. Likely Luke and Adelaide hadn't been awakened by the shot and were entirely unaware of the incident. Despite her hurt and frustration with Will, Lydia couldn't negate the fact that his diligence had spared her family a great deal of loss. Pivoting toward him, she wrenched the words from her throat. "Thank you."

Without waiting for a reply, she turned on her heels and started along the path toward the house. A few steps later, she slowed her pace, secretly wishing Will would follow and plead her forgiveness.

But he didn't.

And her heart broke a smidgen more.

31

L uke shook his head, taking in the charred section of wheat. "I still can't believe someone would be so heartless." Thumbing his hat higher on his forehead, he peered over at Will. "If you hadn't taken it upon yourself to keep watch, we'd have lost most, if not all, of our crop."

Unaccustomed to praise, Will raked his boot through the ashes at the foot of the stook of wheat. "Too nice of wheat to have destroyed."

"Can't argue that." Luke clapped him on the shoulder. "We're all deeply indebted to you. And you've convinced me we need to keep guard until the wheat is harvested and ready to take into town. Not a pleasant way to sleep, but we can alternate. I'll stay out here tonight."

Will shook his head. "You've a wife with child to tend to. I don't mind sleepin' under the stars. Sort of gives a person time to think."

Luke's blue eyes scrunched slightly. "You sure? 'Cause I'd be more than willing to take a turn."

"I'm sure. I doubt he'll be back anyway after last night."

Motioning toward the reaper, Luke stepped in that direction. "You still convinced it's Malloy?"

"Yep." Will fell into pace beside him. "I'm certain of it."

With an exasperated breath, Luke tugged at his sleeves. "Well, we'll worry about him later, once we get the rest of this wheat harvested. If you'll go harness the team, I think I can have this reaper finished when you get back."

Will cast a glance over his shoulder as he headed toward the barn. Was it his imagination, or did Luke seem more like himself this morning? *Despite* news of the nighttime visitor.

Had he made his decision?

As he turned back around, Will gave a soft sigh. Now if only he could right things with Lydia. Though she'd willingly come to his aid last night, it seemed all she could do to squeeze out a word of thanks. And this morning at breakfast, she'd barely uttered a sound. Part of her melancholy mood could be from concern over her mother, but he had a feeling the majority had to do with yesterday's harsh exchange.

He longed to tell her he'd given serious thought to her words and had delved into Scripture. But something told him she needed time and space to work through the incident.

As things were, he figured the wider berth he gave her, the better.

A RECOGNIZABLE HUM outside the farmhouse window pulled Lydia's attention to the worn path. "Mrs. Perkins is here."

Mama nodded and finished pouring milk into a container. "Fetch the butter, will you dear?"

As Lydia retrieved the slab of butter, she kept a close watch on her mother. Other than the dark shadows under her eyes, she appeared her normal self. Still, yesterday's episode at breakfast had Lydia on edge.

Not to mention all the other tensions plaguing her.

Between Mama, Luke, Will, and Guthrie Malloy, Lydia had been fortunate to garner two winks of sleep. Pushing her troubled thoughts aside, she gathered the tin of butter and the container of milk. "I'll take them, Mama."

"Thank you, dear."

With a heavy heart, Lydia toted the basket of items down the hall and onto the veranda. Trading milk and butter for honey and eggs with their neighbors had been an ongoing practice since the war when the two families found it necessary to downsize their livestock and pool their assets.

Hal and Celia Perkins were as fine of neighbors as Guthrie Malloy was vexing. Yet today, Lydia found it difficult to muster a smile as Mrs. Perkins greeted her from the veranda stoop. "Good mornin', Miss Lydia. How fares ya this fine day?"

Forcing a grin, Lydia strode over. "I'm well. And you?"

"No complaints." The dark-skinned woman cocked her head, her brown eyes scrunching. "Your words say one thing, but your face tells another tale."

It was impossible to fool Celia Perkins. Having known Lydia since birth, the woman could see through any pretense. "I suppose I've ... a lot on my mind." Her gaze drifted past Mrs. Perkins to Will steering the harnessed team toward the wheat field.

The neighbor craned her neck for a look and released a humored chuckle. "I can see that."

Realizing the message her comment and gawking must have conveyed, Lydia's eyes darted back to her neighbor. "Oh, I didn't mean—"

"No need to explain, child. I had the same flustered look about me when Hal first came around."

Heat singed Lydia's cheeks. "But it isn't Will. Well, it is, but it's Mama and other things as well."

Mrs. Perkins's face pinched. "Is your mama still ailin'?"

"She ... wears out easily and seems to be worsening."

With a shake of her head, Mrs. Perkins handed Lydia the basket of honey and eggs and took the carrier Lydia held in its place. "I hates t' hear it. Your mama is such a fine woman. Hal and I'll surely keep her in our prayers."

"Thank you."

Mrs. Perkins held Lydia's gaze, the woman's kind eyes seeming to invade every unseen crevice of Lydia's mind. "Is there somethin' else troublin' ya?"

Lydia slid her tongue over the back of her teeth, trying to resist the urge to divulge more than she should. But she needed *someone* to confide in. Someone with wisdom and discernment. With a slight nod, she slipped a glance over her shoulder to ensure Mama wasn't listening. Satisfied they were alone, Lydia set her basket on the veranda and downed the steps.

Bending closer to Mrs. Perkins, she softened her tone. "I've been asked to keep confidences within the family. Confidences that, if honored, could have a huge impact on the future of our farm and family. If told, some changes might be avoided, and the family spared grief."

Lydia swallowed, attempting to calm the shakiness in her voice. "I feel caught, uncertain what the right thing to do is. Should I go against their wishes and tell what I know?"

The older woman's mouth twisted, the wrinkles in her left cheek pulling taut. For a long moment, she said nothing but merely studied Lydia. At last, she spoke, her voice soft yet firm. "I s'pose that depends on whether your motive is for your family's sake or your own."

Lydia blinked. Her motive? She'd never considered the actual reason she wished to break confidence and convey the information. She only knew the thought of Luke and Adelaide leaving devastated her. Tipping her chin higher, she ignored the tension mounting inside her. "I just don't want to see decisions made that would later be regretted." The words left a bitter taste in her mouth. Though the reason sounded valid, in her heart, Lydia knew it wasn't entirely true.

Not even close.

Her stomach gripped. Will was right. She was inclined to break one or both of her mother and sister-in-law's trust more for *her* sake than theirs. Her aspirations to keep the family together and the farm intact had overshadowed any viable reasoning.

"What is it, young'un? Ya look as if you've a burr lodged in your throat."

Struggling to find her voice, Lydia choked down her pride. "What I said isn't true. It's for selfish reasons I wish to break their confidences." She lowered her head. "I realize that now."

Warm fingers cradled her cheek, drawing her gaze back to her companion. "Maybe it's the Lord you need to be tellin' 'stead of me, child."

Moisture blurred Lydia's vision as she offered a weak nod. So focused was she on her own desires, she'd completely closed her heart to the Lord's intentions.

A gentle smile touched the older woman's lips. "Then I'll leave the two of ya to hash things out. Give my love to your mama."

"I will." Blinking back tears, Lydia caught Mrs. Perkins by the arm. "And ... thank you."

With a firm squeeze of Lydia's hand, the kindly neighbor gave a soft chuckle. "I did nothin'. 'Twas the Lord's prompting that revealed the truth of the matter. You and Him go have a nice long chat. He'll set things aright."

Lydia's spirit lifted. "I'll do that."

As Mrs. Perkins started for home, she called over her shoulder. "Remember, child, sometimes the Lord takes us down paths we don't wish to go to get us where we need to be."

Lydia returned a reluctant wave, her cluttered mind failing to make sense of the swirl of words. Drawing a deep breath, she turned her eyes heavenward. She and the Lord indeed had some solemn reckoning to do.

A conversation which was long overdue.

WILL SLID the harness from Chloe's back, the scent of sweat wafting out at him. By the looks of their lathered coats, both horses could stand a good rubdown. He'd fetch the brush and give them a quick grooming before supper. After pulling the reaper in the hot sun all day, they deserved some sort of reward.

Luke slapped Molly on the rump, and the horse trotted out to pasture. Brushing his gloved hands together, he peered over at Will. "One more day oughta do it for wheat harvest. In another week, you'll have your earnings in hand."

Will nodded. "Sounds good to me."

A few days ago, money in his pockets would have heightened Will's readiness to be on his way. But circumstances had changed. Searching for his past no longer had a grip on him. Not that he wouldn't jump at the chance should the opportunity arise. He just refused to let it eat at him. Though moving forward still held its challenges, he would simply place it in the Lord's hands and accept whatever He thought best.

He had Lydia to thank for that.

Opening his heart and mind to Scripture had allowed Will a whole new perspective. From now on, he'd trust the Lord to direct his way rather than struggle to carve out his own path. If God truly had a purpose and plan for his life, that's what he was determined to seek.

With a satisfied breath, Will slipped the bit from Chloe's mouth. Glad to be free of her restraints, the horse shook her head side-to-side and kicked up her heels as she trotted to join Molly.

Hefting the harness onto his shoulder, Will started toward the barn.

Luke quickly fell into step beside him. "Say, Will. Adelaide and I were wondering if you'd join us for supper this evening?"

The unusual request caught Will off guard. While Luke and his wife had joined them on occasion for a meal at the farmhouse, this would be his first invite to eat with *them*. "I'll be there. Soon as I clean up and let your ma know I won't be at supper."

Luke's furrowed brow smoothed. "Sounds good. If you'll take this harness, I'll go let Adelaide know you're coming."

Shouldering the harness, Will glimpsed Lydia making her way to the farmhouse, her labored steps hinting at fatigue. She'd worked tirelessly much of the afternoon, not uttering a word to him or Luke. More than once, he'd considered offering some word of affirmation as she worked to bind the sheaves of wheat. But her silence seemed to indicate conversation wouldn't be welcomed.

Oddly, he'd noticed she'd spent a good portion of the morning near the house. He'd assumed it was due to a reluctance to leave her mother unattended, yet her aimless wandering around the yard lent more to an unsettled spirit. Was she still sulking over their exchange or was something else troubling her?

Maybe it was for the best Luke had asked him to supper. Squaring things with Lydia would take time, and he didn't intend to rush her. Avoiding her might not be the best way to handle the situation, but it allowed him more time to pray ...

And her, more time to heal.

32

Saturday evening, June 20, 1868

Lydia set the bowl of steaming mashed potatoes on the table and slid into the chair beside Will, keenly aware of his presence but unwilling to glance his way. Though they'd spoken only out of necessity since their confrontation earlier in the week, her anger at him had subsided. She'd spent much of that time wrestling with the Lord, finally concluding it was fruitless to argue against Him. Yet, submitting to His will when it wasn't in line with her own was proving a challenge.

Across the table from her, Luke and Adelaide remained uncharacteristically quiet, their expressions difficult to read, anxious one minute and blissful the next. They'd requested this family meal under the guise of celebrating the end of wheat harvest. But their demeanor hinted of something more substantial. Plainly they'd made their decision, and Lydia's heart told her it would be a difficult one to accept.

With an amiable smile, Mama stretched her arms out along the table and clasped Lydia and Adelaide by the hands. "We have so much to be grateful for, not least of all each other. Wherever the Lord takes us in life, whether near or far away, we'll never be far from each other in spirit."

The comment garnered an immediate reaction from Lydia's brother and sister-in-law—Luke raising his brows in question and Adelaide responding with a faint shrug of her shoulder.

Lydia, too, sat somewhat stunned, wondering if she'd inadvertently let the news slip. Convinced she hadn't and that neither Luke nor Adelaide had either, she risked an inquisitive glance at Will. But nothing in his countenance seemed to suggest he'd shared their "secret."

Perhaps Luke's unwelcome news wouldn't come as such a shock to her mother after all.

Or was she referring to something else entirely?

Mama's gaze settled on Luke. "Would you say grace, son?"

Normally the warmth of Mama's touch brought a sense of contentment, but the dread of what almost certainly was to come produced a wave of disquiet within Lydia as she bowed her head. Luke's prayer was lost to her as she silently prayed her own, pleading once again for the Lord's mercy in allowing Luke to stay and for her ability to accept whatever news came.

At his firm "amen," Lydia opened her eyes and, as inconspicuously as possible, swiped the damp outer corners with the back of her finger. Mama gave her hand a gentle squeeze, and a twinge of pain shot through her palm, still tender from the constant binding of sheaves.

The mood was anything but celebratory as they filled their plates and began to eat. At last, Luke ventured to speak, his voice sounding forced, unsteady. "The wheat did real well this year. Better yield than we've seen in a while. Corn came up good, too."

"That's welcome news, son, especially with your little one arriving soon."

"Yes." Luke cleared his throat, casting a sideways glance at Adelaide. "I always intended to be a farmer. Never had ambitions for anything else."

Mama arched a brow, stirring a spoonful of sugar into her tea. "But now you have."

The words hung in the air, more statement than question. Lydia's pulse ticked loud against the stillness. Her fingernails dug into the fleshy part of her thumbs as she clenched her fists tighter in her lap. She held her breath, dreading his response.

Luke leaned forward in his chair, resting his forearms on the table with a sigh. "I got a taste of preaching, and it doesn't wanna let go."

Mama's pensive smile held a trace of wistfulness. "That's not surprising, son. You always did have a heart for the Lord."

Amazed at Mama's calmness, Lydia's gaze darted between the two of them. Deep down she knew Luke was meant to share his faith. His love for God had always been his passion. She envied him that.

Deep in her heart, she aspired to be that dedicated to the Lord herself someday.

Luke raked a hand through his hair, clearly struggling. "Yes, but I never dreamed He'd call me to a ministry and ask me to leave my family."

"Is it the church in Copperville, son? Have they asked you to be their pastor?"

Confusion rippled across Luke's face. "Yes, but how did you know?"

Mama's smile deepened. "A mother tends to have intuition about such things. It was written in your eyes as you spoke, in the enthusiasm of your voice, and on the face of every person in that church. I've known ever since it was only a matter of time before you'd realize your calling. I've been praying for just that, though my heart breaks to see you and Adelaide go."

A blend of relief and regret seemed to spill across Luke's and Adelaide's faces. With a sigh, Luke fixed his gaze at Mama. "It's been a gut-wrenching decision. One we're still not completely at peace with. My heart longs to serve the Lord, but the thought of leaving you and Lydia and this place tears me up inside."

Mama gave a slow nod. "A difficult sacrifice, to be sure. For all of us. But remember, son, Jesus said we mustn't place anyone or anything above our allegiance to the Lord. Not even family. If you feel called to ministry, that's where you belong."

Food suddenly lost all appeal for Lydia. Warring within, she set her fork aside. Try as she may, she'd been unable to fully yield her will to God. Mama saw everything in black and white. She didn't know Will planned to leave come fall. How would the two of them manage? Didn't Scripture also say one was to provide for his family?

Before she could stop herself, the words oozed out like a boiling pan of gravy. "But Luke, I think you should know that Mama—"

Thin fingers gripped Lydia's arm, stilling her mid-sentence. "Supports you completely in your decision."

Mama's pointed stare made clear she wanted nothing more said. Deterred, Lydia edged back in her seat. Her mother's desire to keep Luke in the dark about her failing health made sense now. She'd had an inkling all along the Lord was calling him away, and wanted nothing to influence his decision.

Lydia's stomach dipped. With so much to lose, Mama had still put God's will ahead of her own. Something, thus far, Lydia had failed to do.

His countenance lifting, Luke clasped Adelaide's hand. "We've worked everything out. The elders have agreed to allow me a few weeks off in both spring and fall so I can help with planting and harvest. And Will has agreed to stay on indefinitely, so you'll have someone nearby to look out for you when I'm unable to."

Lydia's eyes snapped to Will, meeting his gaze but an instant before he looked away. Had she heard right? Will was staying? But he'd been so determined to leave.

"Then I'd say we're in good hands." Mama's blithe voice cut through Lydia's fog. "I can't think of anyone outside of my boys whom I'd rather entrust our needs to."

A hint of a grin edged across Will's lips. "Thank you, Mrs. Gallagher."

She wagged a finger at him. "And it's high time you stop being so formal and call me Martha."

His smile deepened. "Yes ma'am."

Lydia tried to catch his eye, hoping to read the genuineness of his expression, but he returned to his meal. Did Will's invitation to eat with Luke and Adelaide last night have a bearing on his decision to stay?

As the conversation shifted to more ordinary topics, Lydia glanced around the table, drinking in each face and expression. She was beginning to glimpse what true devotion to the Lord looked like. Each of them—even Will—was making sacrifices to do what they felt was right.

Blinking back the moisture stinging her eyes, Lydia again took up her fork. If they were willing to yield their wills in obedience to God, perhaps it was time she did the same.

"MAY I COME IN?"

Lydia's soft voice from outside the barn pulled Will from the verse he was reading. He slid a finger in to hold his place and snapped the Bible shut. "Sure."

The barn door creaked open, and Lydia eased inside. "Am I interrupting?"

"No. Just reading." He stood and brushed straw from his pants, guessing by the stunned look on her face earlier in the evening she'd come to learn more about his decision to stay.

She inched closer. "Reading?"

He held up the Bible, finger still wedged in place. "I figure it's time the Lord and I get better acquainted."

"Really?"

Even in the shadowy lantern light, Will couldn't miss her vibrant smile as she edged closer. She wore her hair down, her golden locks caressing smooth cheeks. It was all he could do to keep from reaching to touch one of the soft strands.

Though her expression bore no remnant of anger, Will needed her to know he'd taken her words to heart. Clutching the Bible tighter, he swallowed his unease. "What you said the other day made a lot of sense. I've put off living far too long. Time to stop chasing the past and live the life I've been given."

"Then it's true?" Her blue eyes widened, her voice barely above a whisper. "You plan to stay?"

Warmth flooded his chest at the flicker of hope dancing in her eyes. "As long as I'm needed. Or until I outstay my welcome."

A shy grin slipped onto her lips. "I don't see that happening anytime soon. Without Luke here, Mama and I will be deeply indebted for your help."

With a tentative step closer, Will shrugged. "After our last conversation, I wasn't sure you wanted me here. No hard feelings?"

She shook her head, her grin fading. "I've thought a lot about what you said as well."

Noting the slight tremor in her voice, he touched a hand to her arm. "I spoke out of frustration. I'm sorry."

"Don't be. You were right. Though I didn't fully realize it until tonight." Lantern light glistened in her eyes, and a single tear trailed down her cheek. "I've been struggling so hard to keep this family together, I completely ignored the Lord's bidding. Luke, Adelaide, Mama, even you, have been seeking God's will while I've been busy attempting to do His job for Him."

Will gently brushed away the tear. "Seems we both had some hard lessons where God is concerned."

"So it does." She stared at him long and hard as if struggling to let go of her words. At last, in a meek voice, she said, "Perhaps we should pray together."

Heat singed Will's cheeks. He'd never prayed out loud. At

least not to his knowledge. But to refuse such a request didn't seem proper. Dropping his arm to his side, he shifted his weight from one foot to the other. "My words may not be pretty. I don't have the gift of speaking Luke does."

The muscles in her face relaxed. "They only need to be sincere."

Instinctively, Will reached for her hand. Rather than pull away, her delicate fingers latched onto his. As they bowed their heads, Will sensed something deep and meaningful pass between them as though their spirits were being woven together by their openness.

And for the first time he could recall, he felt he was where he belonged.

33

Monday, June 29, 1868

Lydia packed the iron skillet in the crate, then peered over at Adelaide, shoulders drooped. "I wish you could at least stay until after the baby arrives."

"I wish so, too, but that's likely another month away. The church has been more than patient in waiting for Luke's answer. We would hate to put them off longer." Easing into a straight-back chair, Adelaide blew out a breath and slid a hand along her rounded abdomen. "It's best we get settled in before the baby comes."

With a sigh, Lydia gathered the stack of utensils and placed them in the box. "It's just hard to see you go and not even get to meet my new niece or nephew."

"Corn harvest isn't but three months away. Trust me, when we come, you'll have all the time you wish to get acquainted with our little one."

Lydia scoffed. "*When* you come. You mean *if* you come."

Adelaide's brows pinched. "You don't believe we'll be back?"

With a shrug, Lydia puckered her cheek. "Drew had every

intention of returning home in spring and harvest, too, and it rarely happens."

Adelaide tipped her head to the side. "Drew's situation is different. His job is more demanding. Luke has already prearranged time off, and the church elders have agreed."

"How do you know that won't change?"

Adelaide clasped Lydia's arm, drawing her gaze. "Because I know Luke. He doesn't take his commitments lightly. He may feel called to the ministry, but he also has a deep sense of responsibility to provide for you and your mother." She eased back in her chair, her violet eyes shimmering. "At least until someone else comes along to take his place."

The slight upturn in Adelaide's lips and the lilt in her voice brought a flush of warmth to Lydia's cheeks. Her pulse quickened as she recalled their previous conversation about Will. Had Adelaide perceived the two of them growing closer? Lydia could still feel the warmth of his hand entwined with hers as they prayed together and the sense of rightness surrounding the sacred moment.

Attempting to quell the remark, Lydia returned to filling the crate. "You're right. Luke always keeps his word. I shouldn't doubt him."

"And Will? What are your thoughts of him?"

Unable to ignore the direct query, Lydia stifled a grin. Keeping her eyes trained on her work, she schooled her voice lest her regard for Will appear obvious. "I'm thankful he's decided to stay. I feared we might lose him as well."

"Yes. Luke's decision would have been much more difficult had Will not agreed to remain here."

Lydia peered into the filled crate, her eyes glossing over. "He sacrificed much to stay."

Her short rest over, Adelaide pushed to her feet and pressed a hand to her lower back. "I won't speculate what Will has given up, but I do know he's a good man. Certainly a blessing to this family. Did you know he insisted on sleeping near the harvested wheat for better than a week to ensure no one tampered with it?"

Lydia's heart leaped at the sense of pride her friend's statement evoked. Memories of secretly laying at Will's feet prompted a timid smile. "Yes. I know. We'd likely not have had a crop if not for him."

"It's plain you think highly of him."

A tinge of heat again flamed in Lydia's cheeks. "Is it?"

"Why, yes." There was something delightfully tantalizing in Adelaide's tone. She leaned closer, voice low. "And from what I've witnessed, Will holds you in similar regard."

Lydia fought to breathe, never dreaming her affections for Will were so transparent. Did he truly think highly of her? As long as his past had loomed between them, she'd not dared to hope he would embrace thoughts of a future with her.

But now. Now that he'd decided to stay and give up his search, was there a chance love could grow?

A hint of anticipation throttled in her chest. Though it pained her to see unwelcome changes come to their family, somehow the future didn't appear as bleak as she'd anticipated.

She restrained a grin. Perhaps the Lord intended to prove to her change wasn't always disagreeable.

LUKE CLIMBED on the wagon seat outside the grist mill, a broad smile on his lips and a thin wad of money in his hand. "The Lord was kind to us. There was enough wheat to get credit for Ma's flour with plenty left over for ready cash." He portioned out some of the bills and pushed them toward Will. "Hopefully this will be enough to make your efforts over the past couple months worthwhile."

Quickly summing up the bills in his hand, Will arched a brow. "That's more than generous. Thank you." He slid the money in his pocket, his fingers knocking against his pocket watch. Maybe now he could afford to have it fixed.

Stuffing the remainder of the cash in his trousers pocket with one hand, Luke clapped Will on the back with his other. "Well deserved. Every bit of it. Now, if you'll drive me to the livery, I'll pick up the horse and carriage for our trip."

With a brisk nod, Will took up the reins. "How soon till you leave?"

"Tomorrow morning, if we can get everything in order."

So soon? Will tapped the reins across the horses' rumps, and the wagon jolted forward.

"A gutsy move to leave what you know behind and try something new."

Leaning forward, Luke rested his elbows on his knees. "It was a hard decision. One I never thought I'd have to make. But I've learned, when you feel the Lord's tug, it's best not to argue."

"I'm learning that." Will had had his share of warring against God. Learning to trust wasn't easy. He blew out a breath. "I envy you knowing what God wants of your life."

"Why envy that? You've been a godsend to our family since day one. It was no accident you happened upon Adelaide and me on the road that day."

"Never thought of it that way." The wagon wheels churned louder, and the busy street became a blur as Will soaked in his companion's words. Was that true? The encounter seemed so happenstance. Had the Lord planned for him to come here all along? Is that why it felt so ... right?

"Well, I have. Dozens of times. It's one of the reasons I'm comfortable with my decision to leave. I know you'll not only look after the farm but Ma and Lydia as well."

His friend's confidence bolstered Will's resolve. "I'll do my best."

"I know you will." With a soft chuckle, Luke gave him a good-natured slap on the arm. "Just think. Starting tomorrow, you'll be your own boss, and the cottage house will be yours for the using. No more sleeping on the hard ground."

Will cut him a sideways glance. "Won't you need it when you come home?"

"Nah. Adelaide and I can stay in the farmhouse with Ma and Lydia. No sense letting the cottage sit empty when you need a decent place to lay your head."

His own boss and a place of his own. Added benefits Will hadn't bargained on. He squared his shoulders, a hint of a grin tugging at his lips. "I'm not eager to see you go, but I have to admit that takes some of the sting out of it."

A hearty laugh erupted from his companion. "I thought it might. And you'll have no worries about interrupting anyone's sleep."

"That's certain." Will maneuvered the team around a stack of crates piled along the street. Come to think of it, his nightmarish dreams hadn't plagued him quite so often since he'd been spending his evenings reading Scripture. Maybe saturating his mind with godly images was ridding him of the negative ones.

Another added blessing.

As they neared the livery, Will bristled at sight of the bearded man on horseback jawing with another fellow outside the building. With a subtle nod of his chin, he leaned towards Luke. "Look who's here."

Luke straightened, his gaze fastened on Guthrie Malloy. "Huh. This should be interesting."

Tugging the team to a halt outside the livery, Will scrutinized Malloy for signs of injury. Though none stood out, the underhanded neighbor held his reins in his left hand instead of his right.

Malloy's eyes flared as he swung his head in their direction. Quickly tapering off his conversation with his companion, he tapped his mare's flanks and awkwardly reined her over. He peered into the empty wagon bed littered with bits of straw, his rigid grin settling on Luke. "Well now, it appears you've finally sold your wheat."

No thanks to you. Will wanted to say. He climbed from the wagon, gnawing his cheek lest he spout something he shouldn't.

In his ever-patient way, Luke secured the brake and nodded. "Minus a few mishaps, we made out all right."

"Good. Good." Malloy sat forward in his saddle, raking a hand over his wiry beard. "Say, I uh, hear rumors you're leaving the area. Don't suppose there's any truth to 'em?"

"That's right." Hopping from the wagon, Luke wielded a lopsided grin. "As of next Sunday, my wife and I will be pastoring a church in Pennsylvania."

"Well, ain't that somethin'? Who'd a thought you'd leave the farm to be a ... *clergyman?*"

Though Will would have taken offense at the way Malloy spewed the word, Luke's smile only widened. "It stunned me as well, but when God calls, we'd best listen."

One of Malloy's bushy brows shot up. "So, with both you boys away, who'll be manning the farm? Or are you ready to sell?"

"Nope. No plans to sell." Luke gestured toward Will. "I'll be back to help come planting and harvest seasons, but Will here will be in charge while I'm away."

"Is that so?" Malloy's upper lip twitched, his gaze flicking from Luke to Will. "Pretty brave of you, Gallagher, leaving your place in the hands of a ... hired hand."

Luke crossed his arms over his chest and leaned against the wagon bed. "Oh, I don't know. Will can handle himself pretty well. Even saved our wheat harvest from a would-be saboteur."

The slightest hint of unease flashed in Malloy's eyes. "You don't say?"

"Yep. He's pretty sure he winged the fellow who did it."

Leveling his gaze, Will propped the toe of his boot between wagon wheel spokes. "I notice you're favoring your right arm."

Malloy's brows dipped as his eyes locked with Will's. "Stiff shoulder. I came off my horse a few days back."

The man's hefty mount appeared anything but flighty. Will slid a hand down her face. "For an avid rider like yourself, that seems mighty careless. Or a bit too coincidental."

Malloy's expression hardened. "You've got some nerve accusin' me." He started to dismount.

Like a protective older brother stepping in to keep peace, Luke wedged in front of Will and motioned for Malloy to stay put. "No one's accusing you, Guthrie, but the fact is someone's been out to waylay our wheat." Luke stuck up a hand. "I'm not sayin' it's you, but I want to make one thing perfectly clear. Our land is not for sale to you or anyone else and any attempt to ruin us or our chances at a decent crop will be met with firm resistance."

The man's eyes narrowed, his lips turning downward in a scowl. "Your loss, Gallagher. I'll enjoy watching your hired man here fall on his face. Then you'll beg me to take your property off your hands. Only then, my price may not be so generous." He snickered as he wheeled his horse in the opposite direction.

"Oh, and Malloy?" Will called after him. "I'm a lot better shot when I can see who I'm shooting at."

Though he didn't turn around, Malloy paused, his shoulders seeming to harden with tension. At last, he gave his mare a firm tap with his heels and trotted away.

Will and Luke shared a discerning grin. "Now that he knows where we stand, hopefully you'll have seen the last of Guthrie Malloy," Luke said under his breath.

"Hope so." The warning had indeed been straightforward.

But men like Malloy didn't scare easily.

34

Lydia closed her eyes, melting into her brother's warm embrace and willing tears not to fall. She was determined not to let her emotions get the better of her. Luke kissed her cheek as he pulled away, and her throat tightened. Goodbyes never got easier. But at least this time he wasn't leaving to fight in a war.

He cocked his head and smiled. "Don't look so glum. We'll see you in a few short months, baby in tow."

Drawing a jagged breath, she blinked moisture from her eyes. "I'm gonna hold you to that."

With a chuckle, Luke wrapped his arms around her for another quick, teetering hug before moving on to Mama.

Adelaide stepped up to take his place. One glimpse at her sister-in-law's doleful expression shattered Lydia's resolve to stem her tears. Moisture pooled in her eyes as she pressed her cheek to her friend's, careful not to crowd the babe in her womb. "I'll miss you."

"I will you too." Adelaide rubbed a gloved hand along Lydia's shoulder blades, her embrace gentle and enduring. "We'll let you know the moment the baby arrives. Promise." The words whispered in Lydia's ear sounded strained, choppy.

This wasn't easy for any of them.

Unable to find her voice, Lydia simply nodded and gave her friend a soft squeeze. When they drew apart, Adelaide's cheeks were damp with tears, yet a tender smile graced her lips. "Perhaps you can even come for a visit after the baby arrives."

"I'd like that." Even as she spoke the words, Lydia knew it could never be. Mama was too frail now to make the trip, and Lydia could never leave her alone so long.

Reluctantly, she let go of Adelaide's hand and allowed her to move on.

Still clutching Luke, Mama leaned her head against his chest, arms fastened firmly around his waist. Though her eyes were pinched shut and an array of emotions puckered her brow, her lashes and cheeks remained dry.

Such strength.

At last, they parted, and she clasped Luke by the hand. "Our prayers go with you, son. No mother could be prouder."

"Thanks, Ma." Luke leaned to kiss her forehead, his own face sated with emotion.

Through reddened eyes, Mama turned to Adelaide and managed a weak smile. She pulled her into a gentle, one-armed embrace, never letting go of Luke's hand. "You take care of yourself and that sweet baby of yours."

The slight quiver in Mama's voice tugged at Lydia's heartstrings, and she shifted her gaze to where Will stood, head bowed, at the front of the wagon. Even he seemed moved by their departure.

Holding both Luke and Adelaide by the hand, Mama tipped her chin higher, glancing from one to the other. "Your absence here will leave an awful void, but I'm confident the Lord has good things in store. May He bless and keep you until we meet again."

Then, as if releasing them into the Lord's care, she loosened her hold on their hands.

With a heartfelt nod, Luke touched her arm. "We'll see you

soon." A bit hesitantly, he turned to help Adelaide onto the springboard seat. Packed to the brim with belongings, the rented carriage was yet another reminder this was no weekend venture.

Luke reached to shake Will's hand. "Thanks again. Take care of them for us."

"I'll do my best."

Will's candid response warmed Lydia, and yet hollowness gnawed at her as Luke hoisted himself onto the carriage seat and took up the reins. Months would pass before they'd see him and Adelaide. Drew and Caroline's departure had been equally as sudden and unexpected, and yet somehow this parting had hit Lydia even harder. Perhaps it was that she and Adelaide had spent more time together or the baby's birth being so near and then stolen away. Or maybe it was simply that she and Mama were again left alone.

For good this time.

She swallowed the tautness in her throat. Why did things have to change? She'd been but a girl of ten at the start of the war. Now, with her eighteenth birthday only months away, she felt cheated, as though her childhood had been ripped away and her beloved father and brothers stripped from her too soon.

The wagon rumbled forward, and she lifted a hand in response to Luke and Adelaide's vigorous waves. This would be a new season of life for them all, one which, for Lydia, would take some getting used to.

As the wagon disappeared down the lane, she lowered her arm and released a long breath. Enough gloom. Luke was leaving to do what the Lord intended for him, and Adelaide would prove a certain asset to his ministry. The Lord had finally given Lydia some semblance of peace, and she refused to surrender it.

Brushing unwanted moisture from the corner of her eye, she took a sweeping glance at the distant hills and trees and the fields of golden wheat stubble and knee-high corn nestled in between. This truly was a picturesque place to live. One she never wished to leave.

Mama came and stood beside her, wrapping an arm around Lydia's waist. Tucking her own arm around her mother, Lydia leaned her head on her shoulder. They might not have much, but they still had this place, each other ...

A faint grin wedged out the sorrow in her soul as her gaze drifted to the handsome, sandy-haired man staring into the distance.

And Will.

WILL EASED open the cottage house door, feeling like an intruder. It didn't seem right, traipsing in a house not his own. Even a vacant one. Papered walls, planked floors, and an empty corner cabinet greeted him within, but not much else. Still, after bunking in the barn the past couple of months, a house all to himself seemed a luxury.

Setting his bundle of belongings inside the door, he took in the adjoined kitchen and dining area. He'd been in the cottage only once—the night Luke had sprung the invitation to supper and asked if Will was agreeable to staying. The place looked far different than it had then, as if all the life had been snuffed from it.

The fireplace was cleaned of ashes, and a few logs remained stacked in the tinder box—signs of Luke's thoughtfulness. Will's boot soles echoed against the quiet as he crossed the empty room and ventured a peek into the two smaller side rooms. The one on the left contained nothing but a caned chair near the window, while an unmade bed and a small nightstand occupied the room to the right.

Sitting on the mattress, he bounced gently, and his lips lifted. Feathers instead of straw. At least he'd have a softer place to lay his head.

A light tap on the door brought him to his feet. With quick strides, he crossed the dining area and lifted the door latch.

Lydia stood outside, arms laden with bedding. The impulse to ease her load quickly outweighed his surprise. "Let me help with those."

Her vivid blue eyes locked onto his as he emptied her arms of the quilt and stack of linens. "Mama thought you could use a few comforts of home."

"Be sure to thank her for me." He smiled, noting for the first time the puffiness around her eyelids. Had she been crying?

No doubt her brother's leaving hit her hard. Hopefully, time would ease her heartache, though Will knew from experience the disappointment of loss never fully resolved. Even after making peace with his decision to remain here indefinitely, he couldn't rid himself of the nagging hollowness in his gut at abandoning his search for his identity.

With nowhere else to set the bundle, he trekked in and deposited it on the mattress, returning to find Lydia glancing about, hands on hips. "Not much left to the place, is there?" She nodded toward the empty fireplace. "I see they left the kettle but no cooking utensils."

"I'll get by. I'm not much of a cook anyhow."

She swung toward him and gave a hard blink, her cornflower-blue day dress accenting the blue in her eyes. "You'll continue to take at least your evening meals with us, won't you? We—that is—Mama would be greatly disappointed if you didn't."

Will summoned a grin and patted his stomach. "So would my belly."

The creases in her brow smoothed as the corners of her mouth tipped upwards. "Good. Mama will be pleased."

The lilt in Lydia's voice and the sparkle in her eyes hinted Martha wouldn't be the only one pleased. Since the night they'd prayed together, Will had sensed a deepening bond with Lydia. One which left him a bit lightheaded.

She angled her head to one side. "Can I ask you something?"

"Sure."

"What changed your mind? About leaving, I mean?"

Will's thoughts churned as he contemplated how to respond. How could he explain something he wasn't completely sure of himself? At last, he shrugged. "I'm needed here, so I figure this is where the Lord intends me to be."

Lydia gave a slow nod, her gaze trailing downward. "You *are* needed, that's certain. I was just hoping, I mean ..." Her voice fell away, her ruby lips struggling to form the words. "I thought perhaps there might be more to your decision."

A bit amused by her subtle probe, Will pulled his lips taut to ward off a grin. Should he reveal the whole truth? That he'd grown fond of a certain young lady?

His heart thrummed in his chest. Too risky. His life was still too unsettled. Giving Lydia false hope of a future he couldn't promise wouldn't be right. Yet, she looked so pensive, he longed to give her some smidgen of encouragement. "There is another reason I'd find it hard to leave."

Her face lifted, eyes glistening. "There is?"

"Yes." He edged closer, stirred by her nearness. She was so young. So lovely.

Both inside and out.

Gazing down at her, he struggled to find his voice. "I've come to think of this place as home and you all as family. You welcomed me like one of your own. I'm grateful."

A gentle smile touched her lips, and she placed a hand on his sleeve. "I'm glad. We've become rather fond of you as well."

Resisting the urge to brush the back of his fingers along her cheek, Will returned a warm smile instead.

For a long moment, her azure eyes remained locked on his. A faint blush rose in her cheeks as though unspoken sentiment had reflected in his eyes.

Fearful his transparency had betrayed his feelings, he eased back and immediately felt the void as her hand slipped from his arm. At a loss for what to say, he thumbed over his shoulder. "Thanks again for the linens. I'll sleep in comfort tonight."

"Would you like me to make up the bed before I go?"

Will shook his head and stuffed his hands in his pockets. "Thanks, but I can manage."

A hint of puzzlement creased Lydia's brow as she edged toward the door. "Well, I'll leave you to get settled in. I'll box up a few spare cooking items and bring them by first chance I have."

He lifted the door latch for her. "No need. Just set them on the veranda, and I'll tote them down."

"All right." She studied him as if weighing his motives and then stepped outside. Slipping on her bonnet, she started up the path without a backward glance.

Will closed and latched the door, the vacant cottage still alive with her essence. He hadn't meant to rush her away. Yet, he had a feeling in his attempt to conceal his fondness, he'd somehow offended her. Though appreciated, her offers to help further unnerved him. He needed time to pull his feelings together. Her nearness only confused him.

But truth be told, he wanted her near, wanted to learn every nuance of her nature. Much like the faceless girl in his dream, she fascinated him. Made him feel vibrant and alive.

From the corner of the window, he watched her go, her dress swaying side to side with each spry step. His chest tightened. No doubt about it, he was falling for this girl. Whatever his past, his affections were quickly becoming linked to Lydia.

He just hoped his heart wasn't outrunning his head.

35

Lydia moved her three-legged milking stool aside, casting a wistful glance at the empty stall Will once occupied. Between his work and spending more of his time at the cottage, she'd likely not see much of him outside of evening meals. And after the way he'd rushed her off yesterday, she had no intention of paying him another visit anytime soon.

Taking up the pail of milk, she stifled a sigh. For a moment, she thought she'd glimpsed affection in his hazel eyes. He'd drawn so close, his gaze intently fastened on hers. But, just as quickly, the tenderness had died away, and he'd edged back, finding every excuse not to accept her help. With a huff, she trudged from the barn. The man made no more sense than hanging clothes to dry during a rainstorm.

In her rush, some of the milk sloshed from the pail. Lydia slowed. She missed having Adelaide to talk to. By now, she and Luke were busy settling into their new life, likely not giving her and Mama much thought.

Waving away a pair of pesky flies, Lydia chastened herself for her dour mood. She wasn't being fair. Luke and Adelaide had every right to live their own lives.

As did Will.

Forgive me, Lord.

Lydia hung her head. As much as she might wish otherwise, she and Will had no formal understanding. If he chose to curtail her company and decline her help, who was she to criticize?

But something told her he was holding back, as if he still hadn't completely let go of his past and the inkling that someone somewhere awaited his return.

Her stomach dipped. While his sense of loyalty was admirable, it didn't lend to much of a future for the two of them.

Mama greeted her on the veranda, a shawl draped over her rounded shoulders and a gentle smile on her lips. "You look mighty glum for such a bright morning."

In truth, Lydia had hardly noticed if the day was sunny or gray. She set the pail of milk down, noting the box of cooking utensils she'd collected for Will had disappeared. Her heart sank. He'd come to collect the goods and made no attempt to stop by the barn.

Perhaps he truly *was* avoiding her.

Leaning against the railing, she forced a grin. "Just tired. I didn't sleep well."

Mama cupped a hand under Lydia's chin, scrutinizing her as if she were an intricately woven piece of clothing. "It's not tiredness I glean in your eyes. It's troubles of the heart."

Heat flamed in Lydia's cheeks. Only Mama could discern her so effortlessly. Reluctant to expose her feelings, Lydia sought to mask the truth. "I-I'm merely missing Luke and Adelaide."

"Oh?" One of Mama's brows shot up, her pointed stare penetrating Lydia's resolve. "Then Will has nothing to do with it?"

Dropping into one of the wicker chairs, Lydia crossed her arms over her chest, the truth nipping at her conscience. "I suppose a little."

"I thought as much." With a knowing grin, Mama eased into the chair opposite her. "I've seen the two of you together enough to recognize the signs."

Lydia snapped her head toward her. "Signs?"

"That you care for each other."

Mama's assertion brought a fresh flash of heat to Lydia's cheeks. She dropped her gaze, amazed at her mother's perception. "I'll not deny I care for Will, and I suspect he cares for me, but I'm not sure anything can ever come of it. "

Mama's thin fingers gripped Lydia's arm in a tender squeeze. "Whatever the trouble, I'm certain a bit of time and prayer is all that's needed."

"It's not that simple." Lydia's mouth twisted. How could she explain? "There's more to Will than you know, Mama. Circumstances from his past keep him bound and unwilling to commit to any place or anyone."

"And yet he's here."

"For now. But I sense he's still torn and restless and may never get over it."

A twinkle gleamed in Mama's eyes. "Patience, child. The Lord has a way of working things out in His time."

A glimmer of hope flickered inside Lydia. She had to admit God had used Scripture to persuade Will to forego his search for his past. The decision hadn't been an easy one. She was certain of that. Was he still wrestling with himself? Given time, would the Lord bring contentment?

She leaned forward and placed a hand atop her mother's. "Indeed, He does. Thank you for reminding me, Mama."

Mama winked as she rose to her feet. "A good reminder for us all."

Lydia's lips slanted upward. If she lived to be twice Mama's age, she'd likely not be half as wise and discerning. The very fact Will had agreed to stay when he'd had his heart set on leaving ought to be proof the Lord's hand was at work.

She drew a cleansing breath. If more time was what Will needed, more time was what she would give.

"HAVE MORE POTATOES, WILL."

Will peered at the depleted bowl of mashed potatoes Martha offered and rubbed his full stomach. "Thanks, but I'd better quit. Everything was good, as usual."

Setting the bowl aside, Martha offered a gentle nod. "How are you liking the cottage house?"

"Real well. It has the barn beat by a long shot."

A chuckle sounded from Martha. "Indeed."

Will eased back in his chair, cutting Lydia a quick glance. "The extra lantern and kitchenware you provided will come in real handy. Much obliged."

The faint scent of lilac drifted his way as Lydia leaned closer, her crystal blue eyes brightening. "I'm glad. If there's anything else you need, let us know."

"Thanks. I'll do that." He met her gaze, almost wishing he could think of something more for her to drop by. Hopefully she understood he'd offered to tote the box of items to spare her and not because he didn't enjoy her company. Despite his misgivings about the two of them becoming overly attached, he regretted rushing her away.

"I've been meaning to ask …"

Martha's voice sliced through his fog, and he broke off his stare. "Yes, ma'am?"

Lacing her fingers together on the table, Martha tipped her head, her loose bun of silvery blonde hair shifting slightly. "Have you considered attending the Independence Day celebration in town?"

What else could he answer but the truth? He'd seen signs up around town but never gave them more than a glance. "I really haven't given it much thought."

"Oh, it's great fun," Lydia's enthusiasm pulled his attention back to her. "There's a parade and a picnic with games and, in the evening, fireworks."

Will couldn't help but grin at the vibrant glow in her eyes, her smile radiating through him like the summer sun. "Sounds like quite an event."

"I ... don't suppose you'd care to escort us to the festivities?"

Martha's plea wiped the smile from his lips. So long as memory served him, he'd never attended any sort of public activity outside of church service. The very thought of socializing in a crowd left him sweaty-palmed.

Yet how could he refuse? He couldn't allow the two ladies to go unattended.

Swallowing the acorn-sized bulge in his throat, Will glanced from one hopeful face to the other and then gave a reluctant nod. "I'd be honored."

A satisfied smile wedged across Martha's face, her eyes vacillating between Will and Lydia. "Good."

Something in Martha's tone, coupled with Lydia's gleeful grin, gave Will the feeling he'd wandered headlong into a feminine conspiracy.

But somehow, he didn't seem to mind.

36

Saturday, July 4, 1868

Lydia paused on the veranda stoop and turned to her mother as Will brought Angel and the carriage around. "You're sure you don't feel up to coming, Mama?"

Dabbing a kerchief to her neck, Mama shook her head. "I don't believe so. This heat is liable to sap every ounce of my energy before the day's half through."

Lydia tightened her hold on the railing, troubled at the thought of leaving Mama alone so long. Yet, the day did tend toward excessive heat. Already the layers of petticoats and her high-necked, long-sleeved dress threatened to draw perspiration.

Coming up beside her, Will touched her elbow, sending a pleasant shiver through her despite the morning's warmness. He glanced from Lydia to her mother. "Are we all set?"

With a dismal shake of her head, Lydia turned to Will. "Mama feels the heat would be too much for her and has decided not to go."

Will's smile faded. "I'm sorry to hear that."

As much as Lydia dreaded missing the festivities, not to mention leisure time with Will, she determined her place was with Mama. With a heavy heart, she stared down at Will's polished boots. "I'm sorry, but I should remain home with her."

"You'll do no such thing." Mama blurted resolutely. "There's no need for either of you to sacrifice your day on my account."

"But we're left without a chaperone."

"Only during the ride there and back. I have complete faith in both you and Will in that regard."

"But Mama, I ..."

Mama gave Lydia a gentle nudge. "There'll be no arguments. I'm perfectly capable of looking after myself. Celia Perkins is sure to be by. Perhaps she'll stay a while and help pass the time."

Hope swelled within Lydia. "That's true. It would ease my mind if you had some company."

"Of course. Don't give it another thought. You two go and have a nice time."

Lydia ventured a glance at Will, nearly melting under his gaze. He looked so handsome in his ivory cotton shirt, brown vest, and a narrow cravat about his neck. She swallowed, forcing herself to focus on the problem at hand. "Do you think we should?"

With a slight shrug, he looked at Lydia, then her mother. "Don't see why not. Your mother knows her mind. And I promise to bring you home whenever you say the word."

A smile erupted on Mama's face. "There, you see? It's all taken care of. Not a thing to fret about."

Judging by the glint of satisfaction in Mama's eyes, Lydia had to wonder if her dear mother hadn't put in a request with the Lord for the steamy day so she could remain behind and allow Will and Lydia the chance to be a twosome.

A tingle vibrated through her. She had to admit the thought of spending an entire day at Will's side was more than appealing.

Mama motioned them on. "Now, you'd best be on your way before the sun gets too warm for even you."

Relinquishing with a grin, Lydia gave Mama a hug and a peck on the cheek, then gingerly took the arm Will offered. With folded parasol in hand and Will toting their picnic lunch, they downed the steps, Lydia's heart pounding fiercely beneath the fabric of her dress. She'd never imagined Mama would back out of going.

A web of nerves balled in Lydia's stomach, and she snugged her arm tighter to Will's. Though she'd been on occasional outings with men, none had stirred her interest.

Unlike Will.

Being on his arm left her giddy and longing for more of his company.

As they reached the carriage, she slid her arm from his and allowed him to gently clasp her gloved hand. The intimate touch nearly stole her breath, ending all too soon as she eased onto the seat. Though she kept her head straight, her eyes followed Will's every move while he deposited the picnic basket under the seat behind her.

He veered out of sight, and Lydia mentally tracked his boot steps until he reappeared on the opposite side. Donning his hat, he hoisted himself onto the seat beside her, the carriage jostling under his weight. She breathed in the woodsy scent of soap, mindful Will's shoulder nearly clipped her own while seated on the narrow bench. Whether from the sun's warm rays or her own foolish infatuation, a wave of heat trickled through her.

Opening her parasol, she scolded herself for being overly conscious of Will. After all, they weren't courting, and to allow herself to believe such could only bring disillusionment. Sitting taller, she smoothed a crinkle in her skirt. This was simply a companionable outing, which, until moments ago, was meant to include Mama.

"Have a good time, and don't worry about me. Stay as long as you please."

Mama's gently raised voice cut through Lydia's musings. Returning a warm wave, she prayed she'd made the right decision in going. "Goodbye, Mama. Take care of yourself."

"I will. Enjoy your day."

With a tip of his hat, Will took up the reins.

As the carriage trundled forward, Lydia dismissed any last-minute change of heart. Whether good or bad, she had a feeling this would be a day to remember.

"You and your ma sure know how to pack a lunch."

"Why, thank you." At Will's comment, Lydia dipped her head, her lips lifting in an appreciative grin. "Food always takes on better flavor when eaten outdoors."

"That it does." Will set his fork and plate on the picnic blanket and patted his stomach, swallowing his last bite of peach pie.

Stacking her empty pie plate atop his, Lydia ventured a glance around, sounds of laughter and merriment echoing from all sides. "Though I might have preferred a less crowded atmosphere."

She and Will had searched more than a quarter-hour for an out-of-the-way place to spread their picnic blanket amid the throng of people. They'd finally located a shady spot beneath a sprawling oak tree that hadn't been claimed. Only to have the space soon fill in around them, robbing their solitude.

Hugging his knee to his chest, Will leaned against the tree and smiled. "A quiet meadow would've been nice, but I don't mind. It's the company you're with that counts."

Lydia stared at him, any attempt to suppress a grin futile. Will had as much as admitted he enjoyed her company. The truth of which invigorated her like cool water on a parched tongue. "That's very sweet."

His hazel eyes locked onto hers, conveying more than words ever could.

The commotion around them faded as Will slid his hand next to hers. Not daring to draw attention to the movement, Lydia stilled, her heartbeat pounding in her ears.

Would he hold her hand?

As if testing the waters, his warm pinky entwined with hers. Her breaths shallowed at the tender touch. Having removed her gloves for the meal, she clearly felt the blend of softness and callouses that embodied the hands of a hard worker. Through singed cheeks, she offered him a timid smile.

He clasped her hand fully in his, and in that instant, every doubt of his feelings for her fled. The carriage ride had been nice, the parade grand, and the luncheon delightful, but none equaled this moment when, for the first time, she glimpsed the depth of Will's affection.

Raucous barking sounded near her left ear, and before Lydia could shield herself, a midsized dog bounded mere inches from her face. With a stunned squeal, she lurched backward, bracing herself with her hand to keep from toppling. In a flash, the dog darted past, tromping on Lydia in passing. A glance down at her dark blue skirt affirmed her fears—smudged stains and a spattering of blond dog hair.

"I'm real sorry, miss."

The tenor voice drew Lydia's attention to the out-of-breath boy who'd screeched to a halt beside her. Red-faced and hair askew, the boy looked as though he'd been chasing his furry companion through all of Elmira. She pursed her lips and closed her eyes, biting back the scolding her tongue was eager to unleash. Shaking her head, she opened her eyes and motioned him on. "Go! Catch up to him before he mauls someone else."

A wide smile lit the boy's face. "Thanks, miss." With a quick tip of his cap, he rushed on.

Will touched a hand to her elbow. "Are you all right?"

Uncertain which was more upsetting—their ruined tender moment or having been trounced upon—Lydia gave a curt nod. "Other than the fur and dirt prints that brute left behind."

"You were very forgiving to the young lad. For a moment, I thought you might wallop him."

At the trace of humor in Will's voice, she stopped plucking

strands of dog hair from her skirt and peered over at him. To her dismay, amusement had replaced the endearment in his eyes and a droll grin played on his lips. Uncertain whether to vent her annoyance or share in his mirth, Lydia tilted her head to one side and rested her hands on her hips.

Lightheartedness soon won out, evoking a soft giggle. "I had to be lenient lest the foul beast land on some other poor, unsuspecting soul."

Will's grin blossomed into laughter.

Lydia chuckled at the unexpected display. In the months she'd known Will, she couldn't recall ever hearing him laugh. Such joy radiating from him warmed her in ways she would never have dreamed. So robust was the sound, Lydia couldn't resist joining in. Suddenly, the incident seemed more blessing than curse, and she was grateful she'd chosen to make light of the situation.

The lively clanging of a cowbell silenced their chuckles. The response from the crowd around them was immediate—excited voices, people packing up their belongings, children tugging at their parents' hands.

Will stared at Lydia, brows pinched. "What is it?"

"The games are about to start. They're quite entertaining. Would you like to watch?"

He shrugged. "May as well."

While Lydia packed up the tableware, Will shook and folded the blanket. Leaving their picnic basket at the foot of the tree, they followed the throng of people to a large, grassy area bordered by red, white, and blue bunting. Onlookers pressed in from all sides as Lydia and Will vied for a tangible place to observe. Out of necessity and so as not to hinder the view of those around, she lowered her parasol and immediately felt the difference. Her fashionable bonnet offered little protection from the intensity of the midday sun.

The summertime heat combined with all the warm bodies was stifling, and Lydia was grateful Mama hadn't come. While her concern for her mother's welfare had never fully subsided, as the day wore on, her worries had given way to the excitement of the festivities. Though she continued to lift a silent prayer whenever Mama came to mind.

Will touched a hand to the small of Lydia's back and pointed to their left. "Over there. The sun won't be so in our faces, and we might catch a bit of shade from that tree."

Nodding agreement, Lydia allowed Will to guide her through the onslaught of people. As they reached their desired spot, Will bent to speak in her ear. "Better?"

She smiled up at him, his face mere inches from her own. "Yes. Much."

In that instant, the bell sounded again, and a hush fell over the crowd. "And just in time," Lydia whispered, reluctantly turning from Will to the red-haired man standing with arms stretched high at the center of the field. "Good afternoon, and welcome to ... We've much ... so welcome you all to ...." The man's words faded in and out as he turned his head from side to side. The cries of infants and barking of dogs further obscured the man's instructions.

"What did he say? I can't make it out?" came frantic whispers from the mob of people.

Only there to observe the entertainment, Lydia didn't mind the confusion. She glanced at Will, content just to be with him. Unaware of her scrutiny, his gaze darted this way and that as though taking everything in.

A dozen youths filtered onto the field spreading to various points along the outer edges. Lydia stood on tiptoe to speak into Will's ear. "Those are runners, meant to announce the upcoming races."

Will returned a brisk nod, his eyes still fixated on the scene before him.

"Sprint race for boys ages six to ten." The youths hollered over and over.

At their bidding, a horde of youngsters dashed onto the field, eager to take their place at the starting line along the south end. The man at the center made his way over and waited for the row of boys to get situated. Raising his arm, he held a red flag high above his head. With a loud shout, he lowered the flag, and the line of boys skittered off in a frenzied hurry. The crowd pointed and cheered, urging on their favorites.

A dog ran onto the field, tripping up one of the boys near the lead and causing him to stumble. Other boys sprinted past.

"The winner!" a fellow announced, holding up the arm of the boy who'd been the first to cross the finish line.

The boy who'd fallen picked himself up and stood looking on, having missed his chance to finish. Lydia felt a tug on her sleeve, and Will leaned close to her ear, gesturing toward the boy. "Isn't that the young fellow who was chasing after his dog?"

Lydia peered around the bonnet of the woman in front of her, catching a glimpse of the boy's face. "I believe it is." She gave a soft chuckle. "He might have won had it not been for that brutish dog of his."

The boy and his dog jogged to the side of the field opposite them and stood along the outer edge. Lydia put him out of her mind as several more races ensued for older boys and girls. Eventually, the runners called for the father and son three-legged race. Numerous men strode onto the field alongside their sons.

Will craned his neck as though looking for someone or something.

Lydia followed his gaze. "What is it?"

He gestured across the field. "That boy. He doesn't seem to have anyone to partner with."

She searched out the youngster in the crowd and finally spotted him, head bowed low, hand draped about his dog. "He does look a tad downhearted."

Before she realized what was happening, Will pushed his way through the crowd toward the grassy area. "Where are you going?" Lydia called after him.

He gave no indication he'd heard but instead strode across

the field to where the child stood. Bending down, he spoke to the boy, who shook his head and then nodded, his face brightening. Lydia's brow squeezed as Will clamped a hand to the boy's shoulder and walked with him toward the starting line while another boy kept hold of the wayward dog.

What was Will doing?

Leaving behind what limited shade the tree she'd stood under afforded, she vied for a closer spot. "Excuse me. Pardon me," she called as she shouldered her way through to the front. By the time she reached the string of bunting bordering the field, Will and the boy's legs were being bound together. Raising a gloved hand to her lips, she chuckled to herself. Will was going to race? What would possess him to do such a thing? Where was the boy's father?

As Will and the youngster took their place in line, the red-headed man raised his flag. A nervous twinge worked through Lydia. She hoped they'd fare well. Knowing Will as she did, it had taken a lot of gumption to put himself before so many people. She lifted a silent prayer on his behalf just as the man signaled the start of the race.

To a volley of cheers and chuckles from the crowd, men and boys hobbled forward, some barely taking a step before tumbling to the ground. In the haze of activity, Lydia lost sight of Will and his partner. She perused the mass of competitors, finally spotting them as they were picking themselves up off the ground about a third of the way down the field. They started again, arm in arm, quickly establishing a unified pace. By the time they reached the midway point, only half a dozen pairs remained in front of them.

Lydia pressed a hand to her chest, repeating quietly to herself. "Don't fall. Don't fall."

They continued to gain momentum, passing all but two other fathers and sons.

Setting all ladylike restraint aside, Lydia bobbed up and down, cocking her hands to the sides of her mouth and shouting. "Go, Will!"

In a final rush, they moved into second place, crossing the finish line a few strides behind one of their competitors. With a shout of glee, Lydia clamped her hands together, dropping her parasol to the ground with a *clunk*. Suddenly aware of the stares of those around her, she quietly reached to retrieve her parasol. As she straightened, she caught sight of Will and his companion making their way across the field, the boy chattering excitedly.

Will glanced her direction, eyes searching. She lifted a gloved hand and waved. He smiled at her but, instead of approaching, kept walking toward the starting line. Two father-son races later, he finally parted ways with the boy and trotted back toward Lydia. His face reddened from activity, he ducked under the string of bunting.

She greeted him with a smile, shifting to make room. "You and the boy did well."

With a shrug, Will handed her the second-place ribbon. "Made the boy happy, I s'pose." With a glance around, he lifted his hat, revealing a ring of dampened hair. He swiped his sleeve over his beaded forehead. "Let's go somewhere less confining and cool off."

Barely able to move amid the crush of people, Lydia nodded.

Taking her by the hand, Will led her to a shady spot away from the crowd. He leaned against the tree and released a long breath. "This is more like it."

Lydia rocked back on her heels, fanning herself with her hand. "You surprised me, joining in the games as you did."

He shrugged. "Robbie needed a partner."

"Robbie? Is that the boy's name?"

With a nod, Will moistened dry lips and pointed across the way. "I could sure use some of that lemonade the vendors are peddling."

Lydia eyed the string of merchants and raised her parasol. "Let's go." Taking his arm, she fell into step beside him. "How did you know young Robbie needed a partner?"

Will's cheek flinched. "I recognized the look on his face."

"Where was his father?"

Will slowed his pace, his head dipping downward. "His father was killed at Gettysburg."

Lydia's chest clenched, recalling the horrific day they'd received news of her own father's passing. "Oh, the poor boy." She tightened her hold on Will's arm. "So, you stepped in in his father's stead?"

He stared past her, his eyes glossing over. "Wasn't the boy's fault he had no one to partner with. Everyone deserves a chance."

"Yes, they do." Moisture pooled in Lydia's eyes, the reason behind Will's selfless act becoming clear. He'd seen himself in the child's hurt-filled face. He understood what it was to feel alone and excluded.

Tugging Will to a stop, she turned to face him. "That was incredibly kind of you."

He met her gaze, his mouth taut. "I only did what I would have wanted someone to do for me if I was in his shoes. Isn't that what Scripture teaches? Do unto others what you'd have them do unto you?"

A smile tugged at her lips, her respect for this man mounting. "That's exactly what it teaches."

For a long moment, they stared into each other's eyes, not caring who took notice. Resisting the urge to throw her arms around him, she instead raised a hand to his cheek. "You're a good man, Will Evans."

Without a word, he clasped her hand and pressed it to his lips and then, looping her arm in his, guided her toward the venders.

Lydia leaned in close, proud to be at his side. Whether he realized it or not, Will had given her yet another reason to like him.

Or dare she say ... love?

37

"We should probably head home. I don't wish to worry Mama by arriving too late."

Will nodded, certain Lydia's eagerness to check on her mother played an equal factor in the decision. "We'll collect Angel and the carriage and be on our way." He pointed to their right. "I get twisted around with all these people, but I think the livery is down that way."

"Yes. Only a few blocks from here."

The confirmation put Will's mind at ease. As much as he'd enjoyed the time spent with Lydia, he was more and more eager to be rid of the constant flow of people. All the walking was making his feet sore, and if Lydia's slower pace was any indication, hers were suffering as well.

He grinned. Still, he wouldn't have traded this day for a dozen others.

The waning sun cast long shadows between the rows of buildings as Will and Lydia inched along the crowded street. At this rate, they'd be fortunate to make the trip home before dark. Hopefully, they wouldn't have long to wait at the livery and would soon be on their way.

Lydia pointed up ahead. "There it is."

Relieved, Will stepped up his pace and almost collided with a man stumbling toward him from behind a parked buggy. His stomach twisted when he recognized the fellow as Guthrie Malloy. Will attempted to sidestep around him, but Malloy caught him by the sleeve.

"Watch where yer goin', feller." The man's slurred speech and the strong scent of alcohol suggested too much celebrating. Malloy took a hard blink and released Will's shirt with a shove. "Oh, it's you."

Will clenched his jaw. "Excuse us."

With a swaggered lurch sideways, Malloy blocked Will's path, his bloodshot eyes shifting to Lydia. "Didn't take ya long t' make good with the boss's sister. Mighty handy with him away."

Will's shoulders tensed. That did it. This scoundrel could say what he wanted about him, but to insult Lydia's integrity was a whole other matter. Drawing his arm back, he rounded his hand into a fist.

Lydia tugged on his arm. "Don't, Will. He's not worth it."

One lingering glance at the soused man convinced him she was right. The last thing he wished to do was end their pleasant outing by starting a brawl.

Lowering his fist, he blew out a breath and prayed for wisdom. Luke would know what to do. How would he handle this?

"Love your enemies. Do good to those which hate you."

The verse from Sunday's sermon scrolled through Will's mind like a gentle nudge from Heaven. *Love this fellow, Lord? How is that possible?*

He edged back. Maybe love, in this instance, simply meant having enough self-control not to react to Malloy's offenses. "This being my first celebration, Miss Gallagher was kind enough to show me around. But it's time we leave."

Malloy caught Will by the wrist. "You don't fool me, boy.

You're after more than a good time. You've got yer sights set on taking over the Gallagher place. Well, I'll see to it that don't happen."

Lydia's fingers dug into Will's arm as she pushed forward. "See here, Mr. Malloy. You've no call to ..."

Wrenching his wrist free from Malloy, Will motioned her to silence. This was his battle, and he meant to fight it. He looked Malloy squarely in the eyes, squelching the urge to knock him more senseless than he already was. "You're drunk, Malloy. Your threats are as hollow as your accusations."

Malloy took an awkward swing at Will.

Lydia shrieked.

Will grabbed Malloy's arm in mid-strike and twisted it behind his back. Startled onlookers scattered as Will nudged his assailant onto a vacant bench.

With a raspy moan, Malloy crumpled into a heap.

"Go sleep it off." Straightening, Will gestured toward Lydia. "And if you remember one thing, Malloy, remember this. From now on, stay away from the Gallaghers."

Ignoring the gawks of those who'd gathered, Will clasped Lydia by the hand and led her from the commotion. Heat burned his cheeks as he slowed his pace and ventured a glance her way. "Sorry. I'd hoped to handle that better."

She peered up at him, a smile breaking onto her face. "You handled it beautifully."

With a shake of his head, Will stared at the boardwalk. "I lost my temper and caused a stir."

Jarring to a stop, Lydia turned to face him, her vivid blue eyes piercing through his negativity. "No, you didn't, Will. You kept an irate man from inciting a full-fledged ruckus and likely spared Mama and me further harassment."

His spirit lightened at her encouraging tone and the vibrancy of her lovely features. A corner of his mouth lifted. "I like the way you view things."

Her smile returned. "Good."

Suddenly aware of her hand in his and that he'd taken the liberty without asking, he loosened his hold. Lydia quickly linked her arm through his, her bonnet brushing his shoulder as they strode toward the livery.

Will stood taller, a rush of warmth filling his chest. Something had changed. Not only in himself, but Lydia. There was a relaxed feel between them, an effortlessness that hadn't been there before. Gone were the doubts and insecurities that had plagued them for weeks. Today, his heart had melded with hers in a way he couldn't explain. Surely if he'd felt this way for someone in his past, he'd sense it. Even without his memory.

Wouldn't he?

He shook off the unsettling thought. No more living in threat of the past. He was finally ready to move forward and let his heart know love.

DESPITE THE JOGGLING of the carriage over the rutted trail, Lydia couldn't wipe the grin from her lips. She couldn't recall a more enjoyable day. Or such a feeling of total bliss. She'd finally gotten a true glimpse of Will and, for the first time, knew in her heart he cared for her.

She leaned close to his chest and pointed at the thin band of clouds reflecting shades of lavender and pink along the western horizon. "Such a beautiful sunset."

Will followed her gaze, his tanned cheek pulling upward in a gentle smile. "Sure is."

He offered her his arm, and she nestled closer, wishing this day would never end.

Barely a breeze stirred the humid night air, though the setting sun brought relief from the staggering heat earlier in the day. A chorus of crickets and katydids serenaded them as they traveled. With less than a mile to go, they were sure to reach home by nightfall, the full moon lending light in lieu of the sun.

Lydia peered up at Will. "I'm sorry we'll miss the fireworks, but I wouldn't feel right leaving Mama alone so long." *Not to mention the unseemliness of being out after dark without a proper chaperone.*

"I don't mind."

She lightened her tone. "Perhaps you'll not miss out entirely. On a clear night, we can see the fireworks from our veranda."

"Either way, I won't complain. It's been a full day. I've enjoyed it." He smiled down at her, his face mere inches from her own.

Her heart sped to twice its normal pace as her gaze shifted to his smooth lips. What would it be like to have them pressed against hers? She'd never kissed a man. Never even desired to be kissed.

Until now.

The bold notion brought warmth to her cheeks. Time to refocus on something more chaste. She straightened, not quite looking him in the eyes. "H-How's your Bible reading going?"

Tapping the reins lightly across Angel's back, Will stared out ahead of them. "It's going well. A lot to take in. I'll admit there are parts I don't understand."

"Such as?"

"Remember mentioning a while back how long Abraham waited for his son Isaac to be born?"

Uncertain where he was going with the question, she sounded hesitant. "Yes."

Will's brow creased. "After such a long wait for that promise to be fulfilled, why would God ask Abraham to sacrifice him? It doesn't make sense."

Though somewhat relieved by the query, Lydia twisted her lips, considering how to answer. "It is rather puzzling, but I think the Lord merely wanted to know He held first place in Abraham's heart."

Will returned a slow nod. "Still, that was a hard thing to ask of him, to sacrifice his son."

"Yes, it was. But it's no more than God did for us in sending Jesus. And the Lord *did* spare Isaac."

"True." Will paused, his expression thoughtful. "I guess God just doesn't want anything or anyone to stand between us and Him."

"That's it exactly."

"Sort of like the verse that says we'll find God when we seek Him with all of our hearts."

"Yes." Lydia's heart warmed. Despite his questions, Will's faith had obviously deepened. Scripture had a way of penetrating callous hearts. Had Will finally abandoned his search for his family in favor of pursuing God?

A faint popping sound drew her attention eastward to the spray of lights peppering the distant sky. She squeezed Will's arm. "Look! Over there. The fireworks have started."

Tugging Angel to a stop, Will turned for a look. The muscles in his arm tensed, and he quickly averted his gaze.

Lydia sat forward. "What's wrong?"

"I'm glad we didn't stay. The brightness reminds me of ..."

The fireworks forgotten, Lydia leaned closer. "Reminds you of what, Will? Do you remember something?"

His eyes crimped. "I'd rather not say."

"Tell me. Please."

He swallowed, the dim light shadowing the expression in his eyes. "Reminds me of the flames shooting from the *Sultana* after the explosion."

Lydia's heart sank. "Oh, Will. I'm sorry. If I had any inkling ..."

He put a finger to her lips, stilling her. "Don't worry. It's nothing I haven't witnessed a hundred times in my dreams."

As he withdrew his finger, she blinked. They'd not spoken of his disturbing dreams for some time. "Then you do have *some* memories?"

"Only one that I remember clearly—surfacing in the river,

seeing the steamboat in flames and ..." His head dipped. "The rest is too unspeakable to tell."

"I wish I could take away the horrible images you carry."

He touched a hand to her cheek. "In a way, you have. Or at least lessened them."

Her breath caught. "What? How?"

"By giving me your brother's Bible. The more I read it, the less I'm plagued by nightmares."

"Why, that's wonderful, Will. In time, perhaps the Lord will spare you the horrid dreams altogether."

With a nod, Will took up the reins. "One can hope."

The sound of the fireworks died away as the carriage rumbled forward. Lydia leaned her head against Will's shoulder, lifting a silent prayer of thanks for the Lord's healing in both Will's mind and spirit.

In what seemed a few brief moments, the cottage came into view and the farmhouse soon after. The home's unlit windows had Lydia sitting forward on the carriage seat. "I wonder why there are no lights?"

"Maybe she's gone to bed."

"So early? It's barely dark."

Bringing the carriage to a halt outside the house, Will set the brake. "Would you like me to go in with you?"

Lydia glanced at the darkened house and then at Will. It would be comforting to have him with her if something was wrong. She wavered, then, with a steadying breath, pushed her fears aside. "There's no need. I'm sure she's merely sleeping."

Will hopped from the carriage and offered her a hand down. Retrieving the empty picnic basket from the back seat, he cut her a sideways glance. "May I at least walk you to the door?"

She smiled at his kind gesture. "Yes, of course."

His strong hand clasped her elbow, guiding her toward the veranda. Moonlight streamed overhead, casting shadows on the ground beneath. Together, they strode onto the veranda and to the front door to a chorus of nightlife.

Lydia turned to face Will, invigorated by his nearness. "Thank you. For everything."

"My pleasure." With a smile, he passed her the picnic basket, their fingers brushing. He touched a hand to her cheek, his voice soft and low. "There's a lot I don't remember, but this is one day I could never forget."

"Nor me." Warmth trickled through her as her eyes became lost in his. If not for her nagging concerns for Mama, she might well have wished this moment to go on forever. How she longed for him to embrace her and press his lips to hers.

Instead, he slid his hand from her cheek, timidness or uncertainty seeming to take hold. "Well, I'd best see to Angel, but if you need anything, holler."

A wave of disappointment tore through Lydia. Would Will never break free of his constraints? A daring thought angled her lips in a wry grin and sent a nervous tremor through her. She shouldn't.

Should she?

Bolstering her courage, Lydia stood on her toes and pressed a hasty kiss to his cheek. "Goodnight, Will."

Without venturing a glance his way, she rushed inside, heart pounding. Shutting the door behind her, she leaned against it, heat rising in her cheeks. A bit giddy, she pressed a hand to her mouth, embarrassed by her impulsive act. What must he think of her?

A dim glow filtered from a lantern in the hall, so faint it was barely noticeable, and for a moment, her thoughts returned to Mama. Had she gone to bed and left the light for Lydia to find her way?

Or had the wick burnt low from being left unattended?

Will's boot steps slowly trailed across the veranda and down the stoop.

Hurrying to the window, Lydia moved the curtain aside in time to see him climb atop the carriage, his silhouette accented by the bright moonlight. When he glanced back at the farmhouse, she ducked out of sight.

"Lydia?"

Lydia pivoted, her shoulders sagging in relief at sight of Mama dressed in her nightgown and nightcap. "Mama. You're all right."

"'Course I am. Just tuckered."

"Did I wake you?"

With a shake of her head, Mama turned the lantern dial to brighten the flame. "You know as well as I do, I can't sleep until you're home safe."

The sound of the carriage pulling away again stirred Lydia's senses. As pleased as she was to find Mama well and in good spirits, Lydia couldn't rid herself of the pleasantness of the day nor the sensation of Will's cheek against her lips.

Mama ambled closer. "Well, how was your day? Did Will enjoy the festivities?"

Unable to hold back a smile, Lydia suppressed the urge to share every glorious detail. Instead, she moved to give her mother a hug. "It was quite pleasant. And, yes. Will seemed to truly enjoy himself. We both did."

Mama gave a slow nod. "I see by the look on your face I wasn't missed."

"Oh, but you were. I fretted over you repeatedly."

Cupping a hand under Lydia's chin, Mama studied her. "No doubt you did, but the luster in your eyes tells me my absence was, in some ways ... a blessing?"

Try as she might, Lydia couldn't deny her relationship with Will had deepened in the time alone. "Perhaps." The word squeaked out in a whisper, her cheeks warming.

With a soft chuckle, Mama pulled her into another gentle embrace. "Then my prayers were answered, and my time here well-spent." As she relinquished her hold, Mama rested her hands on Lydia's shoulders. "Now, it's truly time to head to bed. Goodnight, dear."

"Goodnight, Mama."

As Mama retreated to her bedroom, Lydia got the overwhelming notion that Mama and the Lord had been in cahoots all along, playing out this day with a plan in mind. Lydia's lips tugged in a grin. She couldn't say she was sorry. In fact, as she trailed along after her mother, sleep was the furthest thing from Lydia's mind.

38

Monday, July 6, 1868

Will chopped at the weed with his hoe, breaking it off at the root. Pushing his hat higher on his forehead, he stared out at the long row before him. Tufts of green dotted the soil between the stalks of nearly waist-high corn, the tenacious vegetation seeming to have multiplied ten times over in the two days he'd neglected to work at them.

He swiped a sleeve over his sweaty brow and leaned on his hoe handle. Why was it weeds grew so easily in places they weren't wanted?

Taking a swig from his canteen, he squinted up at the sky. It couldn't be much past nine o'clock, and already the blistering sun seemed to beam down relentlessly. He dried his mouth with the back of his hand, his lips spreading in a grin. Somehow, he hadn't minded the heat nearly so much when he and Lydia had taken in the Fourth of July festivities. The memory of her on his arm and the lilt of her laughter still beckoned to him, leaving him hungry for her company.

Yet, it was her unexpected kiss that had him tangled in knots. He could still almost feel the softness of her lips on his cheek. She'd had the gumption to do what he'd wanted to do and hadn't. Her boldness had both surprised and pleased him. And maybe given him the assurance he needed to know she shared his affections.

A hacking noise sounded from behind, and he swiveled for a look. Hoe in hand and floppy hat shading her head, Lydia chopped at a weed at the start of the adjacent row. "What're you doing?" he called.

Pausing mid-stroke, she straightened. "Hoeing. Looks like you can use the help."

Will scratched at his cheek. "That I can, but it's not the most pleasant of jobs in this heat."

"I'll manage." Her determined smile wound its way to his heart.

Reluctantly, he returned to work, resisting the urge to caution her not to overdo. He glanced over his shoulder now and then, watching for signs of fatigue. Instead, her reddened cheeks glowed with vitality, and he thrilled at her resolve to labor alongside him.

They spoke little as they chopped weeds from one end of the field to the other. An occasional cloud hid the sun, providing brief reprieves from the heat. In passing, Will offered her a swig from his canteen.

Her sapphire eyes lit as if he'd given her a rare jewel. "Thank you." She tipped the canteen to her lips and gulped the water as though she'd been deprived for weeks. Drying her mouth, she passed the canister back to Will. "I didn't realize water could taste so good."

He looped the canteen strap over his head and left shoulder. "Hard work has a way of making us appreciate life's simple pleasures."

A humored smile crept onto her lips. "And a day of leisure? What does that do for a person?"

Matching her playful grin with one of his own, Will shrugged. "Makes the work twice as hard when you get back."

With a slump of her shoulders, Lydia's smile dissolved.

Will snickered. "Unless a fella is fortunate enough to have good help."

Her countenance lifted. "Well then, let's go. There's work to be done." With that, she raised her hoe and hacked at a weed.

Shaking his head, Will hoed in the opposite direction. Moments later, something struck him in his lower back. He peered behind him, but seeing nothing out of the ordinary, returned to work.

Before long, another small object pinged him on the shoulder. He turned in time to glimpse Lydia whip her head around and make vigorous chops with her hoe. A glance at the ground behind him gleaned only wilting weeds and clumps of dirt.

Was Lydia toying with him?

Staying alert to the sound of her hacking, he returned to work. When her hoeing paused, Will whirled toward her. Arm already in motion, she hurled the object clutched in her fist. With a gasp, she clamped a hand to her mouth.

A small dirt clod landed near Will's boot. Locking eyes with her, he dropped his hoe and sprinted toward her.

With a giggly squeal, Lydia hiked her skirt and ran toward the end of the field, her hat flying off behind her.

Cutting into her row, Will chased after her, the heat no longer seeming oppressive with the breeze his running stirred. Lydia glanced over her shoulder, letting out a lighthearted scream as he closed in. Will reached the edge of the field mere seconds after her. He stretched out his arm to grasp her just as she dodged behind the trunk of a sizeable oak tree.

Rather than follow her, he bolted in the opposite direction and caught her as she rounded the tree.

Stunned, she gave a soft shriek as Will gently clasped her arms.

He stifled a grin. "You call this work?"

Breaths coming hard and fast, Lydia leaned against the tree trunk. "No. I call it taking a break *from* work."

"Ah. And is tossing dirt clods your way of convincing me to join you?"

Her blue eyes danced. "It succeeded, didn't it?"

With a good-humored shake of his head, Will slid his hands from her arms. "Wouldn't it have been easier to just say you wanted a break and walk over here?"

She gazed up at him, a mischievous grin playing on her lips. "But not nearly as fun."

Chuckling, Will removed his hat and gloves. "If running in blistering heat is your idea of fun."

"I found the breeze on my damp forehead rather refreshing."

Tipping his head within inches of hers, Will braced his hand against the tree trunk, softening his voice. "You did, huh?"

She gave a gentle nod, the smile fleeing from her face. Her lips parted, the affectionate look in her eyes pulling Will in.

He brushed a stray lock of hair from her cheek, letting his gaze rove to her rosy lips. A stab of guilt crept in as the image of the unknown girl in his dream played over in his head. He pushed it away. Whatever his past, it was lost to him. His heart was entwined with Lydia's.

And this time, he didn't intend to shy away.

LYDIA'S HEART raced as Will bent closer, robbing her of a full breath. As his arms encircled her, her knees nearly buckled. No doubt he meant to kiss her this time. It was written in his eyes.

As he drew her closer, she slid her arms about his neck. Tipping her head to the side, she closed her eyes. A tingle washed through her at the softness of his lips melding with hers. Their kiss deepened, expressing the love she felt for this man, and evidently his for her.

All too quickly, their lips parted, and Will loosened his hold, his gaze tender.

A bit breathless, Lydia returned a shy grin. "I-I should probably go help Mama get lunch. I fear I've become more of a distraction than a help."

Will took her hand in his and gave it a gentle squeeze. "Maybe so. But you've given me enough motivation for ten men."

She melted at the inference and the touch of his hand clasping hers. With a tease in her voice, she quipped, "Ah! Then, shall I pack enough lunch for all ten of you?"

Donning his hat, he let loose of her hand and edged toward the field. "If you'll stay and help eat it."

"Hoping to get a few more hours of work from me, are you?" she called as he jogged to retrieve her hat.

When he returned, he gently placed the straw hat on her head, hazel eyes sparkling. "I'll take all the help you want to give, but I'd be just as happy to have you sit under a shade tree and merely lend your company."

Stirred by his words, Lydia held his gaze before slowly backing away. "A bit of both, perhaps." She waved to him and started toward the farmhouse, her steps lighter than when she'd come. Her lips still tingled with his vibrant kiss. Was this God's plan all along? For Will to come and ease the pang of loss in Luke and Adelaide's absence? Will had certainly proven a godsend in more ways than one.

Not least of all to her.

Though she would ever miss her loved ones, Will had taken some of the sting out of their moving away. She only prayed this newfound love they shared was strong enough to keep him here.

39

July 31, 1868 (3 weeks later)

Lydia propped her boot on the split-rail fence, watching Will place a blanket across Angel. "So, you're finally going to ride her."

He veered his head toward her. "Gonna try."

An air of contentment enveloped Lydia. These past few weeks had been some of her most grand, strolling hand in hand with Will almost every evening and feeling sure of his affections. Now that much of the difficult summer work was done, they were enjoying a lull in the farm duties.

And a deepening of their love.

She chuckled. "The last time Luke attempted to mount Angel, he wound up being dragged several feet with his foot caught in the stirrup."

"Thanks for the warning. I'll do my best not to let that happen." Will reached for the saddle and eased it onto Angel's back. She stood still as a statue as he tightened the cinch. But then she'd done the same for Luke.

Until he'd attempted to mount.

Pressing her hands prayerlike to her lips, Lydia looked on silently, not wishing to cause distraction.

Will stroked Angel's neck and spoke in a low tone, slowly working his way to her shoulder and withers.

Lydia held her breath, whispering a silent prayer as Will gathered the reins and lifted his boot to the stirrup. Unable to watch, she squeezed her eyes shut and listened for signs of distress. But the only sounds she heard were the squeak of leather and a hand patting horse flesh. She peeked with one eye, mouth gaping at sight of Will seated in the saddle. Fearful the slightest noise might set Angel off, Lydia stifled the urge to voice her praise.

Fully intent on what he was doing, Will kept a tight rein while rubbing a hand along Angel's shoulder. The horse pawed at the ground and arched her neck, looking almost proud to have Will astride her. He flashed Lydia a winsome smile. "Let's see how she does on a ride. Open the gate."

With a hesitant nod, Lydia moved to open the pasture gate.

Will gave a light tap of his heels, sending Angel into a spry walk.

Lydia cast a glance at the farmhouse, then grinned at Will as he passed. "Mama needs to witness this. I hope she's watching."

Reining Angel to the left, Will guided her down the lane. Eventually, he coaxed her into a steady trot and then a canter. Lydia followed on foot a short way, laughing out loud when Will turned Angel around and goaded her into a full gallop. The two seemed to move as one, both obviously enjoying the rare outing. He slowed her to a walk as he neared the farmyard. Even from a distance, Lydia could glimpse the glow in Will's cheeks and the gleam in his eyes.

He was grinning as he came up beside her. "She rides like a dream."

Angel snorted and Lydia ran a hand down her face. "I can't wait until Drew sees."

No sooner had Will dismounted than the rattle of a wagon

pulled their attention to the lane. Lydia swept a stray strand of hair from her temple. "That looks like Hal Perkins's rig. He seems in quite a hurry."

They waited for Mr. Perkins to approach. He pulled to a stop before them, waving a paper in the air, his face alight. "Telegram for you and yer ma, Miss Lydia. Mrs. Flynn down at the post office said t' bring it to ya straightaway."

Lydia's stomach clenched, her thoughts instantly returning to the telegram that brought word of her father's death. Urgent news was rarely pleasant. With an unsteady hand, she took the note from him. "Thank you for bringing it."

Fearful of her emotions, she angled herself out of full view and slowly unfolded the paper. Her heart soared as she read the line of words.

BABY ARRIVED JULY 28
THOMAS JACOB.
MAMA AND BABY DOING WELL

She swiveled back around, a giggle welling in her throat. "It's from Luke! Adelaide had her baby."

"Glory be." Mr. Perkins said with a slap of his knee.

With a quick glance at Will and a wave to Mr. Perkins, she backed toward the house. "I have to tell Mama."

Breaking into a run, she rushed toward the veranda, giddy with excitement. A boy. Thomas Jacob. Named for Papa and Luke's dear friend Jacob. Mama would be so proud. She'd been less energetic of late. This would be just the news to cheer her.

Lifting her skirt, Lydia bounded up the steps. She'd hoped to find Mama at the door, already alert to the activity. Instead, the door remained closed, the house quiet.

Still happily clutching the note, Lydia bolted down the hall to the kitchen where Mama would likely be busying herself. "Mama? You'll never guess—"

At sight of Mama lying motionless on the floor, Lydia gave a frantic gasp and pressed a hand to her chest. "Mama!"

Rushing over, she knelt down and touched a hand to her mother's cheek. Sweet warmth met her fingers, and Lydia released the breath she'd been holding. "Thank the Lord."

Mama's eyes flickered weakly and then closed.

"Mama?" Desperate to rouse her, Lydia gave her mother's arm a firm shake.

Her eyes blinked open.

Lydia slid a hand under her mother's shoulder. "We need to get you into bed. Can you stand?"

Mama made a feeble attempt to rise and then fell back with a cringe.

Lydia started to rise. "I'll send Will for Dr. Royce."

With a hoarse cough, Mama shook her head. "No, child. There's no need."

The finality in her tone lodged in Lydia's chest like a boulder. "Don't talk that way, Mama. You'll be fine."

Raising a shaky hand to Lydia's cheek, Mama inhaled a heavy breath. "So thankful you have ... Will to ... look after you. The Lord ... planned it ... all along. I can ... go in peace ... now."

Lydia shook her head. "No, Mama. You mustn't give up. You have so much to live for. Luke sent word Adelaide's had her baby. A boy. Thomas Jacob."

A hint of a smile formed on Mama's thin lips. "Thomas. After my dear Thomas." The words spilled out in a whisper, followed by another raspy cough.

"Yes. Papa's namesake." Sensing her mother weakening, Lydia barely squeaked out the words. Moisture pooled in her eyes. She blinked, sending streams of tears down her cheeks.

"Don't cry, child. I'm going ... home." With that, Mama's hand slipped from Lydia's cheek and fell limply to the floor.

A whimper rose in Lydia's throat as her mother's labored breathing stilled. "No." With a shake of her head, Lydia scrambled to her feet. Clamping a hand to her mouth, she backed from the room and dashed down the hall. *Not Mama, too, Lord. Not Mama too.*

With all her strength, she threw open the door and stumbled onto the veranda. Choking back sobs, she poured every ounce of anguish into one word.

"Will!"

40

Tuesday, August 4, 1868

Will twisted his hat in his hands, wishing to be anywhere but here. Viewing Lydia's reddened eyes and tearstained cheeks as she laid the rose on her mother's coffin was almost more than he could bear. He'd done his best to comfort her until her family arrived but felt inadequate to console her. To watch her elation over him riding Angel turn to utter sorrow in a matter of moments had been heartbreaking.

Martha Gallagher had shown him nothing but kindness since the day he'd arrived. According to Lydia, she'd gone quick and without a great deal of pain, a grace the Lord must have given as a reward for her sweet nature. Her absence would, no doubt, leave a void in the lives of many.

Especially Lydia.

Will stood apart from the family, letting the cluster of friends and neighbors offer their condolences. Dressed in black, Lydia was flanked by her sisters-in-law and brothers. Her mournful expression spoke of her great love for her mother and the shock she'd suffered at her sudden loss. And yet, she greeted guests with a resilience and grace that would have done her mother proud.

One by one, the guests departed. Among the last to leave were Hal and Celia Perkins, their faces downcast. As they passed by, Hal clamped a hand on Will's shoulder and gave it a firm squeeze. Though the man spoke not a word, the gesture conveyed a true depth of friendship and concern.

When only the family remained, Will slowly backed away, giving them time to grieve their loss in private, as only families could. Pivoting away, he sank his hands in the pockets of his Sunday pants. He'd spent the past three years grieving a family he'd likely never know or remember. Time and circumstances had helped ease the sting of that truth but, try as he may, he couldn't rid his soul of a sense of loss.

With a backward glance over his shoulder, he ambled down the path to the cottage. The Gallaghers were as close to a family as he'd likely ever know. And yet, he could never truly be a part of them. He'd come to love Lydia, but he was at a loss how to comfort her. Surrounded by her family was where she belonged and where she yearned to be. Only they and the Lord could fully share in her loss and give her the comfort she needed.

"Will?"

His heart leaped at the sound of Lydia's tender voice calling after him. Turning, he was surprised to see she'd parted from her family and stood not a dozen paces from him. Though her face held little expression, her eyes were pleading. "Please don't go."

Will stared at her, the plea stirring untold emotions, sealing off any response.

"We were all going inside to eat." She reached a gloved hand toward him, eyes glistening. "We'd like you to join us."

He ventured a step forward. "I figured you'd want some time with your family."

Lips trembling, she mustered a weak grin. "As far as I'm concerned, you are family." Her voice wobbled. "I know Mama felt so too. She would want you with us."

Will's throat tightened. No kinder words had ever been said of him. With an affirming nod, he started toward her. And as he clasped her hand, he knew there was nowhere else he'd rather be.

LYDIA CRADLED baby Thomas in her arm, his tiny fingers clutching her pinky. Barely a week old, he was more alert than she'd expected, his dark hair and eyes reminiscent of his mother's. Drew's two-year-old, Mary, stood with hands draped over Lydia's arm, peering down at the infant. "Baby."

"That's right. Baby Thomas." Lydia guided the youngster.

"Tom-a?" Before Lydia could prevent her, Mary poked a finger twice at her young cousin's cheek as if checking the yeast in a rising lump of dough.

The newborn's face puckered, and a whimper rang out. Panicked, Lydia swayed back and forth to quiet him.

Sweeping his little daughter up, Drew tweaked her belly. "Enough of that, little one."

With a soft whine, Mary stretched out her arms. "See baby."

Reclaiming his seat, Drew propped her on his knee. "You can see him just fine from here."

When Thomas wouldn't be quieted, Lydia passed him to his mother.

As Adelaide snuggled him against her shoulder and spoke in low tones, he soon stilled.

Chuckling, Luke gave Mary a soft pat on the head. "Just think. In a few months, you'll have your own baby brother or sister to poke and prod."

Caroline pressed a hand to her swollen abdomen, brows raised. "Don't give her any ideas. I'm not sure we're ready for that."

A ripple of easy laughter circled the group, and Lydia felt a stab of remorse that Mama and Papa weren't there to share in it.

And yet, it was almost as if their spirits hovered over the family, treasuring the moment along with them.

The family sat clustered around the dining room table laden with food from the many friends and neighbors who'd paid their respects and shown generosity. Relaxed conversation flowed between them, bringing the house to life and providing sweet balm to Lydia's depleted spirit.

But for how long?

Her throat hitched. Mama had sacrificed so much, selflessly releasing her children and grandchildren to the Lord. It didn't seem right she'd been taken from them without the chance to enjoy them.

Tears threatened to fall anew, and Lydia blinked them away.

Don't cry, child. I'm going home. Mama's final words came rushing back, her voice still sharp and clear in Lydia's mind. With a sniffle, she dabbed the moisture from her eyes and nose with her handkerchief, then slid it into her pocket. She would dwell not on the family's loss but Mama's gain. She and Papa were together again, basking in the presence of Almighty God. Nothing in this life could compare.

A taut grin tugged at her lips. Not even grandchildren.

When conversation lulled, Lydia posed the question that pained her to ask. "How long can you stay?" She searched her brothers' and sisters-in-law's faces, each seeming reluctant to answer.

Luke was the first to respond. "I'll need to leave by week's end to be back at Copperville in time to prepare Sunday's sermon."

Trading a look with Caroline, Drew brushed a hand down Mary's shoulder-length hair. "I'm afraid we'll need to leave about that same time."

Lydia returned a slow nod, her heart wrenching at thought of the silence, which would soon invade the farmhouse.

Adelaide's tender voice broke the stillness as she rubbed a hand along the now-sleeping Thomas's back. "If need be, perhaps Thomas and I could stay a week or two longer." She cast a hopeful look at her husband. "That is, if Luke would be willing to do without us a while and make the trip to retrieve us."

For an instant, Lydia rallied, then she shook her head. "I appreciate the offer, but I can't ask that of you and Luke. It's such a long way, and you have a new baby to enjoy and get acquainted with. I'll be fine. Really."

She peered over at Will. How handsome he looked in his Sunday attire, hair combed back, face clean-shaven. If not for him, she would be utterly alone. Fearful he might feel excluded, she stood and offered him another slice of apple pie.

He flashed an appreciative smile as he slid a piece onto his plate.

For a long moment, she held his gaze, unspoken admiration pouring from her. Softening her voice, she declared, "Will's here. He'll take good care of me as well as the farm." She turned her head, talking over her shoulder. "Did he tell you he rode Angel? She seems as taken with him as the rest of us."

Will lowered his head and forked off a bite of pie, a hint of redness leeching into his cheeks.

Had she embarrassed him?

All eyes were upon her as she pivoted toward her family, a hint of amusement on their faces. Heat crept up her neck and into her cheeks. And at once, she realized her boasts of Will had revealed too much of her heart.

"I'M STAYING." Lydia paced back and forth, her boots tapping against the parlor floor.

Drew put a hand out to stop her, his brown eyes voicing concern. "Luke and I are in agreement it's best you come live with one of us."

She shook her head. "But I can't leave. This is where I belong. Will's here to look after me."

"That's just it. Will seems a trustworthy fellow, but we don't know him that well."

"Luke does." She swiveled toward Luke. "You've been around him for months. You know Will's a man of character."

Luke sat forward on the settee. "That he is, but it just wouldn't be proper to leave you here alone with him."

With a moan, Lydia shifted her gaze between her two brothers. "It's not as though he's living in the same house. He's at the cottage, and I'm here."

Drew arched a brow. "Still, as attached as you seem to be, it would be irresponsible for us to leave the two of you alone on the premises."

She raised her chin. "Mama didn't think so. She was happy Will would be here to look out for me in her stead. She told me as much."

Luke scrubbed a hand down his face. "Well, we've no way to dispute that, but we're your brothers, and it's our duty to ..."

"Please let me stay. I would shrivel and die in the city." Her chin quivered. "One of us needs to be here. I promised Papa I'd look after the place. It's not my fault you both chose to leave."

Her brothers shared a distraught look.

Moments ticked by then, with a heavy sigh, Drew touched a finger to her chin. "If it's that important to you, we'll give it a try." He brought his face closer to hers. "With the understanding you and Will keep your proper distance and inform us should anything go awry."

"Agreed." The tension in Lydia's shoulders eased. How grateful she was to have understanding brothers. And ones that cared about her so deeply.

LYDIA REACHED to douse the lantern but stilled at the tap on her bedroom door. Sitting up, she reached for her bed jacket. "Come in."

The door eased open, and Drew stepped inside, still dressed in his suit pants and shirt. "Am I intruding?"

"Not at all." Lydia grinned as she donned her robe. "I'd forgotten how much you resemble Papa. For a moment I was a child again, waiting for him to tuck me in."

Drew stepped closer, his large frame filling much of the void in the small bedchamber. "Not so long ago, it seems. When I left for war, you were but a girl. Now look at you. Somehow, you've grown into a young woman without me realizing it."

Lydia tugged at her braid. "Much of my youth was stolen away by the war." Her gaze drifted to the floorboards. "It changed our lives more than any of us would like to admit. And once it ended, nothing was the same."

He pulled the desk chair to the bedside and eased into it. "The Lord never intended life to remain stagnant, Lydia. The war changed things, that's certain. But to cling to the past doesn't leave room for a future."

Her eyes lifted. Wasn't that exactly the point she'd tried to impress upon Will? And yet, here she was still mulling over her losses. "You're right."

A baby's cry rang out, and a smile tugged at Lydia's lips. "Still, it's nice to have the upstairs full again, if only for a short while."

With a chuckle, Drew gave her hand a squeeze. "Agreed."

Shadowy light danced along his forehead as he reached into his pocket and pulled out a slip of paper. "This may not be the best time to show you this, but I found some information that might prove helpful in locating your friend Will's family."

Lydia stared at the paper in her brother's hand. She'd forgotten her request to search for information on Will. "You ... found something?"

"I can't promise anything, but it may be something to go on." He handed her the folded page, his face sobering. "It wasn't easy, and mind you, the records aren't exactly thorough, but of the passengers listed on the *Sultana*, there were twenty-five Williams with a last name starting with E. Seven are unaccounted for. The rest are confirmed dead."

With trembling hands, Lydia unfolded the paper and read the names of those unaccounted for aloud. "William Eckers, Everly, Erney, Eagan, Ellis, Emerson, and Everett."

Her breath caught. Was one of these *her* Will?

Drew gestured to the paper. "Only two of them, Emerson and Everett, are denoted as cavalry. Both from Indiana. So, if your hunch is correct, that would be the place to start."

Half-numb, Lydia could only nod. A month ago, she might have relished the news. But now—now that she and Will had all but declared their love—the thought of losing him to his past ripped her apart.

"You don't seem very happy. I thought you'd be overjoyed."

Drew's somber tone cut through her fog. She forced cheerfulness into her voice. "Oh, I am. This will mean so much to Will."

Seeming satisfied, Drew stood and set the chair back in its place. Raising a hand to Lydia's braid, he gave it a gentle tug. "Don't let yesterday's sorrows keep you from missing out on the blessings God intends for you today."

Peering up at him, she mustered a weak grin. "I won't. Thanks, Drew."

"Oh, and by the way, if Will has Angel's approval, that's good enough for me." With a wink, he turned and sauntered from the room.

While normally such a comment would have elated Lydia, in the wake of their conversation, it wielded a crushing blow to her heart. As the door clicked shut, she slumped onto the bed and studied the list of names, wishing she'd never made the request. She hated that Drew had gone to such lengths to find the information. It was exactly what Will needed to narrow his search. Yet, to share it with him meant she would likely lose him.

The way she'd lost everyone else she'd ever loved.

Her stomach tightened. Will was all she had left. Surely the Lord wouldn't be so cruel as to take him from her as well?

Tears stung her eyes. Even Mama said he was meant to be here and considered it the Lord's will he'd look after Lydia in her absence. Was it so wrong to want to hold on to the one person left to love her?

Insides roiling, she smacked her fist down on the mattress. *No!* She couldn't give him up. *Wouldn't* give him up. Not after he'd finally found contentment here and abandoned his endless searching.

Not after he'd come to care for her.

It was too much to ask.

Though it pained her to keep the knowledge from him, she couldn't risk it. Too many times, she'd witnessed his longing to recover his past. One look at this list, and he'd be gone.

With trembling hands, she crumpled the paper in her fist and tossed it to the floor.

41

W ill brushed a hand down the chestnut's face, gripping the bridle to hold the team steady for Lydia's brothers and their wives to board the carriage. He dipped his head, unable to view the anguish on Lydia's red-blotched face as she hugged her loved ones goodbye. It pained him to see her hurting. She'd done well so long as she was surrounded by family. But things would be different now with them away and Martha gone. He only prayed he, along with her faith, could bring Lydia some semblance of comfort.

Luke sauntered over and clapped Will on the shoulder. "Thanks for everything, Will. I'll be back come harvest time. Sooner if need be." He nodded toward Lydia. "Take good care of her."

"I will." Will's heart twisted as Lydia, garbed in mourning black, kissed Thomas on the cheek and passed him off to his mother in the carriage.

Striding over, Drew stretched his arm out to Will. "Good to see you again. I've no doubt we're leaving the place in good hands."

Will stood taller and gave Drew's hand a firm shake. "Thank you."

"I hope you find what you're looking for." Drew's dark eyes seemed to convey some hidden meaning. "Let me know if there's anything more I can do."

Anything more? Uncertain what Drew referred to, Will curbed his response and merely nodded. He was still pondering the words as the carriage pulled away. It seemed almost as if Drew had some inkling of Will's plight. But how? Lydia would've had no reason to mention his situation to Drew. And even if she had, what help had Drew given to be offering more?

Lydia's sniffles pulled Will from his thoughts. He went to stand beside her and draped an arm around her shoulders.

She leaned into him and rested her head against his chest. He gave her shoulders a gentle squeeze, wishing he could somehow wrench the sorrow from her spirit. But only God and time could manage that. A lot of unwanted change had come her way in recent weeks. Healing would come gradually.

And he intended to be there to see her through.

LYDIA TOSSED IN HER BED, every pop and creak of the wood reminding her of the house's emptiness. Moisture pooled in her eyes, and she blinked it away, her skin raw from tears. How she missed hearing Mama's steady breaths drifting from her downstairs bedroom. With the family gone, Mama's absence seemed to cry out from every nook and crevice.

Weary of restlessness, Lydia sat up and lit the lantern on her bedstand. She sank her face in her hands, her mind tethered to countless memories that had sprung to life—Mama kneading dough in the kitchen, sitting in the wicker chair on the veranda, the whole family gathered around the supper table in happier times in years gone by.

How she longed to hold on to each remembrance, never to let it fade.

Swiping a tear from her cheek, she yawned and stood. Her heel knocked against something lightweight under the bed, and she knew at once what it was. Grudgingly, she bent to retrieve the crumpled list of names Drew had supplied.

She'd meant to discard the tossed paper days ago but had let it slip from her thoughts. A surge of guilt gnawed at her. To hide the information from Will seemed traitorous. Was she denying him memories of his family while hoarding her own?

With trembling hands, she held the paper in her palm, half tempted to set it aflame and forget she'd ever set eyes on it. Instead, she painstakingly unfolded it and flattened it on the mattress. Heart thrumming, she stared at the list of names and locations. Which belonged to Will? What untold story lay behind his unknown past?

She'd had such dreams for this place, this family. Yet, one by one, those dreams were slipping away. To share the contents of this paper with Will would most certainly shatter her dreams for the two of them as well.

Closing her eyes, she pinched the bridge of her nose to stem her tears. "I can't do it, Lord. Will's all I have left. Please don't take him from me. I love him."

Her insides churned. *Love.* Hadn't she been taught love was giving rather than taking? Selflessness rather than selfishness? If she truly loved Will, how could she withhold from him the one thing he most longed for?

She'd been quick to tell Will he needed to be patient in waiting on God's timing as Abraham had his promised son Isaac. But now that the Lord had provided the means, could she live with herself if she stood in the way?

Will had questioned why, after promising Abraham a son, the Lord had asked him to sacrifice him? Heaviness weighted Lydia as she recalled Will's conclusion. 'I guess God doesn't want anything or anyone to stand between us and Him.'

With shallow breaths, she pressed a hand to her chest. Was the Lord asking the same of her—to surrender Will and entrust the outcome to Him?

Sometimes the Lord takes us down paths we don't wish to go to get us where we need to be. Celia Perkins' discerning statement came rushing back. At the time, the saying had seemed but a jumble of words. But now, it made perfect sense. Though she would never have chosen the losses she'd endured, they had brought her to a place of surrender.

Exactly where she needed to be.

Kneeling by her bedside, she folded her hands and closed her eyes. "Lord, I've tried so hard to hold on to those I love, only to have them stripped away. Too often, I've asserted my will over Yours, attempting to control what I cannot. Forgive my selfishness and lack of faith. You did not withhold Your only Son, Jesus, but sacrificed all for our sake. Give me strength to do the same."

She lifted moisture-laden eyes, her spirit lighter from the freeing words. "I'm Yours, Lord. Do with me as You will."

With a sniffle, she reached to smooth the tattered paper. Come tomorrow, she knew what had to be done. As heart-wrenching as it was to admit, Will's decision to stay or go was not hers to make.

It was between him and the Lord.

42

Will scooped up another forkful of scrambled eggs, and peered across the table at Lydia. She had him worried, the way she pushed her food around on her plate, rarely venturing a bite. It saddened him to see such a young, vibrant woman donned in mourning clothes and looking so forlorn.

He'd kept a watchful eye on her throughout the day yesterday. Twice she'd visited her parents' graves, leaving bouquets of black-eyed Susans in jars alongside the sandstone markers.

He cleared his throat, eager to generate any form of conversation. "Breakfast is real good."

Her faint grin belied the solemness in her eyes. She picked at her food a moment more, then set her fork down. "Will?"

"Yes?"

Not quite looking him in the eyes, she ran a finger along the rim of her water glass. "If you had the opportunity to find out who you are, would you take it?"

His chair creaked under him as he sat back. Considering everything, it seemed an odd question. "Hard to say. I've sort of given up on the notion."

Creases formed at the bridge of her nose. "But if you knew for certain you had the means to uncover your past, would you still wish to try?"

The shakiness in her voice set him on edge. Why would she bring up such a topic now, when he'd finally found contentment here? He swiped a hand along his jaw. "I suppose a part of me will always long to know who I am. Why?"

After a long moment of hesitation, she reached into her lap and brought up a folded slip of paper. "Then you need to see this." With a quivering hand, she held it out to him.

Reluctantly, he took it from her. "What's this?"

Her eyes flickered and fell away. "It's a list Drew provided of *Sultana* passengers with the name William E."

Will froze in place. Was this what Drew referred to when he said he hoped Will found what he was looking for? He stared at the folded slip, then at Lydia. "How? Why would he—"

"I asked him to." Lydia's words tumbled out almost apologetically. She wrung her hands, seeming about as nervous as Will was speechless. "When he was here in June, I told him your situation and asked if he'd be willing to look into it. I knew how desperate you were to find your family. I ... wanted to help."

The catch in her voice had him wondering if she regretted the action. He slid his thumb between the folds of the paper, wondering how it got so crinkled. "Have you seen the list?"

With a hasty nod, she averted her gaze. "I held off showing you because I ... didn't want you to see it. I tossed it away. That was selfish. Forgive me."

The note's wrinkled appearance bore evidence to the fact. Will's chest squeezed. There could be only one reason behind Lydia's action.

She wanted him to stay.

Will stared at the crumpled paper. For years, he'd longed for information such as this. But now, his heart was torn. To leave Lydia in search of his past was a sacrifice he wasn't sure he wanted to make. Especially now, when she would be alone.

He reached across the table and cupped a hand over hers. "There's nothing to forgive. Say the word, and I'll toss the list myself."

Her moist eyes lifted, a spark of life rekindling. A tear streamed down her cheek as she gently shook her head. "No, Will. You'd always regret not doing everything you could to find your family. It would haunt you all your days."

With an affirming nod, he blew out a huff. "You're right. But I can't leave now. Not so soon after your mother's passing."

Lips trembling, Lydia tilted her head to one side. "Putting it off won't make it any easier."

He shook his head. "I wouldn't feel right leaving you alone. What if Malloy comes around, giving you trouble? It wouldn't be safe."

"He hasn't come since you warned him not to. But, if he does, Luke taught me well how to use a rifle. I'd keep it loaded by the door in case of trouble. Promise."

Still unconvinced, Will wavered. "But there's the place to tend and ..."

"I'd manage." Her tone strengthened. "Harvest is a couple of months away. There's nothing pressing with the farm work. If you were to go, now would be the time."

He rubbed his thumb over the back of her hand, loving her even more for the sacrifice she was willing to make on his behalf. "You're sure?"

She gave a slow nod, tear-filled eyes reflecting the magnitude of her choice.

Clasping both of her hands in his, Will swallowed the dryness in his throat. "Then let's pray. A decision like this needs the Lord behind it."

LYDIA MOVED to stand behind Will as he spread the page out on the table. She nibbled her lower lip, giving him time to look over the list of names and locations.

He peered over his shoulder at her. "I could be any of these." "Or none of them. Drew said there were soldiers on board whose names weren't recorded."

Will slumped back in his chair. "Then is there any need to travel hundreds of miles chasing unknowns when I'm needed here?"

Lydia eased into the chair beside him, chastening herself for dispiriting him. If she was truly going to entrust this to the Lord, she needed to set her negativity and personal wishes aside. "I'm sorry. I didn't mean to discourage you." She pointed to the last two names on the list—Emerson and Everett. "Drew said to start with these. They're from Indiana and both cavalry."

Straightening, Will read the information aloud. "William Emerson, age 22, son of Thomas and Winifred Emerson of Jennings, Indiana. William Everett, age 21, son of Henry and Rebecca Everett of New Castle, Indiana."

"Do any of those names or places sound familiar?"

"Nothing stands out." He turned to Lydia. "Why cavalry?"

"You have such knowhow with horses. And with the way Angel took to you, I figure you must have been with a cavalry unit."

He jutted out his lower lip. "Makes sense. I guess it would be as good a place to start as any."

Lydia's insides roiled. "Then ... you plan to go?"

The flinch of Will's jaw and his long silence lent toward uncertainty. He'd waited so long to find out who he was. Now that it seemed a possibility, why was he balking?

Perhaps, like her, he feared discovering he was bound to someone else. Had he finally begun to look to the future instead of pondering the past?

Still, she could sense that inner tug on his spirit, unwilling to relinquish its hold.

At last, he leaned over the table. "Let's give it a few days and see how we feel about it."

But even as he spoke the words, she knew in her heart what the outcome would be.

And by the conflicted look in Will's eyes, so did he.

43

Elmira Train Depot
Wednesday, August 12, 1868

T he train whistle roused Lydia and Will from their resting place inside the newly built Elmira train depot, the old depot having been destroyed by fire the previous year.

"All aboard!" the conductor called, and a string of passengers clipped past to find their spot on the train.

Lydia bit back a sigh as Will shouldered his duffel bag, his mouth growing taut. "Guess this is it."

She marshaled a weak grin, trying to appear strong while her insides roiled. "Yes." The word caught in her throat. Dare she tell him how it tore her up inside to see him go?

Or did he already sense it?

He brushed his knuckles along her cheek, gazing at her with an intensity she'd not seen since their first kiss. "I'll come back to you. I promise."

Fighting tears, she moistened her lips. "You can't promise that, Will. You don't know what you'll find ... or who."

Her heartbeat raced faster as he leaned in close. "I know if I'd cared for someone the way I care for you, I'd remember."

The endearing words spiraled through her like the hope of spring. And yet, something deep within her held tight to the fear he might not return. "I want to believe that."

A second whistle sounded, and Will glanced over her shoulder at the locomotive. "I've got to go." He touched a hand to her elbow and guided her to the line of passengers boarding the train. Reaching his hand in his pocket, he pulled out his watch and pressed it into her palm. "I *will* come back."

She glanced at the timepiece, knowing how dear it was to Will. His only link with his past. Clearly, his pledge was a heartfelt one. But would circumstances derail his intentions?

Rallying her courage, she entwined her fingers with his. "I'll be waiting."

Her words seemed to satisfy, for he nodded and his expression mellowed.

Tears sprang up anew as Will's turn came to board. Lydia clung to his hand until it was wrenched from her. He turned and upped the steps, disappearing without a backward glance.

A moment later, the locomotive rolled forward, steam and smoke gushing from it. Lydia trailed alongside, eyes searching for one final glimpse of Will. At last, she spotted him and waved. He pressed his palm to the window, keeping his gaze fixed on her until the passenger car moved out of sight.

Lydia stood on the platform watching until the train became swallowed up by buildings and its steady chugging and mournful whistle grew faint. Choking back sobs, she clutched Will's pocket watch to her chest, praying for strength.

And wondering if she would truly ever see him again.

44

New Castle, Indiana
Saturday, August 15, 1868

Will shifted his duffel bag, thankful he'd packed light. The two-day train ride to Jennings, Indiana, followed by a day-long search for the Emersons had proven not only tiring, but a dead end. William Emerson had died aboard the *Sultana*, his meager belongings having been shipped to his family mere weeks after the incident.

Will hated witnessing the pained look on the family's faces when he'd mentioned the young man's name. Yet after learning why he'd come, Mr. and Mrs. Emerson were more than hospitable, insisting Will spend the night and probing him with questions about the incident he could not answer.

Thankfully, Will had been able to purchase an early Saturday train ticket to Dayton, the closest town to his next sojourn. The greater than seven-mile jaunt from Dayton to New Castle had given him plenty of time to think and pray. Mostly about a future with Lydia. Leaving her behind had been the hardest thing he'd ever done. If this lead came up short, he wasn't sure he had it in him to continue the search. Disrupting people's lives and stirring up unwanted memories wasn't something he relished.

As he entered the outskirts of town, several wagons and buggies rumbled past, their occupants nodding a greeting. Rows of brick and framed buildings lined the main street, tidy and well-ordered with an abundance of patrons milling about. A decent-sized town like this should have a post office or mercantile to supply him with the information he needed. He pulled the slip of paper Lydia had given him from his pocket, missing the feel of his watch against his thigh. He'd hated to leave it behind, but Lydia needed some reassurance of his return.

And perhaps he had, too.

Up ahead, on the opposite side of the street, he spotted a sign for Farley's General Store. That would do.

Weaving around oncoming carts and wagons, Will made his way across the street. He nodded to a white-haired man as he stepped onto the boardwalk. The man returned the nod, then jolted to a stop and caught Will by the sleeve. "Will? Is that you, boy?"

Will scrunched his brow. "Uh, yes. I'm Will."

Gripping Will by both shoulders, the man studied him closer, then brandished a wide smile. "Well, as I live and breathe. You *are* Will Everett. I'd recognize Henry and Rebecca's boy anywhere."

Will Everett. Heart pounding, Will swallowed. Had he finally learned his name? "You ... know me?"

The older man let out a raucous laugh. "Know ya? Why I half raised ya. Your pa, Henry, and me were like brothers. Surely you haven't forgotten your ol' Uncle Sy, have ya?"

At Will's blank stare, the man's smile faded. "You don't know me, do ya?"

Feet throbbing and back tired from the long walk, Will motioned toward a bench outside the barber shop. "Let's sit."

Sy eased down next to Will, his expression jumbled. "The war do somethin' to your mind, son? Is that it?"

Lowering his duffel bag from his shoulder, Will released a long breath. "I was aboard the *Sultana* steamboat when she exploded. A head injury left me without my memory. I've been searching for my home and family ever since."

Sy rubbed a hand over his stubbled jaw. "Why, I'll be. And us thinkin' you was dead all this time. Your mama's gonna keel over when she sees you're alive."

His mama? Will's chest burned, aching to know more. "You spoke of Henry, my ... father, in the past tense. Is he no longer living?"

Shoulders drooped, Sy shook his head. "Your pa caught the influenza back in '66, along with your sister Susanna and brother James. Sadly, all three of them were gone within a month. Rebecca, your mama, is the only one who survived."

Will hung his head, bearing the loss of a father, brother, and sister he'd never know or even remember. Had he been here, might he have done something to help?

Or perished with them.

His thoughts turned to his mother. He at least had her. "Is my mother well?"

Sy clicked his tongue in his cheek. "She suffered quite a shock, first with you, then Henry and the children. I worried she might give up on life itself. But she's a tenacious woman with a strong faith. She's done all right for herself, despite her troubles."

A deep sense of longing stirred within Will. He couldn't erase his mother's hardships, but perhaps he could at least ease her burden. If she could manage the shock. "Could you take me to her?"

With a grin, Sy slapped Will on the back. "You betcha."

Gallagher Farm

CELIA PERKINS'S familiar hum drifted through the kitchen window, stirring Lydia from her morning Bible reading. Gathering up the tins of butter and milk, she hurried to greet her neighbor, hungry for conversation. She'd not seen a soul outside of the animals since dropping Will off at the train station four days ago.

Had it only been four? It seemed an eternity. Though too soon to hear anything from him, she prayed by now he'd at least either eliminated or located one or more of the families on the list.

As Lydia stepped outside, Mrs. Perkins waved, her flimsy bonnet flopping in the breeze. "Mornin', Miss Lydia. I've been eager to see how you is gettin' along."

There was nothing to say but the truth. "Managing, but missing Mama."

"Yes'm. She was a grand lady, your mama. I 'spect we'll all miss her for some time to come."

Lydia swapped the milk and butter for Celia's honey and eggs. "Do you have time to stay a while? I could make us some tea."

"Well now, I would sit a spell, but Hal's feelin' poorly, and I don't wish to leave him alone too long."

Lydia's heart sank. "I'm sorry to hear that. I would've enjoyed the company."

Celia swung her head side to side. "Where's Will? Surely he's better company than me."

"Will's ... not here."

"Gone to town, has he? That man doesn't let grass grow under him, does he?"

Lydia considered letting the comment slide but longed deep within for comfort. She dipped her head, the painful truth hard to admit. "No. Will's gone to Indiana."

"Indiana?" The word burst out in a screech. "Whatcha mean?" Celia propped a hand on her hip. "I thought he was s'posed t' be tendin' the farm with Luke away. Not t' mention lookin' after you."

"He is. I mean, he intends to. When he comes back." *If he comes back.*

"Seems mighty strange, him leavin' you alone with all you've been through. How long do ya expect he'll be away?"

"I'm not sure." Lydia could see the disparaging look in her neighbor's eyes and quickly added. "He had good reason to go. In fact, I encouraged it."

One eyebrow lifted. "Well, young'un. You've some explainin' t' do on that."

With a nod, Lydia determined it was time to bare her soul.

New Castle, Indiana

"THIS IS IT. YOUR HOMEPLACE."

Will stared at the small, somewhat dilapidated house and yard, a vague familiarity washing over him. Almost as if he recalled standing in this exact spot.

Sy crossed his arms and widened his stance. "You want me t' go in first and soften the blow? Might be quite a shock."

The offer was tempting. Not having any recollection of his mother, Will wasn't sure how she'd react. But Sy had said she was strong. That was good enough for Will. "Thanks, but I'd rather she find out from me."

"Suit yourself. But if ya don't mind, I'll hang around out here a few minutes, just in case."

With a nod, Will edged forward. "Fair enough."

Three tentative strides landed him at the porch, his hands growing clammy. He'd waited years for this moment—to learn who he was and where he'd come from. Would it bring an end to his searching? Or make him wish he'd never come?

Surely, the Lord must have wanted him to come, to allow Lydia and Drew to unearth the information and to run across Sy as he had. It seemed when Will had given up his search and began pursuing God, things had fallen into place. Maybe that's all the Lord ever really wanted.

Will stepped onto the porch, noting the boards were worn and a couple had broken off, leaving gaps. A sure sign there'd been no man about the place for some time. The weathered boards creaked under his feet as he strode to the door. Mouth cottony, he peeled off his hat and knocked lightly on the door. When no one came, he glanced over his shoulder at Sy. The older man nodded and gestured for him to try again.

A more forceful knock produced the click of boots within. Will straightened and gripped his hat in his hands. As the door eased open, his heart sprang to his throat. A petite woman about Lydia's size peered out at him, her tawny hair pulled in a loose bun.

"May I ..." Her brown eyes blossomed to the size of silver dollars, her face growing ashen. "Will?" The word spilled out barely above a whisper. She swayed and started to wilt downward.

Will reached to support her. "I-I'm sorry. I didn't mean to upset you."

After a moment, she seemed to recover, her color returning. Raising a trembling hand to his cheek, she blinked back the moisture brimming in her eyes. "Is it really you, son?"

At the tenderness in her voice, any doubts he'd had about coming melted away. "Yes. I'm Will."

She ushered him inside, her eyes never leaving his face. "We were told you likely were ... dead. And when months and then years passed and you didn't return, we were inclined to believe it. But I never gave up hope someday you'd come. Longed for it. Prayed for it." Sobbing, she fell against him.

Will wrapped his arms around her, hating all the anguish he'd unknowingly put her through. As much as he'd agonized over his forgotten past, he had a feeling his mother had suffered worse. Though he'd made every effort to find his home, he owed her an explanation why he hadn't returned sooner. He loosened his hold on her. "Is there someplace we could talk?"

Straightening, she drew a handkerchief from her sleeve and nodded. "Yes, of course." She led him to a modest parlor with a stone fireplace, a sofa, and two upholstered chairs. "Please, sit down."

Will perused the room, hopeful something would strike a memory. But it was as unfamiliar to him as the town. He eased into one of the chairs, twisting his hat in his hands. A table against the opposite wall bore a display of photographs too far away to distinguish. He longed for a closer look at the images but abandoned the notion as his mother took a seat beside him.

Sitting forward in her chair, she reached to clasp his hand. "Now. Tell me everything. Starting with why it took you more than three years to come home."

As best he could, Will explained the details of his head injury, memory loss, hospital stay, and how he'd spent the remainder of the time combing town after town in search of information that might lead to his family. About giving up and traveling out east and working for the Gallaghers. About Lydia and the list of names and how Sy had recognized him and been brought here.

His mother hung on his every word with tears glistening in her eyes, not uttering a sound until he'd finished. With a sigh, she shook her head. "My poor, dear boy. I knew something terrible must have happened to keep you from us. I sensed in my heart you were alive somewhere, somehow. Yet I couldn't understand why you wouldn't come to us or at least contact us." She leaned back in her chair, her gaze drifting to the fireplace hearth. "Now I know. Thank you for explaining what has haunted me for years. I only hate that your father and the children will never know you've returned."

Will squeezed her hand. "Sy mentioned I had a younger

brother and sister and that they, along with my father, succumbed to influenza."

She nodded. "It will be two years come October. A dreadful time I thought never to recover from. But somehow, the Lord brought me through." Swiping a tear from her cheek, she stood and made her way to the display of photographs. She snatched up two of them and brought them to Will. "This photograph was taken shortly before you left for the war."

Will held the family picture in both hands, drinking in each face. The resemblances were strong within the family, with Will and his sister favoring their mother and his younger brother boasting their father's fleshy face and stouter frame. Will's eyes snagged on the younger image of him. How odd to see a photograph of himself with a family he had no memory of.

His mother bent closer to his face. "Does it stir any memories?"

As badly as Will wished to say yes, he merely shook his head. "I'm sorry."

A sad sort of disappointment dulled his mother's eyes. She pointed to the man seated beside her in the photo, then at the girl and boy standing next to Will. "This is your father, Henry, your sister, Susanna, age fourteen, and your younger brother, James. He was ten."

Her voice caught, and she covered her mouth with her hand. Drawing a steadying breath, she handed Will the other photo, a picture of him dressed in his Union uniform. "You were so young when you left us. Barely nineteen." She returned to her chair. "The children looked up to you. It's a pity you don't remember them. They were devastated when we heard the news you'd likely drowned or perished aboard the *Sultana*. As were your father and I."

She swallowed. "Your father was never quite the same afterward. When influenza hit, and we lost Suzanna and James, he simply gave up."

Will's heart ached for his mother. Though he didn't recall her face or memories of her in his past, he knew from this one brief encounter, she would be an important part of his future.

Just how that fit in with Lydia, he wasn't sure.

45

New Castle, Indiana
Wednesday, August 19, 1868

"Y ou couldn't have been more than two years old, mind ya, Will. You traipsed after your pa and me to the wagon barefoot and without your breeches in the snow, bound and determined to go with us. Took every ounce of strength your mama had to pull you back to the house, flailin' your arms and legs and wailin' like she was beatin' ya."

Will chuckled at Sy's retelling of the childhood venture. One of many Will had heard over the past few days. It did his heart good to hear the stories. The tidbits from his past gave better insight into the man he'd become. "Glad to know I had a determined spirit at an early age. That's good."

His mother reached to pat his shoulder. "That it is, son. It helped bring you back to us."

Warmth flooded Will's chest as he smiled at her from the sofa. In the few days since he'd come, his mother had garnered a treasured place in his heart. The short time together had awakened a bond that would take a lifetime to unravel.

His thoughts shifted to Lydia. By now she would be eagerly

awaiting word from him. He'd written to her days ago but never had the opportunity to post the letter. Though he'd never asked, he was relieved no mention had been made of a wife or steady girl. But figuring out how to live more than five hundred miles away without breaking his mother's heart was a trick he hadn't yet deciphered.

As much as he loved Lydia and longed to return to her, he was enjoying this glimpse into the life he'd missed out on. He needed a few weeks to at least soak it all in. When the time was right to go, he'd know. Though to leave his mother alone again would devastate them both.

Sy stood and gripped his hat. "Well, I'll get on and let the two of you reminisce."

On a whim, Will reached into his vest pocket where he'd kept Lydia's letter. "Would you mind posting this for me?"

Glancing at the letter as he took it, Sy released a soft chuckle. "Got yourself a girl, huh? Sure. I'll take care of it. See you folks later."

"Goodbye, Sy." Will's mother called as she strolled to the far corner of the room. Stooping down, she picked up a small tin. "Speaking of girls. I'd forgotten about these. Here are some tintype photographs I haven't framed, mostly of you and Emily."

Will jerked his head toward her. "Emily?"

"Oh, I forget you can't remember. Though, Emily is rather hard to forget." His mother giggled and sat beside him on the sofa. Opening the tin, she gazed over at him. "Emily is the daughter of some close friends of your father and mine. She had her cap set for you by the time the two of you were five. I rather think she fancied herself one of the family long before you were old enough to ask her to marry."

Will's hands went cold, and the muscles in his shoulders knotted. "She's ... my intended?"

His mother grinned. "If she'd had her way, she likely would have been had you come home directly after the war." She held out a photograph of him standing aside a fair-haired girl. "Emily can be quite persuasive."

Will held the rigid black and white photo in his hand, studying the girl's face. Was she the girl in his dream? The one he'd envisioned hundreds of times running to greet him? The long, flowing hair was similar, but with no clear features to go on, it was difficult to say.

"She insisted on a photo of just the two of you. You were both twelve at the time." His mother's words sliced through his thoughts. She pulled another tintype from the box. "This one was taken when you were sixteen. A handsome pair, don't you think?"

Though Will had to agree, he was reluctant to say. "Did I reciprocate her feelings?"

His mother tipped her head side to side. "You were ... fond of her, though never gave any indication you wished to marry her."

Will's heart throttled faster, almost afraid to ask the question burning his lips. "Where is she now?"

His mother set the tin aside and laced her fingers together in her lap. "She married late last spring and moved to Illinois with her husband."

The breath he'd been holding released in a gush. *Thank You, Lord.* He handed the photo back to his mother. "Then I'm not obligated to anyone?"

"No." She peered closer at him. "But judging by that coy grin of yours, I'd say you've lost your heart to someone somewhere."

He leaned back on the sofa, his smile widening. "Lydia Gallagher. The one who supplied me the list that allowed me to find you."

His mother nodded. "Back in Elmira?"

"Yes. She's a sister to the man I work for."

The tone in his mother's voice deepened. "And you ... love her?"

He gazed intently at her, certain his words would be telling. "Very much."

As if the admission made clear his commitments, his mother's eyes lowered. "It must have been quite a sacrifice for her to see you come all this way, not knowing the outcome."

"It was." *For both of them.* "She recently lost her mother but knew how deeply I longed to reunite with my family."

A long moment passed before his mother's eyes lifted. "And now that you have, does your heart lie here or in Elmira?"

The pointed question was one he hadn't anticipated. Focused solely on seeking out his lost roots and clearing up any personal obligations, he hadn't considered the attachments he might foster. He sandwiched his mother's hands in his. "Let's just enjoy our time together and trust the Lord to take care of the rest."

She nodded and rallied a weak smile.

Though Will had delayed the inevitable, there was no balm to remedy the threat of his leaving. He knew Lydia well enough that she would never consider moving. And, undoubtedly, his mother would feel the same.

No doubt about it. When the time came, he would have to make a choice—break Lydia's heart or his mother's.

Not to mention his own.

Elmira, New York

LYDIA LEANED over the counter as the jeweler removed the casing of Will's pocket watch and examined the insides. "Do you think it can be fixed?"

Setting the pocket watch down, the man raked a hand through his thinning hair. "It might take some doing. Some of the parts are corroded from moisture, but I'm fairly certain I can repair it."

Lydia pressed her gloved hands together. "Oh, that's grand. When do you think it might be ready?"

The man's face puckered. "Give me at least a week."

"I will. Thank you." Turning, Lydia couldn't hold in her smile. In another week, Will's pocket watch would be working. She could hardly wait to see his expression.

Exiting the jeweler's shop, she stepped out onto the boardwalk. The post office was but a short distance away. A week had passed since Will left. Surely, by now, he would have sent word of some sort. Good or bad.

A nervous tingle worked through her as she made her way along the busy street. The last time she'd strolled through town, she'd had Will's arm to cling to. How lonesome it seemed without him. The closeness they'd shared that day, as well as the month that followed, were memories she would forever treasure. Yet the fond remembrances made her miss him all the more.

Reeling in her thoughts, she quickened her pace, eager to hear some word from Will. She reached the post office and slipped inside, out of the hot sun. When her eyes adjusted to the dimness of the interior, she waved to Mrs. Flynn.

Gathered in a loose chignon, the woman's auburn hair stood out like a flame amid the backdrop of the wooden compartments at her back. She smiled a greeting. "Oh, Lydia. How nice to see you. I was grieved to hear of your mother's passing."

"Thank you." In time, perhaps she would grow accustomed to her mother being gone, but each mention of her loss resurrected the sorrow tainting her spirit. "Would there, by chance, be any letters for me?"

Mrs. Flynn touched a finger to her cheek. "Let's see. I do believe I recall seeing something for you." She turned and ran a hand along the boxes.

Lydia nibbled her lip, doing her best to stem her excitement.

"Ah, here it is." Turning to face Lydia, the postmistress handed it to her with a smile.

"Thank you, Mrs. Flynn." Taking no time to examine the missive, Lydia hurried outside to find a quiet place to read it. She rounded the corner of the building and pressed her back against the wall, finding it hard not to smile. But her heart sank when she noted the return address. "Pennsylvania?" she whispered under her breath.

The letter wasn't from Will at all, but Luke and Adelaide.

She scolded herself for her disappointment. To hear from Luke and Adelaide so soon was a pleasant surprise.

Just not the one she'd hoped for.

Opening the correspondence, she drank in Adelaide's every word—updates on baby Thomas, the church, and her cousin, Clarissa. But it was the final paragraph that most captured her interest.

How are you and Will managing? Another six weeks and Luke will return to help with harvest. Thomas and I will come as well, in hopes of giving you good company. We look forward to seeing you both.

All our Love,
Luke and Adelaide

Lydia folded the letter and slipped it in her in-seam pocket. *Six weeks.* Surely, Will would be back well before then. If not, what would Luke say? He'd trusted Will to not only look after the place but Lydia as well.

She pressed a hand to her waistline, suddenly a bit nauseous. If Will wasn't back, would Luke do something drastic? Like sell their land and take her to live with them?

She couldn't.

She could never leave her home. It was all she had left. And she'd promised Papa.

Closing her eyes, she lifted a silent prayer. *Oh, Lord, please bring Will back to me.*

46

New Castle, Indiana
Friday, August 21, 1868

Will strode onto the porch, the humid August evening drawing him outside, away from the closeness of the house. He pushed on the weathered porch boards with the heel of his boot, again struck by the house's unkempt appearance. Shutters hanging sideways. The chipped porch rails sorely in need of paint. There were enough repairs around here to keep him busy for weeks.

He canvassed the street, looking for anything familiar but coming up short. There wasn't much to see outside of buildings and people. Even here, on the outskirts of town, he couldn't help comparing the ordinariness of the level landscape and confining buildings with the beauty of the rolling hills and open fields at the Gallagher farm. It seemed more home to him than here, where he'd apparently spent most of his life.

Between Sy and his mother, he'd learned a great deal about his youth. Every now and then, he would catch a vague recollection from one of their stories that sounded the least bit familiar, but there were still a lot of holes he needed filled. Especially regarding his stint as a soldier.

The door opened behind him, jolting him from his reverie. "Enjoying the fresh air?"

He turned, his mother's now familiar voice a comfort. "That and doing some thinking."

She came to join him. "Anything important?"

Reluctant to reveal his deepest ponderings, he channeled his response. "Where can a fella get some boards and paint around here?"

His mother's eyes brightened. "You intend to fix the porch?"

"Thinking about it."

She looped her arm through his and leaned her head against his shoulder. "How I've missed having a man about the place. There's a lumber mill on the other side of town. We'll go there first thing in the morning."

"Sounds good." He fell silent, his mind still chockful of unanswered questions.

His mother peered up at him. "Something else is troubling you besides repairs, I fear. What is it, son?"

Will blew out a breath. "There's still so much I don't know about myself. During the war, for instance. For years, I've been plagued with jumbled, nightmarish dreams. That part of my life is still a blank slate."

"I think I've witnessed one or two of those dreams you speak of."

Will dipped his head. "I'm sorry. They don't come as often as they once did, but I should have warned you."

"That's quite all right, son. I'm not surprised by the harsh dreams. You spared us many a detail, but I know the war wasn't easy for you."

"How could you? You said you never saw me after I left for the war."

She patted his arm. "Come with me. I think we can remedy that inquisitiveness of yours."

Curious, Will followed her to his bedroom.

His mother slid open the bottom dresser drawer and pulled out a sizeable box. Setting it on the bed, she lifted the lid. "I don't know why I didn't think of them before. I've read each of your letters dozens of times."

"My ... letters?"

She drew one from the box and handed it to him. "Yes. You were quite faithful in writing twice a month to let us know your whereabouts and what had taken place. Though, as I said, you were often unclear about the specifics."

Speechless, Will studied the letter as if it were a priceless gem. It was a piece of his missing past he'd never imagined seeing.

His mother flipped through the row of letters. "They're arranged by date, the only gap being the month you were taken prisoner." She touched a hand to his shoulder, her eyes moistening. "I knew something dreadful had happened or you would have written."

Will nodded. Prison wasn't necessarily something he wanted to remember. He'd relived enough dismal images in his dreams. But here was his chance to gain insights into his elusive past.

His mother gestured to the final set of letters. "These prison letters were all censored, so some of the content is blacked out. But they provide a glimpse of what you've been through."

Dropping down on the mattress, he opened the letter she'd handed him. "I never dreamed I'd get to read a firsthand account of my soldiering days." He glanced at his mother. "Thank you for keeping them."

She bent to kiss his cheek. "I'll leave you to it. Take all the time you need."

———

As Lydia rose from her wicker chair on the veranda, she spotted a lone horseman riding up the lane. She fumed when she recognized Guthrie Malloy. Six weeks had passed since their confrontation in town. Will's warning to stay away had apparently worn thin.

Caught in plain sight, she resisted the urge to run inside and lock herself in. Instead, she quickly retrieved Luke's old hunting rifle from inside the door, thankful she'd held to her promise to keep it loaded and handy. Swallowing her dread, she leaned the rifle against the railing and stood with arms crossed at the top of the stoop.

More than ever, she wished Will was at her side.

But she wasn't truly alone. The Lord was with her. *Lord, keep me safe.*

Mr. Malloy tugged his sturdy roan to a stop several paces from the veranda and tipped his hat. "Evenin', Miss Gallagher."

Cutting through the niceties, Lydia summoned her most assertive tone. "What is it you want, Mr. Malloy?"

He lifted his hat and placed it over his heart. "I've come to pay my respects on behalf of your mother. She was a fine lady. Should have come before now, but ... I wasn't sure I'd be welcomed."

Lydia held back a smirk. *He had that right.* "I thank you for your sentiments, but I must ask you to be on your way."

Replacing his hat, he took a gander around. "Where's your farmhand? I'd like a word with him before I go."

Not wishing to convey the knowledge she was alone, Lydia did her best to remain poised. But how could she evade the fact Will wasn't there? She unwittingly moved her hand to the rifle barrel. "I expect him back any time." Not quite the truth, but wishful thinking.

Malloy leaned on his saddle horn and raked a hand over his beard. "Then maybe I'll just wait till he comes."

She gulped. Now what was she to do?

With as robust a voice as she could muster, Lydia called out. "I wouldn't advise that. Will asked you not to show yourself around here. He'd not take kindly to you coming."

Malloy sneered. "I ain't afraid o' him."

As he started to dismount, Lydia gripped her rifle and aimed it at him. "Stay right where you are."

He eased back into the saddle, then flashed a wry grin. "Now, you wouldn't shoot your neighbor just for gettin' off his horse."

She cocked the rifle. "Try me."

He tapped his heels against his horse's flanks, edging closer.

Lydia pulled the trigger, the bullet skimming the hat from his head.

Malloy ducked, whipping a hand to his hair. His eyes narrowed. "Why you ..."

"The next one goes through you." Quickly reloading, Lydia held her ground.

Tightening his hold on the reins, Malloy eyed her. "Can I at least get my hat?"

Legs quivering, Lydia finished loading and aimed the rifle at him a second time. "Carefully."

With a disgruntled sigh, Malloy dismounted and scooped up his hat. Like a chastised youngster, he shuffled back to his horse.

Gaining confidence, Lydia peered at him from behind her rifle. "And there'll be no more badgering us about selling our property. This has always been Gallagher land, and it will remain Gallagher land."

With a slow nod, he reined his horse around and headed down the lane.

Lydia slumped against the railing. Had she seen the last of him?

Perhaps her prayers had been answered, and she'd finally earned the man's respect.

WILL READ FAR into the night until he'd devoured every last letter. The final one, dated April 22, 1865, had originated from a place called Camp Fisk near Vicksburg, Mississippi. The letter was sent just days before he was to board the ill-fated *Sultana*.

Lydia had been right in assuming he was a part of a cavalry unit. He'd joined the 8th Indiana Cavalry in August, 1863, and apparently trekked all over the South. He'd done battle at Chickamauga, Tennessee, during Rousseau's Raids in Alabama, and faced defeat and capture at the Battle of Brown's Mill in Georgia in July of 1864.

He spent the next nine months at the Cahaba Prison. Grateful he'd spared his family the details of prison life in his letters, he knew from his dreams it had been anything but pleasant. Maybe now that he'd filled in the missing gaps, his troubled mind could rest.

Setting the box of letters in the bedside chair, he breathed a contented sigh. He'd found what he came for—insights into his past and a sense of belonging.

But as he doused the lantern and sank onto his mattress, all he could think of was sharing what he'd found with Lydia.

47

New Castle, Indiana
Thursday, August 27, 1868

W ill finished hammering the porch board and leaned back on his haunches, the woodsy scent of sawed oak wafting up at him.

"Say now. That's lookin' a mite sturdier. A coat or two of paint, and she'll be like new."

Will turned to see Sy sauntering up behind him. "Wasn't safe to walk on the way it was."

The older man gave the board a tug. "Got her nailed down tight now."

The door creaked open, and Will's mother stepped onto the porch holding a glass of lemonade. "Good morning, Sy. See what a fine job Will's doing with the porch?"

"Sure do, Rebecca. This boy of yours is comin' in real handy. Fixin' the place up right nice. Bet you're tickled to have him 'round."

"I couldn't be happier."

The sheen of his mother's eyes as she handed Will the lemonade was both a comfort and a sorrow to Will. The longer he stayed, the more attached the two of them were becoming. He wouldn't have minded so much leaving an entire family behind and coming for visits. But how could he leave his mother alone again? She'd suffered such loss. It seemed cruel to abandon her now that they'd found each other.

Turning to Sy, she rested her hands on her hips. "Come to help, did ya?"

With a shake of his head, Sy put up a hand. "'Fraid not. I've plenty of mendin' to do at my own place. I just stopped by to apologize to Will here."

"Apologize? For what?"

With a slight cringe, Sy looked Will in the eyes. "I set that letter of yours aside and plumb forgot to mail it until yesterday."

Will's stomach lurched. Then Lydia had gone all this time without word from him? What would she be thinking?

Sy clapped him on the shoulder. "Sorry about that. Didn't mean to make trouble."

Tempering his annoyance, Will merely nodded. What good would it do to get angry? The letter wouldn't arrive any sooner.

"Well, gotta run. I'll be seein' ya." With a wave of his hand, Sy started toward the street.

As if sensing Will's frustration, his mother placed a hand on his arm. "I'm sure Lydia will understand."

"I hope so." But just to be sure, he'd write a second letter tonight and explain what happened.

And post it himself.

LYDIA SAGGED BACK in her upholstered chair, the mantel clock ticking by slow minutes. Her eighteenth birthday had come and gone in quiet solitude, her spirits sinking lower and lower with each hourly "bong" of the clock. Truly, what was there to celebrate?

Yesterday's trip to Elmira had produced Will's repaired

pocket watch. But no letter. More than two weeks had passed. Ample time to receive a missive. Why hadn't he at least sent a telegram to let her know he'd made it there safely? Had something happened?

Her mind bobbed in a dozen directions, attempting to make sense of his silence. Had he been injured? Or found his family and become so caught up in them he'd forgotten her? Worse yet, had he found he was obligated to someone else and hadn't the heart to tell her?

Sickened at the thought, she wrapped her arm around her middle. Will had promised to return. But she knew when he'd made the pledge, there was no way of knowing he could keep it.

She smoothed her fingers over the bronze pocket watch, her only keepsake of Will's. She flipped open its lid, lips tugging in a weak smile at the rhythmic ticking and the second hand's steady movement. Wouldn't he be pleased to have it working?

That is, if he ever returned to claim it.

She ran a finger over his etched name. Had he found what he'd longed and searched for?

Setting the watch on the stand table, she picked up Drew's old Bible that Will had left behind. Somehow, reading from it made him seem nearer. She held the Bible to her chest and closed her eyes, having committed to memory the verse in Jeremiah 29 about seeking God. 'Ye shall seek Me and find Me when ye shall search for Me with all your heart.'

A tear drizzled down her cheek as she prayed. "Lord, help me find You in this place of loneliness. You can see what I cannot. May I learn to trust You completely and know in my heart You want the best for me. May I seek Your will above my own and accept whatever plan You have for me. For Will. For our future. Whether it be together or apart. Watch over him, Lord. Help him find the answers he's seeking. And if it be Your will, bring him back to me."

New Castle, Indiana
Monday, August 31, 1868

WILL SWIPED the paint brush over the rail, his mind more on his troubles than the paint job. Nearly three weeks had passed since leaving Lydia behind, and each day, his desire to return to her deepened. Hopefully, by now, she'd at least received the first letter he'd written. Each day, he prayed she hadn't lost faith in him and his promise to return.

His only hindrance in doing so was his mother. He hadn't the heart to leave her. It would shatter her. For days, he'd wrestled with what to do and prayed for an answer. Surely, there was a way they could all be together.

The paint job complete, he set his brush down and strode a few paces away from the house, giving the gray-coated porch and white rails a glance over. What a difference from the rickety porch that had greeted him a few weeks earlier.

His mother stuck her head out the window, eyes wide. "Why, Will. It looks like new. You've made it a house anyone would be proud to own."

With a nod of agreement, he started to dismiss the comment and then paused. The house *did* look like one anyone would be proud to own. His lips spread in a broad grin, the idea blossoming into hope.

There's the answer.

If only his mother proved agreeable.

He lifted a silent prayer, quick strides landing him in front of the window where she stood.

She blinked at him. "What is it, son?"

"Now that the house looks good enough for anyone to own, what would you say to selling it?"

48

Gallagher Farm
Friday, September 4, 1868

"You miss him, don't you, girl?" With a sigh, Lydia stroked a hand down Angel's face. "Me too."

More than three weeks had lapsed since she'd seen Will. The days seemed to lag endlessly. If Mama had been here, Lydia could have withstood Will's long absence. But as things were, the lonesomeness seemed unbearable.

Lydia sighed. At least he'd finally written, though he'd only explained why she hadn't heard from him sooner and that he'd found only his mother. He'd given no indication when or if he would return.

She rubbed her arms against the chill of the September breeze. Harvest was just weeks off, along with Luke and Adelaide. While she relished the idea of their visit, she hated to think what Luke would say to Will being gone. She just prayed that day wouldn't come. She and Will hadn't discussed the length of time he might be away, only that he would return before harvest. Would he hold to his promise?

Angel turned her head and released a welcoming nicker. "What is it, girl?"

Turning, Lydia saw a buggy joggling up the lane. She shielded her eyes against the waning sun, trying to see who it could be. In the distance, she couldn't make out the faces of the man and woman seated side by side in the rig.

Another nicker from Angel set Lydia's heart pumping faster. Curious, she slipped through the pasture gate and strode toward the approaching buggy. As the couple neared, the man removed his hat and waved it in greeting. There was no mistaking Will's sandy hair and winsome smile.

With a sharp intake of breath, Lydia drew a hand to her chest. "Will." She barely breathed the word.

Hiking her skirt, she ran toward him, tears of joy stinging her eyes.

He'd come home.

WILL DROPPED his hat back on his head, mesmerized by the image of Lydia running toward them. A woman dressed in black with flowing blonde hair.

Just like his dream.

At last, she had a face. It had been Lydia all along.

He tugged the rented horse and rig to a stop and hopped down to meet her.

She ran into his arms, tears staining her cheeks. "Oh, Will."

Will held her close, cherishing the feel of her.

"I had no idea you were coming," she whispered.

"I wanted to surprise you." Relaxing his hold, he rested his forehead against hers. "It was a good surprise, I hope."

She threw her arms about his neck. "Most definitely. The best."

An "ah-hem" sounded from atop the rig, jolting them apart.

In his enthusiasm, Will had nearly forgotten his mother.

Straightening, he slid an arm around Lydia's waist and gestured toward the buggy. "I'm sorry. Lydia, this is my mother, Rebecca Everett. Mother, this is Lydia Gallagher."

Red-faced, Lydia tipped her head forward. "It's so good to meet you, Mrs. Everett."

"And you, Lydia. Will told me much about you on our long trip here. And please, call me Rebecca."

Will turned to Lydia. "I hope it's all right. My mother agreed to sell her house in New Castle and live here with us. Her friend, Sy, is tending to the place and also sending her furnishings by train in a few days."

Lydia's face brightened. "All right? Why, that's splendid. I'm weary of an empty house all to myself. It will be a pleasure having her here."

Will helped his mother from the buggy and carried her satchels while the two ladies strode together to the farmhouse, chattering as if they'd known each other for years.

As they reached the veranda, Will set down the satchels and waited until his mother stepped inside, then said, "We'll be right in, Mother. Make yourself at home." Snagging Lydia by the arm, he led her to the far corner of the veranda.

Lydia flashed him a quizzical look. "What is it?"

Peering over her shoulder to ensure his mother wasn't listening, he spoke softly in Lydia's ear. "This arrangement with Mother in the farmhouse is only temporary. When your time of mourning ends, Mother will move to the cottage to allow me to join you here."

Lydia's jaw slackened. "What? But Will, that wouldn't be ..."

"As your husband." He slid his arms around her waist, drawing her to him.

Understanding dawned in Lydia's eyes, and a smile broke onto her face as the words sank in. "If that's a proposal, then I accept." She rested her hands on his chest and flashed a playful grin. "Though it may take me a while to grow accustomed to being called Mrs. Will Everett rather than Evans."

He chuckled, drinking in every nuance of her face as he pressed his lips to hers. While their first kiss had been tentative, there was no second-guessing the love that flowed between them now. This kiss carried a lasting fervor that left no doubt of the affection they would pledge to each other.

As Will followed her inside, he knew the Lord had, at last, given him the home and family he'd longed for. Though much of his past would ever remain a mystery, with God's help, he'd moved beyond shattered dreams into a future he could cherish.

EPILOGUE

Gallagher Farm
April 9, 1869

"I present to you Mr. and Mrs. Will Everett."

To the sound of whistles and applause, Lydia clasped her husband's hand, savoring the warmth of his touch as they turned to face the small spattering of friends and neighbors on the farmhouse lawn. She shared a glance with Will, his deep love evident in his eyes. With her brothers' permission, she'd gladly shed her black mourning dress a few months early to don her mother's satin wedding gown.

Mama would have wanted nothing less.

As they moved to greet each guest in turn, Hal Perkins struck up a lively tune on his fiddle. While Caroline and Adelaide served up cake and cider, Drew passed around four-month-old Martha Rose while Luke kept tabs on mischievous Mary and eight-month-old Thomas. Will and Lydia clapped and danced along with the guests until a late afternoon thunderstorm drove them all inside.

Barely escaping being soaked by the rain, Lydia ducked into the parlor with Will ahead of the rest, the two of them stealing a tender kiss before the others joined them. These past few months had garnered a deeper love between them than Lydia could have imagined. How she'd relished learning more of Will through his letters, hearing stories of his youth, and witnessing his tender care for his mother.

The first to enter, Rebecca strode over to them, a wide smile on her lips. "You make a lovely couple. I'm so happy for you."

Though her mother-in-law could never take Mama's place, Lydia had come to cherish Rebecca's friendship over their months living in the same household.

Will slid an arm around Lydia's waist. "Thank you, Mother."

Reaching a hand out, Rebecca fingered his new watch chain. "And what a sweet gesture to get Will a watch fob as a wedding gift, Lydia."

With a grin, Lydia pressed a gloved hand to Will's vest. "I thought it high time he had a better means of keeping track of it."

Will leaned toward his mother. "She feared I'd lose it after the trouble she went to having it fixed."

Lydia straightened. "I did not." Then added with a giggle, "Well, perhaps a little."

Rich laughter rang from Will as he slipped the watch from his pocket and popped it open. Not a day passed that he didn't gaze at his timepiece to ensure it still worked. The action never ceased to bring a smile to Lydia. She could still recall the gleam in his eyes when he first glimpsed the hands in motion.

"And well she should, as often as you lift it from your pocket." Rebecca patted Lydia's hand. "I shall miss our daily chats now that I'll be moving to the cottage. Though I'll be glad to be among my own furnishings again. Will has had all these months to enjoy them."

He gave Lydia's shoulders a squeeze. "You're welcome to them. Having Lydia as my wife is all the luxury I need."

Tears of happiness welled in Lydia's eyes as she peered up at him. "If I thought I could love you more than I already do, that comment would have accomplished it."

He pulled her closer, resting his chin atop her head.

As the rest of the family and friends filtered in, Hal Perkins struck up another fiddle tune, filling the house with music. Lydia leaned against Will, drinking it all in. The Lord had indeed been faithful. When it appeared all was lost, He'd blessed them with renewed abundance.

Her dreams of one day carrying on the Gallagher tradition of living and loving in this home had arrived at last. What began with her grandparents had continued with her parents, Drew, Luke, and herself. Now she and Will would have the privilege of experiencing the blessing of raising their family in this place she held so dear.

Lydia breathed a contented sigh. The farmhouse was once again full and bursting with joy.

And so was her heart.

THE END

AUTHOR'S NOTE

The *Sultana* steamboat disaster was the worst U.S. maritime disaster in American history, yet few people know about it. I was unfamiliar with it myself until I started researching for this novel. Coming just at the end of the Civil War, the tragic circumstances surrounding the *Sultana* were overshadowed by newspaper headlines highlighting a country still mourning the loss of President Lincoln and the capture and demise of John Wilkes Booth.

Carrying more than two thousand recently released war prisoners, the overcrowded *Sultana* was en route from the deep South along the Mississippi River, ushering the soldiers home. Despite knowing the steamboat was grossly overloaded by more than four times its capacity, those in charge seemed unconcerned about the safety of the passengers. So crammed they could hardly move, the men had to vie for a spot to sleep wherever they could on the decks and stairwells.

The overcast, moonless night of April 27, 1865, was black as pitch as the steamboat lumbered down the Mississippi north of Memphis, Tennessee. Just before 2 a.m., while many soldiers were attempting to sleep, three of the overtaxed boilers exploded, killing many passengers instantly, while others drowned in the cold, murky waters of the Mississippi.

In a weakened state after months in Confederate prison camps, numerous others clung to debris in hopes of being rescued, only to succumb to death days later from their injuries. In total, nearly two-thirds of the newly freed soldiers on board perished that fateful night.

Beyond Shattered Dreams opens with my hero, Will, among those aboard the *Sultana* just moments before the explosion. The incident provided the perfect catalyst for his story and the injury that led to his loss of memory.

DISCUSSION QUESTIONS

1. When the Lord doesn't answer Will's prayers to locate his family and reestablish his identity, he feels God has let him down. Will's reaction is to shut God out of his life. Have you ever felt let down by God? How did you respond? Looking back on the situation, what might you have done differently? When we can't see God's overall plan, how can we hold onto hope and trust Him to work things for our good?

2. Lydia's joy at Luke and Adelaide's engagement is soon dampened by the news that Drew and Caroline plan to leave for Washington. Her heart's desire to have her family remain intact is torn from her grasp and disappointment sets in. Have you ever felt the sting of disappointment in regards to the way you envision your life to be? Who or what do you struggle holding onto too closely? How might a new, selfless perspective help you give it to the Lord?

3. When Will meets the Gallaghers, he likes them immediately and agrees to work for them. Secretly, he intends to stay only through harvest so that he might resume his search for his family. But the longer he

stays, the more attached he grows to the family, especially Lydia. How has the Lord used unexpected circumstances to change the course of your life? Why is it important to keep an open heart and mind as we journey through life?

4. Initially, Lydia is a bit suspicious of Will and his vague answers to her queries. When he opens up to her, and she sees his struggle, she is sympathetic to his plight and eager to learn more about him. Have you ever made a wrong judgment toward someone you've just met? Why is it crucial we not make snap decisions about a person's nature or character? How should we respond when someone immediately rubs us the wrong way?

5. Both Will and Lydia suspect Guthrie Malloy is up to no good, yet they have a rough time convincing the rest of the family he might be a threat. When the barn is set ablaze, Will is amazed by the rainstorm putting out the flames and wonders if God sent the storm at just the right time. The incident plants a seed of faith in Will's heart. How did Hal Perkins' offer to help further demonstrate the Lord's provision? Has the Lord provided during a hard situation in your life? How did it help demonstrate He cares about you?

6. When Lydia discovers Luke is considering leaving the farm, she longs to manipulate him into staying. What does Will say that pricks Lydia's defenses to help her realize she needs to give the situation to the Lord? How does her encounter with Celia Perkins further convince Lydia of her selfish motives?

7. Will's encounter with Guthrie Malloy at the 4th of July celebration challenges Will's fledgling faith. How does he react differently to Malloy than earlier incidents?

What measures does he take to ensure he responses in a positive way?

8. Upon receiving the list of names that might help Will find his home, Lydia's first response is to wad the paper up and toss it away for fear of losing him. What changes her mind? How does giving Will over to God change things for the better for both of them? Have you ever struggled to entrust someone or something to God? How did holding on to that treasured person or thing make you feel? How did it feel to release them into God's hands?

ACKNOWLEDGMENTS

When I consider all that the Lord has done and the beautiful people He's placed in my path these past several years, I am overwhelmed with gratitude. My dream of becoming a published author stems back to my high school days, and I am indebted to so many for helping make this novel-writing dream a reality. First and foremost, the Lord. Without His abiding love and guiding hand, none of this would have been possible. May His name be praised, and may each word I write bring glory to Him.

I'm so grateful to the staff of Scrivenings Press for believing in my stories. Thanks to my publisher, Linda Fulkerson, for her tireless efforts to aid, encourage, guide, and promote my work, as well as the numerous other authors she's taken under her wing. Thanks to editors, Amy Anguish and Kaci Banks, for your time in making the story all that it could be. The staff and authors at Scrivenings Press are truly like family. God bless you for your commitment to excellence in writing and caring for us as individuals.

What a blessing my wonderful critique partners Kelly Goshorn and Jodie Wolfe and dear friends and beta-readers Savanna Kaiser and Cara Grandle have been in helping fine-tune my writing. Thank you for walking alongside me as friends and writing pals. I'm so grateful the Lord allowed our paths to cross while on this writing journey.

Thanks to Misty Beller, Denise Weimer, and Candace West for taking the time to read and endorse this novel. You all lead busy lives, and I'm honored to have you lend me some of your precious time.

I'm forever grateful to my husband, Marvin, for enduring my countless hours of writing and research. Thanks for your understanding and sticking by me though writing is "not your thing." Thank you for your patience and love through every project and deadline. I love you!

Lastly, thank you to my parents, who bought my first computer and encouraged me from the start to follow my dream of writing. Though my dad is no longer with us, what a joy it was to have his love and support while he was here. Thanks to my mom for your continued support and encouragement and for championing my stories!

ABOUT CYNTHIA ROEMER

Cynthia Roemer is an inspirational, award-winning author who enjoys planting seeds of hope into the hearts of readers. Raised in the cornfields of rural Illinois, Cynthia enjoys spinning tales set in the backdrop of the mid-1800's prairie and Civil War era. .

Cynthia feels blessed the Lord has fulfilled her life-long dream of being a published novelist. It's her prayer that her stories will both entertain and encourage readers in their faith. Her Prairie Sky Series consists of Amazon bestseller, *Under This Same Sky, Under Prairie Skies,* and 2020 Selah Award winner, *Under Moonlit Skies.* Her fourth novel, *Beyond These War-Torn Lands*, is set during the final year of the Civil War and is Book One in her Wounded Heart Series. *Beyond Wounded Hearts* is the second book in the series.

She writes from her family farm in central Illinois where she resides with her husband of twenty-eight years. She is a member of American Christian Fiction Writers. Visit Cynthia online at: www.cynthiaroemer.com

ALSO BY CYNTHIA ROEMER

Beyond These War-torn Lands—**Wounded Hearts: Book One**

While en route to aid Confederate soldiers injured in battle near her home, Southerner Caroline Dunbar stumbles across a wounded Union sergeant. Unable to ignore his plea for help, she tends to his injuries and hides him away, only to find her attachment to him deepen with each passing day. But when her secret is discovered, Caroline incurs her father's wrath and, in turn, unlocks a dark secret from the past that she is determined to unravel.

After being forced to flee his place of refuge, Sergeant Andrew Gallagher fears he's seen the last of Caroline. Resolved not to let that happen, when the war ends, he seeks her out, only to discover she's been sent away. When word reaches him that President Lincoln has been shot, Drew is assigned the task of tracking down the assassin. A chance encounter with Caroline revives his hopes, until he learns she may be involved in a plot to aid the assassin.

Get your copy here:

https://scrivenings.link/beyondthesewartornlands

***Beyond These War-torn Lands*—Wounded Hearts: Book Two**

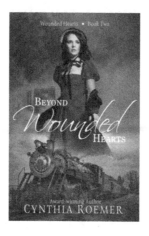

After suffering disabling burns during the fall of Richmond, Adelaide Hanover awakens in a hospital alone and destitute, escalating her already stanch hatred for Yankees. When the Union soldier who freed her from the rubble begins paying her visits, she wants nothing to do with him ... or his faith. Yet, his persistent kindness penetrates her resolve and forges a much-needed friendship. But after a dangerous man threatens Addie, she flees Richmond, intent on finding her only remaining relative before he does.

Haunted by a tragic failure in his past, Corporal Luke Gallagher takes Adelaide's plight on as his own. Though his strong beliefs collide with his growing feelings for her, he offers his family's home as a place to convalesce. Adelaide's initial rejection, followed by her unexpected willingness to accept his benevolence, hints there's more to the decision than a mere change of heart. When trouble follows her, endangering her safety, as well as his family's, Luke must lay his life and his convictions on the line to save them.

Get your copy here:

https://scrivenings.link/beyondwoundedhearts

Becky Hollister wants nothing more than to live out her days on the prairie, building a life for herself alongside her future husband. But when a tornado rips through her parents' farm, killing her mother and sister, she must leave the only home she's ever known and the man she's begun to love to accompany her injured father to St. Louis.

Catapulted into a world of unknowns, Becky finds solace in corresponding with Matthew Brody, the handsome pastor back home. But when word comes that he is all but engaged to someone else, she must call upon her faith to decipher her future.

Get your copy here:

https://scrivenings.link/underthissamesky

Unsettled by the news that her estranged cousin and uncle are returning home after a year away, Charlotte Stanton goes to ready their cabin and finds a handsome stranger has taken up residence. Convinced he's a squatter, she throws him off the property before learning his full identity. Little does she know, their paths were destined to cross again.

Quiet and ruggedly handsome, Chad Avery's uncanny ability to see through Charlotte's feisty exterior and expose her inner weaknesses both infuriates and intrigues her. When a tragic accident incites her family to move east, Charlotte stays behind in hopes of becoming better acquainted with the elusive cattleman. Yet Chad's unwillingness to divulge his hidden past, along with his vow not to love again, threatens to keep them apart forever.

Get your copy here:

https://scrivenings.link/underprairieskies

Under Moonlit Skies—**Prairie Skies**—**Book Three**

She had her life planned out - until he rode in

Illinois prairie - 1859

After four long years away, Esther Stanton returns to the prairie to care for her sister Charlotte's family following the birth of her second child. The month-long stay seems much too short as Esther becomes acquainted with her brother-in-law's new ranch hand, Stewart Brant. When obligations compel her to return to Cincinnati and to the man her overbearing mother intends her to wed, she loses hope of ever knowing true happiness.

Still reeling from a hurtful relationship, Stew is reluctant to open his heart to Esther. But when he faces a life-threatening injury with Esther tending him, their bond deepens. Heartbroken when she leaves, he sets out after her and inadvertently stumbles across an illegal slave-trade operation, the knowledge of which puts him, as well as Esther and her family, in jeopardy.

Under Moonlit Skies won first-place in the Western Fiction category of the 2020 Selah Awards.

Get your copy here:

https://scrivenings.link/undermoonlitskies

YOU MAY ALSO LIKE ...

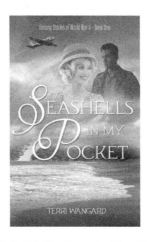

Seashells in My Pocket—by Terri Wangard

German-Brazilian Isabel Neumann delights in creating seashell art, but it's her mathematical ability that lands her a job at the American air base in Natal, northern Brazil, during World War II. She doesn't need a calculator to determine the correct weights and balances for the Air Transport Command's cargo planes.

Daniel Lambert, an American transport pilot based at Natal, endures the taunts of combat pilots that he is "allergic to combat." His flying skills win him respect, however, and his friendship with Isabel deepens, even as new source of trouble looms.

Isabel is caught in the crosshairs of a German saboteur who is obsessed with her. He insists that she belongs with him, and demands that she help him sabotage the Allied base. Her growing relationship with Daniel angers the Nazi, who will do anything to get rid of him. What will happen to Isabel if the madman captures her?

Get your copy here:

https://scrivenings.link/seashellsinmypocket

Scrivenings
PRESS
Quench your thirst for story.
www.ScriveningsPress.com

Stay up-to-date on your favorite books and authors with our free e-newsletters.

ScriveningsPress.com

Table of Contents

Getting Into
Supercompensation Mode

The Refeed

Appendix

Scott Abel

About the Author

For over 30 years, Scott Abel has been using the Cycle Diet himself and with clients to stay lean, enjoy their diets, and make improvements to their physiques and metabolisms.

Scott has been involved in the diet, fitness, and bodybuilding industries for over four decades. He has written for, or been featured in magazines like *Muscle & Fitness*, *Flex*, *Muscle Mag*, *T-Nation*, and many more.

His online coaching specializes in fat loss, staying lean year round, metabolism, and long-term sustainable solutions for permanent physique transformation.

Visit scottabelfitness.com/coaching for more information.

Scott Abel

Introduction:
30 Years of the Cycle Diet

The Cycle Diet is so named because it is all about "cycling" regular diet days of a relative caloric deficit (under-feeding) with well-timed calorie spikes of unlimited calorie intake within a specific time frame (over-feeding). You cycle between under-feeding for most of the week, with well-timed, specific periods of over-feeding. In its most common form, usually this means six days of a relative caloric deficit "on diet," then a full, single-day "anything goes" refeed or "cheat day."

However, one of the things that makes the Cycle Diet different than other "cheat day" diets out there is that before you implement various kinds of spikes you have to put your body into "Supercompensation Mode," so that taking in huge amounts of calories will *serve the body*, and not just get stored as fat.

The Cycle Diet works extremely well to control weight, maintain low body fat and optimize metabolism and create metabolic resiliency. It is a lifestyle diet. It is sustainable, durable, flexible, and adjustable—and it must be all these things in your own application of it in order for it to be successful for you.

The Cycle Diet is natural for me now, and an ingrained part of my lifestyle, so much so that I often forget that other people don't know a lot about it or understand the concepts. In the past few years, there have been a plethora of "cheat day" type diets that distort what this kind of dieting is all about, and why and how it works so darn well.

I've been controlling my weight and staying lean with the Cycle Diet since the early 80s. I did an in-depth presentation on it at the SWIS Symposium back in 2005, and it's hard to believe that was more than a decade ago. And between when I first started doing the Cycle Diet all the way up to that 2005 presentation, and since then, there have been many tweaks to the Cycle Diet's applications and strategies. I decided it was time to write a lot of it down, and provide an in-depth entry point for those who were curious about the diet.

I'm excited to bring it to you. Actually, writing this has helped me recall many stories and events that shaped the Cycle Diet, which correspondingly shaped my career as well. It wasn't until I started going back over some of these events that I realized how closely my career and the Cycle Diet were intertwined, because the Cycle Diet was so closely wrapped up with my physique success, and the success of my clients.

To this day what I like best about the Cycle Diet is that it was born from real-world experience first and foremost, and then tweaked over time, based on that experience. Over the years, research started pouring in to back it up and at least partly explain why it was working so well. These days many diets come and go which are the opposite—they are born in research of "shoulds" and "coulds" based on a few studies, taken out of context, but their real-world applicability leaves—well, a lot to be desired.

Any diet undertaking must meet two essential criteria:

1) The diet must serve the body.
2) The diet must be sustainable.

The Cycle Diet meets both of these criteria better than any other diet I've studied, and believe me I've studied them all. Part of this is because the diet is flexible and adaptable: cheat meals and cheat days can be adjusted if there is some real-life social event coming up in your life, like a holiday celebration. How and when you include spikes can be tweaked as well. You can make the deficit on the diet days greater or lesser, depending on your goals and your own metabolism and where you're at right now, versus where you want to be.

The title of this book uses the word "cheat day" because that's what people tend to understand. I much prefer the terms calorie spike, refeed, or over-feed. These terms can refer to one single meal, or to a whole day, or even a whole week or two completely off diet where anything goes.

With clients I rarely use the word "cheat" nowadays because there are so many negative emotional connotations surrounding the word, and I didn't want people to think of it as breaking the rules of the diet. It's not breaking the rules when the over-feeding is part of the greater overall diet strategy.

In fact, that's an important part of the mindset going in: one of the reasons the so-called "cheat" day is so enjoyable is *because* you are serving your body, and loading yourself up for the week to come. As you get more experienced, you will feel this for yourself.

There was a time when the only application of the Cycle Diet was a full refeed day or cheat day once per week, with a possible midweek half-day spike as well. That's a bit simple, though it might be useful to think of that as the "original" version, or the baseline from which you tweak and adjust it to your needs, once you understand the concepts. I've used other approaches where there is just one over-feed *meal* per week, or one every 10 days; or, you might have half-day over-feeds, whole day over-feeds, weekend over-feeds, or anything in between. Depending on the client, I've often played with the size of the refeed window and the regularity of the window, and I still do.

I've also learned, more and more, that there are so many other things that can affect metabolism outside of diet application. Things I never considered before can positively or negatively contribute to the viability and sustainability the Cycle Diet, and whether it's a good fit for you.

Something as simple as age can be a big factor. In the prime of my career I needed a whole day and a half of over-feeding to stoke and optimize my metabolism. That meant a full cheat day and a midweek spike each and every week, all while staying below 10 percent body fat. But now, at age 54 at the time of writing this, I only need one refeed day per week, and no more. For me to eat off my regular diet outside of that once per week structure would just be for pure indulgence, rather than for any physiological need to spike my metabolism.

The one reality of metabolism that hasn't changed much in terms of applying the Cycle Diet is this: the leaner someone is, the more over-feeds and calorie spikes that person should get in order to keep their metabolism optimized and robust. Otherwise, you risk metabolic down regulation and damage. When that happens hormones get out of balance, and the whole physiological system gets thrown out of whack.

Other factors, such as having a totally unpredictable schedule, with unstructured days and lots of travel, can impact how viable the Cycle Diet would be for you. Lack of sleep can impact leptin sensitivity, hunger, appetite, and even the willpower needed to stick to the diet on your diet days. These are variables that can affect someone being consistent on *any* diet. Lifestyle has a huge influence on whether any diet will be successful. People need to stop reading only about the ins and outs of a diet, and start considering whether they have the essential lifestyle in place to make a diet work, and to allow a diet to work for them.

Thus, the overview of the Cycle Diet comes with a bit of warning!

People hear about the Cycle Diet with its meals and days of "free eating" and they focus on that and only that. That's understandable: knowing you can eat a dozen donuts for breakfast and have it be a positive thing for metabolism sounds a little too good to be true.

Practicing what I preach this year in Aruba!

But the flip side of the fun over-feeding and calorie spikes is that the Cycle Diet is still "a diet."

It requires strict adherence to the diet days in order for the over-feed "free eating" days to work the way they should.

You also need to put your body into "Supercompensation Mode" first. You likely won't add in a cheat day your first week on the diet; you do it when your body and your metabolism are *ready*. How long this takes can be different for everyone. But when it *is* ready… well, it's a fun ride.

A whole section of this project will include people and clients of mine who have followed the Cycle Diet for a long time with great success. You will hear from them in their own words, their experiences with the Cycle Diet, and how they've made it their own.

The Origins and Birth of the Cycle Diet

I'm not going to go on and on about the science behind the diet. I'll mention it here and there. There's still plenty of research that hasn't been done yet that I'd still like to see. There has been a lot of promising new research on leptin and over-feeding since I started doing this, but even with that, the ins and outs of it are still being explored (e.g. I'd like to see research into the effects of periodic over-feeding over the long-term, especially in subjects who were already quite lean). As I said, what I've found is that this kind of eating works extremely well for *staying* lean while optimizing your metabolism and your physique, but the research is still catching up to it.

Rather than focusing on the research, I would rather discuss the ins and outs of the Cycle Diet, and how to make it a sustainable part of your lifestyle that serves your body. I think any diet that has worked well for myself and for clients for 30 years speaks for itself.

When I first got into it, all that existed in the bodybuilding world back then was "bulk up" then spend weeks and weeks and months dieting down. Every year bodybuilders would bulk up in the off season, then diet for months to get lean during contest season. Well, I did that at first, and it was exhausting. I never wanted to do it like that again. I wanted to stay lean all year, while still making improvements in my physique.

The Cycle Diet originated in my own experiences in bodybuilding and observing what was going on around me. It was like putting pieces of a puzzle together during my younger years of competing, and my passion for fitness and activity. I'll outline some of the key "aha" moments below.

1983

I competed in my very first bodybuilding competition in 1983. I was in my third year of undergraduate studies at Queen's University in Kingston, Ontario, Canada. It was my first experience with "dieting" and to be honest I had no idea what I was doing. I was more or less following the magazines. I didn't understand anything about my own biofeedback and how to read it and respond to it. I was a newbie, to say the least.

But something had stuck in my head before I started prep. Just as someone said I would never last four years of university, so I used that as motivation to stay in school, when I told someone in my local gym back home that I was going to compete the following year in the London (Ontario) bodybuilding contest, this person in turn basically went around telling everyone I would never be able to "get abs" and so I wouldn't do well. I lost 50 lbs. in 12 weeks for the show, focusing the whole time on "getting abs." I weighed in as a light-weight, at less than 154 lbs. I won the contest, and best abs.

I hadn't been 154 lbs. since Grade 9. I was emaciated. I'll never forget what my dad said to me. He came up to me after the show and said, "Now that the show is over, I can say I'm really happy for you that you won, but the next time I see you ever looking like that again you better be in a bloody coffin!" People didn't even recognize me when I returned home to compete in that contest. I'd gotten my abs, but I had over-dieted.

I also witnessed other things at that first contest that got my brain churning about the nature of dieting and metabolism.

As I said, I was very naïve. What I witnessed back

stage confused me. Guys were eating chocolate, others were drinking liquid honey, and some were drinking wine. It just struck me in my mind that all these foods that must be "restricted" during the contest diet in order to lean out were suddenly *preferred* in order to make the physique "pop" right before going on stage. These taboo foods were suddenly good for the physique, at least cosmetically. It seemed like a contradiction at the time, but I was fascinated by how the body used foods differently, depending in what state it was in at the time.

What fascinated me even more was what transpired in the few weeks following the contest. In the first few days I could eat ravenously, and I was indeed doing so. My appetite was insane. But for the first few days eating my physique just looked even better. This was the first experience I had with "Supercompensation Mode." My veins had veins and my skin looked shrink wrapped around my muscles! I was feeling better and better.

Then, of course, that stopped. What had begun as a fascination for how all this eating could make me look better, soon turned to concern. I gained back 50 lbs. in less than week. My muscles were cramping all over and seizing. The physique that was looking better by the hour very suddenly didn't look so good. I began to feel terrible as well. There was obviously a limited window where the body could put up with such over-feeding without consequences, but in this case I had gone well beyond that window.

I knew I never wanted to go through that experience again, but I kept it in my head. For the next year or so, my body was in a sort of chaos metabolically. The experience taught me about refeeds, and limited windows and cosmetic effects for both the positive and negative for over-feeding in a specific metabolic context.

A younger me, just starting to enjoy the benefits of the Cycle Diet.

1985

By 1985 I had finished my bachelor's degree, and my body had course-corrected itself. At the time I was also riding my bike everywhere. And I mean everywhere. I had a job in social work about 30 km outside of town, and I often rode my bike there and back when I had afternoon shifts. I also went on long bike rides with friends.

I started experimenting with low carb, low calorie days for the long Saturday bike rides, and then holding off eating until the next day, where I'd have a huge Sunday brunch as a kind of spike. This was not very smart. One low-carb Saturday I bonked out while riding my bike about 40 kilometers outside of town. I couldn't control my leg muscles or the bike, and I was wobbling all over the road. I ended up getting a car ride back to town. I was learning firsthand about "muscle depletion" and what happens to the body when it is truly deprived. These were valuable lessons, but they came from experimenting and making huge mistakes. I certainly didn't have it all down from the get-go.

I was also continuing my bodybuilding training, and the big Sunday brunches became more of a routine and something I looked forward to. I allowed myself to eat whatever I wanted at Sunday brunch and then diet (more reasonably, without the low low-carb shenanigans) the rest of the week. This seemed to have positive effects as I went along, so I made note of it, but didn't really know what to do with the information.

1986

By 1986 I was ready to compete more seriously again. This time I did really well, and didn't over-diet. I won the London show and the overall. The commentators actually made note that I was in a league of my own.

The secret *this* time was that I had continued doing the Sunday "cheat days" on my diet all the way up to the show.

People wanted to know what I was doing, but it hadn't occurred to me yet that the Sunday "cheat days" were actually contributing to my success. To me they were more psychological—keeping my sane while dieting. Since no one else was doing such a thing back then and I just assumed I shouldn't have been doing so either, and that I was "getting away with something" that I really shouldn't have been. Yet in retrospect, knowing what I do now, it's obvious that the Sunday "cheat days" were enhancing my physique by enhancing my metabolism.

1987

By 1987 I was in graduate school, pursuing my master's degree in social theory. But bodybuilding and the training that went with it was my passion. I returned back to my hometown to win The Great Lakes Championship, and by then I weighed 235 lbs. on stage.

Coming in lean at 235 was unheard of in the 80s, at

least in my neck of the woods. If you want a laugh, you can find a few clips on scottabelfitness.com of me guest posing (look under "About" in the menu). All during my prep, the Sunday cheat day was a key component. I remember still not knowing any of the science behind why it was working so well. It was just clear that it did.

I recall to this day how I would walk to and from the gym during prep for that contest. Right near the gym on my route home there was a Baskin Robbins. The second-last Sunday before the contest I stopped in and got two liters of winter white chocolate ice cream, which I ate after having two medium Little Caesars pizzas. I still won the show. I was still "getting away" with the cheats, if not outright benefiting from them. Since the previous year's show, where I had done really well, others sought me out for contest prep. My success during the shows for 1986 and 1987, and the amount of weight I was able to put on while staying lean, catapulted my career as a physique prep specialist. I never really turned back.

It was around this time that I stopped considering these crazy cheat days as something I was "getting away with," or something that I shouldn't be doing. I realized that there was actually something very positive going on in my body when I underfed most of the week and then heavily overfed for that one day. This was effectively the birth of the "cheat day" in my dieting strategy. It was allowing me to stay relatively lean year round, all while making improvements in my physique year after year. I could use it to some degree even during contest prep, but for that I had to be more careful in reading my body and making sure my body really needed it.

Not only that, but I *enjoyed* eating this way. I enjoyed that I didn't have to think there was any kind of food out there that I could "never have again" if I wanted to stay lean. I wouldn't have been able to live that way. There was also something about waiting for that one day per week that made me appreciate the food all the more. The diet was, in short, serving me well. It was serving me well mentally, emotionally and physically. And right around that time, I started using it with clients, and it seemed to serve them well too.

1989

By 1989, "cheat days" were a well-established part of my diet strategy with myself and with many of my clients. That was a pivotal year for my career. I was fortunate enough to be selected as the only Canadian from applicants of over 24 countries to be a camp counselor at the prestigious "Muscle Camp" produced by Joe Weider, held in the mecca of bodybuilding: Muscle Beach.

Muscle Camp helped take many careers to the next level—mine included. It's where I first met someone who would become my mentor, the great Bill Pearl. There was so much else going on as well. Our boss at Muscle Camp was the well-respected Dr. Tom Deters, who was at the time publishing editor of *Muscle & Fitness* magazine.

Word spread really quickly around Muscle Camp about my weird diet approach. When I outlined my "cheat days strategy" and that anything goes, most people didn't believe me, since I wasn't obviously in "off-season" shape or anything. I was still pretty darn lean, with abs showing. This made people doubt even more that I was eating what I said I was eating on cheat days. By this point, there was still no "Cycle Diet." There were just these weird "cheat days" that I somehow was using in my diet strategies for me and my clients.

In one of our mandatory lectures, I'll never forget that Dr. Tom Deters himself used me as an example, and said something along the lines of, "Abel says he eats about 10,000 calories or more on his cheat days. There's no way he's doing that unless he's drinking Crisco Oil right out of the bottle. It's just not possible to eat that many calories." Of course, he was wrong. Competitive eaters, who I'll talk about later, can do that in a single 10-minute sitting, eating normal foods like burgers, steaks, cheesecakes, or whatever.

People who didn't believe me, but who were nonetheless curious, decided they had to see it for themselves. Many went out of their way to witness my cheat day, where I ate whatever the hell I wanted to eat, in front of guys who were still eating tuna right out of the can because they feared adding condiments would somehow ruin their entire diet. I've been a very early riser since my undergraduate days. I remember one time a few guys waking up early so they could see my gobble down a huge carrot cake I'd purchased the evening before.

Note, though, the Cycle Diet wasn't (and still isn't) just about eating a lot on a cheat day. It is about putting your body in that mode so that it needs the calories, and is able to put them to good, beneficial use. This element of The Cycle Diet had a lot to do with understanding essential biofeedback, "Supercompensation Mode," and the physiological "readiness" for an over-feeding day.

One of my first experiences with the importance of biofeedback was also at that same Muscle Camp. It came from eight-time Mr. Olympia, Lee Haney.

At the time Muscle Camp was going, contest prep for the Mr. Olympia, the top contest in all of professional bodybuilding, was also underway. Along with actors and other famous names in fitness, many of the top Olympia competitors were slated to come in to Muscle Camp to give seminars and talk about their training, and often to do a little physique display at night as well.

Given that most of these guys would be right in the midst of preparing for the Mr. Olympia I was excited to see them in person for the first time. But I was disappointed at their lack of conditioning. Even though most of them came to camp during contest prep, most of them looked *way* out of shape. I was surprised.

But then the reigning Mr. Olympia, Lee Haney, showed up. He was different. He was on a totally different level, though I didn't notice at first.

I ended up having breakfast with him one morning. He was an incredibly nice guy. I watched like a hawk everything he did. We all ate at a buffet-style breakfast place in the area that catered to bodybuilders. That morning Haney came to the table with a plate of egg whites, a large bowl of grits, two bran muffins and two bananas. It seemed out of place to me that he was eating this much eight weeks out from defending his crown. (Yes, I was staying lean with the cheat days, but I was still eating in a deficit the rest of the week. If I ate in a caloric surplus all through the week, I'd have gained weight quickly.) The breakfast conversation turned to his pre-contest prep, and he was saying he was basically ready now at eight weeks out, with just minor adjustments to make between now and then.

Since for weeks I'd been seeing other top Olympia pros coming to Muscle Camp out of shape, I was more than a bit skeptical, especially having watched him eat what I considered to be way too many calories for pre-contest dieting. We all sat there talking for a while and then Lee Haney said something along the lines of since he'd been sitting so long talking, he better eat a bit *more* or he won't make it through his training. He went up and got two more bananas and two more bran muffins, and then made his way to the gym. At this point I was more dubious than ever that he was "basically ready" for the contest and eating so indiscriminately.

But that night at the social seminar Haney took his shirt off and hit some poses. I was floored. He looked unbelievable. He did indeed look "basically ready" for the contest, even though it was still eight weeks away. I was humbled by just how far ahead of everyone he was. It was staggering.

I also learned some lessons I never forgot. For one, I "assumed" things before I had all the real-world facts. I assumed since all the *other* guys were out of shape, that the reigning champ would be as well, just based on what I saw him eating. I couldn't have been more wrong.

I learned something else, too. Lee Haney was one of the very few people who actually really considered and could read his own biofeedback during contest prep. He wasn't counting calories and letting that dictate what he should or shouldn't be eating or when. He just knew his own body. He knew that to get through his workout he needed two more muffins and two more bananas, and he didn't think twice about it. He knew he was "basically ready" and that these extra calories were not going to hurt him. He could feel what his body needed. No fancy number crunching and percentages of this and that, just a solid inside-out respect for his own biofeedback. (You'll see as you read that biofeedback indicators play a huge role in the Cycle Diet. You'll need to learn to pay attention to them.)

All these experiences kept adding up, and over time, what had once been just about "cheat days" was beginning to take shape as a solid, methodical approach to my dieting and the dieting of my clients. And it was an approach not just for achieving leanness but for *sustaining* it as well. Seldom had any strategy at the time focused on this. Indeed, most diet strategies are all about how to "get" there and not about how to stay there. So you get rebounds and unwanted metabolic aftereffects. The Cycle Diet let me and my clients live in the real world.

These were the early days of the genesis of the Cycle Diet. The pieces were starting to come together. It was an approach that was just working, and working well, not just with me, but also for many of my clients. Many of my clients then were a lot like me. We were young. We liked food. We liked food a lot! We didn't want to pretend that we didn't, and we didn't want to obsess about it while dieting.

I think this is probably what Cycle Dieters like best to this day. Once body weight and leanness is under control, then some good ol' fashioned food indulgence is always just a few days away at most. Knowing that makes even the "strict" diet days very easy. When the cheat days come, they are guilt free, because you are *serving the body*. Cycle Dieters tend to love, *love*, that they can still enjoy favorite no-no foods and still stay lean. At the time, it seemed too good to be true, even though it was working. There was no real science backing it up, just my purely anecdotal work and experimentation. Some of the science would come later.

Is the Cycle Diet Right for You?

A diet strategy by any name *has* to become a lifestyle if it is going to be sustainable.

All too often people ignore this element of their diet undertaking. They want to diet for some special event like a wedding or a high school reunion. They lose the weight and then gain it all back again. Yo-yo dieting like this hurts metabolism, sometimes irrevocably. I've written whole books about that.

The Cycle Diet, like any good diet strategy, is a *lifestyle*. I've been following it since the 80s, and I've been honing it since. This speaks to the sustainability of the Cycle Diet. The Cycle Diet is a healthy diet as well, because it advocates *relative* caloric restriction with very healthy foods, cycled with regular indulgences.

However, you need to consider whether or not you

can follow this kind of approach as a lifestyle. You can't just make it all about regular cheeseburgers and fries and desserts. Yes, that is an appealing element of the Cycle Diet. But there are all those diet days (and maybe weeks) in-between the refeeds. You need to accept that as part of the whole package of the diet strategy, and embrace it as a lifestyle. Otherwise, you are just using the Cycle Diet as a reason to eat indulgent foods, and that won't work for long before your discipline on diet days breaks down completely.

The Cycle Diet is still a diet. The Cycle diet requires not cheating during the diet days, not wavering even a bit from the meal plan on diet days. For the diet to work as intended, you don't want to risk taking yourself out of supercompensation mode. The Cycle Diet is not for people who have no discipline when it comes to meal regimentation and control. You can't just have what you want when you want it—that is fantasy thinking.

The beauty of the Cycle Diet is that you *can* have what you want by planning it in advance, and by creating the metabolic environment where having what you want and as much as you want never hurts you metabolically or cosmetically—instead, it *helps* you.

This still requires discipline and dedication. All diets require true dedication if you are going to be successful with them. But with the North American Diet Mentality and its destructive nature, I always have to point out that there is a *huge* difference between dedication and obsession.

> Dedication means you control the thing you do.
> Obsession means the thing you do controls you.

All too often, people become diet zealots. What began as worthy dedication becomes an obsession with food and eating. That can happen with any diet strategy undertaking. It's a warning I feel is necessary to point out to anyone considering any diet. If you feel this is you, you can read my other books for more on the psychology of diet, diets, and dieting.

Scott Abel

The Goals of the Cycle Diet

The Cycle Diet is all about building and sustaining **"metabolic resilience."** Some people are genetically just blessed with metabolic resilience. There are people we all know who eat whatever they want and never gain weight and stay lean. Everyone knows someone like that. Generally, this is just genetic.

The Cycle Diet can actually train the metabolism to be more robust and resilient. It takes time, but this is actually my favorite element of the Cycle Diet, and how it differs from almost all the other "weight-loss" diets out there. The Cycle Diet is all about "training metabolism." The Cycle Diet puts metabolism *first* and weight-loss *second*. This is how any diet strategy should be, actually, but of course the common weight-loss dieting approach pays scant attention to metabolism, especially in the long-term.

Once you reach supercompensation mode and begin refeeds, you are "training" the metabolism. Just like when you're training muscles, your metabolism becomes more resilient and stronger. When you've been practicing Cycling under-feeding with over-feeding for a while you can take longer breaks from dieting with no ill effects from these breaks at all. This allows the Cycle Diet to work in the real world.

I often instruct my Cycle Dieting clients to take a week or two off from diet and training after completing a program. They eat whatever they want and as much as they want and this engages the "restorative" elements even more completely. Whatever weight is gained during that week comes right back off again. It's a great way to enjoy planned time off, vacations, holidays and so on. For myself, it's usually at Christmas and then again in springtime when I go to Aruba every year for two weeks or more.

Aruba is famous for restaurants and the *last* thing I want to be doing there is dieting, worrying about, or thinking about food in a restrictive way. I take the whole vacation off from any diet restraints or regimens, and I make that part of my vacation experience. As soon as I go back to my regular diet, any gained weight comes right back off again.

At this point, with all these years and years of Cycle Dieting, I can easily work "time off dieting" into any situations that come up. If I have to travel and it's been at least six weeks on my Cycle Diet regimen, then I just take that travel time off-diet because I know it won't affect me negatively.

My most recent vacation to Aruba.

This easy-to-come-off weight is referred to as "the labile element" of weight change. Labile in this instance means unstable. Yes, my clients and I gain "lots of weight" while on vacation. But it all comes off, very, *very quickly*, because it's just water and the body's adjustment to both more food and to different foods.

Frequently I have clients ask me about their upcoming vacations and how they are going to handle their diets. Many of them are worried and anxious. The experienced ones know not to worry and what to expect. For the ones that are still worried and new to this, I just tell them: take that time off your diet and don't worry about it. They seem skeptical, but they trust me. When they return and they get back to their structured diet regimen and back to checking in with me again, they often report being "shocked" at how fast their weight returned to pre-vacation levels, something that has never happened before. This is all a testament to the metabolic resilience that the Cycle Diet creates. The longer someone has been on the Cycle Diet, the longer it seems this resilience lasts from a break in dieting regimen.

Take my client Aaron, for instance. He took an extended break from dieting, then he came back to dieting after a long break away from it. It wasn't long before we were "cycling" his diet with regular refeed days again. Even after a few months off of dieting, his metabolism retained its resilience and responded immediately to dieting again.

Aaron stayed on the Cycle Diet for the duration of his contest prep diet and ended up winning his Master's Class in competition, competing 100 percent naturally. He didn't suffer, he didn't suddenly balloon up in weight again post-contest. He just used the Cycle Diet and counted on the metabolic resiliency we'd built up with years of following the Cycle Diet.

He told me he found the whole pre-contest diet experience "relatively easy" while most people will tell you they experience a form of "hell" while dieting to get the leanness required to compete on stage.

Is the Cycle Diet a "Weight-Loss Diet," Then?

Short answer: No.

It'd be more accurate to say the Cycle Diet is a *metabolism diet*, which makes weight loss easier in the long term.

You will absolutely lose weight while getting into supercompensation mode and dieting at a relative caloric deficit. That's just inevitable. But once you're in Supercompensation mode, you're very close to your body's metabolic set point, so we don't push things in a way that'll damage or down-regulate the metabolism. Instead, we focus on staying lean while training the metabolism to be more resilient. Depending on goals, we can also make adding muscle or gaining weight a focus (often by increasing the diet day calories just a tiny bit).

Beyond that, it's a diet that helps people constantly improve their physiques, while living in the real world.

Once you are in supercompensation mode the Cycle Diet is flexible in adapting to the real world and actually "enjoying" indulgent foods that are such an entrenched part of various holidays and traditions. It's easy to work "cheat meals or days" and time them for events like Thanksgiving, Christmas, vacations, or whatever other events used to present "diet dilemmas." Changing the refeed or cheat day around is okay, here and there. The Cycle Diet is flexible in that regard.

I have always said that I think it is unreasonable and unrealistic to think you can trick your mind to not perceive "food as celebration." There is a reason that food and eating indulgences evolved to be a major part of religious and cultural celebrations. But how many times at Christmas do you witness all these articles and commercials advising you "how to stay on your diet during the holidays." This kind of food deprivation is unnatural and your mind knows it. The Cycle Diet allows you to participate fully in these cultural traditions, and that includes enjoying the once-a-year food indulgences that go with these holiday celebrations.

Staying Lean Year Round

The Cycle Diet was basically designed first and

foremost for those people interested in achieving and maintaining leanness. I first used it to stay quite lean while making improvements in my physique and metabolism.

I have many, many clients who use The Cycle Diet to stay within striking distance of things like "photoshoot readiness" all the year round.

Consider my client Andy Sinclair. Andy is a professional fitness model. He's been on the cover of fitness magazines, romance novels, and more.

Andy stays with The Cycle Diet year round and also takes regular one to two week off-diet times. When he knows he has a photoshoot pending, he just skips a mid-week refeed, or refeed day, and *bam!* he's photoshoot ready. He doesn't have to "diet-suffer" his way to photoshoot readiness for weeks and weeks.

He has been with me as a Coaching client for more than a decade now! In fact, that photo above is from almost a decade ago. He's stayed lean all this time, near photoshoot ready!

These are just a few of the examples of just how well the Cycle Diet works in the real world we live in. The Cycle Diet is not for diet "martyrs" who are only happy when they're unhappy. It is for people who truly can and want to enjoy real food of all kinds, guilt-free, while still being consistent and still taking responsibility for their health and — yes — a bit of healthy vanity as well.

* * *

There you have it! To my mind, the Cycle Diet is different than other diets for four key reasons:

1. It was born in the real world of experience first, and then the research came along to support it, not the other way around like most diets, which take a smidgen of research or theory without sufficient real-world proof or examples.

2. The Cycle Diet takes an *inclusive*, not *exclusive*, approach to food, and doesn't demonize any kind of food or food groups like so many modern diets do.

3. The Cycle Diet doesn't eliminate whole nutrient groups like carbs, fats, dairy, wheat, gluten, or fruits.

4. The Cycle Diet fits the real world of food abundance that we live in *now*, today! We have never had greater access to indulgent foods. The Cycle Diet makes living in such a world much, much easier — and enjoyable. It doesn't try to negate this fact and tell us that we should eat like our starving hunter-gatherer ancestors (who, by the way, probably hated their diets).

Scott Abel

The Cycle Diet in Application

Diets of all kinds will always speak directly to our own "wish bias." Wish bias is about speaking to what we *want* to hear, getting us to believe in magic solutions because our minds are set up to *want* to believe in them. Most diets will speak about weight loss or fat loss or ultra low body-fat percentages and blah blah blah. All of these diets are designed to cater to our desire to believe more in the promise than the reality.

Most diet protocols try to sell you the sizzle, not the steak.

In some ways, the Cycle Diet is no different!

The selling point for most people who are fascinated by the Cycle Diet is that you get to have meals, days, and weeks where you can eat anything you want and as much as you want. I'll be honest: that's a good reason why *I* like it, and why I have followed it for 30 years.

However, if the idea of a dozen donuts for breakfast, or pizza and ice cream for dinner sounds too good to be true. That's because *without the proper context* it is!

With the Cycle Diet, you *have* to put your body into the right mode with your training and dieting in order for the refeeds and spikes to *serve* your body. You have to earn it, yes, but that doesn't mean you have to "suffer" to get there. Some clients have been put on full day cheats on their *first week* of dieting, and still lost weight. Some clients had to go for months before their body was ready for the cheats, but they didn't "suffer" unnecessarily—part of the biofeedback that told me they weren't ready for the refeeds was that they weren't that hungry yet. Their "diet days" were still pretty satisfying, and they still had lots of energy. This is the reality math of dieting. Some people take longer.

There are many diets out there now that talk all about the "free meal" or the "cheat meal" or a "cheat day."

However, you can't just decide to add a cheat meal or cheat day because you heard someone else doing it with success, or because you think you "deserve" it. The cheat meal or cheat day has to be added at the right time and place. It's not about what you "deserve," it's about what will serve your body. Your metabolism should be trained to handle *both* sides of the diet: the under-feeding, or diet days, and the over-feeding, or cheat days.

Dieting in a caloric deficit impacts metabolism and sets in motion a cascade of hormonal, histochemical, biochemical, enzymatic and metabolic reactions in the body, in order for it to protect itself against weight loss. It is the way our physiological systems evolved. Over time on a diet, your body will lower metabolism, hunger will go up, and you will eventually regain weight. This is known as the metabolic compensation system, and it's all about body weight set points.

The Cycle Diet deals with this by letting you diet until lean, and then when you start experiencing that cascade, you have a refeed day that takes care of hunger, hormones, and causes a reverse cascade of very good things.

Diets generally try to sell you on short-term windows of time like 12-week transformations. The Cycle Diet isn't about that at all. **The Cycle Diet is about a sustainable lifestyle, and constant improvement from there.** It's about working *with* metabolism, not against it. That's why you don't use the Cycle Diet with full cheat days and mid-week spikes and everything to diet down for a bodybuilding show. You use it to stay lean, and to improve, slowly and surely, during the off season, so that when it comes time to diet down to an unsustainable "on-stage" level, your metabolism is revved, and you don't have to lose 50 lbs., much of which is muscle. If you're not planning to actually step on stage any time soon, the Cycle Diet, cheat days, spikes and all, can keep you just as lean as your body can comfortably handle.

You will always lose weight at the start, before you get to super compensation mode, but then you end up right near your body weight set point, and instead of dieting "past" it, you start working *with* it, nudging and coaxing it down, and adding muscle mass if that's your goal.

Most "before and after," 12-week transformation pictures you see would be much more accurate if they also had an "after after" picture, maybe six months to a year later, once the metabolic compensation system had come into play. Once you get to adulthood your body has a specific body weight, leanness level, and body fat level it wants to be at and stay at. If you have ever dieted you know, your body will fight to maintain this, that is, maintain "homeostasis." Just because you "successfully" start dieting past your set point and start losing weight doesn't mean that your body has forgotten where it really wants to be. It will cooperate with you to a point (and we will take advantage of this), but eventually it will begin to adapt to bring you back to where it's comfortable.

It is possible to alter sets points and leanness levels a little here and there. That's part of what the goal of the Cycle Diet is. The problem is that most "diets" put weight-loss and leanness first, and pay scant attention to metabolism. But *sustainable*, real-world weight loss is all about **metabolism first, and weight loss and leanness second.** It's a bit counter-intuitive, but not that much if you think about it.

Mostly, I think people don't talk about it like that because it doesn't sell. The average dieter doesn't want to hear that. Instead, they want to lose weight in the short-term for some understandable reason. A few common ones I hear often from clients are their wedding, their school reunion, a vacation, or a physique competition.

It's when you do this, and diet past your set point, that your wish bias comes into play. You "think" you will diet down to leanness and then your body weight set point will "settle" in at this new lower weight and stay there. But this isn't what happens, is it? Practically all the research on the metabolic compensation system and body weight set points shows this is actually the path to an *increasing* body weight set point, and increased fat percentage, as the body "rebounds" to protect itself against future starvation.

So we have a dilemma. If you are overweight and want to lose weight or lean out then you need to diet. But if you diet incorrectly, your metabolism "compensates" by lowering metabolism and increasing hunger until you've gained weight, and your set point is even higher. Not good!

This is where the Cycle Diet comes into play. The Cycle Diet argues and demonstrates that regular over-feeds (refeeds, calorie spikes, and so on) while dieting in a relative caloric deficit will tell the body *not* to go into emergency rebound mode.

Now, that said, you have to enjoy the re-feeds and the over-feeding. If you feel guilty and worry about it, you release hormones that basically counteract the benefits of the over-feeding.

"Coax the body and it responds, force the body and it reacts."

Pretty much *all* my research into the metabolic compensation system, the biology of weight control, body weight set points and sustaining weight-loss and leanness, and so on, has led me to the following mantra for physique transformation: "Coax the body and it responds, force the body and it reacts."

Memorize that line. You coax the body to sustainable weight-loss and leanness by dieting in a *relative* caloric deficit, and never in an *absolute* caloric deficit. (I will explain in more detail further on. But a relative caloric deficit is a slight deficit that is *relative* to what your needs are. An absolute deficit is just that: an *absolute* one, with no thought to what your body needs to function. The difference between the two is different fro everyone. But if you imagine an insane 600-calorie per day deprivation diet, you can be sure that's an absolute deficit.)

Then, while under-feeding in this relative deficit, when the metabolic environment is just right, you start "over-feeding" your body in regular, well-timed intervals. This tells your metabolism that you are not starving, and it doesn't start to adapt in "reactionary" ways to the dieting sequence. Instead, it *responds* in the kinds of ways we want. In other words The Cycle Diet is one way of *coaxing* the body to sustainable weight-loss and maintaining tolerable levels of leanness!

Scott Abel

Why the Cycle Diet Works

I said in the beginning of this project I'm not going to bog you down with a bunch of research studies and the like, but I do want to touch on the basic highlights of why and how The Cycle Diet works in a way that coaxes the body to sustainable weight-loss and leanness.

One of the ways is that, as I just mentioned in the previous chapter, well-timed calorie spikes or "over-feeding" interrupts the body's compensation systems and has a beneficial effect. These over-feeding scenarios must occur in the "right" and "appropriate" metabolic context. You can't just have cheat meal because you want to, or because it's Friday night and you don't feel like cooking, or because you are bored. In order for the over-feeding to do what's it is supposed to, your metabolism must be trained to handle them, and to respond positively to them. Your metabolism must be *primed* for them. This means dieting to a certain level of leanness that puts you in what I call Supercompensation Mode. I'll discuss that a little more in a little bit.

Once you diet and exercise in a relative energy deficit for a while, you not only get leaner but you gradually deplete muscle and liver glycogen stores. Depleted glycogen stores create a series of signals to the body to down-regulate certain functions. This is one small part of the metabolic compensation system mentioned earlier. Calorie spikes help to refill glycogen stores, and also help optimize metabolism and keep it robust.

Intramuscular fats also get depleted. Once you get to a certain level of leanness by dieting, your body doesn't tap into fat stores as easily as before. Most people who've dieted have experienced this. Your body senses you're in a state of energy depletion, and you are now in some form of "Supercompensation Mode."

Once you are in Supercompensation Mode your body will partition and store energy where it is needed most. By depleting and even regularly semi-depleting both muscle glycogen and intracellular fat stores within muscle, your body is set up to "Supercompensate" energy storage inside the muscle instead of just adding extra it as extra body fat (as you would if you just had a huge binge without being in a Supercompensation Mode).

But what is very important to know and understand

is that as you get leaner, leptin levels start falling as well, because leptin is stored in fat. As you get leaner, you sacrifice leptin, and leptin has a direct emergency line to your metabolic compensation system. If leptin is not replenished and goes ignored, your body will lowers its metabolic rate and metabolic processes, and also set itself up to store fat more readily. One of the jobs of the energy spike is—as it takes that energy and "super" replenishes your muscle glycogen and intramuscular fats—it also spikes your leptin levels. This is very good.

Leptin

Leptin is considered a master hormone and it's stored in body fat. Leptin has receptors in the Hypothalamus, and the Hypothalamus is considered a key command center for your body, and for metabolism in particular. Leptin has huge influences on thyroid, growth hormone, and testosterone. If leptin is low, or it is "there" but is somehow not being received by the cells (as in leptin resistance, which is a lot like insulin resistance) it can create a cascade of negative effects on these others hormones that also influence body weight and leanness potential.

In plain simple English, dieting reduces leptin, and that's bad. Over-feeding brings leptin back up, does so very quickly, and that's good. The stimulation of leptin shuts down hunger cues and stimulates calorie burning.

One of the reasons for metabolic slowdown from dieting is the drop in leptin levels. Periodic spikes to bring it back up are therefore very, very important. But you also want to do it when you're in a state where those extra calories will be put to good use (i.e. Supercompensation Mode).

Since leptin comes from fat, then as you get leaner you'll require more re-feeds to keep restoring your leptin levels. (This is why on the Cycle Diet really, *really* lean people also get a mid-week spike along with the full cheat day.) Experts I talked to early on told me that leptin levels increase better with refeeds of something like 40 to 55 calories per pound of Lean Body Mass (LBM). They also said you top up leptin levels better if these over-feeds are more or less "high-carb" over-feeds. (We emphasize carbs on the cheat days, but by no means do we cut out fats or focus on only "low fat" carbs or anything like that.)

In terms of leptin sensitivity there are certain things that help that as well. Things like nicotine, zinc and Vitamin E help keep leptin levels adequate, and also increase leptin sensitivity. The nicotine effect on leptin and leptin sensitivity may be one reason smokers experience weight gain after they quit smoking. It can be a delicate balance. Note that I'm *not* suggesting that you supplement vitamin E or zinc, (and I'm definitely not advocating tobacco use); I'm saying these two nutritional components should be a regular part of any diet undertaking.

When leptin levels get too low, Neuropeptide Y (NPY) decreases metabolism yet at the same time increases appetite and hunger. Its effect on the hypothalamus is one of the least desired effects of the metabolic compensation system after a diet. The way for you to control it, instead of it controlling you, is (again) with well-timed refeeds or over-feeding that resets your leptin levels, which in turn affects the biochemical environment of the brain to keep metabolism optimized and keep it robust. Replenished leptin reduces appetite and directs energy to be stored in muscles instead of added on as extra body fat.

Also, and as a side note here: as you age, just like sex hormones diminish which in turn negatively impacts lean mass and your body's propensity to store body fat, so too with leptin. As you age there are fewer leptin receptors in the brain. With that in mind, you want to have better leptin sensitivity for those fewer receptors so they can help control body weight and leanness. Increasing leptin sensitivity is difficult, though, to say the least.

Leptin Resistance

As I alluded to above, there is also leptin resistance to consider. Leptin resistance is the opposite of leptin sensitivity. Leptin resistance is a lot like insulin resistance. Receptor cells, instead of being "sensitive" to the presence of leptin (which is good, because of all the benefits leptin has), they become resistant to it. So even if it's there, they act as if the leptin isn't there. Anecdotally, from working with clients for 30-plus years, I suspect that repeated yo-yo dieting may result in some level of leptin resistance, but I haven't seen any research on that.

In another form of leptin resistance, cells stop accepting the leptin message altogether. This is a lot like the difference between Type 2 diabetes and Type 1 diabetes. For example, good majorities of obese people have adequate or even high leptin levels, but their bodies simply don't receive and accept leptin signals.

But all things being equal – if you allow leptin to do its job, it will help the body control weight and leanness. Since leptin is stored in fat and releases its effects from there, then as you get leaner you will need to practice regular calorie spikes to keep leptin levels and leptin sensitivity having their preferred influence on keeping you lean and keeping hunger from intensifying to a level you can no longer control.

Ghrelin

Speaking of hunger, there is Ghrelin to consider. When your stomach is empty it produces the hormone ghrelin to stimulate appetite and hunger and a desire to eat. Ghrelin also makes you want to eat by stimulating NPY levels as well. For chronic dieters and people in a chronic caloric deficit, ghrelin will send stronger and stronger and more consistent messages and signals to u. brain to make you want to eat. It will make you feel hungry. It will make you think about eating. It will make you crave your trigger foods.

This is a powerful evolutionary function for survival. It's so powerful it can override willpower and stimulate a factory of biochemical and enzymatic influences that will make you feel like you have no choice but to eat. It is another element in the puzzle we want to control so it doesn't control us.

The average stomach secretes ghrelin in half-hour waves and pulses. It's like a constant text message from your stomach to your brain about the state of affairs in the gut. When you are chronically deprived of adequate calories (e.g. when dieting to lose weight) these pulses and waves become not only more frequent, but more amplified. Your brain is hardwired to pay attention to these messages to eat. It is another back-up survival mechanism, designed to make eating a priority when your body is lacking calories. We keep it in control by dieting in a relative calorie-deficit instead of an absolute one, and we include over-feeding spike intervals.

* * *

Leptin is on your side when it comes to waist management and staying lean. Ghrelin on the other hand is kind of like a warning from the gut to the brain that you are taking this dieting thing too far.

Leptin works over the longer term. If you can get your leptin levels high and keep re-fueling it when needed, you'll coax your weight and leanness in the desired direction. If you can increase or optimize leptin sensitivity at the same time (as well-timed calorie spikes or over-feeds can do), then you optimize metabolism for the long-term as well.

Thankfully, in the grand scheme of things, leptin "outranks" ghrelin. That means when you control leptin, you in effect control ghrelin.

Now, let's take a good look at a study[1] from *The New England Journal of Medicine* which explains a lot of what I am saying here. Researchers measured the circulating levels of hormones like leptin, ghrelin, cholecystokinin, and others in 50 obese subjects. The subjects were placed on a weight loss program, measured after weight loss, then measured them again a year later. They found that even a year after weight loss "Levels of the circulating mediators of appetite that encourage weight regain after diet-induced weight loss do not revert to the levels recorded before weight loss. Long-term strategies to contract this change may be needed to prevent obesity relapse."

The researchers suggest "long-term strategies are needed." Well The Cycle Diet *is* a long-term strategy. By using well-timed intervals of tremendous refeeds and calorie spikes, reasonable diets can continue long-term.

The problem is that the North American Diet Mentality makes people *afraid* of food. People can't fathom that sitting down to a dozen donuts can actually be beneficial to their long-term weight-maintenance strategies and strategies to stay lean. I put the pictures of me with my Timmies' donuts on Facebook recently, and got a flood of comments from people who refused to believe that eating like that could serve the body.

This is a cultural bias, not a factual one. We associate these things with binging and the like. But in the right metabolic and hormonal environment, and the right mindset of course, it is anything but that. It is *serving* the body.

[1] Sumithran, Priya et al. "Long-Term Persistence of Hormonal Adaptations to Weight Loss." *New England Journal of Medicine* 365.17 (2011): 1597–1604. Web. <http://www.nejm.org/doi/full/10.1056/NEJMoa1105 816>

Scott Abel

Lessons from Competitive Eating

Eating competitions can be sideshows, but they are also intriguing from a research point of view. I wish more academic researchers would investigate the hormonal and metabolic responses of people who can compete and win in eating contests, because they're counter-intuitive, and I think there's something important there for us to learn.

For me, while it's *somewhat* interesting to see what tricks competitors use to get down more food in time-limited constraints, I'm more interested in the metabolic elements. What people miss in observing these sideshows is that over-feeding seems to train many competitors' metabolisms to be resilient, tolerant, and adaptive. Most people want to just "chalk it up to genetics" as to why these people can eat so much. While that may play a small role, there is far more to it than genetics.

Look how many professional eating competitors are not overweight at all. Some of them are even thin, including Takeru Kobayashi and Sonya "The Black Widow" Thomas.

Thomas, for example, is consistently thin. She stays lean, she controls her diet and she works out. She'll do an eating competition where she downs 12,000 calories in 10 minutes, two to three times per month.[1]

Some of Sonya's eating feats include 8.31 pounds of Armour Vienna Sausage in 10 minutes, 8.62 pounds of sweet potato casserole in 11 minutes, and 11 pounds of Downtown Atlantic Cheesecake in nine minutes (my kind of cheat!)[2] This 100 lb., thin "Black Widow" has been doing it for years.

Actually, the more I read about her, the more it sounded a bit like a version of a Cycle Diet to me. Her training depletes her glycogen, and her diet with a variety of healthy whole foods keeps her stomach enzymatically vibrant and healthy.

But the Black Widow isn't the only thin competitive eater. If you look at the general rankings of competitive eaters [3] you'll notice of how many of these top eaters are thin or not overweight. This isn't *just* genetics!

As another example let's take a video look at Matt Stonie, not overweight at all. You can watch him eat a Giant Ice cream Sundae of 30 *large* scoops of ice cream and 17 toppings here. [4] In another follow-up video he eats a gallon of ice cream surrounded by a giant cookie for a whopping 23,000 calories! **[5]** That isn't through the course of the day—that is *one sitting*. Yet he isn't even remotely fat or overweight.

As I look at these eating records and feats I think about how at Muscle Camp a fitness and diet *expert* said "there is no way Abel is eating 10,000 calories in a day unless he is drinking Crisco Oil right out of the bottle." To me, this illustrates the paradigm blindness we have in our industry regarding anything at all outside of the box in thinking and application. According to his Wikipedia page, Matt Stonie weighs 120 lbs. I'm not a competitive eater, but at 250 lbs. while lean *of course* I could eat 10,000 calories in a day. That was nothing! The "Black Widow" Sonya Thomas, who weighs 100 lbs., ate over 12,000 calories of hot dogs in 10 minutes! Yet fitness experts were skeptical and incredulous that a 250 lb., lean bodybuilder who is in Supercompensation mode—and therefore energy depleted—could eat 10,000 over the course of a whole day.

Having said all that, let me be clear here. It's too easy to take what I say here out of context. For the record, I'm *not* advocating that you go out and see how many hot dogs you can devour in 10 minutes, and I'm not suggesting you try to eat 30 scoops of ice cream. I'm not saying that doing either of those will suddenly make you lean, especially if you ignore everything I say in this book about Supercompensation Mode, as some people always do. Even when you *are* in Supercompensation Mode, I'm not suggesting you eat as much as you can until you feel sick, as though you were a competitive eater. Over-feeding and Supercompensation are not about that. I'm just using the example of thin competitive eaters to make my point about over-feeding within the right metabolic profile and context—if anyone was going to get fat from pigging out and massive over-feeding, then it would be these people. Yet they maintain leanness.

Here is another point. If you are of average weight, or overweight, and you have a piece of cake for dessert or for celebration, here and there, those extra calories are well within your body's digestive capabilities to store as fat. But if you are in Supercompensation mode and you eat a whole cake instead of a piece, then your body will *not* likely want to store most of those calories as fat since it needs to "supercompensate" any extra incoming caloric energy to where it is most needed (that is, refill glycogen stores and intramuscular fat stores). Besides that, it would just be beyond the ability of your metabolism to store these excess calories as fat, so it will take care of them or burn them off in other ways, like thermogenesis and extra excretion.

Again, over-feeding of this intensity optimizes metabolism, but it has to be done in the right metabolic and hormonal environment!

[1]

http://mentalfloss.com/article/30750/why-are-best-competitive-eaters-so-skinny

[2]

http://www.majorleagueeating.com/rankings.php?action=detail&sn=20

[3]

http://www.majorleagueeating.com/rankings.php

[4]

https://www.youtube.com/watch?v=FYZ-eGEDO0w

[5]

https://www.youtube.com/watch?v=FJNi7mxgMx0

Scott Abel

NEAT
(Non-Exercise Activity Thermogenesis)

Lately, fitness circles have been making a lot out of NEAT, that is, Non-Exercise Activity Thermogenesis.

I only want to draw your attention to two academic research elements and show you why they are important and how NEAT also supports over-feeding for optimizing a strong metabolic environment.

JA Levine points out that it is,

> not surprising that NEAT explains a vast majority of an individual's non-resting energy needs. Agricultural and manual workers have high NEAT, whereas wealth and industrialization appear to decrease NEAT. Physiological studies demonstrate, intriguingly, that NEAT is modulated with changes in energy balance;

NEAT increases with over-feeding and decreases with under-feeding. Thus, NEAT could be a critical component in how we maintain our body weight and/or develop obesity or lose weight." **[1]**

The more you eat in an over-feeding scenario the more thermogenic the metabolic response will be.

Once you're in Supercompensation Mode, it is more important to over-feed muscle than it is to try to over-starve fat. If dieting is too deep into an absolute calorie deficit and/or if dieting goes on too long, not only does the metabolism lower the rate it will burn off energy while resting, it will do all sorts of other things to lower the rate at which you expend energy. In other words, NEAT goes down.

Anyone who competes in physique contests where extreme leanness is the goal will tell you that as they get near the end of the dieting process, and leanness is peaking, and they've been eating low calories for an extended period of time, their energy is tanking on every level. *I have had competitors literally tell me that they were watching a TV show they didn't want to watch, but they didn't change the channel because reaching over and grabbing the remote just seemed like too much effort.* If you've ever been in this state you know what I'm talking about, where each small movement of your body seems to take tremendous effort. By contrast, when you're full of energy (say, after an over-feeding period), you can't help but keep moving.

If you diet to starve off fat, you will preserve resting

energy more and more, without even realizing you are doing so. Over-feeding has the opposite effect of burning even more calories at rest via thermogenesis.

Here's a snippet from another article by Levine about NEAT:

NEAT Is Biologically Adjusted to Counterbalance Fat Gain

When 16 lean volunteers were overfed by 1,000 calories per day above their weight maintenance needs, changes in NEAT accounted for the energetic counter response to fat gain. *Those people who increased their NEAT the most did not gain fat, even with over-feeding.* Those who did not increase their NEAT with over-feeding gained the most fat. [2]

Notice what I italicized. This suggests to me that metabolism can be trained and optimized with over-feeding, by taking advantage of NEAT. The next sentence also suggests that, of course, there is a genetic component to this—some people won't respond as well to cheat days as others, because the over-feeding phase doesn't increase their NEAT as much. In other words, the over-feeding has less of a beneficial metabolic effect. This is why it is important to pay attention to biofeedback both before and after a cheat.

While this research is merely concerned with NEAT in relation to metabolism, we can extend the findings well beyond that. And this supports the major arguments of The Cycle Diet, especially if you combine this with the professional eating competitors as well. So, what we see here is that if your metabolism is "coaxed" into Supercompensation mode, then over-feeding in that metabolic state is unlikely to cause fat gain. On the flip side of this equation, if the body is "forced" to lose weight by deprivation dieting metabolism will slow down and other processes will kick in to hoard fat and keep metabolism artificially lowered. Even from this research we can see, that in the right metabolic state, *over*-feeding has no ill consequences. And to my argument, it may even have positive effects in keeping metabolism optimized and robust, as I think it does. I have been following the Cycle Diet over 30 years now and I am still lean – and I over-feed on a weekly basis.

[1] Levine, James A. "Non-Exercise Activity Thermogenesis (NEAT)." Best practice & research. *Clinical endocrinology & metabolism* 16.4 (2002): 679–702. Print.

[2] Levine, James A. "The 'NEAT Defect' in Human Obesity: the Role of Nonexercise Activity Thermogenesis." *Endocrinology Update* 2.1 (2007): 1–2. Print.

Other Versions of The Cycle Diet

I want to talk about misrepresentations of the Cycle Diet by those who either do it intentionally to try and put their own stamp on it, or those who truly don't understand it at all.

I've had people write ask me things about the Cycle Diet that I never said, or they write me about comments I did make, but which have been taken completely out of the context. They end up adding massive cheat days without worrying about Supercompensation Mode, or things like that. Here are a few misconceptions I've come across.

"You have to be seven percent body fat or lower."

Recently, I posted on Facebook about the Cycle Diet

and the benefits of it as a lifestyle. Someone posted a comment and said, "Yes, but getting to 7 percent body fat is really hard and not everyone can do it." This comment reminded me that I'd heard this before, though I'd never said that, so I commented. Immediately, the poster posted a link to a very popular weight-training forum where someone was going on and on about me saying "The Cycle Diet only works if you are at seven percent body fat or below." I never said that! Yes, I have made reference to the point that the Cycle Diet works best if you are lean, and if you have dieted to achieve leanness. I may have even thrown out a number like 10 percent body fat or something. You do not have to achieve "extreme leanness" for The Cycle Diet to work and to work well. You only have to achieve Supercompensation mode.

As well, one thing I have learned since is that Supercompensation mode can be achieved at various levels of leanness and body fat, as high as 14 percent or so in some cases. But even then, it's not about the numbers, it's about biofeedback.

Weird Juice Fasts

Another funky permutation of the Cycle Diet somehow attributed to me was someone saying that you had to have a "juice fast" the day before and the day after the "cheat day."

This is ridiculous, and it's reflective of the "fear of food" mindset and the mindset that has you believing that the metabolic compensation system operates in 24-hour windows of time. It doesn't work that way.

As an even weirder variant on this theme, I've even seen it attributed to me that you have to do a "cleanse" the day before or the day after a cheat day. In yet another misrepresentation of this nature, it was also attributed to me that I said you have to "fast completely" the day after a cheat day. All of these notions are untrue and ridiculous. Each of these would trigger the body to go into "emergency mode" and "react" to lack of food. (Remember we are "coaxing" the body. Coax the body and it responds; force it and it reacts.)

Low Carb Diet Days

A more popular variation of the refeed is the notion of eating low carbs during the week, then high carbs, low fat on spike days. This stems from Cyclical Ketogenic Diets, or CKDs. The Cycle Diet is not a CKD. This idea actually has some limited application to be sure, but it should not be identified as some kind of hard and fast rule.

Once your body has been gently coaxed into supercompensation mode, its main priority is to store energy in the places needed most: muscle glycogen and intramuscular fats. Your body doesn't need "specific percentages" of carbohydrates and fats to do this. All your body needs to do this well and effectively is an overabundance of calories. The inner workings of your supercompensating metabolism will take it from there and put those pieces of the puzzle together for you.

"Just start cheating."

Probably the most widespread misrepresentation of the Cycle Diet is that anyone dieting can start a diet with a cheat day in place. I've never ever said that. People who do advocate that are catering to what people *want* to hear, and not appreciating the realities of the metabolic compensation system.

I have always stressed — and want to do so again — that refeeds and calorie spikes must take place in a very specific metabolic environment. This metabolic environment must be earned, by dieting in such a way that you effectively turn down or turn off the fat storing factory of the metabolic compensation system. Once the body is in weight-loss mode and supercompensation is achieved, the and only then will refeeds work to optimize metabolism while having no ill effects on weight or leanness.

To reiterate, "supercompensation mode" is something measured and indicated by biofeedback, not by fancy number crunching. People are all ears to hear about a "have your cake and eat it too" diet. Their ears tend to not hear the part about achieving supercompensation mode of metabolism in order for it to work as designed.

Scott Abel

Biofeedback is Everything

Especially when it comes to implementing the Cycle Diet, biofeedback is always more important than fancy formulas and a lot of number crunching.

In my 2005 lecture on the Cycle Diet, I presented various starting point formulas for consideration when setting up your own diet strategy. But I think presenting formulas like that may have caused some collateral damage. Over the years since that lecture, when people wrote me about the Cycle Diet, they were all bogged down in number-crunching, and were paying less attention to their biofeedback and their own unique background. Biofeedback helps determine whether you are in Supercomp mode far better than does "outside-in" fancy formulas and numbers.

Another issue to be aware of is that with

biofeedback, people often lie to themselves. What I mean is, if I tell a dieter the signals of Supercompensation mode, they will look for and find those signs so they can go out and have a huge refeed, whether the signs are present or not. It's confirmation bias. I see it all the time.

The best way "around" this self-deception is coaching. There's no way around it... I always say people who are serious about results will seek out real coaching. It is the best form of making sure you're not kidding yourself, and the best form of accountability. This is true of whether The Cycle Diet is involved or not.

I was hesitant to write this book on The Cycle Diet precisely for these reasons!

I will give information about the hints to look for in biofeedback and how to make the diet your own. *But* you have to be honest with yourself.

Another way of saying this is that biofeedback is more important than number crunching or fancy formulas, but *honest* biofeedback is most important of all. No one becomes an instant expert on reading and gauging biofeedback just from reading a book like this. You have to be honest, and willing to learn over time. You'll learn about your own body (or the bodies of your clients, as the case may be), and about how to read your own body.

What Workout Should I Use on the Cycle Diet?

There is **no specific workout** that is directly connected to the effectiveness of The Cycle Diet. It would be a stretch to say that. The Cycle Diet is all about training the metabolism to be responsive and resilient, and to be in supercompensation mode.

Having said that, **there are definitely a few things to consider** regarding training in general, and how it may impact the Cycle Diet and vice versa.

Any workouts that are intense enough and frequent enough to gradually deplete glycogen stores would support the Cycle Diet and vice versa. This actually leaves pure strength training, with very low reps and long rests, actually pretty low on the list in terms of compatibility with the Cycle Diet.

Any training workout that burns body fat will eventually deplete glycogen stores as well, so workouts that include complexes are good ideas. But this kind of training should still be with weights. Strength-density training (traditional bodybuilding training) or MET training makes much better sense in terms of getting a metabolism healthy and keeping it there.

However, first and foremost: before considering what workouts to do when following The Cycle Diet, an individual's metabolism needs to be assessed, for very important reasons. For example, if someone has previously yo-yo dieted (losing weight, regaining it, losing weight and regaining it) they may, as a result, have a very slow, sluggish, down-regulated metabolism. In that specific metabolic context, doing only cardio for training is actually likely to lead to this person gaining more fat. I have written about the dangers of cardio in many of my other books.

Cardio *can* be used with the Cycle Diet, but it's not optimal, and only in the right context, i.e. someone with a very healthy, robust metabolism). Once again, I turn to the example of the professional eater, Sonya Thomas, the "Black Widow." At the time of the article I mentioned earlier, her workouts consisted of 10 hours of running per week. She maintained low body weight and low body fat in doing so. But she had a healthy and robust metabolism already, and her over-feeding practices and competitions kept it that way. So running worked for her, in that metabolic context. For someone else, with metabolic issues from previous diets, running and endurance work to "burn calories" would only add to the problem. Ladies reading this who have these issues need to embrace that strength-density training (traditional bodybuilding training), or MET training, makes much better sense in terms of getting a metabolism healthy again!

Though there is "some" research in what I am about to say, it's not so much the research but my experience that allows me to say this with full confidence: training that depletes glycogen on a localized muscle level, seems to work best. In other words, systemized body part training makes the most sense to deplete whole body glycogen stores and "trigger" metabolism to respond accordingly.

There are ways and means to "tweak" this kind of training as well. You will see below in a further section of this book how my 47 year. old client Aaron Chigol used my *Hardgainer Solution* program and the Cycle Diet in conjunction to get incredibly lean and ripped for a natural bodybuilding competition, where he won the Master's class. To summarize it, Hardgainer's Solution is a program that focuses on body part training but in biplexes and triplexes, and with a wide variety of rep ranges.

Here is an example from Day 1 of the program, just to show you what I mean by biplexes and triplexes:

Workout 1

1a) DB or BB Squats	5 X 5
1b) DB Incline Press	5 X 8-10
1c) DB or BB Upright Rows	5 X 20
2a) Pulldowns Behind the Head	4 X 12-15
2b) 2 Arm DB Curls	4 X 20
3a) One Arm DB triceps extension	4 X 5-6 EA
3b) Any sit up or leg raise variation	4 X 12-20

So in Exercise 1, you'd do 1a) for five reps, 1b) for eight to 10 reps, 1c) for 20 reps, all back to back, and that would be one set of the first triplex, which calls for five sets total.

You do not have to follow this workout program to do the Cycle Diet. In fact, the Cycle Diet pre-dates that program by about 25 years!

I am simply giving an example of the kind of training that works well with the Cycle Diet. Many people reading this can stick to the kind of training they are doing already! Traditional body part splits, and traditional bodybuilding training, will work great, but complexes and circuits like you see above are especially optimal for the metabolism and the Cycle Diet. Use your head, and think about your goals. Don't just train so you can do the Cycle Diet and then add in a cheat day or something. Train for your long-term goals.

If you are interested in training designed specifically

for the metabolism, see Metabolic Enhancement Training, or MET. There's a free **Intro to Metabolic Enhancement Training (MET)** book on my website, at scottabelfitness.com (you should see it on the homepage). I also have more in-depth programs with videos, at scottabelfitness.com/workouts (but they're paid programs).

There are indeed some "good fit scenarios" of fitting specific workout methods with the Cycle Diet. But the Cycle Diet is first and foremost about training the metabolism to be responsive and resilient—often this means your metabolism is now able to support your training goals, for whatever program you're already doing. In fact, I'll give you a personal example here to illustrate that "training" with the Cycle Diet can be just an adjunct to the Cycle Diet's effects, and not always a pre-requisite.

Back in 2000 I had surgery to remove two very badly herniated discs in my back, a double laminectomy. There were further complications because of having to wait so long to get the surgery—pieces of the discs had splintered off and attached themselves to the nerve roots of my spine. The nerve roots swelled up. The imagery the surgeon used to explain it to me was that it was a lot like cooking angel hair pasta.

There was a lot of pre-surgery pain that kept me from training, and a lot of post-surgcial neuralgia that also kept me from training. I was walking with a cane for a few months, and sitting was out of the question, so much so that when I did eat, I was eating lying on my stomach.

Why am I telling you this in relation to the Cycle Diet? Because for the better portion of that year I couldn't do any activity at all. But I stayed on the Cycle Diet with the full cheat day and one-half day spike. I didn't gain any weight at all. I actually lost weight. To this day I say this is a testament to how well The Cycle Diet works to "train" metabolism, and it worked in conjunction with my previous years of training, which of course contributed as well.

Therefore while there are no specific workouts for the Cycle Diet specifically, there are "good ideas" of right training to support and optimize metabolism and positive metabolic effects.

To summarize the workout discussion, put simply, the kind of training that is best suited is some kind of resistance training: body part training emphasis in particular.

Getting Into
Supercompensation Mode

Scott Abel

The Need for
Supercompensation Mode

The "real" Cycle Diet operates under one very important premise. A person needs to diet to a level of sustainable leanness and get into a certain state of depletion in doing so.

I want to emphasize the importance of being in Supercompensation Mode for this diet to work.

Dieting depletes glycogen and intramuscular fats, and it causes a decrease in leptin levels. These all need to be replenished through over-feeds. Metabolism will react negatively if you don't do this. A refeed while you're in supercompensation mode serves metabolism and shuts off emergency-mode reactions.

Now, most diets that include refeeds of some sort

don't care about fats at all. Or, worse, they actively discourage you from eating them. These diets are more focused on carbs and glycogen, so you end up eating low fat ice cream or something to get a bunch of sugar without any fat in the refeed, or as little fat as possible. But when you're in true supercompensation mode, it is possible to enjoy the benefits of supercompensating glycogen *and* intramuscular fats.

Intramuscular fats (as in, fats within the muscles themselves) are an important energy source for athletes, or anyone who trains with any seriously consistent level of intensity. Even a 154 lb. man can store 2 lbs. of fat within his muscles, and half of that is readily available for energy supply. Two pounds of fat equates to 7,000 calories of energy—more than twice the storage capacity of glycogen. Normally, depleting these intramuscular fats, and *keeping* them depleted, sends a message to metabolism to down-regulate and preserve energy. Not the desired goal. This is why, during a refeed, we eat fats as well as carbs.

When the body is depleted of energy it "supercompensates" to sites where energy is most needed. This is what allows carb-loading and fat-loading to work in athletic events and physique competitions. Technically, supercompensating fat stored within muscles actually replenishes glycogen faster than carb loading, and fat loading even helps create glycogen stores as well.

For those who train with weights for cosmetic

purposes, an added benefit of this supercompensation effect is that for a few days following a refeed, muscles pump up easier. They look bigger and better, and they *work* better, too. For you intensely-training physique enthusiasts, think of this a lot like inflating a flat tire. A tire that is actually fully inflated just works better!

Supercompensating fats into muscles delivers fluids to the muscles, and this creates a cell-hydrating effect, which in turn spares glycogen. These are all signs of an optimized metabolism. An optimized metabolism will always prevent metabolism from going into any kind of emergency reaction mode.

So, with all that said, the Cycle Diet *won't work as it should* without first depleting the body in a reasonable way and putting yourself into a state of supercompensation, and keeping it right about there.

This can only be done by following a diet that keeps you in a **relative** caloric deficit most of the time, with a few optimally timed refeeds sprinkled here and there. **This means that the Cycle Diet IS a diet! It must be treated and respected as such.** Without inducing supercompensation mode, those surplus calories from a refeed will just be stored as normal fat because they aren't needed anywhere else.

The Cycle Diet is all about training the metabolism, and your metabolism must come first in any responsible diet strategy, ahead of weight-loss! Luckily, for those who want to lose weight, weight loss can be precisely how you train the metabolism. Through a *relative* deficit, the body has to be gently coaxed into a state where it "needs" an over-feed to reset, refuel, or readjust

Heed this warning: you can't just add in a weekly cheat day or cheat meals without being in super compensation mode. If you are already more than 15 to 20 lbs. overweight, you are NOT in true supercompensation mode, because your body knows it has more than enough stored energy to tap into. There is nothing to compensate for. Nothing is depleted. A full cheat day every week in this metabolic environment will only make you fatter!

Here's an example of how twisted the whole "cheat day" thing has become. While I was writing this section, a client emailed me. She is currently dieting off a lot of weight. She met some friends for a meal at a restaurant and these friends were trying to pressure her into ordering more indulgent food than she chose to do. Her friends were two other women, overweight by more than 50 lbs. and members of Weight Watchers. As my client ordered her meal carefully, a plain grilled chicken breast on a spring baby spinach salad, these two other ladies ordered typical restaurant fare of burgers, fries, and drinks and dessert. They "rationalized" it to my client that this was all good because they were making this their cheat day!

When you're 50 lbs. overweight you can't possibly be in Supercompensation mode. There will be more than ample stored energy to tap into, and their bodies know it. Eating this meal they rationalize as a "cheat day" is only going to delay their weight loss. Without training metabolism to be in some sort of Supercompensation mode, cheat meals and cheat days won't "work" to do much of anything except to make you more overweight. So, our goal, then, is to get "into" some decent level of Supercompensation Mode.

Scott Abel

Levels of Supercomp

I think I used to give the impression that Supercompensation Mode was an either-or thing, as in: you are either in supercompensation mode and you can benefit from over-feeding, or you are not.

That is true as a general rule of application, but over the years I've learned there are various levels of Supercompensation.

- Someone may be **deep into** supercompensation mode. Think of an already pretty fit physique competitor who has then dieted down even more, and leaned out for weeks in order to compete at an extremely low level of body fat.

- Then there are people who are **lightly into** supercompensation mode. This is someone like myself, and where I am at right now in life, and taking into consideration things like my age, the fact that I work out less intensely than I used to, and so on.

- Then, finally, there are those who are dieting, but they are only **flirting with** supercompensation mode.

All these various degrees of Supercompensation mode would dictate a completely different way of applying refeed/over-feed scenarios and their frequency.

The leaned-out physique competitor, deep into Supercomp, could likely do a full refeed day *and* a mid-week spike half day of over-feeding as well. As long as he or she keeps calories low on diet days, they can likely keep up that calorie refeed schedule. I used to be this deep in supercompensation mode back in my physique days, when I made my career by staying lean year round for shows, magazine shoots, and so on. But now I am lightly in Supercompensation, so I take only one refeed/over-feed day per week. That serves me well, at this point in my life. For someone who is flirting with supercompensation mode, you're looking at someone who could probably indulge in a refeed/over-feed meal, and it wouldn't *hurt* him or her per se, but it wouldn't help cosmetically or metabolically (though there might be psychological benefits, depending on the trainee).

It bears repeating: the Cycle Diet requires serious

commitment to achieve a level of weight-loss and leanness in order for high-calorie refeeds to work. The more you sabotage your diet efforts upfront, the longer it takes to achieve supercompensation mode, where you can eat freely without cosmetic consequences. In fact people who continue to sabotage their diets with tiny cheats here and there are more likely than not to never achieve supercompensation mode at all.

Scott Abel

Absolute vs. Relative Caloric Deficit

To get into Supercomp, we will first diet for at least a few weeks in a relative caloric deficit. Then, once Supercomp is achieved, you will still eat in a relative caloric deficit for six days of the week, with one refeed day. These will be your diet days.

The next section will give you some starting formulas to figure out a relative deficit for *you*, as a *starting point*, but for now, let's go over the general differences between an absolute deficit and a relative one.

Absolute Deficit: 1,000 calories or more below daily needs	Relative Deficit: 500-800 calories below daily needs
Creates fat storing machine	Creates fat burning machine
Lowers BMR	BMR same or increased
Lowers LBM (which further lowers BMR)	LBM same or increased
Lowers Sodium/Potassium Pump efficiency	NA+/K+ activity is the same
Lowers electrolyte efficiency	Electrolyte efficiency is the same
Decreases lipolysis (less efficient fat burning)	Increases lipolysis
Increases gluconeogenesis (muscle wasting)	Less gluconeogenesis or the same
Increases lipogenic activity (rebounding)	Decreases lipogenic activity
Can decrease immune system function	Immune function same or enhanced
Insulin sensitivity is the same	Greater insulin sensitivity
Increase in catabolic hormones	Decreased catabolic activity
Decreases leptin sensitivity	Increases leptin sensitivity if over-feeds are used
Makes metabolism sluggish	Optimizes metabolism
Decreases or quashes positive effects of NEAT	Optimizes NEAT
Increases intensity of ghrelin, and therefore hunger	Ghrelin levels increased, but tolerable

Induces *in*tolerable hunger	Induces tolerable hunger
Over time likely to increase body weight set point and increase body fat as a mode of self-protection	Not likely to affect body weight set point and newly established levels of leanness can be maintained with over-feeds/refeeds

As you can see, depending on the diet someone undertakes the physiological response can vary tremendously. You can't just think, "I'm losing weight, so everything is fine." That's not how the body works.

If you lose weight in an absolute caloric deficit, you are dieting in an unsustainable way, and your body will fight back. But if you lose weight in a relative caloric deficit, and then achieve supercompensation mode and respond to that with regular over-feeding intervals, then you will be able to sustain the weight loss and improve as well over time.

These physiological differences are not easy to identify and separate over the short-term, because both absolute caloric deficit "deprivation" diets and more reasonable relative caloric deficit diets are likely to produce weight-loss in the short-term window of time. But as you see above, an absolute caloric deficit has enormous negative short-range consequences and future repercussions, while the relative deficit diets with refeeds do not.

I want to reiterate the difference again is all about relevant and personal biofeedback. What is a relative

Scott Abel

deficit for one person may be an absolute deficit for another. In other words, two people of equal size, weight, age and gender, could begin the same diet at the same time, and one of them may drop into absolute caloric deprivation mode and experience all the negative consequences of that, while the other maintains a reasonable relative deficit and experiences no ill effects.

Again, this is where biofeedback becomes so important so you don't do any long-term damage. You can't make it just about numbers and then not pay attention to your own body and the messages it is trying to send you.

Look at the chart above again: the left column is about the biofeedback you'll experience on an absolute deficit. The right column is about the biofeedback you'll experience on a relative deficit. Obviously, you won't be able to see everything in the chart without a lab test, but you'll certainly notice the differences in hunger, in your daily energy levels, and you'll notice the *effects* of things like a lowered immune system function.

Now, here's an example of what I mean about the numbers by themselves not always adding up.

Back in my prime physique days, I was doing the full cheat day and one-half spike day per week. I was dieting for five and half days per week at 1,800 calories per day, with a day and a half refeed. I weighed 260 lbs. with less than 10 percent body fat, and I was often training twice per day, depending on my workout program. That's actually pretty low calorie intake for my diet days, less than what I'd recommend based on the formulas I'll include later on.

But this isn't the end of this example either. At the very same time, I also had a client who was employing the exact same refeed rotation, meaning he also had a day and half of refeeds each week. But here's the thing: this client was a bantamweight competitor in bodybuilding. This means he competed at a weight of 143 lbs. or *less*. I outweighed him by more than a hundred pounds! And yet while my diet days hovered around 1,800 calories per day, this bantamweight client of mine had a buzz saw for a metabolism. His normal diet days were 3,500 calories every day! On the *diet* days! That was almost 2,000 calories more *per day* than I required, even though I outweighed him by one hundred pounds.

As you can see, the numbers and formulas don't always fit, and you should never think they are "the" answer. **They are generalities and <u>starting points</u>**.

Had I not done a metabolic assessment of this client, by getting his background, and getting him to record three days of his actual eating, and if I only relied on "formulas" for designing his diet strategy, I likely would have assigned him a diet that would have put in him in an absolute caloric deficit. That could have ruined his metabolism and his physique for competitions. No matter how you slice it, there is still an art to this kind of thing. Nuance exists at every level of expertise.

There was another diet that was popular a few years ago and still makes the rounds. This diet had very, very low calories and no-to-very-low carbs on diet days, and then these so-called diet days were cycled with weekend feedings, but the feedings were to be restricted to only carbs. This kind of approach is *not* the Cycle Diet. Extremely low calories combined with no-to-very-low carbs will pretty much always produce an absolute caloric deficit, and you'll experience the negative repercussions and consequences from that.

A relative caloric deficit is enough to deplete glycogen stores *over time* and in a *gentle* way. Going extremely low calorie and low carb is forcing the body, not coaxing it. Forcing the body in this way can create long-term metabolic damage. Again: any diet must 1) be sustainable, and 2) must serve the body.

Formulas and Calories for Diet Days

Although I emphasize biofeedback and considering the full context (consider my bantam weight client in the last section), everyone needs a starting point to determine his or her relative calorie deficit.

I'm going to go through a few ways to do that in this section. There is a trend in this industry to over-emphasize numbers and formulas. Only mid-level experts want to try to reduce everything to fancy formulas and numbers and equations.

The truth is I haven't used numbers and calorie formulas in my diet-strategies for clients for years now. It's not necessary. Some portion control is necessary, but all this counting and measuring and debating exact macro proportions is getting out of hand. It doesn't need to be so complicated.

The formulas can never account for every variable, and they're never 100 percent accurate, so this is why it's much more about biofeedback. But people need a place to start, so here is a very _easy_ and _simple_ place to do just that.

The simplest formula you can have for starting a diet in a relative caloric deficit is to take your body weight in pounds and multiply that number by 10 and by 12. Boom. No fancy math. Now you've got a low range of calories, and a high range. If you're 180 lbs., your low range is 1,800 calories per day, and your high range is 2,160 calories per day. From there, we can think about whether to go closer to the high range or low range, based on a number of factors.

As a general rule body weight times 10 is about as low as someone should need to go to be in relative caloric deficit, and body weight times 12 can better if you meet some of the criteria of having pretty fast, optimized metabolism, and a high **Basal Metabolic Rate** or BMR (for any who don't know, your BMR is the number of calories you would burn in a day if you laid in bed all day and did _nothing_). Factors affecting your BMR can be athletic background, genetics, age, body surface area (like height), and gender (women burn fewer calories, generally).

For example, if you are a young male athlete, between the ages of 18 and 30, and you are tall, then you might want to stay closer to the higher range, and go with

BW X 12. But if you're like most average people—maybe you're over 30, of average height and activity level, or whatever—then maybe BW X 10 is better. Or you maybe you feel like you have some things going for you, but some going against you, then you can just split it down the middle and start with BW X 11.

It really does not need to be overly complicated.

As another example, for myself a good relative calorie deficit to begin my diet strategy would be 2,150 calories, because I'm 215 lbs., and 215 X 10 is 2,150. I'm male, and I'm active, but not as active as I used to be, and I'm also 55 years old. By that point in your life your metabolism has slowed down a fair bit. So I just stick to the low end. For a similar hypothetical example for a female, if she's about 135 lbs., her starting numbers might be 1,350 calories. These numbers will pretty much ensure being a relative calorie deficit that will eventually lead to being in supercompensation mode.

What About Activity Levels?

In short: don't worry about activity levels either. Most of you, just like myself, may work out and exercise almost daily. But the rest of your day matters here as well. If you work out intensely for an hour to an hour-and-a-half, for five or six days per week, but the rest of your day is relatively sedentary and not energy-consuming, then you really don't have to worry about "factoring in" activity levels to your overall calorie needs computations. If you do construction work on *top* of those five to six days of working out, then yes, factor that in, and stick to the higher range of calories (BW X 12) or even go to BW X 13 if you really think it's necessary. Again, we still keep it simple.

In a presentation about the Cycle Diet I once gave, I offered the audience several formula options like the Harris-Benedict equation and Katch-Mcardle, with activity multipliers and so on. Even back then I never used these formulas myself, but I knew people wanted them. But now I'm not even going to suggest using them, because more and more I've come to believe that these kinds of formulas just give you the *illusion* of control, making you focus on random numbers on a spreadsheet, instead of learning to read and respond to the actual signs your own body is giving you.

Even in this book, I offer the simple BW X 10-12 formula, but I do so **merely as a *starting point.*** That is all it is: a starting point. Biofeedback matters much more than when it comes to what your body is doing and how you should respond to it.

How Many Meals Should I Eat?

I suggest also keeping it simple in this regard as well. I am a fan of frequent small meals.

- If you're very light, and therefore are only eating a small number of calories like 1,000 to 1,200 calories in a day, you can spread those calories over three to four meals.

- Someone needing something like 1,300 to 2,500 calories in a day can spread those calories evenly over five meals.

- Someone requiring more than 2,500 calories would likely benefit by going to six meals with calories more or less evenly divided throughout the day.

It is that simple.

You <u>don't</u> need to worry about all this pre-workout and post-workout meal timing and all the rest. It's all nonsense, unless you are a high-performing professional athlete in certain sports, always training at your maximal work capacity. Forget about that stuff.

More on Fewer Calories

Can you eat this way forever? No, not really. If you ate BW X 10-12 forever and ever, with no refeeds, you would end up miserable, because you would get deeper and deeper into Supercompensation Mode, your energy stores would be more and more depleted, and your metabolism would down-regulate. But *until you get there*, these kinds of numbers, day in and day out, are perfectly fine. Your body will tell you when it's *not* fine, and when it is time to start the refeeds.

Furthermore, here is another point seldom discussed: as you diet in a relative caloric deficit, your body and metabolism become much more efficient at using those calories. You take in fewer calories, but this is compensated for by your body and by your metabolism, so that they use this smaller number of calories more efficiently. You don't need to try to out-think your body here in this regard.

So, these are just simple starting formulas for you in order to get started if you are trying this out on your own. Do not treat formulas and numbers like a bible. They serve only as a starting point. People who get all bogged down in numbers and calorie equations are people who suffer the most and end up the most confused. It's not necessary.

The same is true about "macro" proportions as well. This is the latest much ado about nothing, illusion of control nonsense that has popped up in the fitness industry. Notice that the numbers are always nice and well rounded. Your body doesn't care about that stuff. All this macro-control is a lot of unnecessary headache. Do you really think your body and metabolism operates on exact agendas like 40 percent protein, 30 percent carbs, and 30 percent fats? Do you really think you've "ruined" your diet if you are somehow outside those numbers? (By the way, can you imagine what a cheat day over-feed day does to those numbers?) Do you really think you have somehow blown your diet if your macros are 38 percent protein, 47 percent carbs, and 15 percent fats? Your metabolism doesn't know or care about the difference. As long as your protein *sparing* numbers (carbs and fats) are higher than the protein numbers, you will be fine. In other words, as long as your fats or carbohydrate intake, or combinations of both, are much higher than your protein intake; then even in a relative calorie deficit your metabolism will work just fine, thank you very much. In these arbitrary macros I just presented above — 47 percent carbs and 15 percent fats — the total comes to 62 percent of your calorie intake. This would be just fine in terms of optimizing metabolism and metabolic function.

In terms of a *starting* point only when it comes to macros, I would say do a 30/30/30 split, which only adds up to 90 percent. And then allow for a 10 percent variance either way between fats or carbs, or both. Again, the point here is to not overcomplicate any of this. It does not need to be complicated. Truth be told, in my 2005 lecture on The Cycle Diet, I presented some pretty fancy formulas for calculating relative calorie deficits and how to implement them. Based on all the letters about the Cycle Diet I've received since then, I think this was a mistake on my part. People were getting overly bogged down by the numbers and totally neglecting the importance of biofeedback, even though I stressed its importance all through the lecture. The Harris-Benedict formula and the like make for good presentation material at a symposium, but they just aren't necessary for real-world application.

To reiterate, if you follow the body weight X 10 or 12, suggestions above and the 30/30/30 suggestion as starting points, then you should be just fine. And you don't need to make it any more complicated than that. In the sample diets provided, I have never sat down and figured out "numbers" involved. I know by portion sizes and by whom I am assigning the diet to, that the relative caloric deficit will be established and that supercompensation mode will be reached.

So again, it's not about the formulas, it's about biofeedback. Once you've determined a starting level for the diet, you need to consider your biofeedback in an ongoing way. Certain diets may require a kind of "a metabolic shift" and this can take anywhere from seven to 17 days. For example, if you are going from eating a lot of processed foods to whole foods it can take time for your stomach and satiety centers of your brain to adapt. The same is true if you are going from a low carbs approach to a higher carbs approach or vice versa.

What Foods to Eat on Diet Days

As you will see in the sample diets section, what someone eats every day for diet fare can vary depending on what their assessment reveals.

There are always exceptions to general rules, but having said this, there are general rules and principles that should apply to most people. For one thing, I am almost always on the side of a carbs-based diet. Carbs—yes,, including starches—should comprise the better portion of the protein-sparing energy component of any diet.

Starchy carbs are the preferred source for the body in making and storing glycogen, and this helps to keep metabolism from downregulating. At the same time, we don't go ultra low fat, either, because they're important too. We don't demonize any macronutrient or food group.

I advocate simplicity. The more complicated a diet strategy is, the more dubious I am of it. Let's start with the very basics. Your diet days should focus around healthy whole foods at 10 to 12 times your body weight (in lbs.), and those calories should spread over about four to six meals. If you're 120 lbs., you might stick with four meals. If you're 240 lbs., 10 percent body fat, and have a fast metabolism, you'll probably need six or maybe even seven meals. Most people can just stick with five meals.

Beyond that, follow Michael Pollan's brilliant directive that simplifies the conclusions of every nutrition text book you've ever read: Eat food, not too much, mostly plants. Unlike others, though, note that "plants" include things like potatoes and legumes, so you get your carbs in there. I'm also a big fan of rice cakes and mini rice cakes as an "exception" to the rules of avoiding processed foods. Rice cakes are a decent carb, they're easy on the stomach, and they do well in terms of satiety and filling you up.

The more healthy whole foods you eat—as opposed to Doritos or processed fast food or something—the more accurately you can measure your actual hunger. This is important for gauging your own biofeedback. Yes, you can lose weight on Twinkies, but it's easier to read your own body's hunger signals when you're filling it up with foods like meat, potatoes, veggies, and so on. So many people have lost the innate ability to even know when they are hungry and to what degree.

Something as simple as this could produce a decent relative caloric deficit that will eventually lead to supercompensation mode.

Example Female 5-Meal Diet

Meal 1

- Four to eight egg whites
- 40 to 50 grams Cream of Wheat, oatmeal, oat bran or grits

Meal 2

- 15 to 25 grams any raw unsalted nuts
- Two to three pieces of fresh fruit or equivalent in berries

Meal 3

- 90 to 120 grams any lean protein source
- 90 to 120 grams potato or yam
- 200 to 300 grams any fibrous veggies

- 1 tbsp. any healthy fat (olive oil, peanut butter, etc.)

Meal 4

- Same as Meal 3 above.

Meal 5

- Large spinach salad with baby spinach
- …plus as many other salad ingredients as desired
- …and sprinkle with dried cranberries, feta cheese, one-quarter cup chickpeas
- …and add low cal dressing of some sort

Example Male 5-Meal Diet

Meal 1

- Eight to 12 egg whites
- 60 to 80 grams Cream of Wheat, oatmeal, oat bran or grits

Meal 2

- 40 to 50 grams any raw unsalted nuts
- Three to five pieces of fresh fruit or equivalent in berries

Meal 3

- 120 to 180 grams any lean protein source
- 150 to 200 grams potato or yam
- 300 to 500 grams any fibrous veggies
- 1 tbsp. any healthy fat (olive oil, peanut butter, etc.)

Meal 4

- Same as Meal 3 above.

Meal 5

- Large spinach salad with baby spinach
- ...plus as many other salad ingredients as desired
- ...and sprinkle with dried cranberries, feta cheese, one-half cup chickpeas
- ...and add low cal dressing of some sort

I don't know what the calorie counts are for these plans. The above is just a sample menu off the top of my head. You see variation in the amounts for portion sizes because I am writing this in a very general sense. Someone actually following one of my diet strategies would have slightly more precise portion sizes to follow.

But these examples for men and women were meant to just show a five-meal, healthy eating breakdown, and the typical variations in amounts that may occur. So obviously a 23-year-old woman who is active and works out all the time is going to need a different portions approach to a 40-year-old mother of three, who has gained a lot weight through pregnancies, and is also less active in terms of exercise. Things like this always require specific attention.

So, this covers the more general approach to diet days. If you are interested in complete cosmetic advantage as well, then for the first little while of dieting, it is a good idea to eliminate the fruit option and stick with fibrous veggies and starchy carbs. (But even then, not *too* many veggies. Human beings aren't rabbits.) But that is a whole other scenario, and really is just about optimizing cosmetics (water retention, etc.)

Scott Abel

Biofeedback As You Diet

Early on while dieting in a relative deficit, there will be peaks and valleys. You should always have "good energy" for exercising and ample ability to concentrate on your work or whatever other activity is demanding your concentration.

Being unable to concentrate is often a sign of being in an absolute caloric deficit rather than a relative one. But this has to be ongoing, not just a one off. The same is true of all biofeedback. If you have one bad workout, don't worry about it. If every workout feels "meh," that's important biofeedback to consider.

If you are someone not used to dieting, or you haven't dieted in a while then you need to get used to the notion of "tolerable hunger." Here's the thing: hunger is normal, and good. But the hunger may take some getting used to. There is a difference between tolerable hunger with good energy and insane levels of hunger, appetite, and cravings, and no energy. We actually work best when we're just a "little" hungry, believe it or not.

Many diets inevitably fail because people just cannot get used to a constant level of hunger, which just grows and grows over time, going from tolerable to intolerable, until it takes over your thoughts. Where the Cycle Diet differs from other diets out there is that once supercompensation mode is established, which is about when the hunger and appetite starts rising a bit high, we have a regular well-timed refeed. This makes getting used to tolerable hunger well worth the price of admission (especially since, as I mentioned, we actually operate at our peak when we're a bit hungry). I will discuss this a bit more when I talk about hunger, appetite, and cravings in a different section below.

For now, embrace the notion that ongoing hunger is normal if and when you are in fat-burning mode. Just accept this reality. There is no such thing as a diet that doesn't leave you hungry. To think so is to just buy into diet industry nonsense. Let me make this point clearer: unless you are in supercompensation mode, then eating to get rid of cravings just takes your metabolism out of fat-burning mode. Hunger is a normal part of dieting to be lean and stay lean. PERIOD. The difference with the Cycle Diet is that you can learn to get used to that hunger and use it productively.

However, the key word here is "tolerable" hunger. This is an important distinction. Absolute calorie deficits tend to produce absolute hunger levels. Intolerable hunger is a hunger level that has gone beyond merely noticing that you are hungry. Intolerable hunger from an absolute caloric deficit is a hunger that prevents you from thinking straight. It is a hunger where your stomach is always empty and your predominant thoughts are all about food and eating. If you are intensely craving foods you wouldn't even normally want or like then you are likely in an absolute caloric deficit, and you're risking your body compensating by lowering metabolism, increasing your set point, and storing more energy as fat. These are pretty much the exact opposite things you want to have in a dieting-down scenario.

An intolerable state of hunger will win out over willpower as well. Tolerable hunger can be managed. Intolerable hunger cannot. There are no "numbers" here that reflect this difference. This is all about biofeedback. You also have to consider the mental and emotional side of this equation. Are you craving foods because of an emotional lack instead of a physical one? (Are you bored? Do you get cravings when you feel lonely?) In that case, it's not the diet that's at issue. These are all things that need to be considered.

Psychologically it's been shown time and time again that chronic dieters become hypersensitive to hunger cues. Because chronic dieters are always paying attention to little else but food and eating and weight, they become mentally and emotional hypersensitive to even the smallest changes in hunger levels. This isn't a good thing because it distorts what should be tolerable hunger and makes the dieter perceive it as intolerable hunger, even when it is not.

For example, one of my clients wrote me recently and gave me all his usual weekly check-in feedback, and then said "I just want you to tell me what to do because I want to make sure I'm not just rationalizing wanting a cheat day." This was a very astute statement for my client to make. Left to their own devices, many dieters simply think all hunger is too much hunger; therefore they need to eat to make it go away. And this of course is just wishful thinking in order to rationalize a diet indiscretion and dieter self-sabotage.

If you're still 20 lbs. overweight, and you "know" you're in a relative deficit, then you're probably experiencing normal tolerable hunger. But if you're not sure, you need to consider the full context. Do you have emotional attachments to foods? Are you a chronic dieter (meaning you might perceive all hunger as intolerable) or is your relationship with food pretty healthy? What are the chances you're actually in an absolute caloric deficit instead of a relative deficit? How are your overall energy levels? How's your sleep (which can affect both hunger and energy)? If you're actually lean already, are you getting into supercompensation mode (in which case hunger levels will probably start to rise)? Again, these are all things to consider. Use your head.

I'll be honest: this is a grey area, and it is seldom discussed. It needs to be assessed on a case-by-case basis, and you have to be really, truly, *brutally* honest with yourself. Many people cannot do this. They start playing head games with themselves. If this were you, you would benefit from one-on-one coaching so that an objective third party can gauge your biofeedback for you and determine whether or not you are experiencing truly intolerable hunger or you just "want" to eat.

Scott Abel

How to Tell If You're In Supercompensation Mode

Remember you achieve supercompensation mode by dieting in a relative caloric deficit and "over time" you deplete the body of energy to a point where it now wants to and needs to "supercompensate" any excess incoming energy.

You don't need to do crazy depletion diets and workouts. You need to make it about the process of coaxing the metabolism—not forcing it. Learn to trust the process, and you will experience a difference in your own biofeedback, especially when it comes to hunger. You will go from experiencing "tolerable hunger" (good and normal), to the next level of hunger, where food becomes prevalent in your thoughts and you can't turn it off. Some people even start dreaming about food and eating. This is your body telling you "I need food, I want more energy!"

As you approach supercompensation, you will also start to experience decreased workout performance. (This will also be true once you're Cycle Dieting with the full refeed day each week, except at that point you'll experience it as the week wears on. At the beginning of the week you'll feel full of energy, and at the end you'll be back to needing that cheat day.) You won't feel sluggish per se, but your performance will *consistently* be slightly off from your best workouts.

Let me re-emphasize: pay attention to your own biofeedback.

Another sign of being in fat-burning mode and supercompensation mode is frequent urination. As long as you are well hydrated, when the body is in fat burning mode and being depleted of glycogen, there is a pronounced diuretic effect. Typically, each gram of glycogen in the muscle gets stored with a few grams of water, so when you run out of glycogen, the corresponding water that usually gets stored with it instead it just passes through your system. The deeper someone gets into supercompensation mode, the more frequently urination occurs. Of course this tends to subside on over-feed/refeed days when you take in a bunch of carbs, and they get stored in the muscle, along with a bunch more water. (Cycle dieters describe having "dry mouth" on refeed days. The experienced ones know to stay hydrated.) The sooner frequent urination returns *after* an over-feed, the deeper into supercompensation mode you likely are.

Beware the Self-Fulfilling Prophecy

Many people use the Cycle Diet, and end up looking so hard for increased hunger and signs of supercompensation that they find it, even when it isn't there. This is another area where professional one-on-one coaching can become imperative, and why I was leery of writing this book. People have a tendency to let their minds trick them into all kinds of things. Over the years I have often had people write me who "think" they are in supercompensation mode, but who clearly are not! They just want a refeed meal off their diet. There is a big difference.

Supercompensation is an actual physiological thing, not a psychological desire. At the same time, to be sure, the physiological effects of supercompensation will have psychological effects—namely, you'll think about food a lot more. This is why it can often be difficult for a dieter to know the difference between their actual physiological cues and their own desires.

With that it mind, it may help to discuss supercompensation mode in relation to hunger, appetite, and cravings.

Appetite

Increased appetite is a definite sign of supercompensation mode. But that said, I want to distinguish between **hunger, cravings**, and **appetite**.

Appetite and cravings can be partly physiological and partly psychological. True **hunger** is almost purely physiological. When we talk about our stomach growling and the like we are talking about actual, physiological hunger. The leaner you get the hungrier you will become. This is a built-in survival mechanism all mammals have. As you get leaner, it makes sense for your body to prioritize food.

It is not possible to be newly dieted down, with a very low body fat percentage, and not be hungrier as a result. People need to get that through their heads. One of the main reasons diets fail is that as you get leaner you can no longer override the intensifying, consistent levels of hunger. The Cycle Diet helps deal with that because 1) you "know" there is an off-day or refeed day coming up, and 2) the refeed day does your body and metabolism good.

Cravings are a combination of physiological hunger with your psychological influences coming into play, especially about what particular foods satisfy you, or that you *think* will satisfy you. The greater and more intense physiological hunger is, the more likely that specific cravings will intensify.

Note, though, that because we live in the world of

food abundance, things other than just physical hunger can trigger cravings. The site and smells of food can trigger cravings, as can memories and emotional states totally unassociated with food. If you have the right mindset toward food and diet, cravings can be fun things to engage. Only if you fear food do you think of cravings as unnatural and something to resist. Cravings are inevitable, and if you have them on a diet day—as all dieters will, including myself—then you just need to adopt the motto, "this too shall pass." Because it will. If you are on the Cycle Diet, part of the fun is that you *do* get to indulge any craving you might have. It's just that you might have to delay "when" you indulge that craving so it is timed with your refeed. This is something most Cycle Dieters actually enjoy.

Appetite in and of itself helps you determine whether you are in supercompensation mode or not, and if you are, just how deep into supercompensation you may be. Appetite is the combination of hunger and cravings combined. It is your ability to eat.

When you are in supercompensation mode, you will have a very, very big appetite. You will feel like you could eat a horse... and then some. When you do start eating on a refeed day, your stomach will feel bottomless. If you're still on diet days, you'll find that your diet meals do very little to satisfy your appetite, even immediately after the meal.

Appetite is a developed "ability to eat" and your

metabolism can be trained for this. This is why I included the section of the professional eating competitors. Their metabolisms have been trained, and one of the ways they train metabolism is by enhancing their appetites: no one who is "not all that hungry" is going to be able to eat 30 scoops of ice cream or 50 burgers or whatever.

When you are in supercompensation you can eat more at a refeed than you ever could before you started dieting. This is a good sign of being in supercompensation mode. And *because* you are in supercompensation mode, then when you do fully feed your appetite in this way, it doesn't negatively impact you—not cosmetically, not in terms of weight-gain, and not metabolically.

Now, lots of people get crazy hungry when they are dieting. To reiterate, this is why diets fail. But not everyone who diets is training his or her metabolism to be resilient and responsive. Many dieters are weakening their stomach's digestive capacities and slowing their metabolisms by dieting incorrectly. And this is the difference between being in supercompensation mode and just dieting to lose weight. Supercompensation mode is sustainable. Absolute calorie deprivation dieting is not. And supercompensation mode with over-feeds has positive metabolic effects. Prolonged dieting hurts metabolism sometimes irreversibly.

Weight Fluctuations After a Refeed

After a refeed, you'll likely gain lots and lots of water weight—more than 10 lbs. is very normal. But you know you're in supercompensation mode if your weight returns to normal within a few days.

So if you're 190 lbs. on the morning of a refeed, and by that evening you're 203, then by the next refeed you should be back to 190 lbs. or *even lower*. The quicker your weight comes back down after a refeed, the deeper into supercompensation mode you are. (This is actually a sign that it might be time to add in the mid-week spike.)

Sometimes you even lose more weight than you weighed before your refeed. I've seen this many, many times with my clients. They can't believe it.

But conversely, all too often, contest-prep gurus panic when a client's weight stops dropping before a contest. They react in a kind of panic as well, so they often drop a client's calories or carbs and increase the client's exercise as well. This is an unnecessary reaction by someone who lacks a true understanding of metabolism. If I have a client who is trying to lean out for some reason and their weight-loss has stagnated and they don't look any leaner either, that is often when I assign a full cheat day / refeed day, along with a prescription to eat anything and everything that isn't diet-food. The result is a break-through from the plateau in leanness and weight-loss. I've had plenty of clients "stuck" at a certain weight. I assign them a full cheat day, sometimes even an over-feed weekend, in order to reset metabolism and leptin levels. Over the refeed period they gain 10 to 15 pounds, but a week later they have lost 15 to 16 lbs. or more. This is how Cycle Diet works when it's working with all cylinders firing.

You eat more to lose more and lean out: too good to be true? No, not at all, because it is still a diet, after all. You have to be in the right mode, and you have to learn to read the signs of supercompensation.

The Refeed

Scott Abel

The Refeed Days

Focusing too much on calorie counts, precise percentages of macros, and so on, are often nothing but what I call the *illusion* of control. That kind of thing simply is not necessary, especially on the refeed days.

On a refeed day, the number one most important thing is simply the volume of calories. That is the first and primary focus. Most of these calories will be carbs, and even simple sugary carbs are just fine. Indeed, often these simple carbs are even the better choice since they don't have much nutritional density and will digest quicker. But don't shy away from fats or something, and only eat "zero fat" carbs and stuff like that. *Enjoy* the day. You need to replenish all sorts of stores, not just glycogen.

There are all kinds of "new and improved" variations of this kind of "cheat day" dieting out there. Most of them are nonsense. Many don't bother worrying about whether your body actually needs a high volume of calories. Some are all about loading up *only* on carbs and negating fats. Based on some of the research on leptin above, I grant that this seems like good sense, but it's really about the calories and the overall energy contribution of the over-feeds. Don't get too one-dimensional. Even macro counting on the refeed days is more of the "illusion" of control.

As you will see in the sample diet section, there are very specific individual "contexts" to consider as well. As long as relative caloric deficits are "cycled" with well-timed refeeds, then any macro approach can work. The question becomes 'what is the best fit *for that particular person* and where his or her metabolism may be at, *at that time.*' You also need to address if the particular approach is sustainable for that person.

That's all a long way of saying that the refeed is all about "indulgence without guilt." If you can't over-feed and truly enjoy it and do it *without* guilt, then the Cycle Diet is not a good place for you to start. You should look forward to the refeed, and you should know and have confidence in the fact that you are *serving your body* by over-feeding and taking in a large volume of calories. In the next section I'll talk about why.

The Goal of the Refeed

The main goals of the refeed are to reset metabolism and particularly to reset leptin levels. Refeeds also help replenish glycogen stores and intramuscular fats stores, which in turn helps with the resetting of metabolism and leptin and so on.

The body also gets enough incoming caloric energy to start optimizing other functions. I haven't seen research on it, but based on 30 years of doing this, I would argue that these refeeds also influence the sex hormones and thyroid function in positive ways. This comes from assessing my clients' feedback when they're on the Cycle Diet, but also by doing some reverse engineering here as well. What I mean here is that if you ask any person in the throes of a long-term diet about their libido and sex drive (or better yet ask *their spouse!*)

and almost inevitably you'll see that sex drive and libido are some of the main causalities of a long-term "get lean" diet. Feeling cold in your extremities signals another common symptom of a long-term "get lean" diet, and of metabolic down-regulation. This can also result in situational low thyroid.

Regular refeeds seem to bring sex drive back up, or prevent it disappearing to begin with. Refeeds also can make people quite thermogenic (heat-generating) as well. These are both obviously good things for people who want to live in the real world, but still change their bodies and keep that change <u>permanent</u>.

Moreover, all of these physiological and hormonal effects also have tremendous psychological benefits as well. A person who is dieting but having regular over-feeds just "feels better" in terms of well-being and overall functioning. It's easier to balance life when your hormones are actually functioning as they should.

The other psychological benefits of cycling diet days with over-feeding "anything goes" meals and days should be obvious but let me point it out here: we live in a world of incredible food abundance, and our brains are hardwired through evolution and through our earliest experiences to emotionally enjoy the eating experience. The Cycle Diet services psychological wellness by allowing you to…. enjoy eating!

So many modern diets and approaches to weight-loss want to demonize certain foods or food groups; or worse, they make you "fear food," which in turn makes you anxious about eating. This is unnatural to the evolved brain. Many modern diets put you at odds with your own instinctual wiring to enjoy eating. How is that ever supposed to last long-term? Diets that engender guilt and shame are diets already at odds with your instinctual wiring to enjoy the eating experience. We need to stop pretending when it comes to the modern diet arena and controlling weight. We live in a world of food abundance and we can't pretend we don't want to enjoy indulgent foods here and there. It was said in the late 1800s that without the culinary arts the brutality of life would not be worth living. In other words, even back then people tapped into being able to fully embrace and enjoy the eating experience, as we are all meant to.

Scott Abel

How "Much" of a Spike to Have

How "much" of a spike to have within the Cycle Diet that has evolved a great deal since the early days of the diet.

The Cycle Diet used to be very one-dimensional in terms of application, but there are many nuances to it. But even people reading this may be slightly confused. People who are not my clients, and who are assessing themselves, will often ask how much of a cheat should they should take. A meal? A day? Every week? Every other week?

These are great questions, but the answer often depends on the person, what their biofeedback is saying, along with where their diet and weight history has been most recently. These things matter. I'll try to give you some solid examples here. I'll start at the smallest level of a cheat meal and move up in scale from there.

Single cheat meal / refeed meal every five to nine days

This is often the way I first start instituting refeeds with clients. It's often a way to "test" whether a client is in supercompensation mode or not, as you can assess how their body responds to the refeed.

However this is also my approach "especially" for clients who were previously *very* overweight. We take this approach to instituting refeeds for clients who have achieved substantial weight-loss for two reasons:

- Simply, to keep them sane and living in the real world.

- Clients who fit this profile are more likely to be "leptin resistant," meaning that even when leptin levels rose, they didn't enjoy the benefits of the hormone (which could very well have contributed to their weight issues to begin with).

So a "cautious approach" needs to be taken with these previously overweight clients to assess biofeedback as to positive or neutral effects of the over-feed meal. As you can see previous dieting and weight-history should be considered when it comes to "when" and "how" to begin assigning regular "cycling" of over-feeds into the mix with diet days.

Take my client JP as example. Many people were inspired by his transformation when his story was shared on my blog. And I used the words transformation, because he didn't just lose weight, he gained muscle and leanness, and sculpted his physique.

Look at these before and after pictures:

But I had to be very careful when assigning JP regular over-feed meals because of his history of being overweight. He could very well be leptin resistant. At first, I just let him go off diet, very sporadically, every so often. Then, after months of sticking to his diet with just mild fluctuations here and there, because of work and other things, we finally started instituting regular cheat meals into JP's diet cycle. At the time I am writing this, he now "cycles" a refeed meal every five to nine days and he'll soon be ready to transition to a full cheat/refeed day.

The Half-Day Refeed

The half-day refeed is where I usually begin refeeds with clients I suspect are now in supercompensation mode, but who have none of the concerns I mention above.

The half-day refeed is also the next step in a Cycle Diet process for those who begin with a mere cheat "meal" every five to nine days. So, in that particular context you can look as the half-day refeed as a Cycle Diet "progression," once supercompensation has been firmly established.

Many clients like the half-day refeed because it still keeps them diet- and responsibility-focused.

In a half-day refeed, clients will eat two or three of their regular diet meals and then take the rest of the day off dieting. Alternatively, of course, you can do it the other way around: they may start with a refeed for breakfast and a next meal, and then get back to smaller diet meals for the rest of the day as well. (This latter option is provided that psychologically they have no trouble just getting back to diet halfway through the day. It's not too hard if you're full, but sometimes it's easier to just start the day with diet meals, take the refeed during the second half of the day, and then "start fresh" with diet meals again after waking up the next morning.)

It doesn't have to be any more complicated than this.

The half day refeeds also tend to work well with social events like parties that are in the evening, or weddings and things of that nature, where there may be no need or desire to take a whole refeed day, and the client may not be deep enough into supercompensation mode to have a full refeed day anyway.

The half-day refeed also works well for clients who are still a little fearful or tense about going off a diet they have followed for so long. Yes, there definitely are people like that. So a half-day refeed is often a good way to introduce refeeds to this kind of client. This helps the dieter stay responsible and keep one foot firmly grounded in the notion that this is still a diet to adhere to, but at the same time using the other foot to "step into" the idea that refeeds are good for the body and metabolism, and have no long-term consequences either.

The Full Day Refeed
aka the famous "Cheat Day"

This used to be where and how I started all clients on the refeed agenda. In retrospect it was a mistake.

It took *years* to realize that there are "degrees" of supercompensation mode, and that not everyone's metabolism responds the same, even to relative caloric deficits.

Nowadays, the full refeed day or "cheat day" is assigned to those who are deeper into supercompensation mode, and who will likely need and require a full day of overeating to reap the benefits of the refeed without storing any negative consequences from this kind of eating.

I would say this is the most common level of "regular" Cycle Dieters, once they're in supercompensation mode. I'd estimate that over 80 percent of Cycle Dieters are people who function well and benefit from the full cheat "day," and do not need more refeeds than this, but definitely not fewer refeeds than this either.

There are other factors involved to take into account. Take me for instance. For many years I benefitted from a full day cheat day plus the mid-week spike, But now, at age 55 as I write this, I have had a natural metabolic downturn. A single "full day" calorie spike is more than enough for me to keep my metabolism optimized and robust. I wouldn't benefit from the mid-week spike anymore—and if I tried, I would likely find myself out of supercompensation mode in a short-time.

The Cheat Day + Mid-Week Spike
aka the "full" Cycle Diet

This is the pinnacle of the Cycle Diet. The full refeed day plus another half day refeed is for people *deep* into supercompensation mode, and wanting to stay lean as well.

This means they keep calories lower than most people would and they flirt with absolute deprivation mode, without ever dropping into it. The full-on cheat day-and-a-half is only for people who are training consistently and intensely as well. This full-on application is also for people with very few restricting factors, such as the ones I mentioned above: age, spending years overweight, etc. Other restricting factors would be specific medications that slow metabolism and/or offset leptin levels. Some anti-depressant and anti-anxiety medications seem to do this, as do some birth control medications.

People who do really well long-term the full day-and-a-half of refeeds tend to be people with a *good amount of developed lean body musculature from years of working out*. I'm not just talking about bodybuilder bodies here, but also an extensive background in athletic history as well. Genetics will also have a lot to do with this as well: both for how much they need it, and for how they respond to refeeds and over-feeding.

Often it will take some experimenting to see if you need that extra mid-week spike.

Using myself as an example, in the early days of having one weekly cheat day in the years before the Cycle Diet had a name, I eventually discovered that this one cheat day was not enough. Late in the following week, before my next cheat day had arrived, I noticed my muscles were flat and stringy looking. My workouts were still good, but my musculature looked and felt flat – to my eyes, at least. I started experimenting with different kinds of mid-week refeeds. I began with just larger portions of my diet meals, but that didn't work. Then I tried one single cheat meal mid-week, and that only "kind of" worked. Too soon I concluded, "I must need two full cheat days then" and I tried that for a while, but it was quickly obvious that two full cheat days wasn't just plain too much. So the full day-and-a-half refeed schedule was born. It's very seldom if ever, I see anyone requiring more than this.

When you do the full refeed meal plus midweek spike, your schedule would look like this:

Day 1: Diet day
Day 2: Diet day
Day 3: Diet day
Day 4: Diet day + mid-week spike
Day 6: Diet day
Day 6: Diet day
Day 7: Full Refeed Day

I *have* had clients who have done well by putting these day-and-a-half refeeds back to back, like beginning their refeeding half-way through Saturday, and staying off diet and refeeding until Monday morning. It isn't what I would recommend myself, but it does fit with the recent research that refeed windows can last from 18 to 36 hours. My concern there is that the metabolic bump doesn't seem to last through the week nearly as well as when that half-day is placed four days later. The mid-week spike approach just makes better sense to me, and it's what I have observed over the years with clients as well.

Scott Abel

What Do I Eat During a Refeed?

For people new to The Cycle Diet, the inevitable question becomes "what foods can I eat for refeed meals?"

The short answer to this is anything and everything!

Yes, it actually means that. Anything. Everything.

Other fitness and diet gurus have confused the idea of refeeds by making statements like "clean refeeds" and the like. These notions have some very limited application, a clean refeed is very unlikely to give you enough calories to have the metabolic effects we're looking for. Frankly, I think the idea of a "clean refeed" also feeds into the fear of food mantra that has no place in a healthy diet mindset.

So, more often than not the rules for refeed meals and days are that there are no rules!

This seems to confuse people. But keep it simple here and know that the whole idea of a refeed is that it does your body good. That's honestly the most important idea to keep in mind. It does your body good for all the "reset" reasons I have laid out previously, plus the psychological effects. At least this is how it should be. When it comes to the Cycle Diet, at least, I can't do much for people who equate worry and anxiety with food and eating—not in the context of this project. In order for it to work, you have to <u>enjoy</u> it!

Learning As You Go

The other great thing about refeeds is that you learn as you go. You start learning more and more about your body. You learn to read your own biofeedback.

You learn more and more through biofeedback which kinds of indulgent foods your body really likes and handles well, and which ones…not so much. This can change over time. Some of my favorite cheat day foods from years ago are far different from my "go-to" foods now. Other foods have stayed consistently. Cycle Diet refeeds are a great way to learn about biofeedback and your own body's preferences. (How many other diets can make that claim?) Most other diet strategies have you approaching various foods with caution or ruling out certain foods from the get go, with no inclusion or notion that you may like those foods and even do well on those foods. The Cycle Diet may restrict some of these foods on your "diet days" in order to produce a cosmetic advantage, but any and all foods are allowed on cheat/refeed meals and days.

One Suggestion for the Mid-Week Spike

I do offer this one "suggestion" and possible "amendment" to the above. For people fortunate enough to be on the full-on full day refeed plus mid-week spike, I often "recommend" restricting simple sugars like desserts, only on the half day refeed. This isn't a hard and fast rule by any means, but I find in general it limits bloating and other digestive issues, and actually allows you to eat more during that mid-week spike. This doesn't mean restricting any and all things with sugar—not at all. It just means the more pure sugars like desserts.

For instance in my old days of full-on Cycle Diet I always went out for a nice steak dinner on my mid-week spike. One place in particular made their own bread and their own honey-butter to go on the bread. I would order three or more loaves of this, plus appetizers and a full steak dinner, and then often finish with a cappuccino or something. Then later, before bed, I would have four large rice cakes with peanut butter and jam. This isn't restricting all sugar by any means, just *delaying* pure sugars like cookies, ice cream, desserts, cake, pies until the very end of the day. As I said this is by no means a hard and

pure sugars lead to bloating

153

fast rule. I have just found that for myself and for many clients it just works very well in terms of optimizing the refeed.

And again: if you aren't on the full-on Cycle Diet of a day-and-a-half of refeeds, then it's not even an issue. Enjoy your cheat day or cheat meal however you like!

Starting the Day If You're New to the Full Day Refeed

I also often recommend *beginning* the day with a similar approach for people *new* to the full refeed day. That is, you have your first meal with limited sugary foods like cakes, and pies and cookies. This is not a hard and fast rule, but it does seem to help a person be able to eat more food throughout the whole day. I'm not saying don't eat them—I'm saying eat the fattier foods first.

Note that I myself violate this one all the time. For instance, one of my favorite first meals is a dozen donuts; that isn't something I want to wait for later in the day to enjoy. I have also begun my full over-feed day with birthday cakes and pies (particularly sweet potato pie). Again: this is certainly not a hard and fast rule, but you might find it lets you eat more food over the course of the whole day to delay the sugary stuff just a bit. It's just a recommendation particularly suited to people who are new to a whole refeed day and may be prone to "overdo it" at that first meal. It happens!

What to Expect After the Refeed Day

This is one of the most common questions out there for newbies on The Cycle Diet. Many have visions of waking up suddenly fat and obese. That won't happen, but there are a few effects you *can* experience after a refeeding indulgence, especially if you are new to it and you haven't learned what your body likes best. Some of these feel great, and some not so much.

Energy Levels

The first thing most people feel across the board is increased energy. Dieting can slowly but surely tap into your normal energy levels. A refeed meal or day will bring your energy levels back—and not just for the day after, either. This usually lasts for a few days, even though you're back on your diet meals. When you have good energy on dieting days, it makes dieting all the easier to endure and stay with as well. Indeed, if that energy isn't lasting your through most of the week, it might be a sign you need the mid-week spike, or you need to move up from a half-day refeed to a full day refeed. It means your glycogen is getting depleted more and more quickly.

The Mirror

Many people also want to know what to expect from the mirror. Most are concerned that all their hard work at dieting and weight-loss will suddenly disappear. This can be a bit more unpredictable. Sometimes you'll actually look better the day after your refeed, sometimes you'll be holding fluids. Often this is because of the foods chosen to indulge in. It can also be genetic, as some people just hold water more easily than others. I find that clients who practice Cycle Dieting for a while notice the fluid retention tends to subside over time.

This is how you learn about yourself, which foods cosmetically enhance you in the short-term, and which foods cosmetically detract in the short-term. This can vary widely from person to person. I had one client who just loved milk: real, full fat, homogenized milk. He would drink a gallon of milk on his cheat day. And he looked *great* after, always tighter and leaner, his muscles full, and not a lot of fluid retention. But that much milk for me, or for most people, would bloat and smooth us out cosmetically, and likely lead to digestive disruption as well. But this client *thrived* on the stuff.

This is the part of the Cycle Diet that is ongoing and can be a lot of fun. **Over time, as you practice refeeds, you get into a "flow."** You learn which foods give you more energy, make you feel better, make you look better, and so on. It's a continuous learning process.

"The Food Hangover"

There are sometimes consequences to over-feed days as well. These are not always expected, but they can and do happen. One of the most common is the food hangover, especially with people new to refeeds, who don't know their own bodies, and have been looking forward to the "cheat" for awhile.

A food hangover is a lot like an alcohol hangover, to be sure. You feel tired, and heavy and lethargic at first. You may even have ankle swelling or puffiness. These things don't always happen, but they can. As your own system adapts to cycling diet days with over-feed days though, these food hangover days tend to happen far less frequently. They also happen less as you learn and consume foods that work well, and avoid the ones that don't. They seldom happen to me, or other more experienced Cycle Dieters at all anymore.

The food hangover can also make you look bloated or puffy in the belly. It can often take a half-day or so for that to settle down, as all the food is still moving through the gut. This is often referred to as a "food baby" or a Buddha belly. It's not very common, but again, it can happen. The reminder about all these things is that they don't last very long into the day after a refeed. Food hangovers become less frequent over time, and even if you are holding some water, it will go away in a day or two.

Night Sweats

There can often be night sweats as well, during the night after a refeed. This is classic thermogenesis in action. It is your body turning up its temperature to help get rid of the calorie surge.

Although this can be uncomfortable during the night, this is often a very good sign. Thermogenesis you can feel means it will likely keep your metabolism burning high for a few more days as well. Overeating in the right metabolic environment increases thermogenesis to a point where metabolism burns off far more energy than it stores.

* * *

Don't forget the whole idea of refeeds is to optimize

and reset metabolism and to restore leptin levels. It's always about the inside-out effects and benefits of the Cycle Diet. And that cannot be forgotten or overstated.

Many people practicing the Cycle Diet really don't care if they look a little fluid-retentive, or less cosmetically impressive for a day or so after a full cheat day. They know the Cycle Diet serves them well, and that they can live on it and sustain it long-term. They don't stress over little things like temporary cosmetic effects the day after a full over-feed day. If they're really looking forward to going to the beach, maybe they delay the refeed, or for one refeed, they actually focus more on the foods that they know will be good to them cosmetically, and actually make them look better.

What matters to people who "get it" is that they can have their cake and eat it to, and do so regularly without worrying ever again about getting fat or gaining weight. That is a pretty fair trade-off for a few hours of not looking as good naked as you did yesterday (but being fine tomorrow).

"Non-Regular" Energy Spikes

There are many variations of the Cycle Diet, and many ways to apply its basic principles in other diet strategies.

I have clients right now who do full cheat days every second week. I have clients who do a refeed "meal" one week, and then a refeed whole cheat day the next. I also have a few clients who don't like the whole "chow down" experience of a whole cheat day and they seem to do well with two half over-feed days per week, or every seven to 10 days. I wouldn't recommend this for everyone, but these exceptions do seem to work well for those to whom they apply. This is all about properly reading biofeedback and considering context.

The reasons these exceptions apply better for some clients and not others would require a completely separate book on metabolism to explain. That is not the purpose of pointing out these exceptions. What I want to make clear is that the Cycle Diet keeps evolving in terms of overall application, and in terms of individual application. But it will always revolve around the metabolic state of supercompensation mode induced over time by a relative caloric deficit.

Energy Spikes Before Supercomp

Sometimes people diet in a relative deficit but they still aren't in supercompensation mode. They are not ready for the *regular* refeed/over-feed cheat meal or day, but they've been dieting a while and consistently enough to maybe need an off-diet meal or day just to stay sane.

This is not the same as being in supercompensation mode of course, so it means not really benefitting metabolically and hormonally from an off-diet day. But these people benefit psychologically from the off-diet day to be sure, and if they've been consistent it won't set back progress to a substantial degree.

The distinction here is to note the difference between refeeds as part of supercompensation mode, versus a simple 'off-diet' break to keep the dieter on track. There is a big difference.

The off-diet approach requires minimizing the consequences of the off-diet meal or day. The goal is to give that meal or day to someone so they don't sabotage their hard efforts. The right call for an off-diet meal or day can be the difference between someone lasting on a diet long enough to reach their goals versus packing it all in, because they are just dieting with no end in sight.

When More Refeeds Are Necessary

Other exceptions to the Cycle Diet can run the other way as well. Often, one or two days of refeeds may not be enough. I've seen this as well. When someone is deep, deep, *deep* into supercompensation mode, very often a longer refeed may be in order as well.

The faster someone's weight returns to normal after a calorie spike and refeed, with no sustained energy bump to go along with it, the more likely it is that a longer refeed duration may be in order.

I once had a client dieting for a National championship. Her body fought with her in the initial stages of the diet, and then it all came together, and fast. She ended up being contest ready five weeks out from the show. I knew from her biofeedback there was no way she was going to be able to last five more weeks of dieting with just one cheat day. Psychology aside, her body would have become flat and stringy. There was no doubt in my mind.

What I had her do had everyone commenting how crazy I was, and that I just ruined her prep and all her hard work… blah, blah, blah. At five weeks out from her competition I had her take five days *completely off diet and training*. She ended up hopping on a plane to Florida and completely enjoyed herself and let loose. She gained about 15 lbs. in those five days. She came back home, resumed training and lost 12 lbs. the first week and another five lbs. the next week. She went into her contest and won Nationals and won her pro card. No one else looked even close to as prepared as she was.

This was all possible because I was starting to understand the real world of metabolism and how it works, when and how to optimize it, and what signs to look for when you may be stressing it too much. Many, many contest-prep gurus even to this day have no real idea of how this all works. The closer a contest date looms, the tighter they make their client's diets and training, *regardless of what that client's biofeedback may be saying.* This is why all my articles stress biofeedback, and why I sound like a broken record.

I knew my client needed more than a one-day refeed and I knew that she was burning out from her training. I also knew that we had time on our hands with the contest being five full weeks away. So I gave her five days off training and diet, and the result was exactly what I thought it would be. Her body responded positively and she was easily ripped up for her contest.

Now was this an exception? Absolutely. That is why I include it here. There are exceptions to every rule. But it speaks to expertise and experience in assessing biofeedback of an individual and knowing what to do with it, and why I say it's often more an art than a science. If you're applying the Cycle Diet to yourself, be aware of the whole context and consider all your biofeedback: how you feel mentally and physically, how your training is going, *when* you get cravings, consider your whole metabolic background (e.g., were you overweight as a child? How do you respond to this or that kind of food?). As you gain more experience, if you're smart and you pay attention, you'll learn more about your body, and you'll learn to be creative in application. (I won't lie. It is extremely difficult to do this for yourself. I recommend getting a coach 99 times out of 100. But it *is* possible.)

Scott Abel

Appendix

Scott Abel

Cycle Diet FAQ

I'm not a bodybuilder or anything. Can I really do the Cycle Diet?

Whether you compete or not doesn't matter. I "discovered" the Cycle Diet through competing and getting myself to low body fat levels, but the competing aspect is not at all necessary. The Cycle Diet is for anyone who wants to improve his or her body while maintaining a decent level of leanness year round, with none of this "bulk/cut" nonsense.

I watched the Cycle Diet DVD, and there you have more complicated formulas. Shouldn't I use those?

Nope. One of the points I was trying to get across in the DVD is that, even after all the fancy calculations, BW X 10 to 12 got you pretty darn close. And, since we're just talking about a *starting point*, the simpler the better.

Adjusting up or down from there based on biofeedback and context will give you far better results than focusing on fancy formulas. Remember, formulas and numbers like that offer the illusion of control, not real precision.

For people's refeed day, does your day not essentially revolve around food? So, no ball games or Sunday day trips or anything else going on because you simply need to eat all day?

Not at all. It's not a "mission" or anything. As a matter of fact, back East, taking in a ball game on cheat day on a warm Sunday early afternoon was once one of my favorite ways to relax. "Beer and a dog" (or two.)

So I should try to eat as much as I can on a refeed, right?

Well, it's not about "eating as much as you can" so much. Biofeedback (i.e. your subjective hunger and appetite) as usual will determine when enough is enough. Don't *force* anything.

It's just that when in Supercomp, eating double or sometimes triple what you are used to is not hard to do, because your appetite is so big.

Of course many people do indeed over do it, especially when they're just starting out, or it's their first refeed in a while. It takes some getting used to.

Does the refeed day have to be a day off training?

How and when you cycle spikes and full calories off days can vary. I've had success with many variations. I've found that when in Supercomp, it's best to have full "eat day" on a day off, in order to eat more and enjoy it. But no, it doesn't *have* to be that way.

Is it possible to still get into supercomp mode if you have a light week in training?

Yes, of course that is possible. It's a good question, actually. But yes, very possible. One week here or there is not the determinant.

I'm going to be playing high level soccer / hockey / football. Is this okay?

It's possible, but it wasn't really designed for athletic purposes. You have to make sure there is gas in the tank when it matters. When in Supercomp, at the end of the week before a refeed, you can be a bit too depleted, especially if you have an important athletic event on that day. So this needs to be customized a bit. The athletes I've put on the Cycle Diet have functioned just fine, but they were very committed and disciplined athletes.

I've read some research that says a refeed can last up 18 to 36 hours. Should that be how long my refeed is?

I've had clients do the mid-week spike immediately before or after their full day refeed, effectively creating a 36-hour window. *However*, especially if you're still on only a one-day refeed per week, there is no reason to push the envelope.

For most of the time, the diet calls for "one normal metabolic day." That means you wake up at the normal time, and you go to bed at the normal time. Don't wake up in the middle of the night at 12:01 a.m. or something to start eating.

So what body fat level do I need to be to be in Supercomp?

There is no "set" body fat percentage. This will vary from person to person. What matters more is the biofeedback discussed earlier. If you're 20 lbs. overweight, you're obviously not in Supercomp, but while one person can be out of super comp at 10 percent body fat, another person might be in it at 13 percent. It varies. Genetics, overall background, recent dieting or body weight changes, etc.

On the Cycle Diet we shoot for cut, full, good energy, and near-ripped at best. That will vary for everyone. For many people they will just have a greater affinity to higher body fat levels, that is natural for them, and pushing them out of that sets up metabolic havoc.

Which supplements work best for the Cycle Diet?

Supplements are as equally useless on the Cycle Diet as they are on any other diet. The only exceptions are common things like caffeine, which is a far better "pre-workout" supplement than any over-priced powder being sold in stores right now.

For the meal plans, when should my Post-Workout or Pre-Workout meals be?

That doesn't matter. The body and your metabolism don't function on 24-hour clock. I do recommend trying to at least get some breakfast in you before your workout, barring any digestive issues.

Sample Diet Day Menus

The Cycle Diet works best when diet days and the corresponding over-feed cycles are customized and individualized to the client. This is the value of coaching, of course.

That said, I wanted to provide you with a few starting points for designing your diet days.

Below are some examples of Cycle Diet application with a very brief explanation of the "metabolic context" of the diet included, just so you can get an idea how the diet is made to fit the client, and that the client is *never* forced to fit the diet. This is an important element of any sound diet strategy.

(It was a balancing act between providing *some* of the metabolic context, but not going into so much background detail that it would seem like it was not applicable to anyone except the example client. I wanted you to be able to get some insight into extrapolating from what I provided here.)

Example 1
Basic Setup

This particular example represents the easiest, most basic set-up for the Cycle Diet. **I recommend starting with this one, or tweaking it to your needs.** You'll see it was for a male, but even if you're female this should provide a good starting framework, albeit you'll just adjust the portion sizes based on your weight and calorie needs. Whether for male or female, that's still bodyweight X 10 to 12).

In this particular example, the client has expressed an interest in the Cycle Diet. The metabolic context of this person is male, under 6 ft. tall (since height affects BMR,) and he was already dieting fairly healthy and pretty lean when he came to me. The application here was just to tweak what he is already doing in order to tighten up the diet, and ensure a relative caloric deficit, and also to create the most cosmetically advantageous diet days (i.e. avoiding foods that cause water retention).

As you can see I do not use calories or macros in my diets, merely portion sizes. I suggest adjusting these based on your calorie needs, but once you've got a basic meal plan set up based on those calories, just throw out the calorie counts and tweak your meal plan *as* a meal plan.

Meal 1.

- Eight egg whites (250 mls) with veggies, salsa or whatever added OR whey protein in equal amount

- Three Shredded Wheat biscuits with hot water/equal/cinnamon, OR equivalent in oatbran or oatmeal or grits (two servings or 60 grams dry weight)

Meal 2.

- 150g chicken breast
- One small to medium size potato or yam (pre-cooked size)

Meal 3:

- 150g chicken or turkey breast
- One small to medium size potato or yam OR two-thirds cup cooked brown rice
- Add any fibrous veggie 200 to 400 grams, and add one tbsp. EVOO

Meal 4:

- 150 grams grass-fed lean beef or steak
- Three rice large rice cakes, <u>OR</u> 25 mini rice cakes (any flavor except the sweet ones)

Meal 5:

- 150 grams grass-fed lean beef or steak
- Three rice large rice cakes, <u>OR</u> 25 mini rice cakes (any flavor except the sweet ones)

Meal 6:

- Eight egg whites or one cup one percent cottage cheese

NOTES

o Space the meals out as evenly as possible throughout the day. Try to eat meals no *less* than two-and-a-half hours apart, and no *further* than four-and-a-half to five hours apart.

Substitutions:

o One cup low fat cottage cheese can also be used as a protein source one or twice per day as well. A post workout meal of cottage cheese and two-to-three pieces of fruit, fruit combinations or equivalent, like berries, can also be subbed for any above meal, but not till after Week 6

o Two-thirds cup cooked weight of any kind of long grain rice can be subbed for potato or yam, but potato or yam are preferred

o Rice varieties include brown rice, basmati rice, jasmine rice, wild rice

o Any white fish, up to 180 grams (pre-cooked weight) can be subbed for any protein source above

o White fish varieties include halibut, haddock, sole, tilapia, orange roughy, etc.

Condiments:

o Ketchup, mustard, hot sauce, salsa sauce, Equal® or other artificial sweetener, non-fat mayo, low cal salad dressing

Fluids:

o Keep intake of water high, especially at the gym

o   Diet drinks like sugar-free Kool-Aid, Crystal Light, diet pop, coffee or tea with artificial sweetener only, non-fat milk. These are all okay.

Fibrous Veggies:

o   Cauliflower, broccoli, asparagus, green beans, yellow beans, egg plant, zucchini, red/yellow/orange/green peppers, squash, salad ingredients, cabbage, coleslaw mix etc. – even frozen veggies combinations are fine to add as long as they don't have peas or corn in the mix.

o   Add one tbsp. of either flax oil, macadamia nut oil, or Extra Virgin Olive or Coconut Oil to Meals 3, and 5

To Set Up the Cycle Diet with the Above:

Follow the diet "as is" *without Meal 6* and without **any** cheats for four-to-six weeks. At that point feel free to add in Meal 6 if you're hungry enough. Then, from Weeks 7 to 10 or so, have one free off-diet meal every five to eight days. This should last two to three weeks or so, and as long as weight keeps coming back to normal after five to six days, then by Weeks 9 or 10 you should be able to have a full-day calorie spike "cheat day" every seven to nine days.

Of course, once you do, you should be monitoring weight each week, but that means weighing in only *once* per week, just to ensure weight is coming back down or close to all the way back down before engaging in the next refeed.

If the body continues cooperating, then within two to three months, you may want to consider adding in a mid-week spike over-feed as well. On that day, usually Day 4 of the diet, you will eat your first three diet meals as usual, and then from the scheduled time of Meal 4 onward for that day you eat whatever you want. (I recommend on mid-week spike days to avoid simple sugars like chocolate, candy, cakes, pies, desserts.)

Example 2
Large Frame (But Lean)

This example comes from a male client with a larger frame. He is well over six ft. tall, and he also has a lot of lean, active muscle mass, and lots of experience in the weight room.

His metabolism isn't revving as though he's some genetic freak, but it's about what you'd expect for his large size and level of leanness and muscle mass. If I recall correctly, I put him straight onto the Cycle Diet with the mid-week spike, but that's not a given. (Most people, even when "fairly" lean, need at least a couple weeks before the spikes come into play.)

Meal 1:

- 16 egg whites (500 mls) OR two scoops whey
- Three pouches Cream of Wheat, OR three Shredded Wheat biscuits, OR equivalent in oats

Meal 2:

- 250g chicken breast
- 25 mini rice cakes OR 200g yams/potatoes

Meal 3:

- One can tuna/salmon, OR 175 grams any white fish fillets,

- 200g potatoes/yams OR 25 mini rice cakes (any flavor)

Meal 4:

- 250g chicken OR 280g any white fish, OR 16 egg whites

- Five rice cakes, large size, OR 25 mini rice cakes OR 300g peas, OR one cup cooked rice (long grain, brown or white)

Meal 5:

- 200g orange roughy or any white fish, OR one can tuna or salmon

- 200g potatoes, OR one-and-a-half cups peas (from frozen) OR 25 mini rice cakes

Meal 6:

- 12 egg whites <u>OR</u> one can tuna, <u>OR</u> two scoops whey

NOTES

o Meal 6 is optional

o This veggie mix which follows can be subbed for any carb portion at any meal: 200 to 300g green veggie mix, including anything like green beans, mushrooms, yellow beans squash, broccoli, cauliflower, cabbage, asparagus, cucumber or Italian veggie mix, zucchini, roasted or barbecued peppers, eggplant.

o One cup beans can also be subbed in as a carb source for any of Meals 2, 3, or 4. "Beans" means canned matured beans, without sauces, like kidney beans, Romano beans, Black beans, Fava beans, Lentils, Navy Beans, Black Eyed Peas, etc.

o White fish fillets means any fish like orange roughy (which is the best), sole, haddock, halibut, whitefish, cod, etc.

o All food weight is cooked weight.

o Condiments such as ketchup, salsa, hot sauce, mustard, ultra low fat mayonnaise, equal, cinnamon, are all fine.

o Rice cakes can be any flavor except the sweet ones (e.g. caramel is a no-no, but BBQ is okay).

o   Follow the diet for three-and-a-half days, so that on day four you eat your first three meals, then from dinner on, anything you like except sugars and desserts...then go back to dieting for two days, then all day on the seventh day eat anything you wish and as much as possible

o   Try to take in at least four liters fluids per day, sugar free, and mostly water, <u>no</u> Crystal Light®, especially on diet days. (This is not important on Day 7.)

o   Two scoops whey can be subbed for any other protein source as well, but go easy on using the protein supplements, twice per day *max*.

Example 3
High Fat Cycling

In this particular Cycle Diet application, the dieter preferred a metabolic diet approach for diet days (low carbs/high fat). I don't assign these often, but the background and use of such diets before, and his maturity, indicated it was viable in this case.

In this particular application the dieter is less than six ft. tall, but with a good amount of leanness and muscle mass.

He will eat three days of this high-fat diet below, and then the fourth day is still a diet day, but it has an alternate High Carbs meal plan. Then he will resume the high fat metabolic diet for two more days, and then have Day 7 as a complete "off diet" day where anything goes.

High Fat Day
(Days 1, 2, 3, 5, 6)

Meal 1:

- Six egg whites
- One whole egg
- One tbsp. coconut oil
- One-half cup cottage cheese

Meal 2:

- Six oz. top sirloin (170g)

Meal 3:

- 140 grams ground turkey or chicken or any fatty protein source
- Green veggies, such as green beans or broccoli

Meal 4
(same as meal 3)

- 140 grams ground turkey or chicken or any fatty protein source
- Green veggies, such as green beans or broccoli

Meal 5:

- 5 oz. top sirloin (140g)

Meal 6:

- Six egg whites
- One whole egg
- One-half tbsp. coconut oil

NOTES:

o   Fiber supplement may be required (Metamucil)

o   No condiments on these high-fat days, except sweetener and hot sauce

o   One-half cup full fat cottage cheese with 20g walnuts can be subbed for any meal as well.

o   200 to 300g green veggie like green beans, or broccoli, cabbage etc., can be added to Meals 5 and 6

High Carb Day
(Day 4)

Meal 1:

- Eight egg whites (250 mls), or one cup one percent cottage cheese

- Three pouches Cream of Wheat, cream of rice, or three Shredded Wheat biscuits, or two servings oat bran, or two servings oatmeal or millet. (60 grams dry weight)

Meal 2:

- 150g chicken breast or turkey breast

- 25 to 30 mini rice cakes, or one medium to large size yam or potato or one to one-and-a-half cups brown rice (cooked weight), add one tablespoon EVOO (Extra Virgin Olive Oil)

Meal 3:

- One can tuna/salmon, or 150 to 175g any white fish fillets (tilapia/sole/haddock etc. is fine)
- One medium to large size yam or potato or 25 to 35 mini rice cakes (any flavor), add as much fibrous veggies as desired from the veggie mix below.

Meal 4:

- 150g chicken or turkey breast or 150g to 175g any white fish or shellfish, or 8 egg whites
- One-and-a-half cups cooked rice, any kind

Meal 5:

- 150g salmon or chicken (or any white fish or shellfish)
- One-and-a-half cups peas (from frozen is fine) or one cup cooked brown rice, or one cup cooked quinoa (can mix in one cup veggies if choose the rice/quinoa option) add one tbsp. EVOO

190

Meal 6 (optional):

- One cup one percent cottage cheese
- Add fresh fruit, any kind. You want about the equivalent of two to four medium-to-large pieces (say two large oranges or equivalent in berries, etc.)

Day 7 is completely off-diet trying to take in as many calories as possible, as many simple carbs as possible!

Example 4
Female Competitor with Digestive Issues

In this particular example the dieter is a female competitor *normally* of average height and weight, but who came to me very lean and deep into Supercomp. At the same time, she had a likely a compromised metabolism from prolonged low-carb dieting. She had been following a low-carbs pre-contest diet plan for awhile when she came to me. So she was obviously in supercompensation mode, but all these weeks and months doing low carbs had given her a very sensitive stomach, especially to a carbs-based diet.

This meal plan uses a relatively lower carb diet on diet days, only because that is what this particular dieter's stomach is used to. We then use the Day 7 cheat day and a modified mid-week spike on Day 4 to effectively cycle in some higher carbs days. (You'll see what I mean in the instructions below the meal plan.) If you're not as deep into Supercomp as she is, you wouldn't start with either of the spikes.

The client was in Supercomp already, and this diet maintains that leanness and Supercomp mode while reintroducing her gut to digesting carbs and processing larger amounts of carbs sometimes. Cycling higher carb days and full refeed days kept her metabolism optimized and robust. At the time of writing this, the client loves this version of diet cycling, as it's keeping her both sane and lean at the same time. It's an interesting use of the Cycle Diet to get someone "back" to being able to stomach carbs!

If you're not in Supercomp like she was, you'll see some instructions below the diet for info on how to get there with this diet.

Normal Days
(Slightly Lower Carb)
Meal 1:

- Six to eight egg whites, (200 to 250 mls) veggies, salsa whatever, or equivalent in whey protein with water

- Two to three Shredded Wheat with hot water/artificial sweetener/cinnamon, etc. or equivalent in oat bran or oatmeal or grits (about 40 to 50 grams dry weight)

Meal 2:

- 100 to 120 grams any lean protein source

- One-third cup cooked rice, add as much fibrous veggies as desired

Meal 3:

- 20 to 30 grams any raw unsalted nuts (roasted is fine)

Meal 4 (same as meal 2)

- 100 to 120 grams any lean protein source
- One-third cup cooked rice, add as much fibrous veggies as desired

Meal 5:

- 100 to 120 grams any lean protein source, as much fibrous veggies as desired, add one tbsp. any healthy oils

Meal 6:

- Eight egg whites or one cup one percent cottage cheese

NOTES:

o   Space meals as evenly as possible throughout the day. Try to eat meals no less than two-and-a-half hours apart and no further than four to five hours apart. These are maximum windows for meal times.

o   Rice varieties include brown rice, basmati rice, jasmine rice, wild rice.

o   **Lean Protein Sources:** include chicken breast, turkey breast, six to eight egg whites (200 to 250 mls in liquid measure), two whole eggs, any fish like sole, halibut, haddock, trout, salmon, bass, tilapia, tuna all at 100 to 120 grams pre-cooked weight. Once per week you can sub in a lean read meat source like flank steak or pork tenderloin.

o   **Condiments:** ketchup, mustard, hot sauce, salsa sauce, equal or any artificial sweetener, non-fat mayo, low calorie salad dressing.

o   **Fluids:** keep intake of water high, especially at the gym, diet drinks like sugar-free Kool-Aid, Crystal Light®, diet pop, coffee, tea, are all okay.

o   Artificial sweetener only, non-fat milk only for coffee.

o   **Fibrous Veggies:** choose any of cauliflower, broccoli, spinach, asparagus, green beans, yellow beans, eggplant, zucchini, red/yellow/orange/green peppers, squash, carrots, mushrooms, salad ingredients, cabbage, coleslaw mix, etc., even frozen veggies combinations are fine to add as long as they don't have peas or corn in the mix (ask if there are any others you would like to use).

o **Healthy Oils Options:** Add one tbsp. of either flax oil, macadamia nut oil, or Extra Virgin Olive Oil, or Coconut Oil etc., at meal five.

o **Leave out Meal 6 for the first two to four weeks.** If hungry enough after that period add it in.

o **On <u>Day 4</u> ONLY, make the following changes:** For **Meal 3** only have 20g raw nuts, but add in as much fresh fruit as you'd like. At **Meal 4**, instead of rice, have a small to medium baked potato or yam. At **Meal 5**, have any free meal of your choice, but not sweets or desserts *preferred*, especially early on.

o **Days 5** and **6** are back to diet days, then **Day 7** is an off day or cheat day.

Adapting this diet yourself...

If you are not yet in Supercomp (like the client was) then to get into Supercomp follow the diet as-is without any cheats at all, and Day 4 actually stays *totally normal* until you're in Supercomp.

Here's what the transition into super comp will look like on this diet:

When you start feeling the hunger and "flatness" in the gym after a few weeks, start with <u>one</u> free "off-diet" <u>meal</u> per week on Day 7, and do that for three weeks or so. If things are going well, then add in the whole Day 7 "cheat day" in place of the free meal. *Then*, if things are *still* going well, keep the Day 7 cheat day, and also add in the alternate Day 4 outlined above.

Example 5
Advanced Carb Cycling

This is an advanced strategy, and really not necessary for most people. The meal plans below cycle carbs and calories to keep the metabolism optimized and robust. This diet is for someone who had a very good amount of muscle, a very good appetite concluded by assessment and hard training five to six days per week, and all the signs of a supportive BMR: height, lean body mass, age, gender. He had a revving metabolism, in other words, and we wanted to keep it that way.

As you'll see below you follow the diet in this sequence:

Day 1:	3,500 cals	Lower carb
Day 2:	3,500 cals	Medium carb
Day 3:	4,000 cals	Lower carb
Day 4:	4,000 cals	Medium carb
Day 5:	3,500 cals	Medium carb
Day 6:	3,500 cals	Lower carb
Day 7:	Refeed	

I won't include how to "get into" super comp with this diet, because to use this you should probably already be there! Again, most people won't be at this stage or have this kind of metabolism. I'm including this for illustration.

~3,500 "Lower Carb"
(Day 1 and Day 6)

Meal 1:

- Five whole eggs
- Egg whites one-and-a-half cups
- Oatmeal one-third cup (measured dry)

Meal 2:

- Chicken 225g or three scoops protein powder
- Four rice cakes or potato, 140g (small)

Meal 3:

- Steak or Salmon 250g

Meal 4:

- Chicken 225g
- Two tbsp. natural peanut butter, cashews, or almonds, 35 to 50g

Meal 5:

- Lean Ground beef 275g
- Potato 120g (small)

Meal 6:

- Chicken breast 225g
- Two tbsp. natural peanut butter, cashews, or almonds (~ 35g)

Meal 7:

- Whole eggs five
- Egg whites one-and-a-half cups

~3,500 "Medium Carb"
(Day 2 and Day 5)

Meal 1:

- Two-and-a-half cups egg whites
- Three Shredded Wheat biscuits, or one cup oatmeal, or four slices dark rye bread

Meal 2:

- 225g chicken or turkey breast, or equivalent calories in protein powder
- 220g grapes, 275g blueberries, 320g pineapple

Meal 3:

- 225g chicken or turkey breast, or equivalent calories in protein powder
- One cup cooked rice, six rice cakes, or 220g potato

Meal 4:

- Two cans tuna or 160g chicken

- One cup cooked rice, six rice cakes, or 220g potato

Meal 5:

- 225g chicken or any white fish
- 200g potato or three-fourths cup rice

Meal 6:

- 225g chicken or 200g flank steak or inside round steak
- 200g potato

Meal 7:

- Two-and-a-half cups egg whites, or equivalent calories in protein powder
- 200g apple, 200g blueberries, 230g pineapple, OR one-half cup oatmeal

~4,000 "Lower Carb"
(Day 3 Only)

Meal 1:

- Six whole eggs
- One-and-a-half cups egg whites
- One-third cup oatmeal (measured dry)

Meal 2:

- 250g chicken or equivalent in protein powder
- Five large rice cakes or 180g potato

Meal 3:

- 265g steak or 265g salmon

Meal 4:

- 250g chicken
- Two tbsp. natural peanut butter or 35g almonds

Meal 5:

- 300g lean ground beef
- 120g potato (small)

Meal 6:

- 250g chicken
- Two tbsp. natural peanut butter, or 35g almonds

Meal 7:

- Six whole eggs
- One-and-a-half cup egg whites

~4,000 "Medium Carb"
(Day 4 Only)
Meal 1:

- Two-and-a-half cups egg whites
- Three Shredded Wheat biscuits, or one cup oatmeal, or four slices dark rye bread

Meal 2:

- 225g chicken or turkey breast, or three scoops protein
- 220g grapes, 275g blueberries, 320g pineapple

Meal 3:

- Chicken or turkey breast – 250g
- Rice- one-and-a-quarter cup cooked, or seven rice cakes, or Potato, 250g (large)

Meal 4:

- 250g chicken
- One-and-a-quarter cooked rice or one bag mini rice cakes

Meal 5:

- 250g chicken or flank steak or pork tenderloin
- 200g potato or three-quarters cup cooked rice

Meal 6:

- 250g chicken
- One-and-a-quarter cup cooked rice, or seven rice cakes, or 250g potato

Meal 7:

- Two-and-a-half cups egg whites or three scoops protein
- 200g apple, 200g blueberries, 230g pineapple, OR one-half cup oatmeal

Scott Abel

Hear From Actual Cycle Dieters

These questionnaires were sent out to several of my clients, as well as people doing the Cycle Diet "on their own."

The hope is that their answers, written in their own words will give you insight into how others have adapted the Cycle Diet to make it part of their lifestyle, as well as give you insight into some of its variations, and some of the elements of it that can change from person to person, such as how long it takes to get into Supercomp, and that kind of thing.

Scott Abel

Andy Sinclair

Tell us about yourself:

I've been a client of Scott's for a decade now and have been applying the Cycle Diet as a lifestyle for almost that length of time too.

I'm not a big guy naturally and really had to bulk up with a traditional high calorie weight gain diet with Scott first to be able to carry enough muscle maturity in order for the cycle diet to work the way it was intended.

When I first signed up with Scott I knew he used it for himself and stayed in amazing shape year round and also knew some of Scotts other coaching clients personally that used the cycle diet as well.

What kind of results did you see on the Cycle Diet?

The Cycle Diet allowed me to look and feel like an athlete year round without having to yo-yo diet by bulking up to try and put on muscle and then cutting for an extended period of time only to strip off all the muscle you gained. I'm able to stay lean and hard year round while still making improvements to my physique.

What do you like about the Cycle Diet?

Well I think most people would automatically say "the cheat days" but I'm an athlete first and foremost, so the eating clean part of the diet is my main focus and the cheat days are just literally the icing on the cake. I would say it allows a lot of diet freedom when you can pigout on whatever you want but in a way where doing so is actually good for your body and enhances both short and long term results.

Why would I want to have a slice of cheesecake through the week when I can time refeeds properly and wait till Sunday and eat the whole thing *and* it's actually good for me!

What did you use the diet for?

As I stated previously it allows me to stay lean and hard year round and close to photoshoot shape, normally I just cut out one cheat day and my body does the rest as its been programmed by following the diet properly which also includes regular time off training and the cycle diet itself to refeed your body for an extended period, no diet sabotage or food restrictions here and my metabolism has never been compromised because of that.

I've been using it since about 2006 which is pretty sustainable if you ask me, I love it and wouldn't want to eat any other way.

Were you a coaching client of Scott's?

Yes I was and still am a coaching client of Scotts. I think for the majority of people it would be best to have Scott's expert application of the diet, as from my personal experience of telling other trainees about the diet they just see the cheat days and completely forget about the other six days of dieting, and the length of time it may take them to get into a supercompensation state which really takes expertise in reading biofeedback. Otherwise you will just get fat over time.

How long did it take to get into supercompensation mode?

After bulking up to a level of muscle I was comfortable with and holding it there for a while, I started dieting for some photos back in 2006. I was able to reach supercomp in about 10 weeks of straight dieting and tweaks by Scott.

What are your diet days like?

Calories haven't really changed a whole lot over the years to get into supercomp and on diet days after reaching supercomp, they've always been kept in a relative deficit and never have dropped them too low or tried to force the body to lose fat. I think you need a certain level of food awareness and maturity to undertake the cycle diet. You can't have emotional food issues.

What did supercompensation mode "feel like" to you?

You feel like you can eat anything and everything—you can even crave things that weren't really appetizing to you previously.

Sometimes workouts near the end of the week right before a cheat day can have you feeling "flat" but that's just a sign you're ready to fill the tank up again. As I said I think you need a certain level of food awareness and maturity to read hunger cues. Yes you're always going to feel like you could eat more and never be full when dieting to lose body fat, but it's a choice, no different then the person who made the choice to go through the drive through for breakfast or pour a bowl of cereal. You've made a choice to eat a certain way to lose body fat and you can either do it or not, and it's about as simple as that.

How has the diet changed over time for you?

Just more maturity and better food awareness, I've been incredibly blessed in this world to be able to choose how I want to eat, I have the freedom to literally eat whatever I want whenever I want it, but I've chosen the cycle diet for myself as part of a healthy lifestyle. I'm not going to feel sorry for myself because I voluntarily eat a certain way that has some restrictions to it.

Did you ever end up implementing a mid-week spike?

Absolutely, it really just depends on energy levels for me. Biggest indicator for me is weight dropping too fast and starting to feel a little sluggish just doing everyday tasks, I really just read it week to week sometimes I need one to finish the week of training off strong, and sometimes I don't, so I skip the mid-week spike.

What kind of foods to you prefer on cheat days?

I pretty much just eat whatever I want when I want it, no rules, easy. I like to wing it and see where the day takes me, enjoy the freedom and indulge!

Give an example cheat day menu!

It changes week to week but my regular go-to's would be donuts, ice cream and pizza. Like I said I'm not really into planning anything out unless I'm *really* craving something and cravings can definitely change week to week for me.

How does the cheat day make you feel?

I definitely heat up as the day goes on to the point where I will be opening windows in the middle of an Ontario winter to cool down! I sweat more in the gym in the workouts right after a cheat, and yes there have been some cheat days when I've certainly over done it and basically lay down on the couch in a carb-induced coma, or "beached whale mode" as I like to call it.

How are energy levels after the cheat day?

If you're truly in need of a re-feed, energy is amazing and workouts and pumps are incredible to the point that you almost feel like you can keep going and going after the workout is over.

Are food hangovers an issue?

My whole mentality is that it comes with the territory sometimes and it's always worth it! The benefits far outweigh a slow start to the day after.

What's the hardest part about the Cycle Diet?

Nothing. It's a lifestyle choice and its just something I do and the way I enjoy eating to achieve my physique goals.

What's the best part about the Cycle Diet?

Bottom line: it works! I find it sustainable and a great way to look and feel like an athlete year round while keeping my metabolism stoked and enjoying foods that most people have labeled as "bad for you."

In your opinion, what's a good reason to start Cycle Dieting, and what's a bad reason?

If you're a serious and focused athlete it's a great way to have your cake and eat it too and stay ripped year round without damaging your metabolism. For others that may have some underlying emotional food issues it wouldn't be a good choice. It also won't be a good choice if you don't thrive on routine or structure.

Funny stories?

Too many to list, but I always get comments and looks checking out at the grocery store when your entire cart is loaded with food from the bakery, or when they need to bring over a small side table at a restaurant to hold all the food you just ordered because there isn't enough room on the regular table.

I've had servers at restaurants tell me "that's a lot of food you know…" "Yeah, I know," I'll say and then I'll wipe it all out, much to their astonishment. Never gets old.

Is there anything else you want to add?

Embrace it as a lifestyle and just "the way you eat" and not some quick fix diet like the amount of bogus stuff out there. It's a choice you're making to reach the goals you've made for yourself and it's one of the tools you can use to achieve them.

Lallana Jorgensen

Tell us about yourself:

I'm a 27-year-old woman, living in Denmark and currently studying to be a food engineer or bio technician with a previous completed education within health and nutrition. Most people would describe me as being goofy, happy, funny and generally a positive person. I'm in love with life and find joy in family, friends and travelling to/experiencing new places and things. And I love food. I really really love food. And that has been a problem of mine in my teenage years and up through my early twenties. I've tried all kinds of diets in the past and have "failed" them all - and worse: I've beaten myself up over it. However, I realized that the problem never was food but how I saw and what I thought of myself. Once I started changing my thought pattern and focus I felt more comfortable in my own skin and generally happier. I then signed up with Scott (I think almost 4 years now?) and my physique started changing – slowly but steadily. And then I heard about the cycle diet which pretty much appealed to me straight away.

How did you hear about the Cycle Diet?

I heard about the cycle diet through a friend that also happens to be a client of Scott and he was on the cycle diet too. I loved the idea of being able to keep in shape while having room for enjoying whatever your heart desires once a week.

In my opinion it seemed to be the optimal "diet" (I actually prefer the term lifestyle to diet) since during the week I'm busy at university and/or with work so I like structure both with what I eat and with my training in order to keep me light, fresh, sharp and in shape. However, since I'm one of the biggest foodie and "indulger" I know I would have a hard time giving up indulgent foods completely which is why it fits me perfectly to be able to enjoy cakes and dinners or whatever once a week with family and friends when I'm completely off, and then the rest of the time when I'm by myself I eat clean and somewhat restricted. I'm allowed to pig out as much as I like to on that day if I feel for it and it's only doing me good. It's like having your cake and eating it too.

What kind of results did you see on the Cycle Diet?

I got to see how I could go to bed looking like a pregnant woman/stranded whale just to wake up finding myself looking amazing. My body had soaked up everything it needed so my muscles looked fuller and I held little to no fluid -This depended on what I ate during my reefed days, how much and the duration of them. Over the weeks and months after starting on the cycle diet I found my body looking better and slowly getting leaner despite eating like a crazy person. I don't weigh myself or believe in scales but depend more on the feeling of how my clothes fit and how I feel in my own skin so I have no idea of how much I lost and/or gained.

What do you like about the Cycle Diet?

I like to be able to stay lean while still enjoying indulgent foods. It is important to me to feel good about myself, look good and that clothes sit well on me (I'm a girl, I'm into fashion). But it is equally important to me to be social with friends/family or to enjoy something delicious every now and then. With the cycle diet I don't have to say no if something comes up during the week or in the weekend. I have learned how to adjust/tweak the cycle diet to my life and me and find it generally easy to follow since over the years I have come to implement it as a way of living. Of course, it took time and sometimes it can be hard – especially at the end of the week when I can feel my body getting depleted but over time you get used to it and it seems to fade too.

What did you use the diet for?

I basically wanted to have my cake and then eat it too. I wanted to get and be in shape and stay lean but at the same time I LOVE food – Especially cakes and desserts – and couldn't see myself having to cut that out completely or worry about it when I then decided to enjoy it. So I use the cycle diet to stay in shape and enjoy indulgent foods without guilt or further worries. In other words: maintaining a balance. In my opinion it is utopia to think that you can stay in shape and eat whatever you like the rest of your life unless you have some sort of freak genetics (Congratulations, you won the gene pool there). Truth is, you have to do something proactively to stay in shape – there's no way around it – and the cycle diet works perfectly for me together with my gym regimen.

Were you a coaching client of Scott's?

Yes, I was and still am one of Scott's clients. I think

that helped me getting to know and properly read the relevant biofeedback. Also, just sometimes to give me a slap in the face when I was overthinking things or losing the perspective on things (Of course, always in a loving manner ☺).

How long did it take to get into supercompensation mode?

It took me a good long time to get into supercomp mode since I had to get used to dieting at first and then I had to tune my body and metabolism into this new way of working in my advantage. I knew in advance I was not prepared to be super strict all the times when dieting down for it since I hold great value in social gatherings and occasions that also happen to include dinners etc. So every now and then I would have a meal – and that I accepted and enjoyed. I think it took me around 8 months if I should put a time frame on it.

What are your diet days like?

I don't remember the exact calories but I would say I got a bit more when dieting down for it than when I was on it. But I also had to get used to being on a diet first before going on a bit of a stricter diet. My diet consists mainly on clean foods such as chicken and fish, brown rice/(sweet) potatoes, loads of greens, some fruits, nuts, etc. Nothing out of the ordinary.

What did supercompensation mode "feel like" to you?

It's a little bit hard to explain for me. I just felt I had gotten so used to being hungry that I wasn't bothered by it anymore, only when it had an effect on my performance and energy level (in relation to strength, focus and concentration), so basically the physiological effects of hunger. In school I need to be able to focus so it was a bit hard to feel that declining a bit. Apart from that and after adjusting to it, it feels good since it's as if you are really in tune with your body. You can feel everything that is going on in your body. You know exactly when to eat and you can feel how that exact meal is like gasoline, fuelling your engine until the next meal. You know the amount you need too in order to function properly. It's really fascinating to be able to control your body like that.

At the end of the week, right before the cheat day I can feel I'm slowly running out of steam as my gym performance decline a bit and overall I start to get slightly unfocused. In deep supercomp I experienced food dreams the night(s) before and sometimes an extreme physical hunger. That is not much of a problem if I'm busy but of course it can be hard when you're just chilling at home and hearing your stomach growling and have time to really feel it. So that is something that you need to prepare for – It does require a little dose of discipline.

How has the diet changed over time for you?

You get more used to it and know it's part of the deal so it doesn't take up much of your thoughts over time. And if you get really hungry, like physically hungry, then you just grab an extra apple or something that day and then that's it. You get to know your body so you can feel what you need and don't need.

Did you ever end up implementing a mid-week spike?

I don't think I was given one by Scott but tried it out by myself a few times. It took some months on the cycle diet before I got there. I just started to feel flakey earlier than normal and had a hard time to focus etc. in class at university. It actually just started out as being a spontaneous dinner night out in the middle of the week and since I experienced getting my focus back and while not gaining anything but still felt and looked good/lean I decided to implement it for a trial period. However, I got more out of upping my overall daily calorie intake and sticking to one day a week. It gave me a more stable energy level during the week.

What kind of foods to you prefer on cheat days?

I wished I had a more sophisticated taste in food but I really do like burgers, nachos, fries and pizzas. I like sushi too though. And of course, I will ALWAYS have some kind of homemade dessert or chocolate or cake since I have a super sweet tooth and I love baking so it gives me the opportunity to try new recipes and munch on that :) I don't avoid any kinds of food since I have a spike day for enjoying food so who cares if I might be a little bloated or hold a little bit of fluid the days after? As long as I'm in shape and feel generally comfortable knowing that it does my body good I don't care too much about that. And usually the deeper I'm into supercomp the less fluid I hold.

Give an example cheat day menu!

Really? Well, don't judge :)

Breakfast usually consists of two fried eggs or scrambled eggs, 6 slices of bacon, handful of (4-5) hash browns or fries, 4-5 buns with cheese, jam, Nutella and peanut butter washed down with coffee and juice. Usually I have also made some sort of cheesecake or cake or cookies, so I'd have a piece or three of that as well finished off by a couple of chocolate bars.

Then I'll keep grazing during the day and have some chips, chocolates, cookies, etc. whatever I feel like and is available.

For a late lunch or pre-dinner it could be a big

portion of nachos when out and some sort of ice cream or cake in town. If home, it would probably end with the nachos or cheese sandwiches and a tub of Ben & Jerry's or more of that cake I made.

Dinner would be a whole pizza or two burgers, fries with mayo and if I didn't have nachos for lunch then also nachos. I'd share a 12 pieces donut box or enjoy the rest of the homemade cake, depending on how rich it was. Sometimes I also have ice cream, other times I just have a couple of chocolate bars.

And if I'm really into supercomp I can continue snacking on buns with cheese later on and some more chocolate and cake finished off with a glass ice-cold milk.

How does the cheat day make you feel?

In the beginning when getting that one day a week I was so excited I basically had a "little bit" of everything and it left me in a complete immobile state of a carb-induced food coma where I would feel completely stuffed and sleepy and lethargic followed later during the night by night sweats and heart pounding. However, once it got part of the lifestyle the excitement wore off a bit and I got better at just eating what I felt like and not stuffing my face (if you've been dieting for some time you cannot believe how exciting the prospect of eating a cheesecake is) which just lead to me feeling how my body was cranking up the metabolism by overheating a bit and still giving me night sweats occasionally but the coma and the feeling of being extremely full had worn off. The days after at gym though are extra sweaty..

How I feel depends on how crazy I go and that depends a bit on my schedule whether I have the entire day off for myself, or if I just have social things to attend.

How are energy levels after the cheat day?

The first day after can be slightly low in energy or groggy depending on how late I went to bed and when I finished eating, however, the following day the energy and strength is through the roof and lasts me until almost the end of the week where I can feel a decline – Then I'm ready for a new day :)

Are food hangovers an issue?

They can be. They definitely were in the beginning when I couldn't contain my excitement and just had to have a lot of everything, especially desserts. And I found that precisely desserts or anything rich in sugar makes you more bloated and gassy - Ice cream too! But the hangovers for me depend on how crazy I went on my cheat day and how I sleep the night after eating. So if I just enjoyed the day with still a lot of food I'm fine just with occasional night sweats etc. but if I go balls to the wall I might suffer a solid food hangover.

What's the hardest part about the Cycle Diet?

I think the hardest part for me personally was to get ready for the cycle diet. If you're not already at a stage where you can jump onto it straight away it does take some time and requires patience and some sacrifices. But once you're there it's relatively easy to maintain. However, when being on the cycle diet I do sometimes struggle with the real hunger and/or flakiness/effects from hunger at the end of the week up to the cheat day. That takes some time and experience to get used to and to learn to balance it all according to your needs and life.

What's the best part about the Cycle Diet?

I can have a whole cheesecake every week and still look awesome.

What would you say to someone considering the Cycle Diet?

It is NOT a miracle or a quick-fix solution and it doesn't work for everyone. It does require getting used to and can be tough at times with the hunger, etc. So I would suggest to whomever that is interested in the cycle diet to really consider if it's something that would fit into their life and to their personality. It takes time and gets better and better as you get deeper in to it but it does take time to get there. So be honest with yourself when considering the cycle diet. It does sound pretty awesome but it does require sacrifices along the way and it just does not work for all. So be completely honest – Does it fit YOU? There are other ways to balance diet and life etc. that might suit you better, so have an honest talk with yourself about it.

In your opinion, what's a good reason to start Cycle Dieting, and what's a bad reason?

A good reason to start the cycle diet would be a desire to balance staying in shape and having the room to enjoy the food part of life too. There are other ways to do that of course but this works for me and I think that wanting a balance is a good reason.

A bad reason for me would be to think that it is a quick fix solution and easy to achieve without any sacrifices or patience. It is not quick fix and it just is not for everyone. Also, if you have issues with your body image or struggle following a diet I would have a hard time seeing how that could play out well by yourself. Then I would highly recommend to have Scott with you on your journey - whether or not you want to get on the cycle diet or you want to create a loving and accepting environment towards yourself since he knows what he's talking about and knows how and when to cut through your excuses/defenses in a loving and supporting way. He is the real deal.

Funny stories?

I have many funny stories.. from sitting and eating chocolate bars in a packed locker room at gym right after finishing my session to impressing the cashier at the donut shop on a vacation to Malaysia by buying 2x12 donut boxes and finishing them both in the store just to buy another box for the trip home. But just on this summer holiday I went to France with my family and just finished a huge steak after eating all the bread and having a couple of appetizers at a restaurant and was more than ready for dessert. I got the dessert card and saw my all time favorite French dessert: crème brûlée. So when the waiter came I ordered 4 pieces. She laughed and said: "good one". I laughed too, then looked at her as serious as I can be and said: "Seriously, I want 4, thank you". She could not stop staring and was very impressed when she came to find only empty plates and a happy and satisfied girl :)

Is there anything else you want to add?

Now when mentioning my vacations I have got to say that this way of living on the cycle diet makes it so much easier to go on vacation and just not care about gaining weight or holding back. I know my body will love me for taking some time off both diet and exercise and will only soak up all the good stuff. Yes, I might hold fluid when I get back but after a week or two, I'm straight back to when I left for the holidays and I promise you – I am NOT holding back when away. If it has been a super long holiday, like a month I might have to cut out one or two weeks worth of cheat days but trust me, after eating whatever your heart desires for a whole month you're more than ready to get back into your normal routine and to eat clean and then you're ready for the cheat days again.

Aaron Jewell

Aaron a week out from a show.

Tell us about yourself:

I am 35 years old, and am married with a beautiful, four-year-old daughter. I have competed in bodybuilding on and off since 2001.

As a teenager and in my early twenties I was a big believer in bulking up to gain as much size as possible, and then cutting large amounts of weight to get ripped. I took this philosophy to the extreme and would get outright fat in my quest to gain size. I would go from 175 to 190 contest weight all the way to 220 to 265 in the offseason! Needless to say, this strategy became frustrating and very hard on my body. I started to remain at higher levels of body fat without even trying to bulk up. I tried several diet strategies in order to find a way to level out my extreme approach, but was unable to find anything that really helped me find a way to stay leaner yet still make progress with my bodybuilding goals.

How did you hear about the Scott or the Cycle Diet?

After reading several articles and interviews with Scott Abel, I became very curious about his approach to bodybuilding. I remember watching the B.C. bodybuilding championships in 2006, and seeing an acquaintance of mine destroy everyone with insane conditioning and win the overall. I was amazed at his improvements over the previous year, and after hearing that he had worked with Scott for the past year, I decided

I needed to work with him as well.

Shortly after working with Scott, he put me on a variation of the cycle diet, and I began looking better and better. I really enjoyed being able to eat whatever I wanted one day per week, while staying lean, and actually getting leaner!

I read up a lot about the cycle diet, and got a copy of "The Science Behind the Cycle Diet" in order to learn more about the diet.

Eventually, Scott had me add in a mid-week spike, and I stayed really lean while also made progress in my physique. In 2007, Scott guided me into the Canadian nationals where I placed 3rd to two current IFBB pros, and I was in my best ever condition. All this was done by staying true to the Cycle Diet. All we had to do was cut out the mid-week spikes, and drop the spike days out for a little while, and then added them back in as I became leaner.

I used a variation of the cycle diet in 2012 as well, and ended up winning a national bodybuilding title (2012 CBBF Elite National Under 185 lb. Champion). The Cycle Diet worked amazingly well for me in my contest pursuits, and now as a lifestyle I enjoy!

What kind of results did you see on the Cycle Diet?

One of the most impressive effects I noticed from the Cycle Diet was a drastic change in my body-fat and weight set point. Prior to starting it, I would remain between 225-240 lbs. and very soft unless I was preparing for a competition. After being on it for a couple years, my set point remains around 200-210 and much leaner. Now no matter what I do diet-wise, my set point seems to remain at that 200-210 level.

On the Cycle Diet I am able to stay really lean, and as soon as my muscles start to flatten out from low calories/low glycogen, I am able to have a spike meal or spike day to keep my muscles full and round, while also revving my metabolic rate through the roof.

What do you like about the Cycle Diet? How does it fit into your lifestyle/goals?

I like the predictability of the cycle diet. It allows you to be very in tune with your body. I find my digestion is perfect (except on spike days when I push the envelope with calorie intake). I am not overly hungry but never full (again… except on spike days), I get amazing pumps and energy in the gym, and I simply feel very good almost all the time. I also really enjoy being able to eat anything I want at certain times, as this allows for me to embrace the social aspect of eating, and to never feel like I am missing out due to having to follow a stringent diet. Of course looking good all the time is also a definite plus too!

What did you use the diet for? Any unique needs that it had to address?

I use the diet to maintain the bodybuilding look without having to feel like I am suffering for it. I also find my training is improved when following it.

Were you a coaching client of Scott's?

I am both a current and previous client of Scott's. I think having Scott guide me in using the Cycle Diet has allowed me to maximize the benefits of his experience and knowledge of the diet, and avoid some of the trial and error that could come with attempting an advanced protocol such as this all alone.

Having Scott as my coach also enables me to take full week or multiple week breaks at properly timed intervals. Yes, I *have* done the cycle diet on my own, but that was after a few years of following it under Scott's guidance, and the insight I gained in doing so is what has allowed me to know how to implement the diet properly on my own. I think it works best when you have Scott guiding you!

How long did it take you to get into supercompensation mode?

I have been on the cycle diet since February of this year. I was able to get into mild super-compensation mode after only a few weeks, and added a spike day. At the time my body fat was not all that low, but since I have an efficient metabolism (not naturally, but by way of years of previous Cycle dieting), and am an advanced trainer, I was able to benefit from the full spike day reasonably quickly.

It took several more months until I was lean enough to benefit from a mid-week spike, which I added in August. Since adding the mid-week spike I have actually gotten a little bit leaner, and am staying fuller, stronger, and more energized. Throughout the process, I was able to have 2 full week breaks, and am scheduled for another one in 2 weeks from now.

What are your diet days like?

I am not sure on the exact calories, but it is somewhere around 2,100-2,200... So between 10-12 cals per lb. body weight. My diet has not really changed in super-compensation mode other than me subbing the odd food source here and there.

Diet is generally something like this:

- 2/3 cup oats, 1 cup egg whites, 1 tbsp. coconut oil, 1 tbsp. apple butter

- 150g extra lean ground turkey or bison, 150 g potato or 2/3 cup white rice

- 1 can tuna, 150g potato or 30 mini rice cakes, 1 tbsp. mayo (made with healthy oils), 1 cup green veggies

- 150g extra lean ground turkey or bison, 150 g potato or 2/3 cup white rice, 1 cup green veggies

- 30-35g protein from whey isolate, 30 mini rice cakes or 3 large rice cakes, 1-2tbsp. natural PB and 1 tbsp. jam.

I add condiments such as ketchup, salsa, low-cal teriyaki sauce, soy sauce, hot sauce, and various seasonings and spices including salt.

What did supercompensation mode "feel like" to you?

When I was younger I noticed my hunger a lot more, and tended to focus on it a fair bit, and was somewhat food obsessed. As a result, my spike days were insanely big on the cycle diet! Doing the cycle diet now, I have a more mature approach, and put very little focus on hunger/cravings. I am never really full on diet days, but never feel starving either. Prior to a spike I tend to notice I am a little more hungry, but mostly just feel notice a bit less of a pump in the gym, and energy levels start to drop off a little.

Did you ever end up implementing a mid-week spike?

How long did it take, and what kind of biofeedback indicated you were ready?

It took over 5 months before we implemented a mid-week spike. Several factors indicated my readiness for it. I was starting to notice a drop in energy and muscle fullness mid-week, and I had become quite lean (under 10 percent), and my strength started to dip lower than usual by mid/end of week. Since adding the spike, I have gotten leaner, my muscles stay fuller, and I have great pumps and energy all week long.

What kind of foods to you prefer on cheat days?

I tend to prefer a mix of savory foods that are high in fat and carbs (pizza, burgers, Chinese food), and sugary/fatty foods such as ice cream, cookies, and pies. In other words I like high calorie foods! My food choices are generally the same these days on spike days, whereas when I was younger I would try to eat wide varieties of foods as much as possible. I now know what foods I feel the best on and digest well.

Give an example cheat day menu!

Breakfast:

- 5-6 whole eggs with cheese
- 1 whole pack of bacon
- 6-8 waffles with a lot of butter and maple syrup
- Hashbrowns with lots of ketchup
- Orange juice
- Coffee with cream and sugar

Lunch:

- Large double bacon cheeseburger (usually ½ lb. or so)
- Large fries with gravy, ketchup
- Large milkshake
- Chocolate bar

Snack:

- Choc almonds mixed with trail mix (several handfuls)
- Potato chips or nachos and usually a couple of beers

Dinner:

- A whole pizza, Chinese food, sushi rolls, or steak and all the trimmings

- A couple beers or 1 to 2 large coca cola

- An appy of some kind (wings, cheese bread, cheese and crackers, etc.)

- A dessert: half a pie w/ice cream, a lot of cookies with milk, or a huge bowl of cereal

Bedtime Snack:

- A tub of ben and jerry's ice cream, more cereal, or 2-3 chicken chimichangas, and some Gatorade or fruit juice

How does the cheat day make you feel?

I generally feel pretty hot, very full stomach by the end of the day, and very relaxed.

How are energy levels after the cheat day?

Energy levels are very high, and my muscles feel very tight and full. I have amazing pumps in the gym for the 2 days following as well.

Are food hangovers an issue?

I sometimes wake up groggy, but don't really suffer from any type of food hangover or anything. I do sometimes experience gas and bloating towards the end of a spike day, and while I am sleeping I am often really warm and sweat a fair bit. None of these effects really bother me, and I have no issues dealing with them. If I don't push the calorie levels through the roof (like over 10-12,000) on spike days, those issues are pretty minimal anyway.

What's the hardest part about the Cycle Diet?

The hardest part about the cycle diet for me is trying to stay on point for diet days when travelling. That said however, it's really not that difficult as you can substitute and wind up pretty close on your total macros/cals anyway… So I actually don't find anything really difficult about the cycle diet!

What's the best part about the Cycle Diet?

The ability to indulge regularly without limitations in order to benefit your body/physique is the best part in my opinion, as it eliminates feelings of being bound to a stringent diet.

If there were ONE thing you could say to someone considering using the Cycle Diet, what would it be?

I would tell them to avoid the cycle diet if they have any hang-ups or emotional issues with food, as it is not meant for individuals with these mentalities. If they do not have any food issues, then fly at it, as it's an amazing way to achieve your physique goals while still being able to enjoy your favorite foods in any quantity you desire.

In your opinion, what's a good reason to start Cycle Dieting, and what's a bad reason?

I think a good reason to start cycle dieting is if you have built a decent foundation of muscle mass, and wish to avoid the pitfall of bulking up and then cutting down (yo-yo dieting). It is a great diet for those who wish to make qualitative improvements to their physiques over the long term. A bad reason to start cycle dieting is because you like the idea of the spike days and simply want to stuff your face. You do have to be pretty diligent on the lower calorie days, and comfortable with a certain level of hunger. For those that struggle with this, I would suggest a different approach.

Funny stories?

When I was in my 20s I took the spike days to the extreme. Often I would start the day with what I called "Oreo soup". It consisted of an entire box of Oreo cookies and 1 liter of whipping cream! Of course I would eat this in one sitting! Can you guess the calorie content of that creation??? My friends were in disbelief about this and could not believe their eyes when I actually ate it! I do recall falling into a "carb coma" shortly after I would consume this, and would always wake up in a pool of sweat. My metabolism would go crazy!

Is there anything else you want to add?

I have found that although it is important to stick to the plan on the cycle diet, it is also important not to become obsessive about sticking to the exact plan. I feel much better when I am relaxed about the foods that I eat, and switch my choices up from time to time. I do of course, stick to the proper amounts as close as I can, but I don't melt down if one meal is a little bit off. In that case I just balance out the next meal to make sure that my totals line up. This relaxed but diligent approach makes the cycle diet very easy to maintain for long term for me.

Scott Abel

Rocco C

Tell us about yourself:

I was always an athlete throughout my life. I participated in athletics since grade 4 through 5 seasons of college football. I love athletics and being around that atmosphere. Working out was always a way to improve my performance on the athletic field and served me well. It was ingrained in me once I began to train at age 11 and that has become a part of my everyday life as I write this at age 36. It has served me well as many things we do translate to other areas of life. Training serves my health, well-being, stress management, competitive side, and offers me the ability to still feel engaged athletically although at this stage of my life I am well beyond competitive sports. Training always teaches me something, such as what smart training is, and managing when I can be intense and also how hard I can push my limits, if life allows for it.

I was not always lean. When I was playing sports I was in the 240 lb. range, and solid. While I was not fat by any means, my goals were for performance in a power sport like football, so it was not my intention to be under 10 percent body fat. I was solid, strong, fast, and powerful at about 235-240 lbs. In my late 20's, after sports, I was not in great shape mostly due to my diet and work demands, but knew I wanted to get back to a serious commitment to training, and that's what I did with Scott. I transformed myself over time from an overweight 230 lb. frame to my current weight which can be 180 lbs. at my leanest and 190-195 lbs. which is more of a natural set point for me but still lean.

I have done various diets like keto diets, velocity diet, Atkins, anabolic diet, etc. The diet strategies I chose were more for the purpose of muscle building early on, and late in life I tended to try diets for leaning out, but that was trickier for me due to the amount of food I was used to consuming just from training and playing sports.

How did you hear about the Cycle Diet?

I employed Coach Abel for training and diet coaching and learned about it as I began reading more and more of his material.

The Cycle Diet interested me because it was simpler than many of the other diets. I thrive on simplicity. I didn't want to hear about tracking calories or percentages of macro-nutrients. I liked that it was if you're in a state of super-compensation you can have a calorie spike day and eat as much as you like of whatever you like. Simple!

What kind of results did you see on the Cycle Diet?

I think Scott can share some of his observations of me on the CD as we went through it but it was simple for me. I was very lean and training intensely so I would re-feed, spike calories, cheat, whatever you want to call it – once per week on a Saturday or Sunday.

For me it was just about refueling and having the freedom to do as I wish diet wise once a week and within about 5 days my weight was back to the starting point. So if I had a spike day Sunday and ate 10,000+ calories in a day my weight could increase by 10 lbs., but by the mid to late week I was back down again.

What do you like about the Cycle Diet?

I like to have a day on the weekend where I can indulge and not concern myself with any structured diet.

What did you use the diet for?

When dieting when I was very lean it was definitely useful to re-feed for the purpose of having an energy spike and maintaining good intensity in my workout program while dieting. You need that extra energy to train hard when you're lean.

Were you a coaching client of Scott's?

Yes, I have been a coaching client of Scott's since 2008. He could help me assess whether or not I was in supercomp, which is essential to being able to eat that much food and not gain fat. He also just takes the guesswork out for me so I do not worry about things all that much if it comes to CD or training... I just ask him! We have an email exchange about it and we set a plan to follow. Simple.

How long did it take to get into supercompensation mode?

Originally it took me about 12 weeks. When I did it again it took me about 10-12 weeks again. There were breaks for sure. I am not on it all the time. There are definitely some adjustments you have to get accustomed to when eating like this.

What are your diet days like?

Most recently I was eating about 2,100 calories per day to get into supercomp at a body weight of about 195.

My body weight was just under 180 when I was in supercomp. The 2nd time I did this I continued at about 2,100 cals.

Nothing changed from pre supercomp to supercomp diet day and cal intake wise.

Back in 2008 I was doing the same calories (2,100) but my weight was lower. I think I started at 200 lbs. and got down to around 188 lbs. before I hit Supercomp. I was probably at the same level of leanness back then as I am now. I am definitely better developed cosmetically today than in 2008.

What did supercompensation mode "feel like" to you?

Hunger was always a constant feeling – not too strong but something you just get used to as normal. I always drank a lot of water and diet cola which seemed to help when I was hungry.

There were days as you got closer to a cheat day that the hunger or appetite would be more pronounced but the real feeling was on the re-feed day or as I like to call them calorie spike day… When I wanted to eat a lot of food I could just eat and eat and eat like there was no end in sight. Your gut feels like a bottomless pit when you start eating.

How has the diet changed over time for you?

I still feel like I can eat a lot but not as much as originally – this may be due to age as well and just getting older. And you learn what you can eat a lot of and what tends to fill you up more than other foods.

Did you ever end up implementing a mid-week spike?

No, I did not. I probably could have if I was more strict on my diet during the week but it never got to that point.

What kind of foods to you prefer on cheat days?

I like sweets. I like doughnuts, pancakes, waffles, muffins, syrup, butter, lots of carbs. I like eating pizzas and breakdsticks and cinnamon sticks. I would literally make a list of things I wanted during the week and eat them all on my spike days. I would eat ice cream and milkshakes and burgers and burritos too. I would mix candy in there too like chocolates, fudge, and some other sweets like caramel and cheddar popcorn but the real sweet candy always tend to make me eat less volume so I would sometimes avoid that. Other days I might eat a ton of fried chicken or steak. It changes due to things I learn about my digestion an ability to eat certain volumes of food. I do not eat too much dairy so I have to gauge how much ice cream or milkshakes – same with candy but there is not much I avoid.

Give an example cheat day menu!

Here, right from two of my emails to Scott from end of last year:

Copied from Email 1:

Spike day: candy and chocolates in AM, ice tea, ice cream cake, waffles with syrup, stack of blueberry pancakes with blueberry syrup, apple cinnamon sticky muffin, cheese omelet, chocolate milk, bacon, 1 cup of ice cream, 1 donut, cheesecake, blueberry cobbler, chicken and rice, pasta shells, sausage, beer, mixed drinks, donuts and probably other stuff I forgot about. Needless to say I ate and drank a lot of calories.

Copied from Email 2:

This past Sat morning my weight was down to 179# again so definitely the supercomp has been established. I think this past Sat was my 3rd or 4th spike day and I seem to be eating about 9-10K calories on these days. This past Sat I had pancakes with butter, syrup, Gatorade, apple pie, toaster strudels, cheesecake, chocolate milk, carton of Oreos, chocolate chip cookies, rice pudding and that was breakfast. I had a medium sized pizza with cinnamon sticks myself for lunch. I topped off the day with a couple wings, a quesadilla slice, a large DQ blizzard with a large cake batter ice cream milkshake and had Gatorade and fudge and cotton candy as snacks during the day. Weight dropped down to 181 already today (2 days later). Crazy. I will be moving spike day to Thursday this week for Thanksgiving and then forgoing Saturday as we discussed before.

How does the cheat day make you feel?

Very full. Muscles feel full. Powerful. Vascularity pops too. I do get very sweaty at night especially the night after my cheat and the next day during workout.

How are energy levels after the cheat day?

If you're truly in need of a re-feed, energy is amazing and workouts and pumps are incredible to the point that you almost feel like you can keep going and going after the workout is over.

Are food hangovers an issue?

YES. The next day you can feel like it's a legit hangover. For me its about letting your body digest the food and drinking a lot a lot of water the next day to begin flushing everything out. It helps a great deal to make me feel good.

What's the hardest part about the Cycle Diet?

It can tend to increase my cravings through the week. So once I get into supercomp I am normally so tuned into my diet and not veering from the plan the CD spike days does give me a taste of the cake so to speak and after a few days from the spike day during the week the cravings can intensify. So the mid week spike would actually be a helpful thing in that regard if you can swing it.

The other thing is just understanding and dealing with what and how much you will eat and how that impacts your digestion over the day and the day to follow.

What's the best part about the Cycle Diet?

Being able to just eat a massive amount of whatever you want and actually feeling very full muscle wise and feeling powerful and looking more vascular and having others wonder how the F it's possible is pretty cool. You know "oh that dude is a genetic freak he can eat a whole pizza and bucket of wings and beer and ice cream and whatever and not get fat" but they do not see the prep work that goes into that. So they just assume it's genetics that allows that to occur.

If there were one thing you'd say to someone

considering the Cycle Diet...?

The state of being in Supercomp is absolutely critical or it will NOT work. You cannot just be dieting and think you can add calorie spikes and expect the same response. You must be lean and when I say lean I mean damn lean and you must be training intensely and hard consistently and you must be on point with a regular diet.

In your opinion, what's a good reason to start Cycle Dieting, and what's a bad reason?

Good reason – you are a serious and experienced trained individual. You are in supercomp and it would be useful to spike your energy in order to improve workout performance while offering an outlet to indulge once in a while.

Bad reason – because you just want to eat a lot food of whatever you like.

Don Rose

Tell us about yourself:

I'm what you would call a veteran trainer, who did a couple shows along the way. I have been naturally lean and wiry but have gotten fat in the name of bulking a few times to get that weight up. I have always done some sort of lifestyle diet starting with low fat high carb and protein, doing a high fat diet for a couple years. Then with Scott I did and am doing the Cycle Diet, with both the higher carb and higher fat versions under my belt.

I actually sought Scott out for training coaching and getting over some overuse injuries. At the time I hired Scott I was lean enough to go right into the Cycle Diet.

What kind of results did you see on the Cycle Diet?

I initially gained a lot more muscle, but *without* the usual body fat accumulation — about 10 lbs. over the first 4 months, which was very impressive having already trained for over 10 years at that point.

What do you like about the Cycle Diet? How does it fit into your lifestyle/goals?

I may be a bit of a sadist but I actually like feeling the acute hunger right before a cheat day, and then waking up to eat whatever I feel like the next day. I like that it gives you one day a week to be normal socially where you go out to eat and spend time at restaurants with people you enjoy being with. It gives you a sense of freedom with the confidence that it's actually fueling your body for continuous improvement.

What did you use the diet for?

I used it to stay relatively lean and still put on a little mass in the beginning, and then I used it to dial into my show, and then used it to stay at a low bodyfat percentage without downregulating my metabolism. It can be used for many purposes when properly tweaked.

Were you a coaching client of Scott's?

Yes, I became a coaching client of Scott's and it was very easy to put my trust in the process because he had fine tuned it for my goals

How long did it take you to get into supercompensation mode?

I wasn't too far away from supercompensation when I started so it only took about a month for my body to respond with getting into that mode. There were some periods where my daily calories were increased and I wasn't really in true supercompensation mode and the cheat days didn't really amount to much more than a couple thousand cals over my highest 'normal' calorie day.

What are your diet days like?

I was on a calorie cycling plan which varied between 2,200-3,200 cals during the week with 40p-45c-15f macro breakdown (pro/carb/fat percentages) once I reached supercompensation and held it for a while. Then those ranges were kicked up to 2,500 to 3,800 with the same macro profile. I believe I was about 215 lbs. at that time.

What did supercompensation mode "feel like" to you?

Supercompensation in the beginning felt amazing and that was when I had higher calorie deficits. The hunger built up for a couple days and it was such a great feeling to just start eating with no rules, getting more and more full as the day went on. Training while hungry was actually something I liked, because I knew the hungrier I felt the day before the more epic the cheat day and couple days following would be.

How has the diet changed over time for you?

As time has gone on and my diet days have come up calorie wise I no longer have those intense hunger pangs and therefore my cheats are moderate comparatively, but I still get the feeling of pumps and great workouts in the couple days after.

Did you ever end up implementing a mid-week spike?

Yes, I did long periods with a mid-week spike because it was necessary based on my energy levels during training, and shorter time period after the cheat day to feeling intensely hungry during the week. It probably took a couple months to feel like a mid-week spike was necessary in the beginning.

What kind of foods to you prefer on cheat days?

I started out eating anything under the sun except true junk like McDonalds. Burgers, pizza, fruity pebbles, ice cream — all higher quality versions. As time went on I eliminated for the most part many sugary items, and started eating more steaks, whisky, burgers and pizza as well as heavily buttered potato dishes. I've found that avoiding sugary foods makes me feel better and I don't get the hangover effect.

Give an example cheat day menu!

10 sushi rolls, 2 bread rolls with butter, bacon and potatoes fried in coconut oil, Large pizza, 12 oz. sirloin with loaded baked potato, Kobe Beef burger with fries, slice of cheesecake, bag of popcorn, Kostritzer beer, Maccallan scotch.

How does the cheat day make you feel?

I feel sweaty and hot once I start getting into the cheat and it feels very fun for the first 2/3 of the day and then the latter third I find that bloating can be an issue but also the fullness starts to show up and you just feel like you are gigantic.

How are energy levels after the cheat day?

They are always really high and whatever I'm training the day after cheat day gets a fantastic pump and the loads feel 'light' so to speak.

Are food hangovers an issue?

Yes all three of them I've experienced and they are uncomfortable when trying to get to sleep after a cheat day. I've found that over time I taper off on food quantity near the end of the day and I've also found that eating less sugary foods drastically cuts down on these issues for me. I stick to burgers, sushi etc. and skip the cakes and ice cream.

What's the hardest part about the Cycle Diet?

I didn't find any part of the cycle diet to be particularly difficult, but you do need the discipline to be ok with the hunger in the day or 2 prior to the cheat day and not give in the feeling to eat just a little more on those days.

What's the best part about the Cycle Diet?

The feeling of being able to eat anything and the insane pumps that window gives you for a couple days after.

In your opinion, what's a good reason to start Cycle Dieting, and what's a bad reason?

If you're a serious and focused athlete it's a great way to have your cake and eat it too and stay ripped year round without damaging your metabolism. For others that may have some underlying emotional food issues it wouldn't be a good choice. It also won't be a good choice if you don't thrive on routine or structure.

If there were ONE thing you could say to someone considering using the Cycle Diet, what would it be?

Pick your cheat day foods carefully and refine them based on biofeedback to reduce the uncomfortable sides like bloating, gas and hangover feelings.

In your opinion, what's a good reason to start Cycle Dieting, and what's a bad reason?

A good reason is to maintain leanness while actually revving up the metabolism and give yourself a break mentally and socially once a week diet wise. A bad reason is to just focus on getting to cheat day, or just doing it for that reason alone.

Funny stories?

There were a few, but the one that stands out is one day at Outback Steakhouse when a friend and I went in about mid-afternoon and I remember ordering the herb crusted 16 oz. prime rib with baked potato, chicken quesadillas and then 2 slices of cheesecake. The waiter came back and was ready to give the check and I said no thanks and ordered the Alice Springs chicken with Aussie fries and then the chocolate thunder dessert. Now about this time my shirt was started to get soaked from sweating so much and the waiter kind of goggled at me and disappeared. I could see him whispering in the corner with the other wait staff and pointing our way. Just to fuel the stunned factor by the onlookers we ordered a blooming onion and split it. We walked out of there with soaked shirts and our waiter came up and asked what we were doing and how one person could eat so much. So we explained the cycle diet.

Other examples involves bringing 12" cheesecakes to sushi restaurants and finishing off the whole thing as inspired by old school Scott Abel.

Is there anything else you want to add?

As I mentioned, continuously test your food selection on cheat day. I and others have discovered sugary foods contribute most heavily towards the unwanted side effects. Also use the hunger as a positive reinforcement and understand that when you are that hungry the cycle diet is working as intended!

Allen Cress

Allen before his spike meal.

How did you hear about the Cycle Diet?

I initially heard about it from a friend. Being able to stay very lean year round and to have a full day where I could eat freely without repercussions to my physique and actually enhance my metabolism.

What kind of results did you see on the Cycle Diet?

When I first did the diet it was about 10 years ago coming off a contest. I stayed very lean all off-season while performance was still high and made some small gains. It made the next year's contest prep very easy compared to past competitions, as I didn't have to diet as long and had multiple spike days through prep making things easy mentally speaking as well.

What do you like about the Cycle Diet?

I like staying leaner as I feel healthier. I'm also able to enjoy social events and just hanging out with friends and not thinking about what I eat all day. The mid week spike made it a piece of cake. I'm a coach and competitor so it fits easily into my lifestyle as I enjoy eating my regular diet foods anyway.

How long did it take to get into supercompensation mode?

I first started it right after a contest so I was already in a supercomp and could just jump right into it, but obviously I had dieted for over 3 months first for the contest.

More recently, going back on it, I dieted strictly for 4 weeks then started with 1 cheat meal every Saturday, then assessed response, then go to a half day. Then assess and then eventually to a whole day. Then after a few more weeks started the mid week spike. I have always been very responsive to this diet.

What did supercompensation mode "feel like" to you?

Hunger levels were pretty high all the time. Energy levels were dropping before I had my first cheat which was one indicator I used before implementing it.

How has the diet changed over time for you?

My hunger levels are a bit lower—due to aging, in my opinion.

Did you ever end up implementing a mid-week spike?

I always used a mid-week spike. Originally it took about 3-4 weeks after the full day was started. My energy and performance was dropping off at the end of the week.

What kind of foods to you prefer on cheat days?

I do better with most foods that aren't dairy-based (like ice cream) so I usually wait until the end of the day to have it if I really want it.

Give an example cheat day menu!

- Large omelette, 6 pieces bacon, 2-3 sausage links, 4 pieces toast with peanut butter and jelly

- Turkey sandwich, chips, cookies

- 4-5 sushi rolls
- Nachos, bread with butter, burger, fries
- Large popcorn at movies with Reese's pieces
- Large roast beef sandwich, fries, pint of ice cream

How are energy levels after the cheat day?

Not great… but much better *two* days after.

Are food hangovers an issue?

At first food hangovers were, but it goes away and it depends on how much I eat. There's always some bloating and gas and sweat sometimes at night. It all depends on the type of foods I eat.

What's the best part about the Cycle Diet?

Staying lean and enjoying anything and everything you want every week which allows me to take a mental break

What's one good reason and one bad reason for trying the Cycle Diet?

A good reason would be to stay lean and enjoy life. A bad reason would be if you have a bad relationship with food and you think it will make it better.

Funny stories?

One spike day I went to a sushi restaurant for my second meal and was alone. I had 94 pieces of sushi (12 different rolls). When it came out to me the chef asked when my guests where going to arrive and I said it was just me. He looked like he saw a ghost and said, "I'll get you some take out boxes before you leave." I just laughed and 20 min later the plate was clear and when he came over and saw it, he was shocked and said "that was a ****** feast!!"

I ended up eating 3 more meals later that day, and I calculated my calories for the day at 17,000.

Is there anything else you want to add?

At this point in my life I actually don't enjoy eating all out for a whole day so I have tweaked it for myself to have one spike meal every 3 days.

Scott Abel

Aaron Chigol

Tell us about yourself:

I'm 47 years old. I have been active my whole life, and continue to lead an active lifestyle. I have always been involved in sports, from hockey to tae-kwon-do to natural bodybuilding. I am employed as a power engineer who has been doing shift work for over 28 years. I had never followed any type of a diet program before being a client of Scott's, other than prep for body building competitions. I have always had a naturally lean body type.

I did not start the Cycle Diet right off the bat with Scott. Before being a client of his, I just ate healthy, and did not really even think about it. Going on the Cycle

Diet was discussed with Scott after about a year of being with him, as he thought it would fit into my lifestyle, and we also discussed what could possibly help enhance my physique and maintain an athletic build outside of competition. I am able to maintain a lean, athletic look by following the Cycle Diet.

What do you like about the Cycle Diet? How does it fit into your lifestyle/goals?

It fits for me because I find I don't really have to think about it. I like the routine of knowing what I am eating throughout the week and having it prepared, and then the flexibility of being able to have a day where I can have whatever I feel like eating that day. I don't find that I obsess or worry about what I can or cannot eat, because I can have a day every week where I can eat at will.

What did you use the diet for?

I have actually used it *during* body building prep, but mostly just with everyday life.

For the year previous to me starting the diet, I had been training with Scott to get ready for a body building show. I had done a 16 week prep leading up to the show, and after it was finished, I wasn't sure whether I would compete again or not, but wanted to maintain a lean, athletic look.

I also found, through previous experience, that I just like how I feel when I am lean. I find I have better energy, strength, and focus. The Cycle Diet easily allows this to be achievable.

Were you a coaching client of Scott's?

Yes, I have been a client of Scott's for 9 years, and having Scott as a coach just made doing the diet stress-free.

What are your diet days like?

For my show prep, I was eating around 1600 to 1800 calories a day, as a 5'8" male competing in the lightweight body building category. For my refeed days, I would guess that I was eating between 6000 to 8000 calories a day. I don't really pay attention to calories on that day, I just eat whatever I feel like eating on that particular day.

What does supercompensation mode "feel like" to you?

Towards the end of the week I would sometimes feel like I had less energy for workouts, and that's where a "spike meal" comes into play on the Cycle Diet. In supercomp mode, you don't feel like you are starving hungry, but you never feel really full after you've eaten either. The meals you eat just get you through to the next meal, and sometimes with this constant mild hunger, this is when people start to feel "cravings," which, with time, you can recognize as appetite, as opposed to actual hunger.

Over time you start to recognize what appetite is versus actual hunger.

Mid-week spike?

I did practice using a mid-week spike meal in order to boost energy levels for workouts. Usually I did mine Thursday evenings, and then I did my refeed days on Sundays.

What kind of foods to you prefer on cheat days?

90 percent of the time you can bet I'm eating a pizza! But there is nothing I really prefer to have, except I eat any sugary foods later in the day, as I find these tend to fill me up too quickly if I eat them early on.

Give an example cheat day menu!

- **Breakfast:** 12oz steak with 8-12 over-easy eggs, with toast or a cinnamon bun

- **Lunch:** Burger or a Clubhouse sandwich with poutine

- **Supper:** 18" pizza and cheesecake or a lemon pie
- **Snacks:** pepper pistachios, dried mangoes, chocolate bars, cookies, Nibs, ice cream, chips and dip, cupcakes or doughnuts (any or all of these are just eaten at will throughout the day)

How does the cheat day make you feel?

Happy and full, but not stuffed. My goal is just to eat to feel full and satiated, not to over-do it. I do find that the night after eating this way I get night sweats, and I am sometimes restless. I also find that the next day I can feel as if I have a "food hangover" for a few hours in the mornings. On Monday morning, once the food hangover clears, my energy levels are very high and I feel good.

I do get night sweats, and feel the affects of food hangovers, but these can be controlled through moderation. I feel sometimes people tend to try and set records with the amount of food they eat, and this is what can lead to obsessing over food, and unhealthy habits that leave you feeling unwell.

Hardest part about the Cycle Diet?

When I am doing a refeed day at work it is a little more difficult, as I have to try and bring so much food with me to the workplace (and fit it all in a backpack!), and so I have to plan more carefully the day before.

But for me, I've always thought of food as fuel, as I was taught this from an early age, and so I've never had too much difficulty sticking to a diet that contains healthy food choices throughout the week. As a child, we always ate healthy during the work/school week, and then had a "treat day" on the weekends, and this is a similar mentality to the Cycle Diet.

I have heard some people say that they struggle with food cravings when they are in supercomp mode, but this can be managed through experience and knowledge of appetite verses hunger over time. For example, if you find that you are miserable throughout the week because you are just so focused on the one day that you can binge eat, then it can be too consuming and overwhelming.

<u>Best</u> part about the Cycle Diet?

For me, it's the routine that makes it stress-free. Throughout the work week, I know what I am having, and it's all prepared and ready, which is important when you're working 12 hour shifts and don't have a lot of time to prepare food.

In your opinion, what's a good reason to start Cycle Dieting, and what's a bad reason?

A good reason would be to maintain a certain lean look and still be healthy. I have been told that a quote I use has stuck with a few people, when I said, "You can either eat what you want and continue to look and feel how you currently do, or you can have a little discipline when it comes to healthy eating, and have the physical look you want." Or, as Coach says, "Have your cake and eat it, too."

If there were ONE thing you could say to someone considering using the Cycle Diet, what would it be?

That they need to understand the physical science of getting into supercompensation mode. Too many people think that if they eat healthy throughout the week, who are not yet in supercomp mode, that they can reward themselves with a "cheat day" on the weekend, and then wonder why it isn't working.

Also, you also have to be careful not to "overthink things" once you are in supercomp mode, as some people start to stress about what to eat on refeed days, and then it can become an obsession. The main thing to realize is there are not rules, and that you just need to relax and enjoy it, and trust the process.

Funny stories?

A time that comes to mind was one time when I

went to Boston Pizza with a friend, and I continued to order food over the course of a couple of hours while we were there watching an MMA fighting event. I would just order a meal, finish it, and then order another that I wanted.

Eventually, the waitress just brought me out a couple pieces of cheesecake and said, "Here, back in the kitchen we figured this was the only thing you haven't eaten yet— it's on the house!" They just couldn't believe that someone my size could eat that much in one sitting. The guys at work always marvel over this as well when I'm having my refeed days; they can't believe I can fit that much into a backpack!

Is there anything else you want to add?

You just have to trust the science behind it, trust Scott, and enjoy the whole process.

Tobias P.

Tell us about yourself:

My name is Tobias P. and I'm 26 years old. I always wanted a lean and muscular physique but I always had trouble to get it. In the past I tried some diets out there but I never could stick with them a long time. I realized that I will never get the results by trying diet after diet without finding a balance in life. Now, I don't pay attention to other diets or websites out there any longer and enjoy my life while keep making progress

How did you hear about the Cycle Diet, or what interested you in it?

I started reading Scott's books and articles years ago and became a huge fan of him. With his knowledge and expertise in the fitness and diet industry I was far beyond impressed and I knew he was the guy to take me into a better life and a better physique.

What kind of results did you see on the Cycle Diet?

The results I already achieved with the Cycle Diet is absolute awesome. Currently I can see changes in my physique nearly weekly, while having one insanely huge cheat day on Saturday. A week ago I was at 193,4 lbs. The morning after my cheat day I was at 207 lbs. and I ate about 15,000 calories on this day. The funny thing is that now – a week later I am at 192 lbs. and that's even lower than the week before. And I'm obviously leaner.

What do you like about the Cycle Diet? How does it fit into your lifestyle/goals?

I diet for 6 days during the week and it's great to have a solid diet routine that fits perfectly into my daily life. The good thing is that I don't have to eat low carb or be on an extreme caloric deficit. On one day of the week (for me it's Saturday) I have one full cheat day without any restriction. It's great to have a diet that fits perfectly into my lifestyle because I love eating, I love food and I don't like stressing about it.

What did you use the diet for? Any unique needs that

it had to address?

I use the Cycle Diet to keep pretty lean while adding quality muscle slowly without the extra fat gain that usually comes with bulk diets.

Were you a coaching client of Scott's?

Yes, I am a coaching client of Scott Abel. It's great to have someone like him behind me and I trust in him 100 percent. I take my part as a coaching client seriously and I am always regular with my check-ins. I'm also very disciplined with my diet and stick to the plan. Consistency is the key.

How long did it take you to get into supercompensation mode?

Well, because I've already had a good working metabolism I was very quick in supercompensation mode.

Some time ago I became ill and couldn't workout for 4 weeks. Mentally it was a very hard time for me. I also didn't follow my diet and ate whatever I wanted in this time but I also didn't feel well in my body. Scott supported me in this time. When I was back in the gym and followed my normal diet, I was very quick getting back to where I was before. Another great thing about the Cycle Diet is that you train the metabolism and in my case my body knew exactly how to handle it.

What are your diet days like?

To get into supercompensation mode I ate 5 balanced meals throughout the day. I have carbs, I have fat and of course I have protein in my diet but in balanced portions. My caloric intake is always in a relative caloric deficit. No carb cycling, no keto dieting or only have carbs around the workout. It's all about balance in the diet.

In supercompensation mode I eat the same way but with one cheat day on Saturday.

What did supercompensation mode "feel like" to you?

I can really feel that my body needs and uses all the nutrients for fuel. I can also eat a huge amount of food without getting really full. The hunger level is very high during the week and especially the day before the cheat day. The days after the cheat day the training intensity is awesome but at the end of the week it's getting harder to keep the training intensity on a high level.

How has that changed over time?

Well, the deeper I go in supercompensation mode the more hunger I have throughout the week. Especially at the end of the week my hunger level is very high.

Did you ever end up implementing a mid-week spike?

No not yet but I think my body is ready soon to implementing a mid-week spike.

What kind of foods to you prefer on cheat days?

On my cheat day anything goes. I like sweet stuff like ice cream, cheesecake, chocolate bars, cookies and so on. I also like pizza, pasta, sandwiches, burgers, sushi and especially Bavarian pretzels with butter on my cheat day.

Give an example cheat day meal!

On my last cheat day I had this meal for lunch:

3 large 30cm sandwiches with double beef, cheese, salad, tomatoes and honey mustard sauce and 2 orders of fries

1 lb. ice cream

…then I went home and ate 6 donuts!

How does the cheat day make you feel?

For me every cheat day is like Christmas. I feel absolutely awesome on my cheat days, but I am also sweating a lot especially the days after that cheat day at my workouts.

How are energy levels after the cheat day?

The energy level after the cheat day is absolute awesome. The training is insane and the veins are popping out of the skin like never before. The pump is incredible.

Are food hangovers an issue?

When I started the cycle diet I had some food hangovers after my cheat day but once my body knew how to deal with this the hangovers has gone. The other issue I had was gas. But the whole cycle diet is a learning process and for me it's better to have all the sweet stuff like ice cream and cookies at the end of the cheat day. Since I do so I have no issues anymore.

What's the hardest part about the Cycle Diet?

The last days before the cheat day are the hardest part of the cycle diet. The energy is pretty low, the hunger and appetite level are very high and sometimes it's hard to keep the training intensity up.

What's the best part about the Cycle Diet?

I love eating and I love food. So eating thousands

and thousands of calories on the cheat day is the best part of the plan. Also I like the mental liberation of eating whatever, wherever and whenever I want and not feeling guilty.

If there were ONE thing you could say to someone considering using the Cycle Diet, what would it be?

To using the Cycle diet the person must be on a relative caloric deficit all week long as well as being in a supercompensation state. Hunger, appetite, performance in gym, and current level of condition are other factors as well to determine if someone can use the full cycle diet approach.

In your opinion, what's a good reason to start Cycle Dieting, and what's a bad reason?

It's a great diet for someone who loves food and want to be in shape year round.

If you have a bad relationship or a negative emotional connection to food and want to start right with the cheat days then I think that would be a bad reason to start the cycle diet.

Funny stories?

Oh yeah. I was shopping for my weekly cheat day and my whole shopping cart was full with a lot of delicious foods. A few guys behind me saw my shopping cart and I could hear that they were talking about me. One guy asked the other guy "How can he eat all that food and look the way he does?" So great.

Is there anything else you want to add?

For me it's the best diet out there. Like Scott says all the time a diet must be functional, it must fit into your lifestyle and a diet must be long time sustainable. I think the Cycle Diet is perfect for this.

Shawn G

Tell us about yourself:

I'm a certified personal trainer, I've been a trainer for 8 years in Edmonton Alberta.

I was very overweight through out my high school years. A couple years after high school I decided I was going to loose some weight. The problem was I went about it the wrong way and really had a tough time keeping the weight off several years after.

Diets I followed prior to the cycle diet were low fat, high protein, low carb. This type of diet approach left me always hungry and dissatisfied. I could never maintain this diet more than a couple of weeks before I would cheat, more often than not this would turn into a 2 day all out binge.

How did you hear about the Cycle Diet?

I was an avid visitor/lurker on several bodybuilding message boards. Scott's name frequently came up, usually it was the athletes who were successful and winning. I knew he was the guy to hire, so that I could get my life back. His methods were unique and he had been in the industry for several decades. Scott was not scared to tell it like it is, or candycoat a situation to pad his wallet. His clients always seemed to have control of the physique at all times of the year, and this was what I wanted. I was sick of struggling and not having any balance.

What kind of results did you see with Cycle Diet?

I lost 25 lbs. initially, going from 205 to around 180 lbs. The biggest part was I didn't struggle to attain this. It felt much easier than the past.

What do you like about the Cycle Diet?

I enjoy the freedom that I have without feeling of guilt. Especially around social events or outing with my friends. The cycle diet allows me to indulge and enjoy life and still maintain a nice lean physique. Its great during NFL season, every Sunday I go out and enjoy whatever I want with my friends.

What did you use the diet for?

I used the diet to stay lean year round, I was tired of yo-yo competition/off season dieting. It wasn't healthy to be gaining 30+ pounds after competitions or photoshoots.

Were you a coaching client of Scott's?

Yes I was a coaching client. He put me on a modified version of the cycle diet in the beginning which fit my body's needs at the time.

How long did it take to get into supercompensation mode?

It was about 4 months without any type of spike before Scott introduced some refeeds into my diet. I've been pretty consistent with my spike days for the past 5 years. I can recall one year after a month of eating whatever I wanted and not training a whole lot, it took around a month for my body to get back into supercompensation.

What are your diet days like?

If I had to guess I would say around 1,800 - 2,000 cals per day, 6 days per week. I weigh 180-185 lbs. and get in close to 10,000 cals on my spike day. The weekly calories haven't changed that much, just some different food choices—especially so with the foods that I spike with. My choices are much different than they were 5 years ago.

What did supercompensation mode "feel like" to you?

By Saturday morning hunger was very high. Through out the day it feels like no matter when you eat you're always hungry. This got better after 6 months to a year, I would pay attention to my energy levels and how I was functioning more than how hungry I was. It's pretty amazing how much you can eat on your refeed day. You almost feel like a bottomless pit.

How has the diet changed over time for you?

Yes, over the past few years it has changed, I don't eat near the amount I used to and I tend to lean towards cleaner options. The hunger levels are not as severe.

Did you ever end up implementing a mid-week spike?

I did briefly for a couple of months after the first year. My weight was dropping every week and I was hungry all the time. I would just have a 1 meal of a couple thousand calories on Thursday evenings.

What kind of foods to you prefer on cheat days?

I prefer foods that are homemade and not overly processed. I lean towards things like guacamole and chips, homemade burgers, steaks, and the odd baked good.

This has changed the past few years. I would go right after tons of sugar when I first got up and pretty well anything that wasn't nailed to the countertops as Scott would put it. This left me feeling extremely hung over and I usually napped for a few hours in the afternoon.

Give an example cheat day menu!

- **Breakfast**: a dozen blueberry or apple fritters with 20 timbits. 2 cinnamon buns with butter or a loaf of toast and jam.

- **Lunch**: 4-5 pounds of chicken wings and a huge pan of homemade nachos with beef

- …and usually 5-6 Eatmore bars throughout the afternoon. I would also consume 3-4 litres of kool-aid or diet pop.

- **Supper** would generally be a steak or pizza with French fries.

- Later in the evening I will have 1 litre of Greek yogurt with fresh berries or something sweet to end the night off.

How does the cheat day make you feel?

I definitely heat up as the day goes on to the point where I will be opening windows in the middle of an Ontario winter to cool down! I sweat more in the gym in the workouts right after a cheat, and yes there have been some cheat days when I've certainly over done it and basically lay down on the couch in a carb-induced coma, or "beached whale mode" as I like to call it.

How are energy levels after the cheat day?

Energy levels are actually low until around 3 p.m. the next day. The mornings can be a bit rough. (I start my days usually at 5 a.m.)

Are food hangovers an issue?

Food hangovers were an issue but not so bad anymore. The better the quality of food I ate the less hungover I am on Monday mornings. You get to know what foods agree and disagree with you over time and how much you can get away with. Bloating and gas is a given for me until Monday afternoon.

What's the hardest part about the Cycle Diet?

Being in a caloric deficit for 6 days takes a lot of discipline but I'd have to say getting the body ready for the cycle diet is the hardest part. I like to use the analogy of building a house is a lot harder than maintaining it.

What's the best part about the Cycle Diet?

Eating whatever you want once per week and keeping the lean physique at the same time. You never really feel deprived.

If there were ONE thing you could say to someone considering using the Cycle Diet, what would it be?

It's not for everyone, and it's not something you just step into. Most of my friends think they can go straight into refeeds the first week. They don't see the discipline and hard work that it takes to get the body *ready* for the cycle diet.

What's a good reason to start Cycle Dieting, and what's a bad reason?

A good reason would be to maintain a consistent healthy lean physique year round. It's the easiest diet I've found that helps me reach this goal.

A bad reason to start it is to put on large amounts of lean tissue or doing it to warrant the guilt of eating a ton of calories one day a week.

Funny stories?

I've had some people come over to my table at a buffet during the men's Olympic hockey game and ask me where I am putting all this food, we have watched you eat 6 plates of food, etc.

I took my girlfriend to Tim Horton's for coffee while we were dating and I ate a dozen fritters in 10 minutes, she was shocked.

Is there anything else you want to add?

It's very adaptable to many different situations, most Sundays now I only do around half a day of spiking due to golfing a lot in the summer. You can work around many lifestyles and make it work.

Amir S.

Tell us about yourself:

I have certainly not always been lean. I'm a classic endormorph and had reached out to Scott for his mentorship program quite a few years ago. Before Scott I was focused purely on getting stronger and ate upwards of 7,000 calories per day. I was around 365 pounds I believe at that time.

How did you hear about the Cycle Diet, or what interested you in it?

The cycle diet was not the reason I approached

Scott. It was his training knowledge. When he sent back my diet – once he agreed to mentor me – lo and behold it was the classic cycle diet he was known for. This made me happy.

What kind of results did you see on the Cycle Diet?

I lost 50 pounds on the cycle diet in the first 3 to 4 months. That was with 6 days of moderate calories and one day completely off from diet – I called it Christmas every weekend.

What do you like about the Cycle Diet? How does it fit into your lifestyle/goals?

Well, psychologically taking a day off for me is essential. I'm an extremist and moderation is simply not my cup of tea. So I was happy to diet 6 days so long as I had a day OFF. This mirrors taking a day off training as well and is really a beautiful combination. We need to drop the stressors once a week to allow the system to replenish, regenerate, and reload.

What did you use the diet for? Any unique needs that it had to address?

I came to Scott to LOOK LIKE A COACH. I had gotten too fat.

Were you a coaching client of Scott's?

I was a mentorship student. So that was SERIOUS pressure – learning from the BEST in the industry. It gave me a level of motivation that I never thought I had.

How long did it take you to get into supercompensation mode?

For me there was no getting into supercomp phase, simply because I was in a high energy flux from the beginning. I was already training 8 to 10 hours per week with high volume, super heavy weights, and eating tons of food. By simply restricting 6 days of eating, my body was very primed to handle the "cheat day" right on the first week. This is why it is SO IMPORTANT to have an experience coach assess this. 99.9% of people WILL NOT BE ABLE TO have a cheat day on week one like I did. They simply aren't coming from the same metabolic place I was.

What does supercompensation mode "feel like" to you?

Day 6 was always mentally challenging WHILE BEING EXHILIRATING. Because to this day, and I've been eating like this for over 7 years now I think, I still feel like "cheat day" is Christmas. It's absolutely wonderful for a foodie like me :)

Did you ever end up implementing a mid-week spike? How long did it take, and what kind of biofeedback indicated you were ready?

Yes. For me the mid-week spike came in at around month 5 I believe. It was based solely on appetite. I was getting VERY hungry as I got leaner.

What kind of foods to you prefer on cheat days?

I believe that cheat days should be high fat ordeals. Too much sugar and carb just makes you bloated and unable to move – so I leave that stuff to evenings. And most of the day time, I rely on fatty proteins or sweets with high fat percentages. That's just me.

Give an example cheat day menu!

Oh goodness. I start off with an entire bottle of port and an entire cherry cheesecake. And that's just breakfast 1. Then I go out and have another massive 3500 calorie breakfast at my favorite restaurant. With crab cake benedict, waffles, French toast, scrambled eggs. From there it's Shake Shack burgers for lunch. Another 3500 calorie meal usually. Then I come home to Ben and Jerry's ice cream. An entire pizza. Plenty more wine, cocktails, and chocolate. And if I have room, Ill end with another Ben & Jerry's and go to bed. I usually hit around 15 to 20,000 calories on cheat day. It's wonderful.

How does the cheat day make you feel?

You must become comfortable with sweat, some bloat, and some fullness. You need to assess what foods to eat and *when*. You have to time it well. And you have to be in very comfortable clothing as well. If you want to go out at night, which I love to do, I'll avoid eating for four to five hours before the evening out for dinner.

How are energy levels after the cheat day?

You *can* feel fatigued or sluggish if you force feed. If you go by appetite, you will feel AMAZING. You will look even better. It's very important to figure out foods types and amounts. And NEVER force feed.

Are food hangovers an issue?

Yes. As I wrote above – this is possible. The best remedy is plenty of water in the morning, and make sure you have water next to bed at night so that you can sip on it if you wake. I also usually skip breakfast the morning following cheat day *if* I'm in hangover mode.

What's the hardest part about the Cycle Diet?

It's only hard the evening prior to cheat day, because it's usually the beginning of the weekend and most of your friends are going to want to come over or go out. That is where you simply exercise your discipline. It's hard for "Regular people" in my experience. Not if you take your physique results seriously.

What's the best part about the Cycle Diet?

The day itself. It's my favorite part of the week. You get to eat, drink, and be merry. And **you KNOW** you wont get fatter. It CANNOT get better.

If there were ONE thing you could say to someone considering using the Cycle Diet, what would it be?

Consult a coach. If you have anxiety issues or do not take training seriously, it is not for you.

In your opinion, what's a good reason to start Cycle Dieting, and what's a bad reason?

A good reason? From a bioenergetics point of view, the system hormetically upregulates to the caloric volatility and disturbance. It's literally "Good for your system". A bad reason is if your entire focus is only on the cheat day. If the only reason you want to do it is because you know you will get a day off, well, then you will screw up.

Funny stories?

I once did a social media "all day on my cheat day" episode. I downed 20,000 calories. It was pretty popular. It was basically a challenge that had been building up for a couple of weeks. AND I DID NOT force feed. The training volume enabled the huge appetite and the next day I felt GREAT.

Is there anything else you want to add?

Listen, the cycle diet will make most people miserable. It will literally create a food disorder if you try it without consulting a coach. It's as dangerous for you psychologically as it is beneficial. You need the coaching to get you into the right state of mind and physical readiness for it. Even if you think you're an expert, trust me, you still need someone to provide you feedback.

Scott Abel

Gabriel Craft

Tell us about yourself:

I am a personal trainer in Lexington Kentucky. I hold a bachelors degree of exercise science from Morehead State University and Precision Nutrition level 1 certification. I started weight training in January of 2000 at 130lbs. I now hang around 185-190lbs now. At one point I had gotten myself to 230 lbs. but I was also carrying around way too much body fat. For the longest time I did a constant "bulking diet" just because I always feared being too skinny, only taking in excessive calories and ended up making myself fat in the process. I dieted the weight off of me by just lowering my caloric intake overall. Nothing fancy.

How did you hear about the Cycle Diet, or what interested you in it?

I heard about the cycle diet from posts in a gym I used to attend. A coach in my gym was putting some of his clients on the cycle diet and I had no idea what it was. So I looked it up online and there were several bastardized versions being described that wasn't even close to what it actually was. I figured that out once I bought the video from the Abel online store. I was interested in the idea of "have your cake and eat it too" idea.

What kind of results did you see on the Cycle Diet?

I actually stumbled into doing the cycle diet a few years ago. After I bought the original video of Scott's SWIS presentation I watched it probably 5-6 times and studied it. I started doing a diet that was balanced 45/40/15 (CHO/PRO/F) around 2,900 calories per day. I had no intention of even doing an all-day refeed.

At first I was only doing 1 cheat meal per week, on Saturday nights. I did that for two weeks and found myself as hungry mid-week as I was when dieting for a contest on 1,700 calories per day and then I bumped my cheat meals to two on Saturdays. That went on for about 2 more weeks and then I tried half of Saturdays. After three weeks of doing that I would wake up on the Sunday mornings after still ravenous. So I started using Saturdays as an all day refeed.

When I initially started doing the 1 cheat per week my weight was 183 lbs. When I began using the full refeed day, nearly two months later my weight was the same. After an all day refeed my weight would go up eight to 10 lbs. Usually by Thursday mornings I would be back down around 184, sometimes 185. My workouts on

Sundays were unreal, it felt awesome because my pumps were out of this world, and my shirts would be so sweaty I could ring them out with sweat like I got them out of my washing machine.

What do you like about the Cycle Diet? How does it fit into your lifestyle/goals?

I like the fact that social events (typically on Saturdays) are very easy to take part in. It's easy for me because Monday-Friday I am working from 6am up until 6-7pm most days. I am already packing my food with me every day anyways and I've always eaten eggs and oatmeal for breakfast for I couldn't tell you how many years now.

What did you use the diet for? Any unique needs that it had to address?

I used it just to see how it worked. At that time I was taking in 2900 calories based off of my BMR and my activity level to maintain weight. I actually wanted to work my way down on calories to try the full-on cycle diet out the way it was intended by using a relative deficit, but when I found myself having stomach cramps because of hunger there was no way I was going to lower my daily calories.

Were you a coaching client of Scott's?

No I was not, but I was part of the Elite Inner Circle he had going at that time.

How long did it take you to get into supercompensation mode?

I'm guessing it was around seven weeks. Like I said above, it was all a fluke for me, because I was actually trying to maintain my weight and I only used the all day refeeds because of intense hunger after two to three cheats on Saturdays.

What are your diet days like?

My calories were around 2900. I didn't even realize what I was doing was considered supercompensation mode. I might not have even been there in actuality.

What did supercompensation mode "feel like" to you?

I'm assuming I was actually there, so here goes. By midweek, on Wednesdays I would usually feel like I was dieting for a bodybuilding show. I would be hungry right after a meal, literally some days I would feel like I had not eaten directly after a meal. But by Thursdays I would usually not even worry about it because I knew what would be coming on Saturdays.

How has that changed over time?

I stopped doing it because of the intense night sweats and body heat I would have all day on Sundays and unable to sleep on Sunday nights.

Did you ever end up implementing a mid-week spike? How long did it take, and what kind of biofeedback indicated you were ready?

I did not use the midweek spike. Didn't know what to look for as far as being ready for that.

What kind of foods to you prefer on cheat days?

Chocolate bars, cakes, cheesecake, pizza, cheeseburgers, Buffalo wings, doughnuts, anything that could give me diabetes and heart disease.

Give an example cheat day menu!

This is from Saturday July 20, 2013

- **Breakfast:** Five toaster strudel pastries, breakfast burrito, two Reese's® peanut butter cups, one Trader Joe's ice cream sandwich.

- **Lunch/After work:** One Hot-n-Ready® Little Caesars pizza, box of yogurt covered raisins, two [Bell's®] Oberon beers.

- **Mid afternoon meal:** Four fried mozzarella balls, sweet potato fries, half rack of ribs, one pack M&M's®, one pack of Raisinets®.

- **Dinner:** Two chicken quesadillas from Taco Bell, one taco, one caramel apple empanada, one pint of Ben & Jerry's ice cream.

How does the cheat day make you feel?

Pretty awesome during and even right before bed. Sometimes I would get hangovers the next day, but not often. Every time though, on Sundays I would be hot and sweaty all the way up into going to bed. My wife didn't like sleeping beside me on Sundays because I would put out so much heat it made her uncomfortable, I would leave sweat spots on bed, nearly like I wet the bed.

How are energy levels after the cheat day?

Unreal. If that feeling could be bottled I would sell it.

Are food hangovers an issue?

Hangovers would only happen if pushed the envelope with super high sugar days. The night sweats were the reason I gave up on the cycle diet.

What's the hardest part about the Cycle Diet?

Night sweats. On Sundays after a refeed I would be miserable because of the heat. Energy levels were fine throughout the week. Hunger wasn't an issue because I knew what was coming on Saturdays. The hunger was fine, it was intense but I knew there was an end to it every Saturday.

What's the best part about the Cycle Diet?

There are no limits on refeed days. It makes social events almost entertaining for others to watch how much I would eat and have such a small waist (laughs).

If there were ONE thing you could say to someone considering using the Cycle Diet, what would it be?

Don't let anyone buy you dinner on a refeed day unless they have deep pockets! On a serious note, it would be this: get in tune with how your body feels before you go for it. Learn what actual hunger is and not confuse it with thirst or boredom.

In your opinion, what's a good reason to start Cycle Dieting, and what's a bad reason?

Good reasons: Can keep diet structured and rigid, enjoy date nights with no restrictions, staying lean is very easy.

Bad reasons: Anyone with eating issues or body dismorphia or image issues.

Paolo Pincente

Tell us about yourself:

I'm a 38-year-old father of two young boys; I recently sold my small business to spend more time with my family. I grew up playing a variety of competitive sports and started lifting weights in my mid-teens, both of which I continue with today, albeit much more recreationally. Being active has helped me stay relatively lean throughout my life, I wouldn't say lean as in how people in the fitness industry might mean it, but certainly leaner than the average person. With my Italian heritage, I've always really enjoyed food for as long as I can remember, and I've always been known in my circle of friends/family as a big eater. I'm the guy that always gets asked to finish off what's left at the end of meals :)

I haven't really dieted prior to becoming a client of Scott's, as I didn't really have the need to. As I got a bit older and my physical activity become less intense, I knew that I would have to change my eating habits if I wanted to stay relatively lean. So my first 'diet' was really just balanced meals with reduced quantities.

How did you hear about the Cycle Diet?

I first heard about the cycle diet through some of Scott's early articles, and the original video. I became interested in it because I saw it as a perfect way to continue to enjoy food the way I do without the concerns for my health.

What kind of results did you see on the Cycle Diet?

The results have been that my scale weight has remained very close to my lean point yet my physique continues to develop – a perfect scenario for me.

Also, I feel that my metabolism has become a lot more 'refined', it responds well to both unplanned spikes (say social events etc.) and long breaks, such as the 10 weeks I just took off to travel around North America with my family.

What do you like about the Cycle Diet?

I like the feeling of being in sync with my body. Knowing that I've optimized my metabolism in such a way that I can be extremely healthy, yet not have to make any real sacrifices when it comes to food. Since I like to travel, it is great to know I can take prolonged periods with little regard to finding a place to train or watching what I eat. The process has given me the confidence to know that once I get back on my routine, everything will fall back into place.

What did you use the diet for? Any unique needs?

I didn't really have any unique needs, in fact I don't even recall if there was a specific time where I started it. It just sort of evolved - I feel the 'diet' is really just a very natural eating pattern. I obviously can't say this with the certainty of a scientist, but it seems logical to me that we as a species have evolved to thrive under cyclical food availability, and the 'diet' is just taking advantage of that.

Were you a coaching client of Scott's?

I am currently a coaching client of Scott's. Having someone with Scott's experience as a guide helps with eliminating a lot of potential mistakes. It's given me the confidence to just go out and do it without worrying about anything, since I know he's got my back. As I said in an earlier question, it feels as though we didn't really explicitly plan it, it just sort of evolved. That's the beauty of a Coach like Scott, he's got the knowledge to be able to see well in advance where you are heading, and he sets up the circumstances to let it happen organically.

How long did it take to get into supercompensation mode?

In hindsight, it probably didn't take very long at all. In fact, I probably was in supercomp mode without even knowing. I mentioned that I like to travel; so there were at least one to three fairly long breaks per year. I didn't require any changes to the diet other than what was intuitive given the breaks in training.

What are your diet days like?

I eat the same amount of calories whether dieting to get into Supercomp, or in Supercomp on diet days — roughly about 1,500 per day as per Scott's original diet plan.

What did supercompensation mode "feel like" to you?

I can best describe the feeling of training prior to a cheat day as similar to having an 'off' day – same type of feeling if I was tired from a late night or otherwise not feeling 100 percent. I don't feel 'bad', just a little on the weak side. After a cheat day I feel strong as heck and my muscles feel 'full' My wife likes to say I get 'puffed up', and it feels that way. For me, the hunger right before a cheat is definitely the most intense.

The full/flat cycle of how my muscles feel after a spike remains fairly constant, however over time the way

I feel hunger changes. It doesn't get too intense as it would when I am coming off a long break, as it is now.

Did you ever end up implementing a mid-week spike?

It was fairly infrequent, but during the peak weeks of good program I would feel the need to have a spike meal mid-week, usually in the form of a big dinner. For me that would be about 10 to 15 weeks into a given program. I knew I was ready based on cues like how quickly performance dropped off after the bigger weekend spike, how tired I was, how my scale weight was trending week to week. I feel it was a combination of all these, plus a bit of intuition – I just knew I needed to eat something or I wasn't going to make it to the weekend :)

What kind of foods to you prefer on cheat days?

Anything and everything. Whatever I can get my hands on. I do tend to prefer carbs – pasta, bread, etc. Did I say pasta? I can always find room for more. Growing up I didn't really have a sweet tooth, but I have learned to appreciate good desserts. I don't really avoid anything.

Give an example cheat day menu!

I would get up before my wife and kids and get a salad bowl full of cereal.

When they woke, I would greet them with breakfast, usually a pack of bacon, a pack of sausages, 10-15 hash browns, a carton of eggs, toast with peanut butter…they manage to get some, I get the lion's share of course.

I'll usually snack continuously through to lunch – chips most of the time, but I've been known to crack open a can of chickpeas and eat straight from the can. Then I'll usually go to Harvey's and get a couple of double burgers with poutine. Snack on to dinner, usually a box of chocolate chip cookies with milk, then dinner is usually a big pizza or a lot of pasta. Then a carton of Reese's peanut butter ice cream as a nightcap.

How does the cheat day make you feel?

When the eating starts, I definitely start to get hot, but other than that I feel great. I surely move a bit slower than usual, and my muscles start to feel full by the early afternoon.

How are energy levels after the cheat day?

Spectacular. I feel like I can lift a house at the gym, I need to be careful that I don't get hurt.

Are food hangovers an issue?

I definitely feel bloated from time to time; a little more gas, but not too bad. I run a bit hotter for sure, but again it's not too bad, you get used to it. I've found that I have to leave room for water – lots – and that usually minimizes the 'side effects'

What's the hardest part about the Cycle Diet?

In my opinion, it would have to be the prep. You have to be patient and allow the time it takes to build up your strength, work capacity, and focused energy output, and you have to make some sacrifices during that process. I feel that's what most people would struggle with in today's world of quick fixes.

What's the best part about the Cycle Diet?

The best part for me is that I'm in an place where my body is just performing in all its glory, it's thriving, doing what it was designed to do. Once I get in the zone and I'm rolling, everything just feels like it's in its place, and it shows.

If there were ONE thing you could say to someone considering using the Cycle Diet, what would it be?

Be realistic about your circumstances. You can look at people's epic cheat days and want that, but it just might not be in the cards for you. I do feel that anyone can do it; you just have to know what version of it is right for you. Get some advice from someone with the right experience

In your opinion, what's a good reason to start Cycle Dieting, and what's a bad reason?

In my opinion, I don't really think there are good or bad 'reasons' to start the Cycle Diet. I do believe that with proper preparation, anybody can (and should) do it, but you have to be prepared to do the work. In some circumstances this could seem daunting at first.

Funny stories?

The first time once of the waiters at our favorite restaurant saw me on a cheat day, he shook his head and commented that he had never seen anyone eat that much – I took it as a compliment.

My wife is quite proud of her husband, and likes to tell stories of how much I eat when we visit friends and family – to everyone's disbelief.

Is there anything else you want to add?

I think some variation of the principles of the diet

can work for anyone. It does take time to get there, as with anything that's worth doing, but the results are life-changing.

That time is going to pass anyway, so might as well use it to get to a place where you can be healthy, look healthy, while enjoying the gift of food!

Scott Abel

Melissa Melnick

Tell us about yourself:

I'm 38 and the mother of two boys and two girls. I was a heavy child and teen who always struggled with weight. By the time I graduated high school I was 215 pounds. My mother was always diet conscience and was always on a fad diet. I was always made to feel I was a chubby child who had to lose weight. I was put onto a weight watchers diet and brought to weekly meeting at the age of 12 and put onto Jenny Craig at the age of 15. I always lost weight on these Low Calorie diets (all around 1000 calories. For a growing child and teen! Seems asinine now)

But always gained the weight back and more, leaving me depressed and anti-social at times.

By the time I was 18 I had enough of being fat and did the blood type diet. I actually did not could any calories and just ate healthy foods and eliminating the refined and processed ones.

In a year or so I lost 70 pounds and felt great. In the next six to seven years I had four kids and went up and down 60 pounds, the last being 100! Yes! I lost 100 pounds in 2005, and I've kept it off since then. Around that time I started to weight train and workout. I put on muscle and transformed my body to where it's at now.

Now I'm doing the cycle diet and I'm lean and muscular and most think I'm not a day over 25. I look and feel better than I did at 18!

How did you hear about the Cycle Diet, or what interested you in it?

I've been and still am an avid follower of Scott since 2007. I've been an active member on his forums and have seen the cycle diet video. I also have most of his books and listened to all the podcasts. I've been interested in the cycle diet from back then, but only felt ready recently.

What kind of results did you see on the Cycle Diet?

I have been seeing great results. I've been easing into it and still figuring out what foods serve my body best. Lost seven pounds. And keeping all that hard earned muscle.

Right now I'm maintaining my weight and recomping. I also have energy to train hard.

What do you like about the Cycle Diet? How does it fit into your lifestyle/goals?

Allows me to be lean and yet still enjoy all my favorite foods. I'm the type that I'd rather eat a whole pint of ice cream than 1/2 a cup. I also enjoy that mental freedom that I can eat whatever I want and how much I want on my spike day. Especially knowing that that spike day is SERVING MY BODY AND KEEPING ME LEAN.

What did you use the diet for? Any unique needs that it had to address?

In the past I have dieted for months on end without any re feeds, and even though I got lean to even see roadmap lower ab veins, I felt depleted and awful and looked gaunt.

I am using and have used the cycle diet to not only maintain leanness, but keep my HORMONES up to par and never get too depleted or feel ill. I've also lost my period in the past with dieting. And so far I still have my cycle and I'm regular.

Were you a coaching client of Scott's?

Not a coaching client per se but, I did purchase a one-time diet from him. And Scott is always easy to approach whenever I had any questions.

How long did it take you to get into supercompensation mode?

For me this time around it took 3-4 weeks since I was already relatively lean by the time I started the cycle diet. I'm still figuring things out and finding out which food serve me best along the way. It's a lifestyle and a process. Luckily through following Scott for so many years I've learned how to connect to reading my own biofeedback and assess from there going forward.

What are your diet days like?

Relative to my body weight to get into supercompensation mode I would eat between 10 and 12 times my body weight.

What did supercompensation mode "feel like" to you?

To describe it I would say it's a feeling of living from meal to meal where I knew I was ready for my spike day. As well, perhaps a little flat and tired, but wired as well, getting up at 4 o'clock in the morning feeling wide-awake was one sign or just not sleeping as deeply

How has that changed over time?

Learning to take in more calories and finding the right types of foods on spike days definitely helps.

Did you ever end up implementing a mid-week spike?

No. Not yet.

What kind of foods to you prefer on cheat days?

I make most of my spike days out of carbohydrate sources such as sweet potatoes, rice and beans, sushi. etc. However, I also enjoy treats throughout the day, being careful not to have too many sweets in one sitting or I won't feel so good. I found interspersing hyper sweet foods with starchy carbs, my blood sugar was much more balanced and I felt much better. I also found that too much fat was not good for me. I know for some people it is, but for me I felt it slowed down my digestion way too much and made feel too full, so I couldn't eat as much. I know this sounds strange, but too much fruit bloated me and made me feel very full almost to the point where it ended my spike day.

Give an example cheat day menu!

- Ezekiel French toast waffles with Greek yogurt and maple syrup

- Sweet potatoes with marshmallow fluff.

- Frozen yogurt.

- Medjule dates stuffed with cream cheese (Yes! It's epic)
- All you can eat sushi!

How does the cheat day make you feel?

At first they made me feel honestly awful. I was sweaty, I had heart palpitations and I felt quite ill. I was ready to give up after that first day, however I knew it was part of the process and from reading a lot of material and learning from people that is totally normal the first spike day you're going to feel awful no matter what. Now I feel full sometimes a little uncomfortable but for the most part I love how it makes me feel sleepy at night and I usually have the best night sleep ever after a spike.

I've learned what makes me feel awful after a spike day and what doesn't so with time and some fine-tuning I figured it out, and still am!

How are energy levels after the cheat day?

Usually really good. I usually want to train hard after us by day since I feel very full and ready to go

Are food hangovers an issue?

Yes at first I had those symptoms however with

time I've learned which foods I can and cannot have. For example like I said above for some reason I cannot have fruit at all on A spike for some reason it really bloats me.

Sometimes I like to start my spec days with a balanced meal so that my blood sugar remains somewhat more stable throughout the day. I also try not to have to many hyper sugary foods in one sitting because that can leave me feeling lousy.

What's the hardest part about the Cycle Diet?

I would say still having to diet and be mindful and count calories throughout the week I'm very used to it though.

What's the best part about the Cycle Diet?

Being lean. Feeling great. And looking forward to that one day where I can eat whatever I want as much as I want. Period!

If there were ONE thing you could say to someone considering using the Cycle Diet, what would it be?

You might have to suffer the consequences of being somewhat bloated or feeling heavy after spike day. And it may even be three or four days until you return back to your lean state.

What are some good and bad aspects of the Cycle Diet?

Good reason: retain or build muscle while still able to lose fat. And being able to enjoy all kinds of foods.

Bad: suffering the consequences of a spike such as bloating or feeing fat. And it taking a few days to perhaps feel your best again.

Is there anything else you want to add?

Keep a diary!! And take notes and write down about how you feel and any other biofeedback about your spike days and on dieting days. Helps you know what to do going through the process.

Dil

Tell me about yourself! Who are you? Have you always been lean?

I haven't always been lean — I was always overweight. I have tried 100s of diets and they were all too complicated. This was the simplest one, and the most consistent diet that was easy to follow.

How did you hear about the Cycle Diet, or what interested you in it?

I found an article on Google by a client of Scott's. I always wanted to be able to eat more as diet and training was always easy for me, but was there a way in which I could eat as much as I wanted that served me? The Cycle Diet was that way.

What kind of results did you see on the Cycle Diet?

Weight is staying around the same and I look bigger in mirror, I can't tell you about "weight loss" as I used it to maintain where I am now.

What do you like about the Cycle Diet? How does it fit into your lifestyle/goals?

It's perfect for me as training and dieting have always been second nature to me, once I got into it. The Cycle Diet allows me to eat like a superhuman. It's allowed for me to connect to more people because I can eat like this and still remain lean. It's the best of all worlds: you look like an athlete and eat like a superhuman when you're in the super-compensation mode, with no fear, just joy. To me it's like having a birthday every week!

What did you use the diet for? Any unique needs that it had to address?

I used the diet for maintain my body fat levels.

Were you a coaching client of Scott's?

Yes. Being coached by Scott gave me reassurance and took out guesswork; assurance like this for a concept like this is a lot of value! (There was no book when I first heard about it.)

How long did it take you to get into supercompensation mode?

It took about 3 months. No full breaks, but for those 3 months I did have regular cheat meals weekly (about doubling my cal intake or more for them)!

What are your diet days like?

1,500 cals/day is what I ate throughout diet and still do on diet days. I am very light at 112lb at 5 ft. 2, and I wanted to look lean.

What did supercompensation mode "feel like" to you?

You eat your food, bit it is like you haven't eaten!

And when you do eat on the cheat day, a normal meal on a cheat day would be the same as an entire day's worth of food; only it would feel like a snack. On cheat days, I would eat 8 meals or so, and my cheat day calorie range was anywhere from 7,000 to 11,000 cals, yet no force-feeding at all! Relax and enjoying!

How has that changed over time?

It feels more like a lifestyle. Cheat days are still always great for me. I make sure to try out new food places and have built up a reputation!

Did you ever end up implementing a mid-week spike? How long did it take, and what kind of biofeedback

indicated you were ready?

Mid week spike I haven't tried yet. I can't wait for when I can. Perhaps that will occur over time.

What kind of foods to you prefer on cheat days?

I like my croissants, breads, butter, chocolate muffins, whole cakes, chips, burgers, KFC, Indian foods, pizzas

I avoid drinking lots of water because I bloat. I also avoid dairy — as much as I love my ice cream, it bloats me. Sodas I keep to a couple of glasses as it tends to bloat me up too.

Give an example cheat day menu!

- **Meal 1:** Four large croissants, butter (lots of it!) four toasted bread slices, four handmade burgers in crusty buns. Three sausages. Lots of sauces (just under 3000 cals!)

- **Snack:** (30 mins after breakfast) , peanut butter chocolates, chocolate muffins, chocolate cookies, chocolate biscuit fingers. (1500 cals +)

- **Meal 2:** Four Chicken thighs, mash potato, four garlic breads, glass of coke (1300 cals)

- **Snack:** New York jumbo hotdog, chocolate muffins (1500+ cals)

- **Meal 3:** KFC™ two pieces and fries and gravy and a Pepsi™ (1300 + cals)

- **Meal 4:** Pizza slices (1000 cals)

- **Snack:** Big bag of marsh mellows, chocolate bars. (1000 cals +)

- **Meal 5:** Chicken and also a an entire one-litre tub of ice cream. (1000 cals+)

11,000 + cals for the day!

How does the cheat day make you feel?

Because I look so forward to them, I tend to get over excited and not sleep the night before, though I do try! The food keeps me full on awake and its like sleep didn't even matter! Afterwards I feel very *powerful*, lots of energy — I feel alive! After the cheat day energy levels are insanely high!

Are food hangovers an issue?

Gas happens if I eat dairy, but it's lessened if I just avoid it.

What's the hardest part about the Cycle Diet?

For me personally? Nothing.

Scott Abel

What's the best part about the Cycle Diet?

Eating like a superhuman, guilt free. And because it actually is a mode you're in, nothing is force-fed—people on the outside only assume it is.

I am now the envy of many of my friends and "*seem*" to have the genetics of someone with a fast metabolic rate. But it's supercompensation mode. Supercompensation is earned. It can't be bought. That makes me feel proud to accomplish.

This is great as for 30+ years of my life I would stare at food and put weight on. With consistency and the right Coach and knowledge, I am now doing what I once envied! I use the Cycle Diet to connect to people, yes it seems like it's all about eating, but this allows me to connect to people. They want to be able to eat like me. I go around eating at new places and as result meeting new clients for my company. In fact, I do meetings ("me-eatings") all day out at restaurants because of the Cycle Diet! The Cycle Diet allows me to have the best of every world: to look like an athlete and also have a super human ability of eating a ton without negative consequences. It shows what the human body is capable of, and of what I am capable of. I am only 112lb yet I can out eat someone whose 200lb no problem without even trying to, super-compensation allows this. ☺

If there were ONE thing you could say to someone considering using the Cycle Diet, what would it be?

Do it! And it's possible to have your cake and eat it — but it is earned!

In your opinion, what's a good reason to start Cycle Dieting, and what's a bad reason?

A good reason is to prove to yourself your aren't stuck with a slow metabolic rate, you will have proof to yourself when you become a bottomless pit once you're in super compensation. It is an absolute reality.☺

A bad reason is if you are not disciplined enough to hold out for the cheat day and you have eating disorders. Granted to those on the outside cycle diet can seem like an eating disorder, but for those who have reached super comp, well we know otherwise!

Is there anything else you want to add?

I can pretty keep my body fat and weight in check doing the cycle diet. Over 17 weeks over cycle diet cheat days my weight kept between 110-113lb. I don't know about you but that's awesome, as my arms and body look VERY defined! (Remember I want to remain toned, I don't care for muscle mass.) If I want to drop to my boxing weight class of 108lb Light flyweight, I just drop to a cheat meal (double normal cal intake and higher, once a week) and get there within 3 or so weeks!

You can stay very lean and eat insane amounts of food to the envy of others, like a superhero! You look like a super hero and eat like one. Use the cycle diet to more than eat but connect to people, I built up a rep and it's served me well with clients and also meeting girls. So for me its rewards outstrip what it takes to get there and what it takes to remain there!

Scott Abel

DISCLAIMER AND/OR LEGAL NOTICES: Every effort has been made to accurately represent this book and it's potential. Results vary with every individual, and your results may or may not be different from those depicted. No promises, guarantees or warranties, whether stated or implied, have been made that you will produce any specific result from this book. Your efforts are individual and unique, and may vary from those shown. Your success depends on your efforts, background and motivation.

The material in this publication is provided for educational and informational purposes only and is not intended as medical advice. The information contained in this book should not be used to diagnose or treat any illness, metabolic disorder, disease or health problem. Always consult your physician or health care provider before beginning any nutrition or exercise program. Use of the programs, advice, and information contained in this book is at the sole choice and risk of the reader.

Made in the USA
Coppell, TX
18 January 2023